MARY SCARLETT'S BACK!

The knock at the door startled Mary Scarlett, though she'd been waiting for it. She ran to answer it.

"Are you married?" she demanded even before saying hello.

Instantly, she saw the shock in his deep-set eyes. He had never seen her as a blonde. No one in Savannah had.

Bolton Conrad lifted his naked hand, then cupped her cheek. "As you may remember, darlin', I considered it once." His voice was husky with emotion. He hadn't meant to do it, but he could no more keep from kissing her than he could stop breathing.

Mary Scarlett melted into his arms. More than anything in the world, she needed to be kissed by Bolton Conrad right now—the way he had kissed her a long, long time ago. Sweet and soft and with so much tenderness, their very souls touching. She trembled from the onslaught of memories and sensations flooding her heart.

Bolt stared down into the dewy glow of her jewel-blue eyes. "Mary Scarlett. Are you propositioning me?" he teased gently.

She looked up at him, her smile too wide, her eyes too bright. "What I'm saying, Bolt darlin', is that I'd really like you to kiss me again." And as their lips met, it was as if time had stopped the minute Mary Scarlett walked out of his life. Now that she was back in his arms, the clock was running once again.

Or was that a time bomb ticking?

ZEBRA'S REGENCY ROMANCES DAZZLE AND DELIGHT

A BEGUILING INTRIGUE   (4441, $3.99)
by Olivia Sumner

Pretty as a picture Justine Riggs cared nothing for propriety. She dressed as a boy, sat on her horse like a jockey, and pondered the stars like a scientist. But when she tried to best the handsome Quenton Fletcher, Marquess of Devon, by proving that she was the better equestrian, he would try to prove Justine's antics were pure folly. The game he had in mind was seduction—never imagining that he might lose his heart in the process!

AN INCONVENIENT ENGAGEMENT   (4442, $3.99)
by Joy Reed

Rebecca Wentworth was furious when she saw her betrothed waltzing with another. So she decides to make him jealous by flirting with the handsomest man at the ball, John Collinwood, Earl of Stanford. The "wicked" nobleman knew exactly what the enticing miss was up to—and he was only too happy to play along. But as Rebecca gazed into his magnificent eyes, her errant fiancé was soon utterly forgotten.

SCANDAL'S LADY   (4472, $3.99)
by Mary Kingsley

Cassandra was shocked to learn that the new Earl of Litton was her childhood friend, Nicholas St. John. After years at sea and mixed feelings Nicholas had come home to take the family title. And although Cassandra knew her place as a governess, she could not help the thrill that went through her each time he was near. Nicholas was pleased to find that his old friend Cassandra was his new next door neighbor, but after being near her, he wondered if mere friendship would be enough . . .

HIS LORDSHIP'S REWARD   (4473, $3.99)
by Carola Dunn

As the daughter of a seasoned soldier, Fanny Ingram was accustomed to the vagaries of military life and cared not a whit about matters of rank and social standing. So she certainly never foresaw her *tendre* for handsome Viscount Roworth of Kent with whom she was forced to share lodgings, while he carried out his clandestine activities on behalf of the British Army. And though good sense told Roworth to keep his distance, he couldn't stop from taking Fanny in his arms for a kiss that made all hearts equal!

Available wherever paperbacks are sold, or order direct from the Publisher. Send cover price plus 50¢ per copy for mailing and handling to Penguin USA, P.O. Box 999, c/o Dept. 17109, Bergenfield, NJ 07621. Residents of New York and Tennessee must include sales tax. DO NOT SEND CASH.

Savannah Scarlett

Becky Lee Weyrich

Zebra Books
Kensington Publishing Corp.

http://www.zebrabooks.com

For
My brother, Bill Lee, and my cousin, Sue Best
They both knew Savannah way back when.

ZEBRA BOOKS are published by

Kensington Publishing Corp.
850 Third Avenue
New York, NY 10022

Zebra and the Z logo Reg. U.S. Pat. & TM Off.

First Printing: December, 1996

Printed in the United States of America
10 9 8 7 6 5 4 3 2 1

Prologue

Mary Scarlett could hear her parents fighting downstairs in the parlor, the very room where the shiny cherry wood coffin had lain on its bier until noon. The cloyingly funereal perfume of gladiolus, chrysanthemums, and carnations still hung in the air in the tall rooms of the old house on Bull Street. Granny Boo wasn't even cold in the ground, yet they were already at it again. Big Dick's voice boomed through the house like a cannon shot, out-blasting her mother Lucy's shrill protests and accusations.

Their hysterical racket brought an alarming change over Mary Scarlett Lamar, reducing the recent, poised graduate of Sweet Briar College to a weeping, fearful child again.

"Make the yelling go away," she moaned, covering her head with her pillow, shivering with terror and revulsion. "Please, Granny Boo, make them stop it."

Of course there was no answer. Except for the angry voices coming from the ground floor, the house seemed unaccountably still to Mary Scarlett. She had never realized before what comfort she had drawn from the sound of her great-grandmother's footsteps overhead in the attic. Now only silence emanated from that dark hideaway under the eaves.

From the time of her birth twenty-one years ago, Mary Scarlett had drawn solace and succor from the knowledge that her Granny Boo was always there—always ready to soothe tears, tell stories, chase away ghosts. Now a young woman on the very brink of adult life, Mary Scarlett knew she should be stronger. She should haul herself out of bed, march down the stairs, confront her parents, and demand that they put a stop to their ridiculous behavior. They should at least call a moratorium out of respect for the dead.

"But what good would that do? It *never* ends." Mary Scarlett turned on her back and stared up at the dark, silent ceiling, feeling tears of frustration slide down both sides of her face.

A crash, then the sound of shattering china made her jump and set her trembling all the harder. She dug her nails into the pillow, holding it hard against her chest like a shield.

"Granny Boo, where *are* you?"

It was a foolish question. Mary Scarlett knew exactly where her great-grandmother was. The dear old woman had simply given out after a hundred and three years. Now, at last, she could have some peace and quiet, sleeping under the moss-draped oaks of Bonaventure Cemetery. It was difficult, though, for Mary Scarlett to imagine her prim and petite granny, embraced by quilted satin and lead-lined cherry wood, lying far below the flowering azaleas. The mental picture made her shiver all the more.

"You're not really there, are you, Granny Boo? You're off flying with angels by now."

A stiff breeze blew in through the open window, bringing with it the delicious smells of springtime Savannah—Confederate jasmine, wisteria, honeysuckle, and the river, always the river. The lace curtains fluttered for a moment like butterfly wings. Mary Scarlett breathed in the sweet air. She sat bolt upright when she recognized another scent. Not flowers, but Pond's face powder, the kind Granny Boo had always used.

Despite her overwrought state, Mary Scarlett smiled. "No. You're not buried deep in the ground. I knew it!"

"Indeed not!" came a thin but distinct voice.

Mary Scarlett jumped at the sound. "Granny Boo?"

"You called?"

She rubbed her eyes, then glanced about the bedroom. "I'm imagining things."

From below she could still hear the quarrel in progress, but the noise seemed muted now, as if she were suddenly protected from the drunken brawl by some invisible, otherworldly wall.

"The only thing you're imagining, young lady, is that you can stay here and know any peace. Why do you think I moved to the attic?"

Mary Scarlett scanned the room again. She was all alone. So where was the voice coming from? Was she asking questions, then answering herself? If so, she must be as crazy as Granny Boo had been.

"I was *never* crazy!" the voice replied emphatically. "I was simply eccentric, a Southern lady's prerogative." A familiar high-pitched chuckle followed. "It suited my purposes to have most of Savannah *think* I was crazy. As crazy as the rest of them. Truth be told, all the sane folks died years ago. I was about the only one left with a grain of sense."

Convinced now that she was truly hearing her great-grandmother's voice, Mary Scarlett climbed out of bed and removed the black bunting from her vanity mirror. Granny had always been fascinated by mirrors. Maybe that's where she was hiding.

"If you're really here, why can't I see you?"

"You can, dear. All you had to do was ask."

A strange lilac-colored light glowed suddenly in the mirror right above Mary Scarlett's reflection. Still staring, she reached up to see if she could feel anything, maybe a warm spot above her head. Nothing. When she glanced up, she realized the glow existed only in the mirror.

She watched the circle of light slowly widen and intensify. Two eyes and a familiar thin-lipped smile materialized. Gradually, her great-grandmother's face took shape around the smiling eyes and mouth.

"There, dear. Wasn't that clever? I learned it from a cat I met here. Claims he came from Cheshire." The ghostly face turned thoughtful. "Isn't that in Effingham County? I believe I had some kin there a long time ago."

Another loud crash from below made Mary Scarlett jump back into bed. The image in the mirror wavered and all but disappeared.

"Don't go!" Mary Scarlett begged. "Don't leave me alone with them, Granny Boo."

"I'll try to stay, but they make it difficult. We're not allowed to remain where we aren't wanted. It was different in life."

"They always wanted you here."

"I wouldn't be too sure of that. I'd heard whispers about a nursing home in the past weeks. That was enough to send me packing. But, actually, they were getting on my nerves, so I decided it was time to go."

"You *decided?*" Mary Scarlett cried. "Granny Boo, how could you do that to me?"

"It's a free country, my dear. You don't have to stay either, you know."

Thoughts of the funeral service in the front parlor and the interment at Bonaventure Cemetery flashed through Mary Scarlett's mind. She shuddered. "I don't think I'm ready to go yet."

"Heavens, child!" Again the lavender image in the mirror wavered dangerously. "I didn't mean for a minute that you should join me. You have your whole lovely life ahead of you."

"Lovely? I doubt it," Mary Scarlett mumbled, thinking of the probable cause of her parents' combat. The major reason for their endless fights in recent months was Mary Scarlett's stalled marriage plans. The two men in her life, Bolton Conrad and Allen Overman, had both proposed. She had given neither man an answer. Her stubborn indecision had set her parents one against the other. Not that they needed her for that.

"It's not *their* choice, you know." Granny Boo seemed tuned in to Mary Scarlett's every thought and worry, just as she had been during her lifetime.

"Then I have to decide," Mary Scarlett replied in utter frustration.

"No, you don't."

"Yes, I do. I can't leave Bolt and Allen hanging forever."

"Why not? At least until you know what you want from life and with whom you wish to spend it. Might I mention a small matter called *love?*"

"Mama says marrying for love is only for foolish women and white trash."

"Poppycock! Your mama should have her mouth washed out with soap. *She* is the foolish one in the family—marrying Richard Habersham Lamar because he could support her in style. Some style! Just listen to them. If she'd minded what I told her, she wouldn't have married any man until she could see his face in my mirror."

"Mama says that's just an old wives' tale."

"Ah, I see. And her method of choosing a husband has proved so much sounder than mine." Granny Boo's words reeked with scorn and her image went from lilac to fluorescent purple. "Have you taken a peek in my mirror lately, Mary Scarlett?"

"Yes," she confessed.

"And which of your beaus did you see?"

"Neither. That's the problem."

Granny Boo's ghost frowned thoughtfully. "Hm-m-m! That *is* a problem."

"So what do I do now?"

After a moment's thought, Granny Boo said, "I suggest you simply disappear for a time. Leave Savannah. Maybe neither man is the love of your life."

"I'm not even sure I know what love is, Granny Boo. How am I supposed to know if I ever find the real thing?"

"Ah, *love!*" The thin lips in the mirror caressed the word as if it were a kiss. "Believe me, child, you'll know it. Let's see now. How can I put this? When you fall in love, he won't be someone you can live with, but the one and only man you can't live without. Does that make sense?"

Mary Scarlett thought for a moment, then shook her head. "Not really."

"Mark my words, it will make sense when the time comes. Yes, I think it best that you go away until you know your heart for sure."

"Daddy would never allow it. He'd be furious and Mama would have one of her spells for sure. She's made all these wedding plans, even bought my gown. Now if only I knew who I'm supposed to marry."

"Is this *your* life or *theirs* we're talking about?"

"Mine, but . . ."

"No buts, my dear! There have been too many broken hearts and broken lives in this family because the women gave in to pressure instead of following their hearts' desire. If you only knew. I won't have you added to that sorry list. I named you and I raised you and I mean to see that you have a good and happy life."

Mary Scarlett was tired of arguing with her mirror, and beyond weariness from worrying over her dilemma. She decided to change the subject. "What's it like where you are now, Granny Boo?"

The old shadow giggled like a girl. "Oh, simply delightful! I was at a party tonight until I heard you calling. Such a grand soirée!"

"A party?" Mary Scarlett asked skeptically.

"Indeed! Why don't you come with me now? See for yourself."

"I don't think that would be appropriate, do you?"

"Oh, I see your point entirely. Nothing to wear. That skimpy black nightie certainly would never do."

"Well, clothes were not exactly my main concern. Actually, I'm not sure I'd fit in. Where is this party anyway?"

"Right here at Bonaventure, the Tattnall Plantation. The house is all decorated for the holidays—cedar, bay, and shiny magnolia leaves everywhere. All the folks from plantations up and down the river are coming in by boat. You can tell who's arriving by the songs their slaves sing as they row. Close your eyes, dear. I'll show you."

Wary, but trusting her granny, Mary Scarlett stretched out on the bed and shut her eyes tight. The minute she did, all sounds of the escalating fight downstairs vanished, replaced by the deep, melodic voices of black boatmen singing their songs as they plied the darkly gleaming ribbon of the Wilmington River.

Mary Scarlett found herself with the group of partygoers waiting near the plantation dock when she opened her eyes. She wasn't really herself any longer, however. The handsome, dark-haired young gentleman standing next to her—a Tattnall cousin—called her "Miss Lou."

When a new boatload of guests from Ceylon Plantation walked up from the landing, her companion introduced her to a stranger as Miss Louise Manigault Robillard. "But we all call her 'Lou,' " he added.

The new arrival, a tall, dark-haired Adonis with sherry-brown eyes, bowed over Miss Lou's hand. Mary Scarlett felt the warmth of his breath through her lace glove.

"*Enchanté*, Mademoiselle Robillard." He had a New Orleans accent that curled her toes inside her satin slippers.

Thanks to her French mother, Louise spoke the language. She answered the young man, Jacques St. Julian, in kind. Mary Scarlett felt immediate intimacy flowering between them. Every other young man at the party vanished from her mind and heart the instant her eyes met Jacques'.

For the rest of the evening, Lou and Jacques were never

apart. He swept her over the polished floor of the gold-and-blue ballroom of the Tattnall mansion while slave musicians filled the scented night air with songs of love. Her heart felt lighter than her feet as the folds of her Savannah-silk gown swirled about her.

They found themselves seated together at dinner, side by side at the long table in the grand dining room of the Tattnall house. An unimaginable array of lowcountry dishes was offered. As silent as ghosts, the servants passed silver platters piled with roasted venison, wild turkey, pink prawns, oysters on the half shell, and every manner of vegetable from Bonaventure Plantation's kitchen gardens.

Midway through the meal, the butler hurried into the room and whispered something quietly to Mr. Tattnall. The man's face went grim for a moment, then he smiled at his guests.

"If you please," he said, "I believe we must move our feast out of doors. We have a slight problem, it seems."

Amidst excited murmurs, the guests filed out through the wide front door. Jacques held Lou's arm as they descended the veranda stairs. If he clung a bit too tightly, no one noticed but the young lady herself.

A general gasp went up as soon as they all reached the lawn and saw flames, vivid orange, leaping through the roof of the beautiful mansion.

"No need for alarm," their host announced calmly. "We're all safely out. Shall we resume our dinner by the light of the fire?"

The servants scurried this way and that, setting up tables, spreading damask, and resuming service. As the great plantation house turned into a massive bonfire, their host proposed a toast to his dying home, then smashed his crystal goblet against one of the ancient oaks under which they dined. The guests followed suite.

No one noticed when Jacques St. Julian brought Mademoiselle Robillard's ungloved hand to his lips. No one but

Lou herself. Flames hotter than any fire licked at her heart. Only the smoky black curls against her cheeks hid her blush.

Later, as the house burned to nothing, Jacques led his new love through the dark garden. They stopped by the burying ground where the moss-darkened stones stood enclosed in a spear fence of wrought iron. The silent dead seemed to welcome the young lovers.

Jacques bent low to kiss Lou's bow-shaped lips. This was her first kiss, and with it he captured her tender young heart.

"Forgive my boldness," he whispered. "But, you see, I believe I love you, Mademoiselle Robillard."

She blushed, her heart hammering, her joy boundless. "Will you be stopping long in Savannah, sir?" she asked breathlessly.

"Alas, no. I must leave for New Orleans with the dawn. But I shall return, my darling Miss Lou. And when that time comes, I mean to ask your father for your hand in marriage. Would that displease you?"

Feeling another, stronger blush of happiness, Louise lowered her lashes. "By no means, Jacques. I do believe you've won me with one kiss."

Mary Scarlett found herself back in her room as quickly as she'd left it. Her heart was still pounding and her whole body burned with excitement and joy. Her lips tingled from Jacques St. Julian's kiss.

"There, you see?" Granny Boo said proudly from her mirror perch. *"That,* my girl, is love!"

"But it wasn't real," Mary Scarlett argued. "It was all a dream, wasn't it?"

"My goodness, no, Mary Scarlett! That party took place long before my time. November of 1800, if memory serves. But every detail you experienced was exactly as it happened on that night. The dashing Jacques St. Julian made his promises to my own Great-Grandmother Louise."

"And did Jacques come back to Savannah to make Miss Lou his wife?" Mary Scarlett asked hopefully, sure that they must have married and lived happily ever after.

"No," the ghost said with a sad sigh. "Upon his return to New Orleans, he lost his life saving a woman and her child when their carriage plunged off the levee. Poor Lou grieved for him the rest of her life. A suitable marriage to an older man was arranged for her."

"How sad," Mary Scarlett sighed, feeling tears sting her eyes.

"But the party goes on," Granny Boo said in a cheery and surprisingly youthful voice. "Each night here at Bonaventure you can hear music and the tinkle of smashing crystal. I expect my own long-lost love will turn up one of these nights."

"I never knew Great-Grandpa Horace."

"Doesn't matter. He was a good enough husband, but not the man I loved."

"Granny Boo!"

"Don't sound so shocked. I'm in Heaven, after all. You get your wishes up here, all the good things denied you during life. But now to business. Where's my mirror?"

Mary Scarlett reached to the floor beside the bed. "I brought it to my room. I was afraid they might smash it."

"Good girl! From the sound of things down in the parlor, you're probably right. Now I want you to close your eyes, hold the mirror before your face, then look to see who the love of your life truly is. We'll settle the matter this minute."

Gripping the gilt-framed antique, Mary Scarlett did as she was instructed. When she opened her eyes, she gasped.

"So! You know at last," Granny Boo said smugly. "I told you it would work. Which man is it—Bolton Conrad or Allen Overman? Tell me quickly, dear."

"It's neither," Mary Scarlett whispered.

"Who then?"

"Jacques St. Julian." She glanced up at the other mirror

where her granny's violet image still glowed. "What does it mean?"

"It means that you must never marry until you love a man the way Louise loved Jacques St. Julian. Obviously, he has come back, looking for his own lost love in *you*, Mary Scarlett."

The thought of such a thing was staggering. "How will I ever find him?"

"Your heart will know. Give it time."

"There *is* no time! Bolt's building me a house. Allen has already shown Mama the antique sapphire and diamond ring that all the brides in his family have worn for generations."

"Which man's kisses make your heart flutter the way Jacques' did?"

"Both . . . *neither!*" Mary Scarlett stammered. "I don't know. Bolt keeps pushing so hard to get married. He wants to put me in a house closed in by a picket fence. Allen just keeps *pushing*. I'm not sure he cares about marriage so much as just getting me in his bed. It's *my* life, *my* decision! I wish they'd all leave me be!"

Granny Boo laughed heartily. "That's what I wanted to hear—a bit of piss and vinegar from my girl. You have your answer, Mary Scarlett. Go, child. Now!" Granny Boo's familiar voice began to fade along with her image. "Don't you marry a soul until you see him in my mirror."

"But I can't just run away. What would Mama say? And, oh, how Savannah would gossip! If I go, it will cause a terrible scandal."

"Go, go, go-o-o-o . . ." The single word swooped and surged through the dark room like a hurricane wind.

An hour later, the sound of the train on its tracks seemed to echo Granny Boo's final admonition. For better or worse, Mary Scarlett Lamar was leaving Savannah, fleeing north through the night into the unknown.

Only one thing did she regret leaving behind—Granny Boo's magic mirror. Without the mirror, how on earth was she supposed to find her man?

One

Bolton Conrad couldn't believe his eyes. By accident he had opened *The Savannah Morning News* to the society page instead of the sports section. Her name jumped out at him with all the force of a mule-kick to the gut. After he started breathing again, he chuckled. It was either laugh or cry, and he just plain didn't have any more tears left to shed over Mary Scarlett.

"Savannah's survived earthquakes, fires, yellow fever epidemics, hurricanes, and General William Tecumseh Sherman. But I'm not sure the old city will live through this."

Wondering if his eyes could be deceiving him, he took a second, harder look at the paper spread before him on his breakfast table.

Hardly a column-inch in length, the seemingly insignificant item was tucked away in the society column along with the mundane details of card parties, out-of-town visitors, and spring wedding showers. Nevertheless, the announcement in Savannah's most read morning newspaper was sure to set phones ringing and tongues wagging all over the city.

The item was conspicuous for what it did *not* say about the lady in question.

Mary Scarlett Lamar, former Savannah resident and debutante, has returned to this city after an extended stay in Europe. Her parents, the late Mr. and Mrs. Richard Habersham Lamar, were lifelong leaders of

*Savannah society, tracing their lineage back to several
of the city's founding fathers, including the Haber-
shams, Davenports, and Robillards. Mr. Lamar was
a member of the Oglethorpe Club. Mrs. Lamar was
a past president of the United Daughters of the Confederacy. Miss Lamar is an honor graduate of Sweet
Briar College, Class of 1988. Her many friends will
be happy to welcome her back to the city after such
a long absence.*

The morning sun off the Savannah River cast watery light
over the ballast stone walls of Bolton Conrad's converted
warehouse loft. His jam-smeared toast poised in mid-bite,
he finished reading the item for the third time, one dark
eyebrow arched in an attitude of consternation. He had figured that if Mary Scarlett ever did come back, she'd sneak
into town unannounced, wanting to call as little attention to
her return as possible.

The phone rang. His gaze still fixed on the paper, his mind
still trying to comprehend the meaning of Mary Scarlett's
return, he put the receiver to his ear. "Yes?" he said absently.

"It's Allen, Bolt. Have you seen the morning paper?"

Conrad pictured Allen Overman at the other end of the
line. The tall, sandy-haired entrepreneur seemed wound as
tight as a spring. That was nothing unusual; Allen always
ran at warp speed. The only thing slow about him was his
deep Southern drawl, the very trademark of leisurely, lush,
historic Savannah. But this morning there was a new note in
his voice. He sounded like a kid who had just found a long-
lost toy or a treasure hunter who had finally struck paydirt.

"I'm looking at the paper right now, Allen."

"Have you heard from her?" There was no need to identify the subject of his question.

"No. You haven't either?"

"Of course not." A subtle laugh edged with nervousness.
"You're the one she'll call and you know it. I might have

been her mama's favorite, but with Mary Scarlett you always came first. The fair maiden's knight in shining armor."

Conrad frowned. Was it starting all over again, this competition between the two of them? "No need for sarcasm, Overman."

"None intended." Another laugh—jovial, placating. "Hell, I never kidded myself. I always knew the truth. We both did. Admit it."

"If I was such a favorite, why did she run off and marry a bullfighter?"

"Good question, Bolt. An even better question is where is he now? Why's she come back alone? And why's she still using her maiden name?"

Now it was Bolton's turn to laugh. "You don't think any Savannah Lamar would give up that name, do you?"

Overman rushed on, "So what are you going to do about this?"

"About what?"

"About Mary Scarlett."

Bolt's frown deepened. After a silent pause, he said, "Nothing. She hasn't called and she probably won't. After all, it's been *eight years*, Allen. My guess is that she just flew in to take care of the house. I'm sure Miss Lucy's lawyers must have notified Mary Scarlett recently to remind her of the specifics of her mother's will. She'll probably meet with them, settle things, then fly out before nightfall. Back to Spain and her bullfighter. We may not hear from her at all."

This obviously disappointed Overman. It was clear he wanted to see her. But he didn't say that. Instead he argued, "She wouldn't dare let that house go. Why, it's been in her family forever. It's built on the trust lot Oglethorpe deeded to one of her daddy's ancestors back in 1733. A Yankee general used the place as his headquarters when Sherman invaded Savannah. At least one president has stayed there. The place is *history*, Bolt. *Savannah* history!"

"The law could care less about all that or Mary Scarlett's pedigree. If she doesn't claim it, the old place on Bull Street will become Savannah's newest National Historic Landmark, the property of the Telfair Academy, a museum. And that's that, the way her mother wanted it to be."

Ignoring what Conrad had said about her leaving, Allen announced, "I'm going to throw a party for her. Yes, that's what I'll do. Black tie, Saturday night, prime guest list. What do you think, Bolt?"

"I think you'd better check it out with Mary Scarlett before you hire a caterer."

"Where can I reach her?"

Bolton frowned. Allen still didn't believe that he hadn't heard from her. "How should I know? I told you she hasn't contacted me. All I know is what I read in the paper."

"You wouldn't hold out on an old buddy, would you?"

"Why should I? She's married now, Allen. The game's over. The fat lady's sung and we both lost out." It still hurt to admit it.

"Well, never you mind. I'll find her, and when I do I have a million questions. If she calls you give me a holler, you hear?"

"Sure, Overman. I'll do just that."

Allen Overman hung up abruptly. Bolton Conrad replaced the receiver and took another bite of toast, then shoved his plate away. His appetite was gone suddenly. Mary Scarlett had a way of doing that to him.

He stood up from the glass-top table, cinched the belt of his gray silk robe tighter about his waist, then walked over to the window that overlooked the river. It was early yet. The shops below on River Street wouldn't open for another couple of hours. In the sunshine a ginger tabby cat preened himself on the warm cobbles. A lone tourist focused her zoom lens on a squadron of pelicans skimming the water. An old black man shuffled along, collecting aluminum cans in a croker sack, whistling tunelessly as he went about his work. The scene below distracted Bolton's attention only briefly. All his thoughts centered on Mary Scarlett. And all his thoughts were troubled.

Why had she gone away eight years ago? Only three people might know the answer to that vexing question—Mary Scarlett, Miss Lucy, and Big Dick Lamar. Now one of her parents was dead, sleeping under the oaks in Bonaventure Cemetery, and the other had been missing these past six years. Only Mary Scarlett herself was left to confide her secrets. Would she tell him what had happened? Did she owe him an explanation?

He sighed and turned from the window. "Can I stand seeing her again, knowing she'll never be mine?"

Weary with all the questions that kept nagging him, Bolt walked quickly toward his bedroom. It was time to get dressed, go to the office.

"Work," he muttered. "God bless work!"

Twenty-three minutes later he stepped out into the humid, sun-drenched morning, locked the Bay Street entrance to his apartment, and crossed the wooden bridge walkway from Factor's Row to the street. Ordinarily, on such a brilliant spring day he would have enjoyed the short stroll to his law office. But he was late. The call from Allen Overman and the shock of finding out that Mary Scarlett was back had interrupted his precise morning routine. He climbed into his cardinal-red Honda CRX, folding his tall frame into the low car. He held the powerful engine in check as he cruised Bull Street to Johnson Square.

As he pulled into his parking spot, he glanced down the street in the direction of the old Lamar place. He couldn't quite see it, but he got a mental glimpse of it. It looked like a once-beautiful matriarch—faded and sad, neglected by the sole survivor of her family, ignored by the world. The house had been locked up tight since the suspicious death of Mary Scarlett's mother over four years ago. So far as Bolton knew, not a soul had set foot inside since the day after Lucy Lamar's wake. Still, it was whispered about town that strange lights were seen at the attic windows on moonless nights and a woman's voice—sometimes singing, sometimes sobbing—had been heard coming from the abandoned mansion.

He shuddered slightly and turned away. In a city of haunted houses and lingering spirits from the past, the Lamar place held more than its share of secrets. Only Mary Scarlett, the last of her long line, still lived to recall those woeful tales.

Pondering the past, Bolt stood too long in the street. A battered jalopy sporting a phantasmagoric paint job, obviously created by a student from SCAD, the Savannah College of Art and Design, whizzed by with a raucous honk of warning. Conrad leered at the speeding teenager, then turned and headed for his office.

His private line was ringing when he walked into the room. No doubt Allen with more news of Mary Scarlett or more questions. He sank into his tobacco-colored leather chair and punched the speaker button.

The voice that wafted into his office was like an echo from the past. "Hello, you good-lookin', sweet-talkin', brown-eyed hunk of lovin'." A pause . . . a husky sigh. "It's Mary Scarlett, and *I'm back!*"

Bolton jerked forward, picked up the receiver, and stared at it. It was like hearing a ghost. He would recognize the sultry-sweet, magnolia-flavored whine anytime, anyplace. Hers was a voice like black moonlight, rough velvet, perfumed poison. This was Mary Scarlett all right, in all her tarnished glory.

His gaze went automatically to the small, framed snapshot on his desk. Mary Scarlett—her bright eyes wide with wonder, her long hair, dark as night, falling over her tanned shoulders as she laughed at him from the Spanish Steps in

Rome. A smoky, dreamy beauty with a woman's smile, but wonderstruck, little-girl eyes. The picture had been taken two months after her graduation from Sweet Briar, a month after her mysterious flight from Savannah.

He couldn't believe she'd actually come home after all these years. He wasn't sure he *wanted* to believe it. He was still in love with her. No doubt about it. Suicidally so! But she was *married*. Wasn't she? Surely, not even Mary Scarlett would bring a *bullfighter* back to Savannah.

With a jolt, he realized suddenly that he hadn't actually believed the morning paper. Hearing Mary Scarlett's voice was his first concrete confirmation of her return.

He glanced out the window of his office, buying time, trying to convince himself that this was just any normal Monday morning in late March. Johnson Square was an eyeburning blaze of color—azaleas exploding in the hot, spring sun. The fountain threw out watery rainbows. The white obelisk marking the grave of Revolutionary War hero Nathanael Greene shimmered in dancing patches of sunlight and shade. A tourist tram rumbled by, the voice of the tour guide droning in the soft morning air. A mockingbird perched in the redbud tree just outside, making musical love to spring.

Bolton cleared his throat. He forced a smile of welcome he knew she couldn't see, but maybe she would hear it anyway. "Hey, Mary Scarlett." He tried to match her playful, Southern-casual-passionate drawl, although he'd long ago sworn off games with the one and only love of his life. "How you doin', honey? It's been—what? Eight years?"

"Don't you 'honey' me, Bolton Conrad! You know exactly how long I've been gone and what I've been up to. Mama used to write me that she read you every last one of my letters from all over—England, France, Italy, Greece, Turkey."

"She did that, Lucy did. Whether I wanted to know all the gory details or not." He chuckled, but it wasn't really a laugh. "I refused to listen anymore after you landed in Spain."

"Aw, Bolt darling, you missed the best part."

"Thank the Lord for small favors!"

"Why, honey, you sound jealous!" *She* sounded pleased.

"Wasn't that the way you planned it, Mary Scarlett?"

He couldn't keep a touch of bitterness from creeping into his voice. It had damn-near killed him when she up and ran off. She'd had her reasons, he supposed. But he had promised her everything would be all right if she would marry him. He'd meant it, too. Bolton Conrad was a man of his word and he had vowed to make Mary Scarlett the happiest woman on earth. That was the problem. She was scared to death of happiness. If you had it, you could lose it. Nothing in her privileged, blue-blooded, dysfunctional upbringing had ever prepared her for being happy. Happiness simply didn't run in her family. Mary Scarlett never was a child like the rest of their crowd. She grew up in that great shadowed house on Bull Street amidst the shades of her ancestors, trying to live up to the best of them and make up for the worst of them. At every turn she had met with failure and frustration.

"Bolton? Are you still there?"

"Just like I've always been."

"You sound surprised to hear from me. Didn't you read the notice I sent ahead to the paper? I did that for you, Bolt. I didn't want to just barge in unannounced."

"I don't believe everything I read in that mullet wrapper."

"Well, you can believe I'm here now, can't you?"

"Oh, yes! But where exactly are you, Mary Scarlett?"

"I don't know," she said peevishly. "Some tacky motel down by the river. But I hardly know this place anymore. Nothing in the city looks the same."

"What do you mean? Savannah never changes."

"Oh, but it has. What are all those Union soldiers doing camped out in the Colonial Cemetery? Their bonfires were

just blazing last night. Is it one of those Civil War reen-
actments or are they shooting another movie here?"

"I don't know what you're talking about, Mary Scarlett.
Bonfires in the cemetery?" He shook his head, wondering
if she'd had martinis for breakfast.

"Bolt, come get me. I want out of this place."

"Just tell me where you are and I'll be right there, Mary
Scarlett."

"I told you, I don't know. A cab driver brought me here
from the airport awhile after midnight. I needed a place to
stay and didn't have a reservation and he said everywhere
was full on account of the house and garden tour. So he
brought me here and I hate it, Bolt. It's awful! There's not
even a bidet."

Her complaint made him grin, but he dared not let her
hear his amusement. "You don't have any idea where you
are?"

"No." He heard that little-girl pout in her voice now, the
same wheedling tone she had used to get her way with him
since he was ten—the kid from south of Gaston Street who
delivered the evening paper—and she was eight—the gifted,
beautiful, justly spoiled only child of one of the Garden
City's first families. "I haven't the faintest. Bolt, will you
come get me?"

"I can't, honey, not till you tell me the name of the
place." He made an effort to be gentle with her, coaxing.
He could tell from the sharp edge in her voice that she was
in a fragile state. "Isn't there a matchbook somewhere in
the room?"

"It's a goddamn non-smoking room!" she exploded.
"Can you imagine such a thing? Why, in Europe . . ."

"Honey, you're not in Europe any longer," he reminded
her gently. "Check the bathroom. Maybe the name's on the
towels or the wrappers on the bars of soap."

Mary Scarlett uttered a martyred sigh, then Bolton heard
the receiver clatter against a hard surface. He waited in si-

lence until she came back after several minutes. She spat out the name of the chain motel as if it tasted nasty in her mouth.

"Okay. You sit tight, Mary Scarlett. I'll be there in ten minutes."

"Hurry, Bolt! I want to see you."

"I will, darlin'."

He replaced the receiver before he said, still staring at the phone and imagining her never-to-be-forgotten face framed in silky, smoky hair as black as Bonaventure Cemetery at midnight, "I want to see you, too, Mary Scarlett. I really, truly do."

But, God, how he dreaded it!

Mary Scarlett Miguel, née Lamar, clung to the receiver for a few moments after Bolton Conrad hung up. It gave her some measure of security, thinking how his voice had been so near only seconds ago. Finally, she replaced it gently, then gripped her arms to try to stop shivering. It was going to be a hot day. The chill she felt came from inside, down deep in her heart somewhere. She had never thought she would be able to face Bolt again, not after what she did to him. Allen was different. He had never loved her for who she was, but for what she represented. Only after all these years had she come to understand the truth about the two men who had wanted to marry her. Knowing the truth would make facing Bolt that much harder.

"Stop it, Mary Scarlett!" she said loudly, angrily. "You've got to get hold of yourself."

Her sudden outburst drained away the last of her strength. She felt almost sick, she was so tired. Even though she had sent the notice of her return to the Savannah paper as insurance to keep herself from backing out on her plans to come home, she hadn't thought to make advance airline reservations. Consequently, she'd had to do some country-hopping to get back to the States. She had been traveling for three days, sleeping in airports, hardly eating the whole way.

Maybe simple fatigue was the reason she was seeing things. Like the soldiers in the cemetery. The last army she knew of that had occupied that space was Sherman's troops when they'd made their infamous March to the Sea. Her family had always taken a lot of pride in the knowledge that one of their ancestors was involved in saving Savannah from that Yankee general's torches. She tried to remember the story exactly, but her brain was too numb to function. She let it go for the moment. There were more important matters to sort out in her mind.

Crossing her long, ivory silk-sheathed legs, Mary Scarlett stroked a leaping orange flame from her gold lighter. After a moment, the slender tip of her Spanish cigarette glowed. Inhaling deeply, she held the smoke inside for several seconds, closing her eyes, savoring the deep acrid burn before she breathed it out in fine twin streams through flared nostrils.

"Jesus! How did it come to this?" With the back of her wrist, she blotted sudden tears that squeezed from the corners of her eyes.

She meant, of course, her unexpected return to Savannah—more unexpected to Mary Scarlett herself than to anyone else. If she was going to come back eventually anyway, why hadn't she returned after her father, Big Dick Lamar, disappeared so mysteriously six years ago? If not then, why hadn't she come after her mother—the fragile, elegant, terrified Amelia Lucy Robillard Lamar—had accidentally killed herself? While trying to kill the pain of her guilt and loneliness with peach brandy and Valium, she had taken a false, drunken step that sent her careening over a balcony railing "carved by the master slave craftsman Cupidon back in 1852 from one solid piece of mahogany from the Indies," as the guidebooks all stated.

Mary Scarlett knew the answer even as she asked herself

the question. In her heart and soul she had never really left
Savannah. Her marriage to Raul had held her prisoner in
an alien land. Only her husband's sudden death had released
her to return to Savannah.

She wore mourning white. Black was for grieving widows,
women who had wept at their husbands' deaths and wailed
at their funerals. Wives who hadn't prayed to be free from
the horrors of a mad, violent, passionate marriage that kept
itself afloat on a vast sea of gin and an endless river of lies.

Raul and their love-hate relationship had been her only
reality for the past seven years. Now it all seemed like a
dream—hot afternoons in the *plaza de toros* in Barcelona,
the smell of blood in the sand, the roar of cheers, the roar
of death, the drunken roar of gin inside her head. The flash
of the blazing sun off Raul's *traje de luces,* his "suit of
lights." His dazzling smile, his graceful, manly moves. How
she had hated it . . . and him, at times. But there had been
other occasions when her passion for her dark-souled Spaniard had known no bounds.

In order to bear those bloody afternoons of the *corrida,*
Mary Scarlett had played a game of her own invention. As
she watched her great *torero* in the ring, she had pretended
she could see beneath the silk and sequins, see that beautiful, naked body under his suit of lights. She would visu-
alize the two of them in bed, making their own wild brand
of love, so that she didn't have to watch the swords tear
the flesh of the bulls or see the flash of blood-lust in her
lover's black eyes—the same look she sometimes saw when
he came to her bed.

A shiver ran through her. She stubbed out the cigarette
in the little gold ashtray from her purse. After brushing a
stray ash from her slim white skirt, she rose and went to
the window. From the second floor she could see only
patches of light through the drifting curtain of Spanish moss
that cloaked the huge oak outside. It was early, just after
nine, but already a few cars moved lazily along behind the

first tour buses of the day. A horse clopped by, pulling a bright red buggy stuffed with gaping, camera-snapping tourists. She frowned as another midnight memory flashed through her mind.

This vehicle wasn't the same as the one she'd seen only a few hours ago. Or had she really seen it—that closed, death-draped carriage drawn by four black-plumed horses? And those strange people in their old-fashioned clothes— who could they have been? Where had they come from? Had she imagined it all or did Savannah have another face that it showed only in the deepest, darkest hours of the night? Was the old city welcoming her home or warning her away?

"Don't be ridiculous!" she scoffed, trying to shake off such grim thoughts. Savannah had always been a place of mystery and magic, spirits and superstitions. But even this witching old city couldn't keep a secret like that.

"I must have imagined it all," she murmured. "It's the strain of the trip. I'll be okay once Bolton gets here. He's always known how to calm me down." She sighed. "I should have married him."

Her own words shocked her. Never before had she been brave enough to admit the truth to herself—the truth of the fact that she'd made a mistake by running away from the only man who might have made her happy. Maybe she was stronger now than she had thought.

She allowed herself a smile. "This could be a break-through," she whispered. She might even dare now to let herself think about all that had happened.

"But not right this minute," she warned. "Not until I've seen Bolt again. God! What if he's married?"

A knock at the door spun her around. She ran to open it.

"Are you married?" she demanded before even saying hello.

Instantly, she saw the shock in his deep-set eyes. Shock

at her question and shock at the color of her hair. He had never seen her as a blonde. No one here had.

Bolton Conrad—taller by a foot than Mary Scarlett, tanned, tough, with just a hint of silver at his dark temples to add distinction—lifted his naked left hand for her to see. Then he cupped her cheek.

"As you may remember, darlin', I considered it once. Once was enough." His voice was husky with emotion.

She clutched his hand and kissed it—rained kisses all over his knuckles, his palm, his wrist, breathing in the clean, ocean-fresh fragrance of his aftershave, the well-remembered musk of the man himself.

"Thank God, Bolt! Thank God!"

He hadn't meant to do it, but he could no more keep from kissing those perfect, pouting lips than he could stop breathing.

Mary Scarlett melted into his arms. More than anything in the world, she needed to be kissed by Bolton Conrad right now—the way he had kissed her a long, long time ago. Sweet and soft and with so much tenderness that she didn't have to ask herself if she still cared for him. Locked in an embrace, their very souls touching, she trembled in his arms from the onslaught of warm memories and old sensations flooding her heart.

After several minutes, Bolton pulled away. He stared down into the dewy glow of her jewel-blue eyes. "Mary Scarlett? Are you propositioning me?" he teased gently.

She shook her head, still clinging to his big, warm hands. "No. I just couldn't stand the thought of you married to some other woman. I know it's selfish of me, Bolt, but in my mind you'll belong to me forever. I've always been that way about my most treasured possessions. And you're definitely one of them," she added in a soft purr.

That pretty well summed it up. His smile faded along with his hopes. Mary Scarlett had never really loved him the way he loved her. She had simply possessed him—mind, body, soul, and heart. She had thought of him the way she'd thought of her Austin Healy or her mink coat or the antique mirror she and Granny Boo had always treasured so.

"I reckon you've just put me in my place, honey. I guess I know for sure now why you came back."

"Bolt? What do you mean?" She stared at him, her smile fading. *She* didn't yet understand why she'd returned to Savannah. So how could he know?

"The house on Bull Street," he answered matter-of-factly. "It's time for you to make up your mind what you plan to do with it. Didn't you come back to see Miss Lucy's lawyers? If you don't claim it and move in within the next two months, the place will go to the Telfair Academy. It will be the newest museum house on the tours."

"Oh. The house." She hadn't lost her soft Geechee accent, pronouncing the word "house" in time-honored Savannah style.

"You mean you didn't know? I was sure your mama's lawyers had contacted you."

"If they did, the letter probably arrived after I left. I've been traveling for a couple of months, trying to work up the nerve to come back here, I guess."

"Well, this is a real stroke of luck. You got home in the nick of time."

"Did I?" she asked distractedly.

"Are you saying you don't want the old house? Mary Scarlett, I know the place holds a lot of bad memories for you, but you shouldn't rush your decision. If nothing else, keeping it would be a sound financial move. If you decide you don't want it, you can sell it later. There are people from all over begging to buy these antebellum houses and restore them. You could make enough to live comfortably for years."

"You mean sell it to a *stranger? Never!*" she snapped.

"Then what are you going to do, honey?"

"I don't know. It's been so long."

"It needs some work, I'm sure. No one's lived in it since your mother passed on. But everything's still there." He looked away, not wanting to say what he was about to, but knowing he couldn't stop the words from coming. "Everything, Mary Scarlett. Even your wedding dress."

"And my mirror?"

Bolt nodded. "That, too, I suppose. Your mother wrote specific instructions that nothing was to be touched until you came home. She left enough money to pay the taxes for a few years. I guess she figured you'd have to come back eventually. She wanted you to have the place, Mary Scarlett. It's part of your heritage."

Mary Scarlett ran trembling fingers through the thick waves of her silver-blond hair. "I can't think about that right now."

"Do you want me to call Miss Lucy's lawyer and tell him you're back?"

"Would you?" she begged. "Lawyers always make me nervous."

He chuckled at that.

"Oh, I don't mean you, Bolt. Let's just get my things and get the hell out of this awful, depressing place."

Bolt gathered up her two pastel tapestry bags. "You're traveling mighty light," he commented.

"All the rest is being shipped. Once I decided to leave, I was in too much of a hurry to bring everything along."

He looked at her oddly. "Then you're planning to stay for good?"

"Of course," she answered, hurrying ahead of him into the hallway. "Where else would I go?"

Again the bullfighter came to mind. "You're alone, Mary Scarlett?"

"Yes!" she answered, without explanation.

Bolton wanted to ask *why* she was alone, but he didn't. He would hear the whole story when Mary Scarlett got ready to tell all. She was never one to be rushed.

They didn't have far to go. Bolton decided the best place to take her for the time being was to his bachelor apartment in the old cotton warehouse overlooking River Street. Only minutes later, they were on Factor's Walk at his front door.

The instant they reached the old ballast stone building, an odd dizziness overcame Mary Scarlett. She had felt this same way when she saw the fires in the cemetery and the black-draped coach hours before. She balked short of the doorway. "Why are we coming here? He knows about this place. He'll find us. I don't want to see anyone. Especially not *him!*"

Bolton turned and stared at her. Her face looked flushed and her eyes glassy. Her voice belonged to a stranger. "There's no one else here, Mary Scarlett. What's going on?"

She blinked at him, her eyes wide and unfocused, her lips pressed in a tight line of genuine fear. "You live here?" she whispered at length.

He nodded. "Yes, I live here. All these old warehouses and cotton factors' offices have been made over into apartments, artists' studios, and shops. I think you'll like my place."

She hesitated, still looking doubtful. "You're sure this isn't a trick? He's not hiding inside, waiting to catch us together?"

"I don't know who you mean, but there's no one in my apartment. We'll be alone, just you and I."

Her expression changed suddenly. Her color returned to normal; her sapphire eyes sparkled in the morning sun. "Slow poke!" she said with a laugh. "I'm getting absolutely faint standing out here in the heat. Why don't you go ahead and unlock the door?"

Thoroughly puzzled by her odd behavior, Bolton did just that. A short time later, they were comfortably seated in his living room, sipping mimosas and watching a cruise ship pass by on the Savannah River. Mary Scarlett seemed herself again and was obviously enchanted by his masculine bachelor abode, with its earth tone decor to match the river view.

"What did you do with our house?" she wanted to know,

referring to the palatial new old-style lowcountry mansion that he had designed and built for them to live in after they were married.

"Sold it."

"Our beautiful house?"

"Had to," he said in a clipped tone. "The place was haunted."

"It was brand new!"

"But your ghost was in every room, Mary Scarlett. I could never have lived there alone."

She smiled at him. "That's sweet, Bolt darlin'."

Her comment galled him. There was nothing *sweet* about it. It was damn sad! If she hadn't run off, that place would be their home now, with babies in the nursery, dogs in the yard, and azaleas bursting into brilliant bloom while Cherokee roses climbed the picket fence.

"This place is more *you*," she went on in a chatty tone. "All the nautical antiques, the river view, the old ballast stone walls. Wasn't one of your ancestors a sea captain?"

"A sailor, but not by choice. He got shanghaied in Liverpool, so the story goes."

"Still, the sea is your family heritage. You paint seascapes, river scenes. Yes, this place definitely suits you, Bolt."

"It's smaller than you like, as I remember." Without coming right out and asking, he needed to find out if she meant to stay with him indefinitely. He wasn't married, but lately he had been seeing someone. Someone he knew Mary Scarlett wouldn't approve of. Not that she would have approved of his seeing *any* other woman.

As if she were reading his most secret thoughts, she asked, "Do you ever run into Kathleen Rutherford?"

He nodded, immediately on guard. "It's O'Shea now. She married Jimbo. Remember him?"

Mary Scarlett twirled her crystal glass, her eyes lit with little-girl delight. "Do I ever! He used to have the worst crush on me in high school. Followed me around like a

sad-eyed hound pup. But I was *madly* in love with Allen
Overman at the time. I can't believe Kathleen actually married Jimbo. I guess they have about a dozen kids by now.
She was always such a homemaker-type and he came from
that huge family. Lace-curtain Irish, you know. My mama
used to say Jimbo's mama had more younguns than she had
sense."

"No children. In fact, they're no longer married."

"Divorced?" Mary Scarlett rasped in a harsh whisper.
"Oh, for shame! And what did their families think of that?
It must have been the talk of Savannah."

"I didn't say they were divorced, Mary Scarlett," Bolt
answered in a serious tone. "Jimbo died of a heart attack
only a year after they were married. On St. Patrick's Day."

For the first time all morning, Mary Scarlett seemed at
a loss for words. Finally, she said, "Poor Kathleen. I'm
sorry. Jimbo was a sweet guy. I guess they were in love?"
She looked to Bolton for confirmation.

"Deeply. It took her over two years to get back out into
society again. It was like her whole world ceased to exist.
She still can't bring herself to watch the parade on St. Patrick's Day."

"Really?" she said. "I can't imagine such a thing."

"Sure you can, Mary Scarlett. You know how your mama
was after your daddy . . ." He paused, trying to think of
the most sensitive word to use. Gossip had it that Big Dick
Lamar had neither been kidnapped nor drowned on a fishing trip, but had left town with a female companion when
he disappeared so suddenly that long-ago June night.

Mary Scarlett relieved him of his dilemma with a dry
laugh. "That wasn't from love. That was pure relief. Big
Dick was a big bastard! Everybody knew it. Especially
Mama. Enough said!"

Bolton made no reply. He didn't want to get Mary Scarlett started on her daddy. That bad blood went way back.

"How about Allen? Is he still around?"

"Never left," Bolton answered.

Mary Scarlett chuckled. "Who ever does?"

"You did."

"And look where it got me. Right back where I started."
She stared down at her melting ice cubes as if she were
contemplating a crystal ball. "I thought for sure Allen would
leave."

"He's old Savannah, Oglethorpe Club and all that. Why
should he?"

Mary Scarlett shook her head. "I don't know. He just
never seemed to fit the mold. I thought sure he'd wind up
in New York on Wall Street, or maybe in Hong Kong or
Paris." She looked up at Bolt and grinned. "Is *he* married?"

"Checking out all possibilities, huh?" he answered grimly.
"If that's the case, you'll be gratified to learn that Mr. Overman is currently between wives. At least he was as of last
week. One never knows with good ole Allen."

"How many has he had?"

Bolt laughed. "Never too many for one more." He paused
and thought for a minute. "I believe four at last count."

"Good God! I thought Bluebeard left Savannah ages
ago."

"Allen's ex-wives wouldn't agree with you. He's still
friends with all four and, if gossip can be relied upon, the
lover of two. But they've all been messy marriages and
even messier divorces. It seems Allen can only get along
with his wives after they've kicked him out."

"Anyone I know?"

"Let's see, in order of their wifedom, Cynthia McCloud,
Helen Armitage, Luanne Webster, and Aurelia LaMotte."

"Aurelia LaMotte? Why, she was Mama's age! They're
all way older than Allen. Why doesn't he try someone from
our old crowd, like Kathleen, for instance?"

Bolton bristled, but held a level tone. "Kathleen's way
out of Allen's league. He came on to her at a party last
year. She cut him right down to size, in ladylike fashion,

of course. No, Allen would be all wrong for Kathleen. He's a mover, a shaker, a wheeler-dealer. If she ever marries again, I'm sure she'll want someone more settled, less flamboyant."

"Flamboyant certainly is the right word for Allen. That's the way I remember him anyhow." Mary Scarlett's face took on a sudden glow that twisted some old jealousy deep in Bolton's heart. "I guess you wouldn't remember, but Allen was my escort at the Cotillion when I came out. There wasn't a girl there who wouldn't have swapped dates with me in a heartbeat. They were just green with envy, the lot of them. I'll never forget that night."

Bolton would never forget that night either. Not well enough born to be approved by the committee as a debutante's escort, he was hired by the hotel as an extra valet that evening. He had parked Allen's father's silver Jaguar. And he'd seen Mary Scarlett—a vision in white lace, her tanned shoulders bare except for a transparent stole. That was the night it really sank in that even though the two of them might live in the same city, they were from totally different worlds. He had wanted to die or kill when Allen had tossed him a quarter tip, then slipped his arm possessively around Mary Scarlett's slender waist and led her off to the party in the hotel ballroom.

Unaware that Bolt was lost in his own thoughts or that she was rubbing salt into old wounds, Mary Scarlett rushed on. "Yes, that night was something. Without my knowing it, Allen told all the girls that he planned to ask me to marry him later that night. Of course, he didn't. And, of course, I wouldn't have said yes anyway. I meant to break my share of hearts before I settled down." She paused and giggled. "He spread the word among the guys, also without my knowledge—I would have *killed* him!—that he and I had already done the *dirty deed* and that he was taking me to Tybee after the ball to do it again, on the beach, in the moonlight. God, if my mama had ever heard that, she would have died of heart failure right on the spot! She thought he was such a proper, upstanding young gentleman. Would you believe Mama even wanted to go ahead and have an *O* for Overman engraved on all my silver flatware? I guess she figured I'd have to marry him if she did that. I think Allen put her up to it. He was always teasing about how he and Mama were going to gang up on me and I wouldn't have any choice but to marry him."

"Allen hasn't changed much. You still have to take everything he says with a grain of salt."

"I still say, Kathleen could straighten him out."

Bolt didn't respond. He had gone as far as he could comfortably go at the moment on the subject of Kathleen. Besides, something was still nagging him. *What about the bullfighter?* Mary Scarlett had talked about everyone else, but she had yet to mention her husband. Had she just up and run away the same way she'd run from Savannah eight years ago?

"I'm only teasing about Allen and Kathleen. I can sympathize with her," she said, pouring herself another mimosa from the crystal pitcher. "I'm a widow now, too."

Guilt seized Bolton for the thoughts he had been entertaining. He touched her hand. "I'm so sorry, honey. You should have told me. How long?"

"Raul died eight months ago."

"It was sudden?"

"Very! He went into the ring drunk one afternoon and the bull gored him. I saw the whole thing."

Bolton was struck speechless, numb. The thought of *anyone* meeting such a horrible death—Mary Scarlett's husband, of all people! And her there to see it. No wonder she was acting erratic.

"God, Mary Scarlett! It had to be awful for you, honey. I'm so sorry," he repeated.

"Let's don't talk about it. Okay?"

"Whatever you say," he answered gently.

She turned to him, her smile too wide, her eyes too bright. "What I say, Bolt darlin', is that I'd really like you to kiss me again. I'm feeling kind of strange and I'm scared to death being back here. I need to know it's where I belong and that at least one person in all of Savannah is glad to see me."

She slid across the tufted leather couch and raised her lips to his, eyes closed, tears seeping from beneath her long lashes.

"Mary Scarlett, you know I'm glad you're back," he whispered.

Their lips met, and Bolton was forced to admit to himself that it was like time had stopped the minute Mary Scarlett walked out of his life. Now that she was back in his arms again, the clock was running once again.

Or was that a time bomb ticking?

Two

The phone rang before Mary Scarlett was nearly ready for Bolt to stop kissing her. He must have felt the same way, judging from the annoyance in his voice when he answered.

"Yes?" he growled. Then in an only slightly friendlier tone, "Why, Allen, your name came up in conversation not ten minutes ago."

Mary Scarlett motioned for Bolton to let her talk.

He nodded, but held the receiver for long minutes while Allen Overman went on and on about his failure to locate Mary Scarlett.

Again, she motioned for the phone.

"Say, Allen, I've got someone here who'd like to say hello. That is, if you didn't get married again since we talked earlier." Bolt gave a hearty laugh at whatever Allen said in response to that, then he pressed the speaker button.

"Al-len?" she said huskily. "Do you know who this is?"

"Mary Scarlett!" he whooped. "Damn, honey! Where you been all my life?"

"Seeing the world and missing you every minute I was away."

Grinning, she met Bolt's eyes. He gave her a scowl of mock jealousy.

Allen immediately issued an invitation to Mary Scarlett. "Hey, I'm throwing a little black tie bash at my place Saturday night. Want to come be my date?"

She arched an eyebrow and glanced at Bolton. "A party?"

Bolt nodded his assent. "I'd love to come, Allen, but I'm afraid I'm already spoken for."

"Shit, honey!" he responded with a laugh. "Seems like I'm always a day late and a dollar short."

"Okay if I bring my feller?"

"And who might that be?"

"You know." She glanced over and fluttered her lashes at Bolt. This was an old game she had played since their school days. Flirting with both "boys," playing one against the other. She was obviously enjoying herself tremendously. However, this time Allen Overman missed her ploy.

"Yeah, I know all right. You went and got *married.* I heard all about it." Allen paused, then chuckled. "Tell me something, is it true all those matador-guys poke rolled-up socks in their tights to get that bulge and that's what makes all the bulls see red and all the gals go crazy?"

Caught off guard, Mary Scarlett gasped and covered her face with her hands.

Bolton cut Allen off before he could say anything more. "Hey, buddy, *I'm* her date. I'll let you know if we can make it."

"Did I say something wrong? What's the matter? Mary Scarlett? You still there?"

"Gotta go. I'll call you later, Allen."

"Hey, Bolt, I didn't mean to piss her off."

"Yeah, sure."

"You should have called me the minute you found her."

"I was going to. We just got here."

"How did you find her?"

"I didn't. She phoned me." Bolton glanced at Mary Scarlett, still huddled up, her shoulders shaking. "Look, Allen, I really have to go now. I'll call you later, okay?"

When Bolt hung up, Mary Scarlett was curled into a ball on the sofa, whimpering softly, tears on her cheeks.

"Hey, it's all right," he said, rubbing her shoulders. "Allen didn't mean anything. He had no way of knowing about your husband. Nobody here knows you're a widow, darlin'. If we don't do something, you're going to be running into remarks like that all the time."

"What am I supposed to do? Hire a sound truck to drive around town and announce it?"

"Why don't I put a discreet announcement in the obituary column? If everyone in town reads it in the paper, they won't ask questions or make dumb comments like Allen's."

She looked at him uncertainly. "No garish details," she begged with a shudder.

Bolt shook his head. "No. Only the essentials—the date that it happened and anything else you want to add. There are going to be a lot of questions in people's minds after that item that ran this morning. The obit will explain things and muzzle the gossips." He touched her hand reassuringly. "Don't worry, Mary Scarlett. Everything's going to be all right. You're back home now where you belong."

Her eyes were wide and searching. "Do I belong here, Bolt?"

"Sure you do, honey," he said gently. "You always did. You always will."

He wanted to add *Right here with me,* but instead he leaned down and kissed her cheek.

Mary Scarlett murmured her thanks. Her crying stopped. When they parted, she was almost smiling, and her sapphire eyes shone with something like hope for the first time all morning.

"Give me a pad and a pen, Bolt. I'll put down what needs to be said."

He obliged, then waited as she scratched a brief paragraph on the lined, white paper. She sat back, read over it, then handed it to him. "There!" she said with obvious relief "That's done."

Bolton got the oddest feeling that she was referring to more than simply the writing of her husband's obituary. The tone in her voice seemed to indicate that she was closing that chapter of her life. It was done, finished, over for good.

"Tell you what," Bolt said, "why don't I show you to the guest room? You can get unpacked, freshen up, and relax. I'll run over to the newspaper office, then stop off for some groceries. By the time I get back, you'll feel like a new woman."

Mary Scarlett agreed hesitantly. She really didn't want to be left alone right now. But Bolt was right. She did need a shower, clean clothes, a nap. Jet lag was dragging her down, making her feel groggy and disoriented.

"You won't be gone long, will you?"

He smiled at her and gave her hand a squeeze. "I'll be back before you can whistle the first verse of 'Dixie.'"

"It's so sweet of you to offer me a place to stay, Bolt."

He didn't frown, but he wanted to. He hadn't meant this as a permanent arrangement, only temporary. Number one, Kathleen would be royally pissed when she found out. Number two, he wasn't sure it was safe for him to share his place with Mary Scarlett. A kiss between friends now and then was one thing, but he could feel those old flames already rekindling. And Mary Scarlett was vulnerable right now, anxious to have someone take care of her. It could become a habit.

"Why don't I stop by the real estate office down the street and pick up their apartment listings—see if there's anything that might suit you until you decide what to do about the house?"

Bolton tried to ignore the disappointed look she gave him, but he couldn't ignore her words. "Honey, I don't think I'm ready to live alone yet. If it's no bother, I'd like to stay here with you a while."

"Sure, no problem." His answer sounded casual enough. Deep down, however, he knew they were heading for trouble or at the very least a dangerous entanglement. "Come on now. I'll put your bags in the bedroom before I leave."

* * *

As soon as Bolton was gone, Mary Scarlett felt the old panic set in. Her own thoughts were her worst enemies these days, and without someone to talk to they crowded in on her, a pack of snapping, snarling wolves, ready to tear her apart.

She sat down on the bright peach-and-blue chintz bedspread and put her face in her hands. She felt weak and dizzy. There was no fight left in her. The past months . . . the past years had left her drained and defenseless.

Familiar old scenes reeled through her mind like a fast-running video. The face she had seen in her mirror that night eight years ago—a face that held both promise and warning, turning her blood to ice. The face of Jacques St. Julian, a man dead for almost two centuries. It was that vision which had sent her running. Her midnight escape on the train to Atlanta, the clatter and rattle of the rails her only comfort as she fled her past and the history of all her ancestors. Then the long, lonely flight to Rome with no sleep, only troubling, terrifying thoughts to keep her company.

There were so many memories after that night that they all ran together in her mind. Backpacking through Italy, France, Spain, stealing blood oranges from groves when food money ran low, accepting the hospitality of latter-day hippies in the caves of Ibiza, tramping through sun-baked, dusty streets, high on pot and cheap red wine. She'd been a mess physically and emotionally by the day she found herself in the *plaza de toros* in Barcelona, surrounded by a motley group of misfits she'd picked up along the way. She remembered thinking on that brassy-gold afternoon that she was about as far from Savannah, with its cool shaded squares and imposing old mansions, its whispered gossip and secret intrigues, as a body could get. She had felt a moment of pride in that fact. She had finally grown up, left her childhood behind. She could take care of herself and she was doing just that, and, yes, she was proud of herself . . . until she got a whiff of her own unwashed body, until the bad wine made her stomach turn, until the filthy Gypsy kid named Cosimo tried to grope her breasts right there in front of God and half of Spain. She'd shoved him away and cursed the whole lot of them—her *friends*—before moving to another seat, farther down, nearer the bullring.

That's when she'd seen *him* for the first time. Raul! Tall, lean, as dark as the pits of hell, as handsome as an archangel, as masculine and sexy as any woman's most wishful fantasy. Raul, preening for his adoring fans, glowing in his suit of lights, making something deep inside her ache to do his bidding.

He had made eye contact with her immediately, holding her gaze for long moments, making her tremble to feel his touch. She knew in that instant that he meant to have her. She had been more than willing. Had he invited her down at that moment, she would gladly, blissfully, have stripped naked and thrown herself onto the bloody sand for him to take her in full view of the cheering multitudes.

There had been no invitation. Simply a single red rose, touched by his lips before he tossed it into her outstretched hands. And that smile—those blinding white teeth in his mahogany-dark face, the black fire in his eyes, the suggestive posture of his firm body that said to her, "You see? It is for you. All my secrets, all my passionate magic, all my love!"

Looking at him, Mary Scarlett had smiled, thinking there was certainly nothing here of the cool, poised, "gentlemanly" young men who had pursued her back in Savannah, with their flirtatious lies and soft-spoken promises. Raul's hard, handsome face told her all that would be expected of her, demanded of her. And she was willing. She had brushed the rose with her lips, smiled back, and nodded her assent.

The rest of that long, hot afternoon had passed in a blaze of longing. Her eyes never left him. Her pulses raced faster and faster. With each flourish of his cape, each thrust of his hips, each sensual movement of his hands, she felt as if he were already making love to her. Stroking her, fondling her, setting her on fire.

By the time Raul's somber bodyguard came to fetch her, she was already his prisoner of passion, *his woman.* She lost more than her heart and her soul that afternoon; she lost her own identity. She became only an extension of the man in the suit of lights.

"Raul wants you," his henchman informed her brusquely.

And I want him, she answered with a silent nod.

She was escorted to a sort of dressing room, a cluttered space used by all the matadors. The chamber reeked of pomade, stale wine, cut flowers, and urine. Clothes were scattered about, along with empty wineskins, bloody capes, baskets of spoiling fruit. She entered hesitantly, her eyes taking a moment to adjust to the shadows after the bright sun outside. Then she saw him—bare to the waist, his tight pants gleaming with their dusty spangles. He was no longer smiling. His black eyes glowed as he gazed at her.

He motioned her closer. She took a few steps toward him, her heart in her throat. Then she was in his arms. He never asked her name, never spoke a word. As he kissed her—a hard, hot, probing kiss that took her breath away and made her tremble—he pulled the peasant blouse from her shoulders. By the end of that first kiss, they were both naked to the waist. He gripped her breasts with both hands, squeezing until her nipples strained toward his waiting lips, squeezing until she moaned, half in pain, half in pleasure. When he smoothed his tongue over her flesh, she forgot the pain altogether. Her blood turned to liquid fire.

He lowered her to a cot in one corner of the room. His cape-work proved good practice for his next maneuver. With expert dexterity, he stripped away her full cotton-gauze skirt, leaving her naked before his hungry eyes. For a time, he simply knelt beside her, examining her body with his hungry gaze. She shivered, aching for his next move, wondering what he would do to her and how long he would make her wait.

Just then, two other men barged into the room, laughing and talking in rapid-fire Spanish. They fell silent when they saw her. Mary Scarlett tried to curl herself into a ball to hide her nakedness, but Raul lashed out sharply in his native tongue. She caught only a word or two, but his tone was universal. He motioned his friends over. All three of them stared at her. She wanted to die of embarrassment, but at the same time she felt strangely aroused by the admiration in their dark eyes and their murmurs of approval.

The men exchanged remarks, again in Spanish. It seemed to her that Raul's friends were offering suggestions. Raul nodded, chuckled, then slid one hand up the length of her leg until it rested between her thighs, the tips of his fingers touching the source of her painful need. She bit her lip, but a soft moan escaped despite her best efforts. The two spectators laughed. They drew up chairs, uncorked a bottle of wine, and passed it back and forth. Raul took a swig and offered it to Mary Scarlett. She rose on one elbow to accept the drink. When she shifted on the cot, Raul's fingers sank into her. She gasped. The two other men laughed, then opened another bottle.

The afternoon wore on into evening. More touching, kissing, taunting. More painful longing for Mary Scarlett—debutante, socialite, prisoner of passion.

The room grew dark. The men lit candles and drank more wine and said things in Spanish to Raul that Mary Scarlett was glad she didn't understand. Raul, too, was naked by now. Naked and ready.

By the time he finally mounted her, Mary Scarlett was very drunk and aroused nearly to the point of madness. His first deep thrust brought a scream from her bruised, wine-stained lips—an exclamation of pure relief. Raul's friends applauded and called encouragement as the magnificent matador rode her expertly. Their voices sounded dim and faraway to Mary Scarlett. Her full awareness centered upon her new lover. His power, his size, his hot male smell. The wonderful slide of his sweaty flesh over hers.

When her climax came, she felt totally transported. She was off in another world—a cool, perfumed, glorious place. Angels sang. Stars danced. The moon cried for joy.

Satisfied, Raul withdrew. He leaned over Mary Scarlett, staring down into her eyes. He kissed her hard and pinched her nipples, then smoothed one firm palm down over her belly.

"De nada," he said, the first words he had spoken directly to her. She understood. Not "Thank you," but "You are welcome." To his way of thinking, he had given; she had received.

She lay there watching him as he rose from the cot and wrapped a towel around his hips to hide his spent erection. His attention turned from her now, centering on his two friends, both big, handsome fellows. With a polite gesture of his hand and a few words, he obviously offered them their turns with his new lover. Mary Scarlett stiffened. The huskier of the men stood, came over to the cot, and grinned down at her. She closed her eyes and turned her face toward the wall.

Again, they laughed and passed the wine bottle. She was drifting off now. As hard as she tried to stay awake, it was no use. Her body longed for sleep almost as desperately as it still longed for Raul.

Sometime late in the night, he woke her. The other men were gone. He tossed her clothes on the cot and said, "Go now."

Until that moment, she hadn't known that he spoke a word of English.

"Go where?" she asked groggily.

"Home to your mama."

"My mama's dead," she lied.

He shrugged. "Go back to your husband then. He will be wondering where you are."

She shook her head.

"No husband either?" He chuckled deep in his throat. "That is good. He probably would not take you back now. Even if he would, he could no longer please you, eh? Not after Raul."

"Please let me stay with you." Mary Scarlett couldn't believe it when she heard herself begging.

He hesitated, considering. "You are American?"

She nodded, blinking back tears, holding her breath as she waited for his answer.

"I saw you with those Gypsies. You are not one of them?"

"No," she whispered.

"Good! I hate Gypsies. American, eh? And all alone?"

Again she'd nodded silently, fighting back tears. She hadn't realized how alone she felt.

He shrugged. "Stay then, if you wish."

When she murmured her thanks to Raul-the-Magnificent, he only scowled at her. Then tossing a few bills on the bed, he said, "If you wish to remain with me, have your hair done. You look like a dark Gypsy. Blondes make me hot."

A week later, Mary Scarlett Lamar from Savannah, Georgia, was a blonde, married to a hard-drinking, trigger-tempered, oversexed Spanish bullfighter. Obsessed with him. Afraid of him, but willing to do anything to be with him.

And that had been the beginning of it. A seven-year rollercoaster marriage during which she had experienced the heights of passion and the depths of degradation. She had been weak when she met him, lost while she was married to him, and freed only when the bull destroyed him. For months after his death, she had wandered Europe, trying to find herself again, trying to remember who the real Mary Scarlett truly was. She had almost decided that the person she had once been had ceased to exist, that the old Mary Scarlett was as cold and dead as Raul.

Until one afternoon on a hilltop in Greece. As she had gazed out over the Aegean Sea, watching the sinking sun turn the water to molten gold, she had suddenly remembered Savannah. Images and sensations had come flooding back— the green darkness of the oaks, the old mansions like faded ladies, the cobbled streets, the smell of marsh and mud and magnolias. The old house on Bull Street, with all its secrets, all its magic. The antique mirror that had been her favorite plaything as a child, her talisman, her good luck charm. The very object that had warned her away was now pulling her back.

Savannah! She had realized in an instant that she would find the real Mary Scarlett there. That's where she had been all this time, waiting for her pale, confused twin to return.

Still sitting on the bed in Bolton Conrad's apartment, Mary Scarlett gazed out at the river—wide, lazy, blue with the reflection of the sky. "Well, here I am," she whispered. "I'm home, Savannah. Now what?"

She caught a glimpse of herself in the vanity mirror across the room and gasped softly. Even after all these years as Raul's blonde, seeing her own image was like looking at a stranger. No wonder Bolton had been taken aback when he first saw her.

Tugging a long lock of her hair forward, she glared at the pale strands. "A *blonde!*" she said with disgust. "This belongs to Raul's Mary Scarlett. Bolt always said I had hair as dark as Bonaventure Cemetery at the witching hour."

She reached for the phone book on the bedside table and flipped through the Yellow Pages. Quickly, she found the listings for beauty salons. She skimmed her finger past "Dotty's Curl Up and Dye" to a more sedate-sounding establishment, the same place her mother had taken her every

Saturday as a child. When she phoned, a seemingly bored female said, "Frankie can do you at two."

She experienced a wave of relief when she hung up the phone. She'd never felt right as a blonde. She'd changed her appearance only to humor Raul. It might have made him feel sexy, but it made Mary Scarlett feel just plain odd. A brunette soul in a blonde disguise. Well, she was through with living her life to suit other people. It was high time she started doing whatever it took to make herself happy.

And the item at the very top of her make-Mary Scarlett-happy agenda was "Marry Bolton Conrad, like you should have done eight years ago."

Bolt felt uneasy as he left Factor's Row and headed up Bay Street. It was great having Mary Scarlett back, but her return could cause him big problems. A lot had happened in the past eight years. He still didn't know for sure why she had run away. He'd blamed himself all this time. What was that old saying of his mother's? *For love to grow it needs roots and wings.* Mary Scarlett had roots, all right, that went back to the very birth of the city. But in loving her so much, had he tried to clip her wings? He had crowded her, pressured her, taken away her breathing space. If he meant to try to win her again, he would have to go about it differently this time. He would have to gentle her along, let her set her own pace.

"No more crowding," he muttered to himself.

People passing on the street who knew Bolton Conrad must have wondered at his frown. He was known for his pleasant disposition. But today he passed right by O'Leary the cop and Jani the praline lady without so much as a smile or a nod, lost in troubling thoughts.

Mary Scarlett was different. She had changed during her time away from Savannah. He realized that she'd been through a lot. Seeing her husband killed had to have trau-

matized her. Still, the self-assurance and the stubbornness
that had once attracted him seemed missing. The old Mary
Scarlett Lamar had never been a woman to lean on any other
person. She knew what she wanted and she went after it,
period. Now she seemed lost, distracted, casting about for
something or someone to give her strength. Bolton could
and would gladly be her rock. Yet that, too, nagged at him.
Was that the only reason she had come back to him, because
he made her feel safe?

Lost in thought, Bolton passed the entrance to the newspaper office before he realized it. He backtracked and
pushed through the glass and chrome doors.

" 'Morning, Mr. Conrad!" The perky secretary at the
front desk greeted him warmly. "Can I help you?"

"Hello, Brenda. Yes, you're the very person I came to
see."

She beamed at him, positively glowing.

"I have a short item to go in the paper."

"Sure thing, Mr. Conrad." She handed him a form to fill
out, then stood next to the counter watching while he
printed the item in neat, square letters.

Reading as he wrote, Brenda's eyes grew wide. She gave
a low whistle. "Mary Scarlett Lamar is back in Savannah?
Man, that *is* news!"

Bolton looked at her quizzically. Was Brenda the only person in Savannah who hadn't read the paper this morning?

"How do you know Mary Scarlett?" Brenda couldn't
have been more than a kid eight years ago.

"I don't know her, not personally. But my mama told me
all about her—how she ran off and married a bullfighter
and broke her mother's heart. Not to mention the heart of
the man who expected to marry her . . ." Brenda's words
trailed off and she lowered her eyes. A hot-pink flush crept
into her cheeks. "Sorry, Mr. Conrad. I forgot. You were the
guy, weren't you?"

This time Bolt cut her off. "It's all right, Brenda. Our

engagement was never official and that's all in the past. Get this in as soon as you can."

"Yessir," she answered, all business now.

He absolved her with one of his most dazzling smiles. "You have a nice day, now."

She smiled back just before he turned to leave.

Outside again in the sunny morning air, Bolt took a deep breath. He was going to have to get used to this sort of thing. Mary Scarlett had been one of Savannah's main topics of gossip since the day she left. Rumors had grown and multiplied every day for the first couple of years, then flared up with Big Dick's disappearance and yet again with Miss Lucy's untimely death. That had been the ugliest time of all. Whispers of suicide had been rampant. Only the high alcohol content in her blood had saved the Lamar name from disgrace. Among Savannahians, drinking was socially acceptable; suicide was not. But still some people wondered. Lucy Lamar had never been a stable person, and to lose her daughter, then her husband, might have been more than she could bear.

Again, Bolton forced such unsavory thoughts from his mind. His next stop was a few blocks away, Garden City Properties. He debated about going to some other real estate office. But Kathleen would find out sooner or later of Mary Scarlett's return, if she didn't already know. He decided he might as well get this over with.

The office was quiet this morning. Most of the agents were out showing property. But he was in luck. The moment he entered he spotted Kathleen at her desk, working at her computer.

"Hi, Katie-girl." He greeted her warmly with his pet name for her.

She turned and smiled, her green eyes warming at the sight of him. "Bolt! What a nice surprise! It's too early for lunch. What brings you to this part of town?"

"Business," he answered. Then leaning close over her

desk and smiling into her eyes, he added, "And the pleasure of seeing you."

"Well now, that pleasure is mutual. How can I help you?"

"I need to browse through your apartment listings."

Kathleen's smile faded. "Bolt, you aren't moving? Why, we just got your new place all fixed up. I love it! I thought you did, too."

He shook his head to put her mind at ease. "No way! I plan to stay put for a good, long time. I wouldn't swap my apartment for the Owens-Thomas mansion, antiques, ghosts, and all. No, I'm looking for a place for a friend. Something nice. I don't think money's a problem."

Kathleen raised a dark-gold eyebrow and grinned at him. "Ah, a rich bachelor-friend. You've been holding out on me, Bolt. He's probably good-looking, too. A real catch."

Bolt shook his head and muttered, "A woman." Suddenly, he had cold feet. He wasn't sure he could admit to Kathleen that his "friend" was Mary Scarlett.

"A woman?" Now the laughter left her voice, replaced by a tone that bordered on jealousy.

He nodded silently, not meeting her curious gaze. "That's right, Katie."

"Anyone I know?"

Bolt looked up slowly, hoping his face was an emotionless mask. "Yes, you know her. Haven't you seen the paper this morning? Mary Scarlett's back."

Kathleen made a soft sound of surprise. "Where is she staying now, the Hilton or the Radisson?"

"No." Bolt's answer was only a whisper. "With me."

The color drained from Kathleen's pretty, heart-shaped face. "I see."

"No, you don't, Katie. She got into town in the middle of the night. She was in a less than desirable motel. She called me."

"Of course," Kathleen said stiffly. "Who else would she call?"

"It's not like that. I brought her to my place, just until we can find an apartment."

"We," Kathleen repeated in an empty tone.

"We—as in, I get the listings, then she goes and picks out a place and moves in, *alone!"*

"I understand, Bolton."

"No, you don't!" Dammit, he was almost shouting and he didn't want to. He was acting as guilty as sin. "You don't understand at all, Kathleen. There's nothing between us. It was over a long time ago."

"I take it her husband's not with her? Then she won't be staying long, right?"

Bolt fought for control. "He died. She's staying."

Instead of an answer, Bolton heard Kathleen's computer keys clicking, then the printer whirring into action. A moment later, she ripped off the printout and handed it to him. "These are the best apartments in town. I'm sure she'll find something to suit her."

"Thank you, Katie." He meant that sincerely. He didn't want to hurt Kathleen. She was one of the dearest people he had ever known.

"You're welcome, Bolt." She smiled and let her hand brush his. She was trying to make up for sounding like a jealous fishwife. "By the way, I had a call from Allen a few minutes ago."

Bolt stiffened.

"So? What about the party Saturday night? Allen seemed surprised that you hadn't invited me already. He said you'd probably phone me this morning. Sounds fancy, and fun. I think I'll wear that rose chiffon gown you like so much. What time?"

"Time?" Bolt's head was spinning. Damn Allen Overman! The bastard had set him up. "Kathleen, I'm really sorry about this, but do you mind making it a threesome? You see, Mary Scarlett . . ."

"Of course," she cut in, the innocent words sounding like

a lurid curse. "I should have realized. Mary Scarlett's all alone, isn't she? So naturally you have a duty to perform." Kathleen returned quickly to her computer, presenting her back to Bolt. "Don't worry about me. I can find my way to Allen's alone."

"Please, Katie . . ."

The phone on the desk rang. Kathleen grabbed the receiver as if it were a lifeline.

"Thanks again, Katie," Bolt said.

She waved without turning.

He left.

Something happened while Mary Scarlett was in the royal blue tiled shower. At first the hot spray felt wonderful and relaxing. She closed her eyes, letting the jets sting her face. But suddenly the water turned icy cold. The shock made her dizzy. Blindly, she fought her way out through the paisley shower curtain and grabbed a towel. But still the frigid water pelted her.

Before she wiped her face and opened her eyes, she sensed a change in the atmosphere. Naked only an instant ago, she now felt a heavy, coarse garment clothing her damp body. The plush bathroom carpet had vanished along with the fragrances of lavender talc and sun-dried towels. Wherever she was now, the place reeked of tar, mildewed straw, and mice.

Gone was Bolton's recently refurbished apartment. She stood in the middle of a dim, musty warehouse, filled with baled cotton and casks of rice. Rain drummed on the closed shutters at the windows. She pushed one open a crack to look out. Beyond the sill she could see the river, but now a forest of tall sailing ships rode at anchor where earlier she and Bolt had watched a coastal cruise ship pass by. Below, River Street was cluttered with filth and debris, teeming with black workers loading and unloading ships. Mule teams strained to move their heavy loads through the mud. Dusky women with baskets balanced on their heads cried out their wares in the guttural Geechee patios.

Mary Scarlett shrank back from the window, fearful that someone might see her, but having no sense of the source of her fear. Her sudden turn caused her long skirt to swirl. The fabric caught on the tine of a pitchfork. It crashed to the floor with a loud thud.

"Lisbet? Is that you?" A man's voice drifted down to her from the room above where she saw a ladder leading up.

Mary Scarlett moved farther into the shadows, trying to hide herself. Yet the familiar male voice with its thick Irish brogue sent a thrill of excitement through her.

When he called again, something moved her to answer. "Sean? I'm here." Her voice quivered with anticipation as she spoke his name. Slowly, carefully, she began climbing the rough ladder.

Even before she saw him, she could picture him in her mind. She knew that Sean Mahone was a tall, raw-boned Irishman with twinkling shamrock eyes and hair as wild and red as any sunset over the marsh.

A moment later she was up the ladder and in the loft. Sean stood across the room near the window. He was carving something into a blue-black stone in the wall. When he turned to her, his whole countenance beamed with happiness. He approached her hesitantly, but there was no hesitation once they were in each other's arms. His mouth came down on hers in a hot, insistent kiss.

Her heart sang at the taste of him. Yet the fear of discovery would give her no peace.

"Sean darling, I can only stay a moment."

"Come see how I've immortalized our love."

He led her to the far wall. There in the smooth stone he had fashioned a rough heart. Inside he had carved their entwined initials.

"Oh, Sean!" She clung to him, tears brimming in her eyes.

"If only our love could last as long as this stone. But, alas . . ."

"You've not told them then?" There was no mistaking the disappointment in his voice, the sadness in his deep-green eyes.

She looked away, tears spilling over her lashes. "I couldn't," she admitted. "I had to sneak away from the house to meet you. Papa would have . . ."

"Papa would have *what?*" he demanded when her words trailed off. Then without giving her time to answer, he rushed on, "You must tell him that Sean Mahone wishes the lovely hand of Elisabeth Lamar in holy wedlock."

"Mahone and Lamar," she murmured hopelessly. She knew the truth of their situation all too well.

Even though a new decade approached—the 1860s—most business establishments in Savannah, her father's included, held to the policy that "Irish Need Not Apply." When they could find work, it was of the lowest, dirtiest sort. Yet Sean, her wonderful, dear, loving Sean, thought he had only to ask for the hand of the daughter of one of the town's founding Anglican families and she would instantly be his. Her papa wouldn't allow an Irishman in his back door. There was no way on earth he would invite Sean Mahone into his front door and into his family.

"We haven't a prayer," she whispered. "We mustn't meet again, Sean. It's hopeless."

"Nothing's hopeless where love is concerned, Lisbet. I'd fight the devil himself to have you, darlin'."

"The devil would be a kinder foe than Papa." She stared up at him, her eyes wide with pain and longing. Every word she spoke tore at her heart. "He'll have you arrested, Sean."

"What? For being in love? For wanting to give you a wonderful life, a happy family?"

She shook her head sadly. "Say no more of this, Sean. Please. Only hold me a moment before I go."

He took her into his arms, stroking her dark hair, mur-

muring her name over and over. "There, there, my little
one, my love, my heart. We'll not let them come between
us. We're meant to love each other, you and I."

The soft lilt of his voice was like a balm to her soul. She
made no protest when he eased the rough cloak from her
shoulders. She sighed when he touched her breasts. With
tender kisses he urged her on toward love. She was a virgin
of sixteen and he a sailor nearly twenty. It was first love for
both of them, with all the burning need and blossoming passion that attend the heart's awakening.

"Had we a babe even your pa could not keep us apart,"
he whispered between kisses. "A wee, dear grandson for
the old tyrant. Think of it, darlin'. A bit of me for you to
hold close while I'm off to sea. A red-haired, blue-eyed,
Irish-English babe, who'd grow up knowing none of the
meanness of this world. Only his father's pride and his
mother's love. Come to me now, my little darlin'."

There in the dusty straw of the loft, Elisabeth Lamar fell
from grace and flew to the stars with her one and only love.
As their lithe young bodies moved together, she knew that
forevermore she would carry a part of her lover along with
the scorn of her family. She and her wee babe would be
shunned by everyone in her father's Bull Street house for the
rest of their lives. But what did that matter? Sean owned her
heart and her soul. He was the only man she would ever
love. Only this moment in all of time counted. There would
never be another so tender, so sweet.

While Lisbet and Sean still lay in each other's arms, glo-
rying in the afterglow of love, a dark shadow fell over them.
She knew before she heard her father's voice that they were
caught.

He pulled her up roughly, his eyes averted. "Cover yourself, girl. Then go home to your poor mother, if she'll have
you. I've business to attend here."

Sobbing, begging, pleading for Sean's life, Elisabeth left
only when her father shoved her down the ladder, then

slammed and locked the door behind her. The muffled sounds from the loft as she pressed close to the door sobbing told her that she would never see Sean again. A sick pain shot through her. If Sean's life was done, what cause had she to live on?

Mary Scarlett returned to the present with a jolt. She was crumpled naked on the ecru carpet of Bolton Conrad's bathroom floor. Her skin felt dewy with the sweat of love. Her body pulsed with recent pleasure yet her heart ached with hopelessness. Slowly, she dragged herself up and pulled on her robe.

Her gaze went to the old ballast stone wall beside the bathroom window. One large, blue-black stone stood out from the others. She raised a trembling hand to its sweetly scarred surface. With one finger, she traced the rough heart carved into the stone, then the initials, all but worn away by time.

"Elisabeth Lamar," she murmured. "My father's greatgrandmother. So that's why she and her son both carried the family name. She was never married." She closed her eyes and smiled, recalling her recent passion. "Oh, but, Lisbet, *you were loved, weren't you!*"

As she stood thinking about the long ago couple who had made love and conceived a son in this very room over a century ago, she realized how closely her own life mirrored that of her ancestor. She recalled her own father's drunken rage over her plans to marry. But Big Dick and his fanatical ravings were a thing of the past. He couldn't touch her now. Nor could he stop her from marrying the man she loved. Granny had been right to send her away. She could imagine her great-grandmother smiling down on her.

"I've come home to set things right, Granny Boo. And there's not a thing anyone can do to stop me."

Three

Allen Overman had pulled a supremely dirty trick on Bolton Conrad and he couldn't have been more pleased with himself. Sure, Bolt had been his buddy since they played high school football together. Conrad had run interference for him ever since, during countless business deals, several lawsuits, and all four of his divorces. But when it came to Mary Scarlett there were old scores to settle, old axes to grind.

"And may the better man win," he said with a chuckle, figuring it would be no contest, since everyone in the Garden City knew that members of the Oglethorpe Club were Savannah's *crème de la crème.* As for the bullfighter, Allen refused to give him another thought. He was obviously out of the picture, for at least as long as Mary Scarlett remained in Savannah.

"And, if I have my way, she won't be leaving anytime soon."

He had called Kathleen O'Shea a few minutes earlier and was still grinning with glee over his evilly brilliant maneuver. He would love to be a fly on the wall when Bolt found out he was expected to escort *two* ladies come Saturday night.

He chuckled. "All's fair in love and war, Bolt, ole buddy! Let's see how you get yourself out of this one."

Allen settled back on the gold velvet Empire sofa and traced his hand lovingly over the carved, gilded eagle on the back. The elegant antique screamed "old money" as did the rest of the furnishings in the room—the massive gilt-framed mirror from Austria over the Carrara marble mantel, the English crystal chandelier, the fragile Gothic side chairs, the Brussels carpet, and the John Singer Sargent portrait of an elegant Savannah miss whose ghost probably lingered in these rooms to this very day. The scuppernong-green walls—a traditional Old Savannah color—made the parlor seem an extension of the verdant square beyond the window. This was truly one of the most beautifully restored mansions in the whole city.

"And now it's mine!" Overman's grin widened, giving his tennis-tanned face a boyish appearance. "At least for as long as I'm house-sitting."

The mansion's idyllic location on Lafayette Square was also its only shortcoming as far as Allen was concerned. From where he sat and from all the front rooms, he could see the great old house across the way—his family's ancestral home, lost to bad debts long before his birth. It was a constant reminder of the Overmans' shortcomings that had been inherited through generations to inflict him as well. A love of fine things, a penchant for gambling, and a vast and varied taste in women. The place across the way was sometimes still referred to as "Overman House," even though no one by that name had slept under its mansard roof for nearly a century. The old manse seemed to stare at him accusingly from the far side of the square. He leered back.

"I've got my own place now. Stow that in your chimney and smoke it!"

Of course, no one else in the city knew the exact details of Allen Overman's sudden acquisition of the elegant residence on Lafayette Square. He had put the word out that a recent smooth deal with Atlanta developers had enabled him to buy the place for cold cash from old Ida Hampstead. In truth, the owner, a rather dowdy widow from Upstate New York, had entrusted Allen with the keys while she visited relatives in Saratoga Springs before embarking on a six-month tour of certain European spas that guaranteed foolproof age-reversal cures. While madame was off soaking her wrinkled body in volcanic mud, being injected with sheep fat, and drinking ill-tasting but rejuvenating concoctions, Allen would help himself to the luxury of her mansion, including her well-stocked spirits chest and celebrated wine cellar.

Savannah knew none of this. Savannah knew only that "that lucky sonuvabitch Overman" had once more cemented a big deal and was now living high on the hog with his hard-earned profits.

"And a party is just the ticket," he said, adding another top-drawer name to his growing list.

He had already secured the services of the best caterer in town, phoned the florist and the liquor store. The next item on his agenda was to procure his staff of "servants" for the evening. The White brothers, " 'Tator" and " 'Gator," could serve with the best of them, when the spirit moved them. And they'd do it free for Allen to keep him from blowing the whistle on them. He knew their secret. He had been a witness to the gas station job they'd pulled a couple of years ago. How fortunate Allen considered himself to have found his gas gauge on empty that night when he'd started home from a rousing evening at Hard-Hearted Hannah's, the liveliest nightspot in town. A few weeks later he had hit paydirt again when he stopped by a convenience store to pick up a six-pack of beer and blundered into another hold-up in progress. It hadn't taken long for Allen to put two and two together and confront the boys.

The identical twin brothers had the local cops baffled because they could appear to be in two places at the same time. One would knock over a gas station or convenience store while the other was miles away, establishing an airtight alibi. And how fortunate for Allen that he knew them and their tricks from way back. When they were kids—just knee-high to the gate post—their mama had worked as the Overman household's ironing woman. 'Tator' and 'Gator' used to employ the same trick against Allen himself. So to keep him from blowing their cover, the twins were always willing to help out.

He made a mental note to stop by River Street later in the day. He could always find one or the other of the White brothers there—even Allen himself wasn't sure which was the musical twin—playing his banjo, with his battered straw hat out for tourists' tips.

Actually, 'Tator' and 'Gator' were a pair after Overman's own heart. What he wouldn't give to have a twin of his very own to cover for him.

"Ah, the things I could do, the scams I could pull!" he mused aloud as he traced over Mary Scarlett's name at the very top of his list, making it stand out in bold, dark script.

He smiled and poured himself a glass of Madeira from the decanter on the table. As long as he had to go to River Street anyway, he might as well pop in on Bolt and welcome Mary Scarlett back to Savannah in style. She'd always loved surprises.

Mary Scarlett had recovered from her episode with Lisbet and Sean by the time she heard the knock at the front door. The whole thing would have seemed like a dream if she hadn't found the heart carved in stone on the bathroom wall. Closer inspection revealed that Sean had even dated his work of art—"1859."

"I'm coming," she called, wondering why Bolt didn't use his key. Maybe he had his arms full of grocery bags.

When she opened the door, she had to shield her eyes against the bright, midday sun. Before she even knew who was there, familiar arms swept around her.

"Oh, God, you feel delicious! Better than ever, Mary Scarlett."

"Allen?" she said, trying to pull out of his embrace. After all, they were standing in the open, putting on quite a show for all of Factor's Row and Bay Street.

He refused to be fought off, but he did guide her into Bolt's entryway and close the door for privacy.

"Baby, let me look at you." Allen held her at arm's length and gave her an appraising onceover. "Gorgeous," he murmured. "You haven't changed a bit. Except for your hair. God! What ever possessed you?"

His remark tempted her to fly to the phone and cancel her afternoon appointment at the beauty salon. But she only smiled at him. That was Allen's way. If he didn't like something, you knew about it immediately.

She twirled a tendril around her finger and laughed. "Just a lark. Don't worry, I won't disgrace you at your party. I'm having it dyed back this very afternoon."

Allen glanced about the room. "Where's Bolt?"

"Gone out on a couple of errands. He should be back any minute."

Overman moved in closer, gathering Mary Scarlett's soft green dress close to her body. "We'd better not waste any time, then. I sure do want to kiss you, but I sure don't want him to catch me doing it. You know what a prig he can be."

He gave Mary Scarlett no time to agree or disagree.

Allen still kissed like a horny high school jock—wet lips, open mouth, questing tongue. He'd been drinking; she could taste it. That probably accounted for his busy hands, kneading the smooth fabric over her breasts. In spite of her best efforts to repel his amorous onslaught, Mary Scarlett realized that he still knew all the right buttons to push. He made her feel like a kid again, making out in a dark corner of the high school gym at the prom.

Finally, she maneuvered out of his embrace. "Hey, it's not even noon yet and I've still got a big time case of jet lag. I'm no match for you, Overman."

"All the better," he crooned, trying to reel her back into his arms.

She stood firm, warning him off with a steady, authoritative gaze. "What are you doing here, anyway?"

He pulled a hurt face. "Aren't you glad to see me, Mary Scarlett? Shoot, I dropped everything to get right over here after we talked on the phone. I'd been calling all over town trying to find you."

"I told you I'd come to your party Saturday night."

"What?" He looked horrified. "You think I could stand to wait that long? Mary Scarlett, I've been pinin' away ever since you left Savannah."

She laughed at his dramatics. "Sure you have, lover boy. That's why you've had four wives since you last saw me."

He nodded until his wavy gold hair fell into his eyes. "That's exactly right. Why do you think none of my marriages took, honey?"

"I can't imagine. Maybe because one woman's never enough for you?"

"Only one woman's enough. I married all my wives 'cause I was looking for you in every last one of those gals. But, Mary Scarlett, when God made you, He broke the mold. There just aren't any substitutes for the real thing. And, honey, you're *it!* Now come here and give ole Allen some more sugar."

"Allen, behave yourself!" she warned. "Bolt could come through that door any minute. What would he think?"

"I reckon he'd think that he better not leave you alone for a minute, if he knows what's good for him. He should have figured it's no use anyway. You ran off last time he tried to marry you." He pulled a sad face and stared down at the floor. "You could have come to me, Mary Scarlett. Lord knows, you must have known how bad I always wanted you."

Mary Scarlett managed to keep smiling even though Allen's words brought an old anger back to the surface. She was half-tempted to say, "You mean you wanted Big Dick's money." But she held her tongue. All that was in the past now. She hoped she and Allen could start over fresh, just as friends, like they'd been when they were growing up.

"Can I fix you a drink?" she asked, trying to change the subject.

"Why, honey, you know I *never* drink before noon. But

then with your jet lag and all, I reckon you don't have your time straightened out yet. It's probably the cocktail hour *somewhere* in the world. So if you want one, I'll have one with you. It wouldn't be proper to let a lady drink alone."

She gave him a look that was pure Southern sarcasm. "Would you like *more* wine or something else?"

Bolton opened his front door just in time to see Allen slip his arm around Mary Scarlett and draw her back into his arms. He slammed the door so hard the crystal prisms on the chandelier in the foyer chimed.

Allen released Mary Scarlett slowly, letting his hand slide down her arm as she moved away. He gave Bolt his most charming, challenging smile. "You didn't think you could keep her all to yourself until Saturday, did you, ole buddy? I was just welcoming our gal back to Savannah."

Bolton glanced toward Mary Scarlett, but she had turned away. She was staring out over the river at the replica of a sailing ship passing by. She seemed to be lost in her own private world.

She was lost, all right. The odd dizziness had come over her again the moment she spied that old ship. She was no longer Mary Scarlett. But who was she *now?*

Faintly, as if from a great distance, she heard Bolt say to Allen, "You should have called before you came dashing over here. She's not up to company yet. She's worn out, exhausted from her trip. The jet lag probably won't wear off for a couple of days." But his words meant no more to her than the whispering breeze off the river.

Instead, she was listening to music. At first it, too, came from far away. But as she closed her eyes against the glare off the water, the sound grew and grew until she seemed totally submerged in the merry notes of hornpipe and fiddle. She found herself breathing hard and laughing harder.

"No more!" she cried. "Please, Jean, I'll swoon with exhaustion."

She stared into his sun- and wind-hewn face. His dark eyes seemed to blaze into hers. Their dancing had fired his passion. She knew that if she left his arms now, he would sweep her below deck to his cabin and make love to her until she begged for mercy.

"But the party's for you, *ma chère.* Would you end it before it's well begun? The best is yet to come."

He leaned over her, bending her back in his arms, still staring into her eyes. She watched him come closer, closer, until . . .

Her eyes closed when his lips captured hers. There was such heat in his kisses that they always left her weak, her mind drifting in a soft haze of golden clouds. His sailors cheered the great Jean Lafitte. She could feel her whole body blushing. Why did he take such pleasure in embarrassing her this way?

"Please, Jean! Not in front of the others," she begged between kisses. "What will they think?"

His laugh thundered in her ears. "My men will think they'd like to change places with their captain. As for their women, every one of them would give her golden earrings to be you at this moment. The amorous feats of Lafitte are legend, after all." His voice dropped to a husky whisper. "Come below with me, *ma petite.*"

He still held her close, his strong arm crushing her against his hard, lean body. He snaked one hand between them to fondle her breasts. Her low-necked frock presented only a tempting challenge. She moaned softly into his shoulder as the feel of his rough fingers set her bare flesh tingling.

The sailors with their pipes and fiddle struck up another lively tune.

Lafitte threw back his head and laughed. "Another turn around the decks, then, my darling?"

Before she could answer, he whirled her around, sending

her skirts and hair flying. Her heart raced with the beat of
the music and the tempo of their dance. She could feel his
chest thundering against hers.

What was it about this man? How could he take an upstanding, prim and proper young maid of Savannah and turn
her into a wanton—a woman who lived only for his smile,
his touch, his kiss? From the first moment she had spied
him swaggering up Bull Street, she knew she was lost. Lost
to love and to a stranger who could make her feel like a
queen and yet ruin her life.

Marie came of solid Savannah stock. She had been sheltered and cared for all her short life by loving parents and
even more loving servants. Her husband had been chosen
when she was still a child. He, too, had the unblemished
bloodlines, the family home, and a fortune to inherit. Their
lives, once they were married, would be ordered and perfect
as dictated by Savannah tradition. She would take her place
in society beside her proper husband. She would make him
a beautiful home and give him devoted children. She couldn't
have been happier with her lot in life or her plans for the
future. Until . . .

Until that moonlit night when she had seen *his* ship sail
silently up the river. Until she had felt the thrill of adventure
and the unknown tug at her heart. Until she had taken the
mirror to the attic and gazed into it to see the face of her
love at the stroke of midnight. Her future husband had never
appeared. In fact, the tales her grandmother had told her of
seeing her one and only love in the mirror seemed no more
than an old wives' tale until that night. When she lit the
candle and gazed at her image—hoping, praying for some
sign—she had seen over her shoulder the dark visage of a
stranger. A rugged, laughing face framed by unruly, wind-
tossed locks. A single, golden earring. A scar upon his
cheek. In his eyes she had seen such love and such passion
that her heart had leaped in her breast.

Frightened by seeing a stranger's face, frightened even

more by her own reaction to that face, she had hurried downstairs and quickly replaced the old gilt-framed mirror to its usual place on the foyer wall. Then she had run off to bed and covered her head with the counterpane. But sleep had eluded her. She had felt feverish until the early dawn chased away the night's shadows.

Only hours later, she saw him for the first time in the flesh. He stood tall and erect with an arrogant air to the tilt of his head. He wore blue velvet breeches and a brocade waistcoat. Silver buckles shone on his boots. And as he passed her house on Bull Street, where she was in the garden cutting roses, he had tipped his hat, said, "Good day," and gone on his way. He might be a total stranger, but Marie remembered that face and she relived that painful ache in her heart when she saw him.

After he passed, she lingered on the front veranda for hours, awaiting his return. Surely, he would come back this way. It was near noon on that broiling hot day when she spied him approaching, retracing his earlier steps. She hurried to the front gate and busied herself at pruning the roses along the wrought-iron fence. As he drew nearer, she managed to drop her basket, spilling blood-red blossoms in his path.

"Oh dear!" she'd cried softly.

"Allow me," he'd said, branding her arm with his gentle touch.

She watched, transfixed, as he gathered her scattered flowers, then handed her the basket. Again their hands touched. Again she felt his heat.

His smile was more dazzling than the noon sun. He swept off his hat and bowed deeply. "Captain Jean Lafitte at your service, mademoiselle."

"Thank you, sir," she whispered, her voice all but vanished.

"Might I be so bold as to ask your name?"

He was bold all right, no doubt about that! If her mother spied her conversing with a stranger on the street, Marie would find herself locked in her room with her prayer book, subsisting on bread and water for the next few days. Still, she *wanted* him to know who she was. It seemed all important to her. After all, he was the man she had seen in her mirror—the man meant to be her one and only love.

"Mademoiselle Marie Angelique Lamar," she answered softly.

"Ah, you are French, then, as am I."

"Acadian. My mother was sent here on one of the refugee boats from Nova Scotia."

His frown of concern made him even more handsome. "Poor woman. What a dreadful experience!" His radiant smile returned. "But I see she survived it to bear a most beautiful child."

"I am not a child!" she answered defensively, impulsively.

He assessed her with his gaze, then chuckled. "Indeed not! How could I have made such a mistake? You are by far the loveliest woman I've yet seen in Savannah."

"But you only arrived last night." She covered her lips with her fingers. How could she have made such a blunder? Now the great Jean Lafitte would think she had been spying on him. She had, but she certainly didn't want him to suspect such a thing.

"Would it be too forward of me to ask your mother's permission to invite you to visit my ship?"

"Oh, yes!" The very thought of such a thing terrified her. Then she quickly changed her answer. "I might come, but my mother mustn't know."

Again he laughed. "Most mothers, I've found, *don't* approve of Jean Lafitte. You have a standing invitation, *ma chère*. I will look forward to seeing you again."

Then he clasped her dainty fingers in his. Ever so gently, he slipped off her gardening glove, bowed over her hand, and kissed it. The heat of noon was cool compared to this.

"I doubt I can come," she whispered, trembling all over.

"Then I shall be the most heartbroken man in all of Savannah, Mademoiselle Lamar. Would you wound me so?"

Without giving it a second thought, she shook her head to indicate that she would never do such a thing. He sounded so sad, so hurt, so harmless.

"If you are an early riser, you might come for a visit and be home before your mother knows you have gone. The river is lovely at sunrise. Tomorrow then?"

"I don't know, Captain." Even though she was in a quandary, Marie knew. She could no more refuse his tempting invitation than she could stop breathing.

Again he tipped his hat, bowed, and flashed her the very smile that had endeared him to countless women all over the world. "Until dawn, then, Marie."

At that, she turned and ran so quickly into the house that she left the Savannah grey bricks of the path strewn with roses.

Lafitte brought Marie's thoughts instantly back to the present with a fierce hug. The music had stopped. Rum, long banned in Savannah, was being passed about on deck, sloshed as tankards clinked in one rousing toast after another. But Marie needed no spirits to make her burn inside.

"Will you come below with me, *ma chère?*" Even after weeks of these secret visits to his ship, he still asked and she still refused. The question was her cue to flee back to the safety of the house on Bull Street. But tonight he added something new. Whispering close to her ear as he held her in his arms, he said, *"Please, Marie. I burn for you so."*

If he burned, she was charred through to the core. How could she deny her own desires any longer? How could she go into the loveless marriage that she knew would soon be her fate without having given herself to the one and only man she would ever love? If, just this once, she could know total happiness in the arms of her star-crossed lover, she could bear the thought of spending the rest of her life with a man for whom she had always felt respect, but never love.

Tears brimming in her eyes, but a smile on her face, she whispered, "Yes, my darling. Oh, yes!"

* * *

A gentle hand touched her shoulder. She covered it with her own and smiled through her tears. "Yes," she repeated.

"Mary Scarlett? Are you all right?"

Bolt's voice jolted her. She felt as if she'd been jerked roughly back through time. Her whole body still ached for Jean Lafitte. With her very soul she longed to be his.

"You were a million miles away, honey. When Allen said goodbye you didn't even answer him. What's wrong? What's happening to you?"

She turned toward Bolt slowly, trying to wipe away her tears before he could see them. But it was no use. The more she dabbed at her eyes, the faster the tears flowed.

"Mary Scarlett, what's the matter? Did Allen say something stupid again? So help me, I'll break his damn neck!"

She shook her head, not sure she could trust her voice yet. Gripping Bolt's hand to steady herself, she eased down on the couch.

"Something's happening to me, Bolt," she admitted at length. "Something I can't control and don't understand. I'm scared."

"Tell me," he urged gently.

She settled in the curve of his arm and sighed. "I can tell you what's happening, but that's all I can tell you."

"Anything," he prompted. "Tell me whatever's on your mind."

"Since the moment I set foot back in Savannah, nothing's seemed right. At first I thought it was the town, but now I know it's me. Things keep changing."

"What kind of things, honey?"

"I keep losing myself, drifting back in time." She squeezed his hand tighter. "It's so scary, Bolt. But at the same time there's something wonderful about it. Each time I go back, I learn something new about my life."

"So that's where you were when Allen left? Off drifting?"

She nodded, then felt a blush creep into her cheeks. "If you hadn't snapped me out of it, I'd be making love to a pirate at this very minute." She paused, stunned by her own words. Then she laughed softly. "Don't look at me like I'm crazy. You were always a history buff. Tell me, did Jean Lafitte ever visit Savannah?"

Bolton stared at her blankly. He didn't say it in so many words, but the tone of his reply accused her of insanity. *"Jean Lafitte* was going to *make love to you?"*

"If I had the courage to let him." She looked up at him with pleading eyes. "Bolt, tell me he never came to Savannah. Please. Tell me I dreamed all this."

Now it was Bolt's turn to nod, speechless for the moment. Finally, he gave her the answer she already suspected to be the truth. "He was here, all right. Twice, so historians say. In 1817 his brother's ship *Jupiter* stopped here to take on board a Greek friend named Captain Nicholas. He was with Jean Lafitte when he died in the Yucatan in 1826, if historians' tales can be believed."

"You don't believe he was really ever here?" she asked hopefully.

"Oh, Lafitte was here. I'm convinced of that. I don't believe he died in 1826. I think he lived to a ripe old age under an assumed identity. Possibly even with the woman he fell in love with in Savannah."

"There was a woman?"

Bolt nodded. "Yes. When Lafitte came again on the schooner *Nancy Eleanor* in 1821 he met her. Some people claimed he even married the girl. I doubt it, though. He'd lost his wife not long before at Galveston. Most likely he was still mourning her. But what does any of this have to do with you, Mary Scarlett? I'll admit, I'm at a loss."

"I don't suppose you know his lover's name."

Bolt leaned his head back and closed his eyes, trying to remember. "Come to think of it, I believe her name was Mary."

Mary Scarlett found tears gathering in her eyes again. Her

voice was only a thin whisper when she said, "She was French. She called herself Marie. And, no, I don't think she married him. But she certainly was in love with Jean Lafitte."

"What are you saying, Mary Scarlett? How could you know anything about that if you didn't even know whether or not Lafitte had been to Savannah?"

She turned slowly and stared up into Bolton's troubled face. "I know because until you brought me back a few minutes ago I was with Jean Lafitte. I *was* Marie."

"This is crazy!" Bolt exclaimed. Then he got hold of himself. "I'm sorry, honey. I didn't mean that. It's just hard to believe that such a thing could happen. Why, you're talking *out-of-body experience* or something equally as bizarre."

"I know," she answered calmly. "And it's not the first time. I realize now who the soldiers in the Colonial Cemetery were last night. Only it wasn't last night when I saw them. It was well over a century ago. I saw Sherman's men, Bolt. And shortly after my taxi passed the old burial ground, I saw a funeral procession—the carriage draped in black bunting, the horses black-plumed."

"Whose funeral was it?"

"I don't know. But I have a feeling I'll find out before too long."

Bolt took both her hands in his and stared down at them. He was silent, lost in thought for a long time. Finally, he looked up at her, trying to smile reassuringly. "Mary Scarlett, you've been under a lot of stress these past months. Losing your husband that way, traipsing all over while you tried to decide what to do. And coming back to Savannah can't have been easy for you, not after all these years, all that's happened."

"You don't believe me," she said in a stony voice. "You think I'm imagining things. Well, come with me. I'll show you. I have proof that it's all real."

She jumped up from the couch and ran toward the bathroom. When Bolt didn't follow, she turned and demanded, "Well? Aren't you coming? I want you to see this."

He rose slowly, with a slight shake of his head. Mary Scarlett stopped him outside the bathroom door. Before she let him see what she wanted to show him, she told him about Elisabeth and Sean. Every detail, everything she remembered. How she'd felt, how the riverfront outside the window had looked, even the smell of the old cotton warehouse. Then she motioned him into the room and led him to the ballast stone with its carved heart and initials.

Bolt looked only half-convinced.

"Don't you see? It's *real!*" she insisted. "Remember my odd reaction when you brought me to your front door this morning? I didn't want to come in. I was terrified. In some part of my mind or heart I knew already what Elisabeth's father was going to do to Sean. I didn't want it to happen." Her voice dropped and she cast her gaze sadly on the heart. "But it did. It happened long ago to my own father's great-grandmother. There was no earthly way I could have stopped it. And there was certainly no way I could have known about it. My family wasn't the sort to pass down stories of unwed mothers and their murdering fathers. Sean's disappearance was probably never even noted in the newspaper of the day. He was Irish, after all. What difference would one dead potato-eater make to the upstanding families of Savannah?"

The bitterness in her tone alarmed Bolt. He took her into his arms to try to soothe her. "Hush now, honey. That was a long, long time ago. It has nothing to do with you now."

She pulled away, her eyes blazing vivid blue. "It has *everything* to do with me! Don't you see? Part of everything they were is in me. I'm made up of all those who went before me, just like Savannah is made up of bits and pieces of all the English debtors, Irish laborers, slaves, murderers, saints, and sinners who ever walked her streets."

"That's true of all of us, Mary Scarlett. But that doesn't

mean we have to be burdened by our ancestors' sins or saddened by their failed love affairs. It's *now* that counts for both of us. The past doesn't matter. We can't let it."

"Can't we, Bolt?" she asked softly. "Can you honestly say that what I did to you doesn't matter? That you were able to forgive and forget? That the past is dead and everything is just the same between us after eight long years?"

The deep, smoldering hurt in his dark eyes made Mary Scarlett's heart sink. He didn't say a word; he didn't have to. He might be trying his best to forgive her, but he would never, ever forget what she had done to him. Maybe she *was* losing her mind. Maybe this was her punishment for the pain she had inflicted on the man who loved her.

"Give me time," Bolt whispered. "I'm trying, Mary Scarlett."

She touched his wonderful face with her fingertips. "Time is something I have plenty of—present, future, *and* past, so it seems. I still care for you very deeply, Bolton Conrad. I always have and I always will. But I'll understand if you can't bring yourself to love me again. I don't deserve you. I never have."

Before he could answer, she whirled away and headed for the door. She couldn't bear that look in his eyes a minute longer. She had to get out, be alone to think.

"Mary Scarlett? Where are you going?"

"To the beauty shop," she called over her shoulder. "My mama always said that when the whole world's going wrong, it's time to get your hair done. Makes all the difference."

She said it with a laugh in her voice so Bolt wouldn't know she had tears in her eyes.

Four

Lime-and-lavender? Mirrors and chrome?

Mary Scarlett knew she had made a mistake the minute she walked through the door. The new, redecorated Broughton Street beauty salon—the same shop she and her mother had visited regularly years ago—transported her through another kind of time warp. She remembered the place as being fashionably antiquated like most of the rest of Savannah. The sedate cream-colored walls, burgundy chairs, and flowered chintz curtains had provided a quiet backdrop for the styling of hair and the swapping of gossip in and about the best circles of Garden City society. The two sisters who had owned the shop, both widows after their husbands were killed in the Korean War, had started their business in the back parlor of their parents' Victorian home on East Park Avenue, before Mary Scarlett's time. Eventually, the shop had moved to the Broughton Street location. Somehow, Mary Scarlett had expected to find the widows still there at this "new" shop they had opened back in the sixties.

Had she been thinking straight and calculating the years, she should have guessed that the sisters would be dead now or at the very least retired. But the once-familiar salon took her totally by surprise with its chrome, mirrors, lavender walls, and lime-colored trim. An even greater shock came when she found out that "Frankie"—as in "Frankie can do you at two," was a balding, ponytailed man in black leather pants and a purple silk shirt open to expose a tanned, hair-

less chest with a tattoo over his heart that read "Donny."
Donny, a blonde dressed all in tight-white, worked at the
next chair, snipping, curling, frosting, and combing out,
humming show tunes all the while.

Of course, neither of the men knew Mary Scarlett. She'd
given her name as "Mrs. Miguel." But both Frankie and
Donny knew from the paper and their earlier customers that
"Mary Scarlett's back." Apparently, she was the topic *du
jour.*

"Ah, my favorite kind of customer!" Frankie enthused,
inviting Mary Scarlett into his chair with a sweep of his
arm and a flash of movie star teeth.

"What kind is that?" she asked.

"New!" Frankie said emphatically. "Let us do you once
and we'll have you forever. That's our motto. Right, Donny?"

"Betcha!" Donny said with a toss of his magnificent head
of hair.

"So what'll it be, Miz Miguel? Cut? Wash? Tint?"

"Dye!"

"Oh, please, no! I'm too young!" Frankie covered his
tattooed breast with his fist and cowered dramatically,
bringing a round of applause from Donny and the blue-
haired matron he was combing out.

"This isn't my natural color," Mary Scarlett explained,
completely unmoved by Frankie's shenanigans.

He fingered a lock and sighed. "Well, it isn't Donny's
natural color either, but doesn't it look fantastic on him? It
suits you, too, Miz Miguel. Are you sure you want to
change?"

"It doesn't suit me at all. I'm walking around with a brunette soul in a blonde disguise."

Frankie pressed his metal comb to his chin and stared
thoughtfully at the mirrored ceiling. "That's very profound.
A brunette soul in a blonde disguise. I never thought of it
that way. I wonder what color my soul is. Hm-m-m."

"Passionate pink," Donny supplied sotto voce.

While Frankie was still trying to picture his soul, Mary Scarlett brought an old snapshot out of her purse. "This is my natural color. Very dark. Almost black."

"Midnight," Frankie pronounced her natural color. "Or perhaps Raven's Wing."

Donny peered over at the picture. "Won't do. Too blue. The color in that photo is Irish-dark, with bronze highlights."

"Donny's right, of course. He's always right about his colors. He designed all this." With a wave of his wrist Frankie indicated the lavender-and-lime decor. "You *do* have Irish blood, don't you, Miz Miguel? Why, you're not Spanish at all."

Mary Scarlett felt a sudden stab of guilt. It was as if they knew about Elisabeth's long-ago assignation with Sean Mahone, about their half-Irish child born out of wedlock. She caught herself quickly before she blushed. What was the big deal anyway? She laughed at her own foolishness. "Doesn't everyone in Savannah have a touch of Irish blood? At least on St. Patrick's Day."

Frankie nodded with enthusiasm. "Ah, you should have seen the heads we turned green last week. Fantastic! The Parade Marshal's wife has a lovely head of perfect white hair. I tried everything to convince her to surprise her husband. Her hair would have taken the green beautifully. She would have made my holiday. But, alas . . ."

Mary Scarlett couldn't help smiling. She could just imagine the genteel matron's horror when Frankie came at her with his bottle of green goop. Even more amusing was the thought of the woman's husband if she had allowed herself to be talked into a shamrock-do.

"It's not too late, you know." Frankie's voice broke into Mary Scarlett's thoughts. "You might start a new fad—green tresses *after* St. Patrick's Day. I've got plenty of dye left, and Easter's not far away. You'd look stunning in a flowered chapeau with lovely, long green hair." He shrugged. "If you don't like it, we could go to brunette. Brunette from green is easy."

"No, thank you," she answered. "I believe I'll go straight to brunette."

"Don't forget the bronze highlights," Donny put in.

"You don't have to remind me," Frankie snapped back. "When have you ever known me to forget the bronze highlights? What? Am I a novice? Did I start doing hair yesterday?"

"Sorry," Donny muttered.

"Well, you should be! Tell *me* about bronze highlights!" Frankie mumbled. "Why, I taught you your bronzes from your coppers. You didn't know a frizz from a flip before you met me!"

"Sor-ry!" Donny repeated more emphatically.

All this while, Frankie was covering Mary Scarlett with a shiny purple plastic apron, arranging his combs and brushes, checking his bottles of dye. Suddenly, out of nowhere, he said to Mary Scarlett, "Have you heard the latest? God, everybody's talking about it today! I'm all but sick of the name Mary Scarlett."

When Frankie said her name, she stiffened before she realized he had no idea *she* was Mary Scarlett.

"She's come back, you know," he went on in a hushed tone. "After eight years. I wonder why." He trilled a laugh. "I wonder where she got a name like that—right out of *Gone with the Wind.*"

Donny ventured an explanation. "Nowadays girls are all Tiffanys and Tylers and Taras, named for soap opera stars. Maybe her mother was nuts about *Gone with the Wind.*"

"I suppose that could be," Frankie mused, fluffing his customer's hair to test its texture.

Mary Scarlett couldn't resist. Without letting them know who she was, she was determined to let them know how she got her name. If all Savannah was talking about her, they might as well spread the truth for a change.

"I've heard about this Mary Scarlett," she confided in such a secretive tone that Frankie, Donny, and even the blue-haired matron drew nearer. "They say her mother's grandmother was charmingly insane. You know the type— never stopped fighting the War, flew a Confederate flag out of the attic window, believed in magic mirrors, that sort of thing. Her name was Beulah Robillard, and when she read *Gone with the Wind,* she swore that every word of it was true. She thought it was about her own family."

Frankie clucked his tongue. "Balmy, the poor dear."

"Bonkers!" Donny added.

"That's not the half of it," Mary Scarlett continued. "She was convinced that she was related to Ellen Robillard, Scarlett O'Hara's mother. So when her great-granddaughter was born, she insisted she be named for 'dear Cousin Scarlett.' If not, she swore she would never come out of the attic again. She said she would refuse food and water until she withered away to nothing. She assured Mary Scarlett's parents that her death would be on their heads."

Frankie gasped. "Can you believe such a cruel old woman?"

Donny kept combing as he mused, "What about Mary Scarlett's mother? Keeping her own grandmother locked away in the attic. Sounds like a weird streak runs in that family. Sick-o! The whole lot of them."

For the first time the woman in Donny's chair broke her silence. She turned slightly to glare up at the tall blonde teasing her hair. "Young man, I happen to have known Lucy Lamar, Mary Scarlett's mother. She was the sweetest, dearest soul on the face of the earth. She spent a good portion of her life tending to that outrageous old woman, who, by the way, *chose* to live in the attic. Then, shortly after she finally passed at the age of one hundred and three, poor Lucy's husband ran off with another woman. A cocktail waitress, no less! Can you imagine the scandal? Lucy, God rest her, never recovered."

This statement jolted Mary Scarlett. She and her mother had both known of her father's affairs, of course. But as far as she knew, Big Dick's disappearance had been accepted generally as a boating accident. Did all of Savannah know the truth? Was Mary Scarlett the last to find out? She couldn't let this pass.

"Pardon me, but I thought Mr. Lamar lost his life in an accident. Seems I remember something about a fishing trip and a storm."

The woman arched a well-plucked eyebrow at Mary Scarlett. "That was the *official* story, the one in all the papers. Everyone pretended to accept it for Lucy's sake. But we *all* knew," she whispered. "If Dick Lamar was fishing that weekend, it certainly wasn't for marlin. And as for that daughter of theirs, well, I could say a few choice words about her, but I won't sully Lucy's memory by even mentioning her name."

"Meow!" said Frankie.

"It seems to me," Mary Scarlett said, "that a child growing up in a family like that would have to have problems."

Donny showered the perfect blue hair with super hold spray, then said, "I think you're finished, Mrs. Thorndyke."

"That's *your* opinion," she answered, casting a cold look at her beautician. "I haven't even gotten started good on the subject of Mary Scarlett Lamar! Can you imagine a girl, given every advantage, putting her ailing mother through all the trouble of planning a huge wedding, then running off the way she did? Poor Lucy suffered terribly from the blow. She was purely traumatized. It was the biggest scandal to hit Savannah since the murder at Mercer House. Lucy never recovered. It just broke the poor dear's heart. And in my opinion, Mary Scarlett has her nerve coming back to Savannah after all she did."

Mary Scarlett was seething. She remembered this woman suddenly. Hattie Thorndyke, not quite high-born or well-married enough to be in the circle of Lucy Lamar's friends, but always hovering about the fringes, spreading gossip, giving parties, hoping to be accepted.

"Maybe there's a side to Mary Scarlett's story nobody knows," she said sweetly to the social-climbing busybody.

"All one needs to know about that girl is that she was spoiled rotten, disgraced the family name, and broke her dear mother's heart. Not to mention what she did to that sweet man, Bolton Conrad. Why, he's never gotten over her." Hattie smiled primly into the mirror, patting her lacquered hair. "Thank goodness he's finally found someone good enough for him."

This came as an even bigger shock to Mary Scarlett. "Who?" she demanded.

Mrs. Thorndyke smirked. "Just never you mind. I'm not one to spread tales. All of Savannah will know soon enough, when Bolton and his ladylove announce their engagement." She turned toward Mary Scarlett. "And I have it on good authority that will be *very* soon."

Mary Scarlett was reeling. Bolt? About to be *married?* But how could that be?

Before she could collect her wits, the woman dashed on, adding insult to injury. "She wrecked Allen Overman's life as well. He was such a lovely young man. I was *intimate* with his parents, you know. To their dying days, they blamed Mary Scarlett for the way Allen turned out. All those wives, all those divorces. And he's still carrying a torch. Why, can you believe he's giving a party this Saturday night to welcome the little witch back to Savannah?"

"I forgot to tell you, Donny," said Frankie, while Mary Scarlett still sat there with her mouth open. "Allen called a little while ago. Saturday night, eight sharp, black tie."

"Great!" Donny enthused. "I guess we'll see you there, Mrs. Thorndyke."

The overdressed, oversprayed matron bustled out of her chair, her face livid. Obviously, she was not among the invited guests. She paid her bill and left without another word—off with her new hairdo to spread more venom about town, Mary Scarlett was sure.

"Beastly woman!" Frankie exclaimed once the door closed after Hattie Thorndyke's ample backside. "Why do you put up with her, Donny?"

"She tips good." He pocketed the ten she'd given him.

"Well, if I had any hair on the top of my head, I can tell you it would be standing on end right now. The woman lives only to make others' lives miserable with her constantly flapping mouth."

"She's not the only one talking today," Donny reminded him. "I'm anxious to meet this Mary Scarlett person. Sounds like she sure left her mark on Savannah."

Mary Scarlett remained silent, still numb from Hattie Thorndyke's news about Bolt. Who could the woman be? Why hadn't he said anything? She realized, miserably, that she hadn't given him a chance. She had been so sure that she could come back and just pick up where she left off.

"Do you know Bolton Conrad, Miz Miguel?" Frankie asked.

"Slightly." Her answer was no lie. She certainly didn't know him as well as she had thought.

"Nice fellow, Bolt," Frankie went on. "He handled the closing when I bought this place. We had a few drinks together. I knew from the start that there was some dark secret in his past—something he kept bottled up inside and didn't want to talk about. I figured it must be woman-trouble. Now I know the woman's name. *Mary Scarlett.*" He finished with a deep sigh.

"How can you be sure of that?" Mary Scarlett snapped.

Frankie shrugged. "Just a guess. But it sounds likely. I wonder what she's like."

"Like *weird*," Donny supplied. "I heard from my first customer this morning that after she ran off and left Conrad practically standing at the altar, she married a bullfighter."

"To each her own," Frankie said with a grin. "Come to

think of it, I go for guys with tight pants, too." He cast a glance at Donny's clinging white ducks.

"Please," Mary Scarlett said, "can you two change the subject?"

She spent the next hour in misery while Frankie trimmed, washed, and dyed her hair. She could hardly wait to get back to Bolt's place. She had so many questions for him. And, too, the conversation between Frankie and Donny kept drifting back to the fantastic exploits of the notorious Mary Scarlett Lamar. She thought she'd scream if they didn't shut up. It seemed that the citizens of Savannah had taken the bare-bone facts of her life and embroidered them beyond recognition. She was now guilty of everything including the gross national debt and the ruination of at least a dozen men in Savannah, ten of whom she had never even met.

Ah, Savannah, she thought as Frankie put the finishing touches on her long, dark tresses, *it's so nice of you to welcome me home again!*

Bolt would be at his office this afternoon. He had told Mary Scarlett earlier that he had a meeting with a client that wouldn't wind up until five, so there was no need for her to rush back to his apartment. And she didn't dare risk more gossip by dropping in on him at work. She decided to take a stroll to see if the center of the city had changed as much as the beauty shop on Broughton Street. She knew her main destination—the old Lamar house. But when she reached the corner of Broughton and Bull, she couldn't quite work up the nerve to visit her former home just yet. She crossed Bull, headed east, then turned south at Abercorn. Without even thinking about it, she found herself heading for the Colonial Cemetery.

Probably because her parents had forbidden her to go there as a child, the old burying ground had always held a special fascination for her with its list of notable Geor-

gians—James Habersham, Hugh McCall, Archibald Bul-
loch, and Declaration of Independence signer Button Gwin-
nett.

She found the cemetery in much better condition than
she remembered. The wrought-iron fence had been repaired,
the grass was neatly cut, and no litter defaced the silent
tombs. It looked more like a park than a burial ground.
Tourists wandered among the tall oaks, snapping photos,
making grave rubbings, and consulting guidebooks and
maps. Some of the older stones, which had been knocked
over by Sherman's troops back in 1862, now stood upright
again for the first time in over a century. But many markers
still bore the vandalism of Yankee soldiers who had defaced
them by changing the dates and the names as they whiled
away boring hours at the campsite.

Traffic flowed smoothly around the boundaries, the driv-
ers keeping their horns silent out of respect for the dead.
The place had an eerie stillness about it, even at this busy
time of day.

Although the afternoon was hot and muggy, Mary Scarlett felt a chill as she walked past certain monuments. A
sense of sadness overcame her at one point, so deep and
hopeless that she glanced up from the tabby footpath she
had been following. She realized the source of her inexpli-
cable depression the moment she saw the marker. Near the
spot where she stood lay the mass grave containing the remains of seven hundred victims of the terrible yellow fever
epidemic of 1820. After a moment's pause to regain her
composure, she moved on quickly, drawn to another,
slightly earlier grave.

As she neared the spot, clouds seemed to cover the sun,
although a glance at the heavens told her the sky was still
clear. A deeper chill, a deeper sadness gripped her. She
could no longer hear birds singing or the sounds of traffic.
She focused her gaze on the plain, weathered tablet ahead.

The closer she came, the darker the skies turned until it seemed to be nighttime.

" 'My life is like the summer rose, That opens to the morning sky; And ere the shades of evening close, Is scattered on the ground—to die.' " She murmured the lines softly, trying to think where she had heard the verse, and why the words evoked such painful emotions that tears filled her eyes.

And then she saw it. The stark, gray stone beside a taller, green historical marker which read "DUELLIST'S GRAVE." She spied the very verse she had just recited. It was printed at the bottom of the marker, attributed to the duellist's brother, Baltimore poet Richard Henry Wilde.

With a sigh of grief, Mary Scarlett sank to the grass beside the stone. "Oh, James," she whispered. "Why, my darling? Why?"

Her fingers trembling, she traced the weathered inscription. The stone should have felt warm from the sun, but instead seemed cold to the touch. Even with her eyes closed, she could read the epitaph. She had seen it in her dreams, her nightmares.

This
Humble Stone
records the filial piety
of
JAMES WILDE, Esquire
late District Paymaster in the Army of the U.S.
He fell in a Duel
on the 16th of January, 1815
by the hand of a man
who, a short time ago, would have been
friendless but for him
And expired instantly in his 22nd year
dying as he had lived:
With unshaken courage and unblemished reputation

By his untimely death the prop of a mother's age
is broken;
The hope and consolation of sisters is destroyed
The pride of brothers humbled in the dust
And a whole Family, happy until then.
Overwhelmed with affliction.

Once again, Mary Scarlett felt herself drifting into the past. Still gripping the stone, she heard voices, far away at first, then close at hand. She opened her eyes to a cold, stormy night. The dark shoreline of the Savannah River. She was alone with young James Wilde, although a group of perhaps a dozen other men stood a distance away from the couple, near the boats at the water's edge.

She was weeping, begging, mourning him already.

"Don't do this, James. Please! I can't bear it."

"Dry your tears, sweetheart. I'll be back when the sun comes up. I'm a far better shot than he is."

"But no less a fool," she sobbed.

Clinging to this man she loved with all her heart, trying to make him give up this dangerous business, she sensed that all was lost.

"James, you will *not* be back." She stared up into his dark eyes, trying to make him understand. "I had a dream last night. I saw the duelling ground at Screvens Ferry. I saw it drenched in blood—*your* blood, my dearest. Think of your mother, your sisters, your brothers. James, think of *me!*"

"I *am* thinking of you and only you. He'll not speak that way of the girl I love. As for your dream, it was woven of a woman's fear. No more, no less. Watch for the rising sun, my love. I'll be back in your arms before you know it. We'll be together forever."

Mary Scarlett's vision of happiness faded into a cold, gray mist. The wind whipped around her. The water churned to dark foam. She stood alone now on the riverbank, searching through her tears for the first hint of the rising sun. A moment before daybreak, she felt a sharp pain through her chest. She could barely breathe. She sank to the damp ground, gasping.

When dawn finally broke, it was not the glorious gold that she had seen in happier times, but blood-red storm clouds tinged with dirty-gray. What little hope she had held in her heart faded in that fierce dawn.

The sound of oars drew her gaze. She struggled back to her feet. Straining to see across the river toward the South Carolina side, she spied a boat returning. She could not make out the figures, but she knew. She had known all along. She had guessed the outcome of this deadly folly even before James left for the duelling field.

Wrapping her black cloak more closely about her, she walked to the edge of the water. She held herself stiff and erect, like the soldier who had been her love. Her gaze never left the boat. Closer and closer it came, like a ghostly apparition out of the river fog. Finally, she could make out forms. Two men rowed while a third supported the head of the man lying prostrate in the craft.

"Oh, James, my James," she murmured. "Why? Why, my love, my life?"

The cold of the grave passed through her as the men pulled the boat ashore. "I am sorry," one of them said in a husky whisper. "This should never have been."

She didn't wait for the men to haul the boat onto dry land. Wading into the icy water, her long skirts dragging her down, she went to him. She climbed into the boat and wrapped James in her trembling arms.

"So sorry." His dying whisper was little more than a soft rush of air. "Love you . . . always . . ."

She leaned down, putting her lips to his, trying desperately to steal her James from the Dark Angel. But it was no use. The blood on his chest seeped into the fabric of her bodice, staining them both with his death. She thought for a moment she felt his lips move under hers.

"James, my dearest," she murmured. "James, you cannot leave me. Stay, my love, stay!"

"Come away," another male voice said gently. "The lad's done, miss."

The men forced her arms from around her dead lover and lifted her from the boat. She fought them, screaming his name, begging for death to take her, too. Finally, she fell to the ground, sobbing.

She felt a gentle hand on her arm. "Mary Scarlett? What in the world?"

Looking up through a torrent of tears, she was forced to squint against the bright sun at the dark figure leaning over her. Slowly, his features came into focus. Bolt stared down at her, his face darkly troubled.

She shook herself slightly. "Bolt? Is that really you?"

His voice seemed to come from far away. "Who were you expecting it to be?"

James, she thought without saying it aloud.

"What's wrong, darlin'? Why are you so upset? And what are you doing out here in the cemetery?"

She glanced about. People strangers—were staring. She must have made quite a spectacle of herself.

"Help me up," she begged. "I'm all shaky. I don't know what came over me, Bolt. I came here just as a sightseer, thought I'd see if Savannah had changed while I was away. But something happened . . ."

"Well, that's pretty obvious. But what?"

She wiped at the tears drying on her flushed cheeks. "I don't know. I'm not sure I can explain it. It was sort of like a vision. But, Bolt, it was *so real!*"

"Mary Scarlett, you're hurt!" Bolt exclaimed. "You've got blood on your dress. What have you done to yourself?"

The horrible vision of her beloved's bloody chest flashed back through her mind. For a brief, hysterical moment, she wondered if modern day DNA testing would identify the stains as the blood of 1815 duellist James Wilde.

Her knees went weak and she sagged against Bolt. "Just take me home," she begged. "I'll tell you about it when we get there. But if you don't get me away from here, I swear to God, Bolt, I'm going to faint right here in the middle of the cemetery."

He half-carried her to his car, parked on Abercorn Street. Once he had her in her seat, seat belt in place, he started the car and flipped the air-conditioning up to maximum.

He glanced at her, his face still solemn, but warm lights danced in his eyes. "I almost didn't recognize you. Your hair."

Still reeling from what she had experienced at James Wilde's grave, Mary Scarlett made no sense of his remark at first. Then she remembered. Before coming to the cemetery, she had been to the beauty salon on Broughton Street. That memory brought back another. She could still hear Hattie Thorndyke's shrill voice, harping on and on. She could still feel the shock of the woman's words and the pain that lingered from her revelation.

Bolton Conrad was engaged and hadn't told her.

"We need to talk," she said in a stony voice.

He nodded, but said nothing.

"A lot's happened since I went away, hasn't it, Bolt? A lot more than anyone's told me."

"You only returned last night. You can't expect to catch up on eight years in that short a time."

She was trying to give him a chance to tell her. He wasn't taking her bait. The rest of the short drive to Bolton's apartment passed in silence. She had no idea what he was thinking, but her mind was awash in questions. Questions about the past, the present, *and* the future.

Five

Bolt pulled off his coat and tie as soon as they got home. Then he went straight to the refrigerator, took the vodka bottle out of the freezer, and mixed a pitcher of martinis. He had a feeling they were both going to need a drink by the time they finished the talk Mary Scarlett was insisting upon. Although she hadn't come right out and said it, he suspected she had learned that he and Kathleen had been seeing each other.

Mary Scarlett had gone directly to the bedroom to change out of her bloodstained dress. She had yet to explain what had happened. Not to his satisfaction anyway. When he had questioned her again as they were coming up the walk, she'd made an offhand comment about cutting her hand on some thorns. But he hadn't noticed the slightest scratch on either of her hands. And what kind of thorn could make her bleed that much?

Along with the martinis, Bolt placed a plate of cold, boiled shrimp and cocktail sauce on the small table out on his balcony. There was a pleasant breeze off the river, and River Street provided its own kind of music this time of day. He loved to listen and lose himself in the slow-paced, long-ago feel of the place.

Mary Scarlett joined him just as he was arranging two blue canvas director's chairs next to the table. He stopped breathing for an instant when he saw her. Her naturally dark hair gleamed with bronze highlights against her apricot-colored lounging suit. Seeing her this way made him feel young again, as young and hopeful as he had been eight years ago, before she went away. Back then it had seemed that nothing could ever come between them to mar their happiness. She had been everything he wanted in the world. *God help me, she still is!* he thought.

"Why are you looking at me that way?" Her tone was still icy.

"What way?"

She brushed her hair off her right shoulder with an unblemished hand. "I don't know. Like you're seeing a ghost or something."

He forced a smile. "Maybe you seem like a ghost to me. The ghost of Mary Scarlett past. With your hair blonde, you were a stranger. I guess I'm only now realizing that you're really, truly back here, standing so close I can reach out and touch you."

She took a step back, a tacit warning that he shouldn't try. Her face was placid, but he read anger in her eyes.

"I fixed martinis," he said cordially, trying to coax her out of her sullen mood. "And some shrimp with hot sauce the way you like them. Come sit. The breeze is fine."

He tried to take her arm, but again she avoided his touch, circling to the far side of the tiny table and moving her chair a few inches farther from his. She couldn't put much distance between them, though. The balcony was minuscule.

She took one sip of her martini, then went straight for his jugular. "So, why didn't you tell me you were spoken for? Who's the lucky girl? Anyone I know?"

"Mary Scarlett, you're just upset." Bolt glanced at her quickly, then looked away.

"Damn right I am! Mad as hell, that's what!"

When she raised her voice, Bolt noticed several tourists on the street below look up and shade their eyes to see what was going on. Maybe the balcony hadn't been such a good idea after all.

"Mary Scarlett, *you're* the one who left *me,* remember? *You're* the one who ran off. After eight years, I really don't think you have a right to act like the injured party just because I've been seeing someone else. You were *married,* after all. I had no idea you would ever come back. What did I expect me to do? Join a monastic order?"

Her fingertips went to her cheeks. She was blushing furiously. In anger? Embarrassment? Bolt had no idea.

"Don't bring all that up," she begged. "You don't know what happened. No one does. I'm the only one, and I have to live with what I did."

Bolt gazed out over the shimmering river and took a long, slow sip of his drink. He waited, hoping she would go on. He had no idea where he should try to guide this conversation.

"Who is she?" Mary Scarlett finally demanded, but this time in a whisper.

"Kathleen," he admitted. "Kathleen O'Shea."

Mary Scarlett remained silent, trying to let this information sink in. She was obviously shocked to hear her old friend's name.

"So that's why you were so outraged when I said she might be a good match for Allen." She laughed softly, a humorless sound. "Poor Bolt! You should have told me then and saved yourself from all my blathering. But, no! You just let me go on and on making a fool of myself" She laughed again, then exploded. "Goddammit! What a stupid little idiot I am!"

With the rush of words came a torrent of tears. She buried her face in her hands and sobbed. Bolt reached over and touched her shoulder. She didn't pull away this time.

"Mary Scarlett, nobody thinks you're a fool or an idiot. You're just—well—*Mary Scarlett.* You're right. I should have told you up front. But you were so exhausted when you got here and you've been through so much. I was trying to ease into things."

Bolt pulled the clean handkerchief out of his back pocket and pressed it into her hands. She wiped her eyes, then blew daintily. After a few deep breaths, she was able to speak again with only a slight quiver in her voice.

"When's the wedding, Bolt?"

"Wedding? What wedding?"

"You and Kathleen."

He stared at her, frowning in disbelief. "We haven't even discussed marriage."

"That's not what I heard."

"What exactly did you hear? And from whom?"

"Hattie Thorndyke was at the beauty shop this afternoon."

Bolton rolled his eyes. *"Christ,* Mary Scarlett! That woman is one percent truth and ninety-nine percent bullshit and you know it."

"You care about Kathleen, though. That's pretty obvious."

"Sure, I care about her," Bolt said defensively. "Kathleen's been through a lot. She was a sweet kid when we were in school and she still is."

"And she'd fit right into the picket fence life you've always dreamed of. Right?"

Stung, he turned to stare at Mary Scarlett. "Is that the way you see me?"

"Isn't that the way you've always seen yourself? With a proper little wife, kids, dogs, home, all enclosed neatly in a whitewashed fence?"

A fleeting glimpse of the house he had built flashed through his mind. He had insisted on the white picket fence with Cherokee roses climbing it. But that wasn't really the fence she was talking about and he knew it. It was the tight-fitting emotional fence he had built around Mary Scarlett.

Guilty as charged, he thought.

He stopped toying with the olives in his martini and looked directly at her again. "I have no plans to get married, Mary Scarlett. Neither does Kathleen. Yes, we've been seeing a lot of each other these past few months, but we both see other people, too."

Wrong thing to say! he realized immediately.

"Who else?" she demanded angrily. "What have you turned into, Bolt? Some kind of Savannah Don Juan?"

Her renewed rage broke the tension. Just how was he supposed to respond to that? He laughed, long and hard.

"Stop it!" she fumed. "How dare you laugh at me, Bolton Conrad?"

After a few minutes, he got control of himself. Still smiling, almost chuckling, he said, "I'm not laughing at you, honey. It's this whole damn conversation that strikes me as funny. Think about it. I find you sobbing in a graveyard at some stranger's tomb, with blood all over you, and what do we discuss? My nonexistent wedding plans. Doesn't that strike you as just a bit funny?"

Mary Scarlett's expression changed. She no longer looked angry. Nor was she amused. When Bolt mentioned the grave and the blood, her face drained of color. She crossed her wrists over her chest and rocked slowly back and forth in her chair, her head down.

"What is it, Mary Scarlett?" he asked gently. "What's wrong? Can't you tell me?"

She reached over, gripped his hand, and squeezed until her nails dug into his palm. "Bolt, could I be losing my mind?"

"Of course not. Why would you think such a thing?"

"Ever since I got back last night, strange things have been happening. I told you about what happened in the bathroom. I showed you the heart carved into the stone. Then the ship and Jean Lafitte. It happened again this afternoon in the Colonial Cemetery."

"What do you mean? You saw Sean and Elisabeth again? Or was Lafitte lurking about?"

She shook her head. "No. I saw James Wilde, the duellist who's been buried there since 1815." Her voice faltered. She paused to control its trembling. "And I saw—no, *I was*—the girl he loved. The girl he would have married if he'd lived. I was there when they brought him back across the river from Screvens Ferry. He was in my arms when he died. The blood . . ." Overcome with emotion, she obviously couldn't go on.

Bolt stared hard at her. "You're telling me that was *his* blood?"

She nodded.

"That's impossible, Mary Scarlett."

"I know," she whispered. "You tell me how it got there."

"Well, even if we can't explain it, that certainly doesn't mean you're losing your mind."

"Granny Boo was crazy. Maybe it runs in my family."

"Miss Beulah was as sane as you are."

"That's what I mean, Bolt. Maybe I'm like her."

"But she wasn't crazy. She only liked to make people think she was so they'd leave her alone. Eccentric perhaps, but not insane."

Mary Scarlett looked up, her eyes bright with tears, but also warm with memories. "I never told anyone this, Bolt, but Granny Boo came to me the night of her funeral."

"*Came* to you? I don't understand."

"Mama and Big Dick were having a terrific row downstairs. I never did find out what they were fighting about. My wedding probably. It upset me terribly. I was already so miserable, to think that Granny Boo was gone. I was crying, calling to her, begging her to take me where she'd gone. The next thing I knew, she was there in my room. She took me to a party."

Now Bolt was looking at her as if she really *had* lost her mind.

Mary Scarlett stood up suddenly. Gripping the wrought-iron railing of the balcony, she gazed out over the river. "Bolt," she whispered, "maybe Granny Boo is doing this. Now that I'm back in Savannah, we're connected again. The feeling when I go back in time—it's the same as when she took me to the party at Bonaventure."

"You went to a party at the cemetery?"

She shook her head and turned back toward him. "It wasn't a cemetery yet when she took me there. It was Bonaventure Plantation, the old Mulryne land grant from 1760. John Mulryne was an English colonel when he built the brick mansion and the terraced gardens on the bluff overlooking the Wilmington River. When his daughter married Josiah Tattnall from Charleston, her father planted oaks to commemorate the occasion. The same oaks that shade the graves today. If you look closely, you can see that the old trees are planted in a pattern, an entwined *M* and *T* to symbolize the joining of two great families."

"I never knew you were so interested in Savannah history, Mary Scarlett. Where did you learn all that?"

She looked thoughtful, almost puzzled. Then she smiled. "I guess Granny Boo told me the night she took me to the party."

Trying to cover his shock, Bolt said, "As I remember it, that's only part of the story. The Revolutionary War split that family, like so many others, right down the middle. The elder Mulrynes and Tattnalls all returned to England. The Americans confiscated Bonaventure. It was returned to Josiah Tattnall, Jr., who fought valiantly for the colonies under General Nathanael Greene. Later the house burned during a dinner party."

Mary Scarlett smiled and nodded. "I know. I was there. Granny Boo told me the party has never ended."

A long stillness followed her words. Even the sounds from below on River Street seemed muffled and distant. Bolt jumped when the phone rang.

"Excuse me a minute?" he said.

He was glad he hadn't brought the phone from the kitchen onto the balcony when he heard Kathleen's voice at the other end of the line.

"I'm glad to hear from you," he said warmly.

Ignoring that comment, Kathleen remained all business. "Another apartment listing on East Jones Street came in this afternoon that I thought *your guest* might find to her liking. That is, unless she's decided on a place already."

Bolt paused a minute before he said, "Actually, we haven't had time to go over the list yet, much less look at any of the places."

"Oh, I see," Kathleen answered stiffly.

"What's that supposed to mean?"

"Nothing. I had thought that there was some urgency in the situation. I see I was mistaken. She'll be staying with you for a while, then?"

"For tonight. Yes."

"Then I suppose I'll see the two of you at Allen's Saturday evening."

"Kathleen, are you sure you won't come with us? I could pick you up . . ."

But the phone had gone dead. Their business talk at an end, Kathleen had hung up on him. Bolt sighed and rubbed a hand over his eyes.

When he looked up, Mary Scarlett was standing in the kitchen doorway. "Checking up on you, is she?"

"Mary Scarlett, you were eavesdropping. No, as a matter of fact, Kathleen was only trying to help. Earlier today she gave me a list of apartments for you to see. Another one came in late this afternoon. She thought you might like to look at it, too."

"Awfully anxious to get me out of here, isn't she? How about you, Bolt? Do you feel the same way?" Mary Scarlett moved closer and draped her arms over his shoulders.

He tried to ignore the cloud of Shalimar that enveloped

him. It was his favorite scent and Mary Scarlett knew it. He had bought her her first bottle years ago, when he was a struggling law student who could ill afford such expensive luxuries. After she ran away, the scent had haunted him. If he passed a woman wearing Shalimar on the street, he would feel the pain of losing her all over again. It would take him hours, sometimes days, to get over his depression.

"You know you can stay here as long as you like, Mary Scarlett." His voice was husky, her nearness and her perfume taking their toll.

"I'll stay only as long as you want me, Bolt darling. Tell me to go and I'll pack my bags this minute."

"No!" he said, breathing deeply, closing his eyes. "No, don't leave, Mary Scarlett."

He gripped her slender waist and drew her near, closing his arms around her in a fierce embrace. Their kiss was long and slow and tender.

"I wish I still had my old Chevy," Bolt whispered between kisses. "I'd put you right in the backseat."

A shiver of pleasure passed through Mary Scarlett. His words brought back the nights after football games or movies when they'd park in a secluded spot beside the river and neck for hours. Everything short of actually making love. She remembered how light-headed and light-hearted she used to feel afterward, her whole body tingling, on fire with love and desire for Bolt.

Mary Scarlett was on the verge of suggesting the bedroom as an alternative to the Chevy's backseat when Bolt suddenly drew away and laughed. "Too bad those days are long gone, eh? We'd be a bit cramped in the CRX. How about we look at that list of apartments, honey?"

Mary Scarlett was crushed, enraged, dumbfounded. How could he kiss her so passionately one minute, then try to give her the bum's rush the next?

"Fine!" she said coldly.

She had no way of knowing how close Bolt had come

to hauling her off to the bedroom without even asking. Another minute, another kiss, another whiff of Shalimar and he would have been out of control. He wanted Mary Scarlett. God, how he wanted her! But he'd learned from his past mistakes. He knew better than to rush into anything this time.

He could see the confusion in her face. He knew she would have been a willing lover moments before. Disappointed now, she could be dangerous.

"No need to rush things," he said with a shrug. "We have all the time in the world. Right?"

"One never knows," she answered.

Her words and their delivery left him feeling chilled to the bone. What was she thinking about? The sudden death of her husband? Or was she reminding him that he had lost her once before and warning him that it could happen again?

Trying his best to sound calm and casual, Bolt said, "I thought we could look over the list, see if anything strikes your fancy. But there's no need to rush into this until you feel comfortable staying alone."

They sat together on the sofa and read down the list. All the places were luxurious and priced accordingly. Kathleen knew Mary Scarlett's tastes—that was obvious.

"What about it?" Bolt asked. "See anything you'd like to look at?"

Mary Scarlett leaned back on the leather couch and stretched her arms out along the back. "I've made a decision, Bolt. I'm not going to rent a place."

His stunned expression made her smile. She could guess the thoughts going through his head—either that she meant to stay with him indefinitely or she meant to leave Savannah immediately. Obviously, he found either option disturbing.

After giving him another moment to think, she announced, "I'm moving into the house on Bull Street. As soon as possible."

A grin replaced his frown. "Mary Scarlett, that's great! You won't be sorry. It's a real showplace. And it's your home."

"There's no place like home," she replied, but Bolt missed her lack of enthusiasm.

"You're right about that."

"One thing, though, Bolt. I'd really like you to be with me when I go back for the first time. I don't think I can do this by myself. Actually, that's how I wound up in the cemetery this afternoon. I'd meant to go to the house, but I just couldn't go alone."

He reached over and took her hand, giving it a reassuring squeeze. "Of course I'll go with you, honey. It will be a treat to see the old place again. Just like old times."

"Let's hope not," Mary Scarlett murmured under her breath.

The rest of their evening proved uneventful. Bolt ordered some barbecued ribs, coleslaw, and fries from a nearby soul food place. He dived in, but Mary Scarlett only picked at the spicy pork. Conversation was at a minimum since he was busy eating, while she seemed uninclined. In fact, Bolt noticed that Mary Scarlett seemed to have drifted off into a world of her own.

That fact was confirmed when she said, "I think I'll take a shower then go to bed. I'm beat."

"You do that," he answered. "I have some papers to look over, but I plan to turn in early, too. See you in the morning."

It was a lot earlier in the morning then he'd figured on when Bolt next saw Mary Scarlett. The tall case clock in his foyer had struck two only moments before he heard the scream. Fighting his way through layers of dreams, Bolt sat up in bed, groggy from being jolted awake so suddenly. He wasn't even sure what woke him.

His flesh crawled as a second, soul-wrenching cry echoed through the apartment. "No! No! Get away from me! Help me! He's hurting me!"

Bolt grabbed the pistol he kept in the drawer of the bed-side table. He hit the floor running, tearing toward the guest bedroom two doors down the hall, more than ready to shoot to kill. He'd had two break-ins before he bought the gun, determined not to have his home violated again. Mary Scar-lett's screams seemed to indicate that the burglar had more on his mind than thievery tonight.

His finger on the trigger, Bolt eased the door open, then hit the wall switch. He couldn't have been more astonished when the lights came on. He found no intruder. Only Mary Scarlett, fast asleep, sobbing, screaming, and fighting the covers. Quickly, he put the pistol aside and went to her.

"Mary Scarlett, hush now, honey." He sat down on the edge of the bed and tried to restrain her wildly flailing arms. "It's Bolt, darlin'. You're all right. Wake up."

When her eyes opened suddenly, Bolt had never seen such terror and agony in his life. "Stop him," she whimpered. "He's hurting me, Bolt. Don't let him do that to me."

He drew her into his arms, comforting her as if she were a child. "I won't let anyone hurt you, honey, not ever again." As he talked to her, he smoothed her tangled hair. She was trembling all over. Whatever the source of her terror, it was genuine, at least to Mary Scarlett.

Her sobs softened to hiccuppy sighs.

"There. That's better. I think we can both go back to sleep now."

But when he tried to ease his arms from around her, she clung to him, desperate. "No! Don't leave me. He'll come back!"

"There's nobody here, Mary Scarlett. Look around. The room's empty. Just the two of us. You had a bad dream, that's all."

She refused to let go. "He's only hiding. The minute you leave, he'll be back. That's the way he is."

"Who, Mary Scarlett? Who are you talking about?"

She looked into his eyes, her own still wide and pale with terror. "Raul," she whispered. "He knows I'm here. I thought I could hide from him, but he's found me." Her lips trembled and more tears came. "He'll hurt me, just like he used to."

"You can't mean your husband. He's dead, Mary Scarlett. You told me so yourself."

She shook her head fiercely. Her eyes darted about the room as if she might see Raul lurking in some corner. Then she leaned close and whispered in Bolt's ear, "He only faked his death. He's *alive*, Bolt! And he's come for me. Please, *please*, don't let him take me!"

"I promise I won't let anyone hurt you. But Raul is dead, Mary Scarlett. Remember? You showed me the clipping about his funeral. You know he was buried. So he couldn't have faked his death."

Not a word of what he said seemed to sink in. "Turn the light off," she begged. "He's watching us."

Bolt switched off the lights. The room was in total darkness now except for a hint of moonlight coming through the mini-blinds at the window.

"Is that better?" he asked.

Mary Scarlett seemed to relax just a bit in his arms. At least she went from rigid to tense. "You'll stay with me?" she begged.

"Until you fall asleep."

"No!" She went rigid again. "He'll come back the minute you leave. You have to stay, Bolt."

"All right. Don't get upset again, honey. I'll stay. I promise."

That seemed to reassure her. She stretched out on one side of the bed and patted the other side, indicating that Bolt should lie down beside her. He obeyed, although the situation was not to his liking—or too much to his liking, depending upon which way he looked at it. He and Mary Scarlett had been many things to each other, but they had never been lovers. As a teenager, he'd had more wet dreams about her than he could count. The only things that had kept him sane over the years were the occasional loose girls he'd blown off steam with and the knowledge that someday Mary Scarlett would be his wife.

But that hadn't happened. And now here they were, finally lying in bed together. He almost wished he had bought that antique bundling board he spotted in an antiques shop a few months back. He had thought about fitting it to this bed simply to amuse his guests. There was nothing the least bit amusing about his present situation. If this didn't test his mettle, nothing would.

"Hold me," she whispered. "I'm scared."

She really was and he knew it. She wasn't just making a play for him, teasing him. There was far too much terror in her voice. Even Mary Scarlett wasn't that good an actress.

Everything seemed out of kilter to Mary Scarlett. What was she doing here? Where exactly was she? There was someone in the bed with her, someone she trusted. That meant it couldn't be Raul. Who then? She was certain that Raul had been here with her, threatening her, only minutes before.

Raul is dead. She had heard someone tell her that. But how could that be? If he was really dead, how could he be here? How could he have come through the bedroom window? How could he have touched her the way he did?

"Hold me," she whispered. "I'm scared."

The arms that closed around her were strong and protective. She snuggled close, breathing more easily. His body felt warm against hers. Even the prickly feeling of his chest hair against her breasts was reassuring. Raul had kept his body smoothly shaved. She pressed closer into him, sliding her right leg between his. The intimate contact sent a warm shiver through her.

"Mary Scarlett?" His breath teased her cheek when he spoke.

"Hm-m-m," she murmured, feeling drugged with weariness and with his nearness. She found his mouth and rubbed her lips softly against his.

He touched her breast. Gently. So gently that afterward she wondered if she had imagined the sensation. Maybe she'd only moved slightly in his arms, making the sheer bodice of her nightgown slide against her nipple. No! There it was again. The light stroke of his fingertips. She arched her back, moving her body closer to his. She slid her right leg slowly up and down between his hugging knees.

The next sensation she felt was indeed the slide of silk against her flesh. He eased the strap of her gown down from her shoulder. When he touched her breast again, there was no barrier between her flesh and his. He pressed his palm against her, then slowly stroked to the very tip of her nipple with his fingers.

She sighed and a shiver ran through her.

"It's been a long time, darlin'," he whispered.

"A dozen lifetimes," she answered.

"Kiss me?"

Mary Scarlett shifted her body upward to reach his mouth again. Her lips moist and parted, she covered his. He seemed to be holding his breath as she teased at his mouth with the tip of her tongue. While they kissed, his hands played at her breasts, sending little licks of flame all through her.

Bolt eased the other strap of her gown over her shoulder. She sat up for a moment to let the cobwebby fabric slither to her waist. He held her in that position, staring up at the moonlight silvering her bare breasts. She could see the gleam in his eyes when he looked at her.

"You're as beautiful as ever, Mary Scarlett. As tender and sweet as I remember." He raised up and caught her about the waist, burying his face against her breasts. "God, I've missed you!"

Mary Scarlett wasn't sure what to do. She wanted to pull away, but how could she? Bolt would never understand. She hadn't been able to tell him how it was with Raul. Bolt wanted to make love. She knew that. She wanted it, too. But she wasn't sure she could. Kissing, touching, holding each other—all that felt wonderful. Yet somehow she knew that anything more would send her over the edge. Raul had been a cruel lover, heartless and sadistic. She still felt his taint. She still feared the act as much as she longed for it.

Sensing something amiss, Bolt said, "I don't want to rush you, darlin'. Tell me if you want me to go."

She gripped him tighter, her fear of being alone overriding her fear of making love. "No! Stay, please, Bolt!"

He nuzzled her breast and sighed. "Gladly, darlin', gladly."

Bolt eased Mary Scarlett back down on the pillows. He leaned over her, kissing her breasts, making her writhe with need. As her body moved, Bolt slipped her gown lower, until it circled her hips. He slid his left hand underneath, stroking her ever so gently. He remembered her body well. He knew exactly the spot that aroused her to the brink of madness. Leaning over her, kissing her deeply, he continued the teasing fondling. Mary Scarlett went hot, then cold all over.

Shoving him away, she cried, "Bolt, no!"

He rolled to the other side of the bed, looking stunned and hurt. "What the hell did I do?"

"Nothing," she sobbed. "Nothing wrong, anyway. It felt wonderful, Bolt."

"Then why are you crying?" He made a move to take

her back into his arms but she recoiled from his touch. "Why did you push me away?"

"It's not you. It's Raul."

"He's *dead*. Mary Scarlett! You know that as well as I do. I told you I don't mean to push you and I meant that sincerely. It's been only a few months. Damn! I really feel like a heel. You're still mourning your dead husband and I'm already putting moves on you. I'm sorry, really sorry, Mary Scarlett."

Her laugh was almost hysterical. *"Mourning him?* Would I mourn the death of the devil himself?"

"I don't get it, Mary Scarlett. If that's not the problem, what is?"

She struggled to a sitting position, taking no note of the fact that her gown was still down around her hips and her breasts were peaked with the desire that Bolt had aroused in her. Leaning toward him, she let her hair hide her face. It was easier that way.

"Raul was not a gentle lover," she began uncertainly. "He delighted in terrorizing me. We had separate bedrooms, all part of his sport. He must have known that I'd lie awake every night, terrified that he'd come to me and demand his rights as my husband."

"What did he do to you, Mary Scarlett?" Bolt's question seethed with quiet rage.

In answer, she shook her head. "I can't tell you that. I could never look at you again if you knew."

Bolt's chin sagged to his chest. Mary Scarlett heard him expel a long, angry breath. "Why didn't you leave him?" he asked at length.

"He never gave me a chance. I was totally dependent on him. He provided everything I needed except a way out. I had no money, no friends, he even took my passport and locked it away. When that bull gored him, God help me, it was the happiest day of my life. I was free at last!" She sniffed back more tears. "At least I thought I was. But life with Raul changed me, Bolt. I'm not the same person you loved eight years ago. I'm not sure I'll ever be myself again."

"What are we going to do, Mary Scarlett?"

She brushed her hair back over her shoulders and smiled sadly at him. "Be patient with me. Take things slow. And, *please,* don't marry Kathleen until I find myself again."

Not even thinking, Bolt reached out and drew her into his arms. She didn't pull away.

"It feels good, the way you hold me, Bolt. And the way you kiss me," she whispered.

He did kiss her then, but with great tenderness. She could feel him holding back, not wanting to frighten her again. When he cupped her breast and she felt a quiver of pleasure, she smiled. Maybe things would be all right after all. As long as Bolt was here to protect her.

Suddenly she stiffened in his arms. What about when she moved back to the house on Bull Street? What would happen to her once she was all alone? Would Raul continue to torment her from the grave?

Six

Kathleen O'Shea had hung up the "CLOSED" sign and was locking the door of the real estate office when the phone started ringing.

"Damnation! Who could that be?"

She thought about ignoring it. Anyone who waited till this late on a Friday afternoon didn't deserve to get an answer; they could talk to the machine. Her parents were coming for dinner and she needed to get home and start the fire for the steaks. Never one to leave loose ends dangling, however, she grudgingly unlocked the door and grabbed the receiver on the seventh ring.

"I'm sorry. We're closed for the day."

"Hey, Kathleen. Am I glad I caught you! This is Allen."

With an exaggerated sigh of relief, she said, "Thank God you're not a client. I could just see myself having to cancel my hair appointment tomorrow to show a house, then turning up at your party looking like a hag."

"P-shaw, gal! You couldn't look like a hag if you had a backstage pass to a Halloween house of horrors."

"Ah-h-h! Compliments! I like!" Allen wanted a favor, she could tell.

"Listen, hon, I know it's late, but I need a big favor."

Kathleen grinned. She knew it. "Like how big a favor? Don't tell me Mrs. Hampstead came home unexpectedly and kicked you out of her house and you need to borrow a mansion to throw your party tomorrow night."

"Sh-h-h! Don't even think such a thing. You're the only one who knows about that, Katie-my-darlin', and mum's the word."

"What then? Make it fast. I've really got to get home, Allen."

"Well, to get right to the point, the favor is party-oriented. And I feel like a total jerk waiting this late to call you. I mean it's not like you're a last resort or anything. I simply forgot that I need a hostess. Someone to stand beside me, laugh at my jokes, and look utterly gorgeous. I know no one who could do a greater job of it. Please, Katie?"

Kathleen arched an eyebrow. Something was fishy here. "I thought you meant for Bolt to bring me," she reminded him.

"Oh, tha-that." Allen always stuttered slightly when he was caught in a lie. "Well, you see, with Mary Scarlett back in town, I just assumed that he would have to bring her. Somehow I can't see you tagging along like it was a three-legged sack race."

"You've got *that* right, my friend."

"Let's be honest, Kathleen."

"Yes, let's," she urged. "The truth, Allen. Out with it!"

He sighed into the phone. "God, how I hate telling the truth! But here goes. I want to make them jealous—totally *pea-green* with envy."

"Because you're green with envy that Bolt's bringing Mary Scarlett."

"Aren't you, Katie darlin'? The whole truth, remember?"

"Oh, I suppose I am," she admitted. "But it's your fault, you toad! You made me think Bolt meant to invite me."

"One can always hope. And I do apologize, providing that you promise not to call me a toad in front of my guests. I need to make an outstanding impression on everyone to-morrow night."

"Everyone meaning Mary Scarlett, of course."

"Well, wouldn't that suit your purposes, too, love? If I

manage to worm my way back into Mary Scarlett's affections, that would put Bolt on the market again."

"He's not *off* the market, as far as I know. He just doesn't want Mary Scarlett to feel awkward tomorrow night. After all, this will be sort of her second coming out party. And she has a lot of gossip to face."

"Mary Scarlett? *Feel awkward?* Come on, Katie darlin', who are you trying to kid? The young widow Miguel will be in all her glory tomorrow night. That's why I need you by my side. Will you do it for me, hon? I'll owe you."

Kathleen sighed, then answered, *"Big time!"*

"Fabulous, Katie! I knew I could count on you. You're a real buddy."

"No, I'm not, Allen. I'm in this for myself and don't you forget it. Mary Scarlett wrecked Bolt's life once. I mean to see that she doesn't do it again. If preventing that means I have to throw in my lot with the likes of you, I'll even stoop to that."

"Gee, Kathleen, I love you, too."

"Don't get me wrong, Allen. I wish you all the best in this quest of yours. You and Mary Scarlett deserve each other. I'll see you tomorrow night."

Kathleen hung up before he could respond. When she did, she was shaking all over. She might have tried to defend Bolt's actions to Allen, but that was only for show. Until Overman called, she'd figured the game was all over for her. The clock had run out. But, surprise, surprise! There was still some time left, time enough to score. Bolt Conrad was the game ball. And she meant to have him, by fair play or foul!

Saturday morning dawned cool and misty. As she gazed out over the fog-shrouded river Mary Scarlett realized that the weather mirrored her mood exactly. She had suffered another nightmare during the night. Bolt had once more come to her rescue—sleeping with her, but keeping his distance. Neither of them had slept much, although they had done a good job of faking it. Around five she had finally given in to frustration and exhaustion.

Before she even opened her eyes, she had known that Bolt was gone. His scent and warmth still lingered, but the man himself had left at dawn. She had been vaguely aware when he rose and slipped out quietly, trying not to disturb her. She had slept lightly after that, wary every moment of Raul's ghost returning to stalk her. Now, in the gray drizzle of the washed-out morning, she felt limp and tired and disappointed that Bolt had made no move during her hysteria, frightened off by her reaction a few nights ago.

A soft knock at the door dragged her out of her dull brown thoughts.

"Coffee's ready," Bolt called from the hallway. "May I come in?"

Realizing she was naked, she said, "Just a minute," then pulled on her robe. The stark morning light required more modesty than the cover of darkness. "All right," she answered. "I'm decent."

Bolt came in silently, he, too, wearing only his robe. Carefully he set the Spode cup and saucer on the bedside table. "You take it black, as I remember."

She smiled at him almost shyly. "I'll bet you also remembered that I like Luzianne with chicory."

Bolt shrugged, tried to smile at her, but it faded before it took hold. "Is there any other kind in Savannah?"

She patted the side of the bed, inviting him to sit down. He ignored her gesture and remained standing, looking awkward as if he didn't know what to do with his hands.

"Looks like March means to go out like a lion," he said, gazing out the window, trying not to look at Mary Scarlett. "Not a very good day."

"No worse than last night," she answered softly. "Bolt,

I'm sorry. I don't know what's gotten into me. I guess my nerves are just shot. Don't you worry, though. I'll be okay."

"About last night?" Bolt hesitated, seeming reluctant to go on.

"I'm sorry," Mary Scarlett whispered again, lowering her eyes.

"You've no need to be. Anyway, I meant about Raul. You don't really believe he's still alive, do you?"

She shook her head. "Only in my nightmares. But I refuse to let him haunt me any longer. I've made a decision, Bolt. I want to go to the house today."

He reached out and touched her shoulder. "Mary Scarlett, are you sure? You don't have to rush this. You know you can stay here as long as you like."

She looked up at him and smiled sadly. "I know that and I appreciate it, Bolt. But the longer I stay, the more dependent I'll become. You don't need that and neither do I. While I was married to Raul, I let him control me completely. I can't allow that to happen again, not ever."

"You know I'd never try to control you, Mary Scarlett." Bolt sounded hurt, almost guilty, but not angry. The white picket fence around the house he had built for her flashed through his mind. Wasn't fencing her in the same as trying to control her?

She reached up and took his hand. "Bolt, I *need* to go to the house. I won't be able to move in for a time, not until it's been cleaned and put in order. But I can't face the people at Allen's party tonight unless I have the courage to face my old home first. You'll go with me, won't you?"

He nodded. "You know I will, if you're determined."

"It's something I have to do."

Bolt turned toward the door. "There's cereal and fruit in the kitchen. Milk in the fridge. I'll get dressed while you have some breakfast. We'll go as soon as you're ready."

A shiver passed through Mary Scarlett, but she smiled and said, "Thank you, Bolt."

Before she could change her mind, she forced herself into action. She pulled on her jeans and sweatshirt, then gave the rumpled bed a lick and a promise.

While she was eating her breakfast and drinking more coffee, she kept telling herself it would be all right. Any ghosts that still inhabited the old place on Bull Street were family spirits, after all. They wouldn't take kindly to a Spanish bullfighter invading their territory. And how could he come, if she refused to think about him? With a determined effort, she put Raul out of her mind.

"Ready, Mary Scarlett?" Bolt said from the kitchen door.

She turned and gave him an overly bright smile. "As I'll ever be."

A short time later, Bolt pulled the CRX into the old carriage drive beside the Bull Street house. The wind and rain had tossed wisteria blossoms all over the front lawn, turning it to a patchwork of lavender and green. The heavy vine that clung to the front of the house groaned in the brisk gusts under its weight of flowers and leaves. Azaleas—pink, fuschia, coral, and white—all but smothered the veranda and stairs. The whole front of the place looked like the Mad Hatter's Easter chapeau.

Mary Scarlett stepped out of the car and climbed up on the old carriage block, remembering how Granny Boo had told her that in the old days ladies always alighted from their traps by way of this square of North Georgia marble. She closed her eyes for a moment, thinking that contact with the block might bring on another of her time-travel episodes. But nothing moved and no strange voices called to her. When she looked again she could see only the tangled mass of the grounds around the house.

"I'll need a yard service first thing," Mary Scarlett noted aloud. "God, it reminds me of an overgrown grave at Bonaventure."

"Pleasant thoughts only, darlin'," Bolt reminded her gently. He chuckled. "Remember how you used to hide behind that big white azalea bush over there and wait for me to deliver the paper?"

She turned on him, her eyes blazing blue fire, but a devilish smile on her face. "I never told you about that."

He laughed. "You never had to. I saw you back there. Why do you think I always popped a wheely whenever I came by? Showing off for my girl, of course."

"I wasn't your girl back then."

"Maybe not, but I could always hope. I must have been all of eleven years old when I first realized I was in love with you. Of course, I didn't know it was love at the time. I just figured it was all the green Japanese plums I'd eaten off old lady Butterworth's tree that gave me that stomachache."

"Well, I like that!" she fumed. "How dare you compare loving me to a bellyache?"

Just then a strong gust of wind swirled past like a miniature tornado. Mary Scarlett's umbrella flipped inside out, and a heavy shower drenched them both. Lightning cracked so close that the hair on Mary Scarlett's arms bristled. The following clap of thunder shook the ground as she raced for the veranda, Bolt in pursuit. When they reached the leaf-strewn porch, they were both laughing and shaking themselves like wet dogs.

They tossed their umbrellas aside and stood looking at each other for several moments. Their laughter faded to silent smiles.

"It is going to be okay, isn't it, Bolt?" Her voice sounded like the pleading of a little girl.

Bolt reached out and drew her into his arms. "Do you remember how we used to hide from the whole world behind this old wisteria vine?"

"How could I forget?" she murmured. "You were the first boy I ever kissed. Right here on this very spot." She sighed. "Life would be so simple if we could turn the clock back, wouldn't it, Bolt?"

He kissed her damp hair. "Yes, Mary Scarlett. How I'd love to come back here and spend an evening on the porch swing with you, with the radio inside tuned to that station that used to play the old songs."

"Elvis, Buddy Holly, the Big Bopper." Mary Scarlett sighed, then added, "They're all gone now, Bolt, along with those happy years."

He drew her closer and kissed her cheek. "But it can be that way again, Mary Scarlett. You'll see. Everything will be fine now that you're home."

She slipped her arms up around his neck and clung to him almost desperately. "Oh, Bolt darlin', I want it to be. I want *everything* to be like it should have been a long time ago. I made such a damn mess of things."

Then she was kissing him. Softly at first, deeper and wilder as moments passed. Bolt held back, cautious with her. But her fervor soon fired his passions. For a long time, they stood together, sheltered from the prying eyes of Savannah by the century-old wisteria vine, luxuriating in their own private world, reliving memories and creating new ones.

Mary Scarlett broke the embrace. Smoothing her hair, she said, "I'm ready now. Will you unlock the door?"

Bolt took the big iron key from her trembling hands and slipped it into the lock. The tumbler made a grinding sound as it moved.

"Put WD-40 on the shopping list," Mary Scarlett said to herself.

The moment before Bolt pushed the creaking door open, Mary Scarlett closed her eyes, the way she always had before opening a surprise on her birthday or tearing into a telegram that might contain bad news.

In that instant, a rush of familiar smells and long-locked-away memories engulfed her. With that first rush of musty air, she could isolate various aspects of family history. Granny Boo's face powder, her mother's peach brandy, her father's expensive Cuban cigars that he literally had smuggled into Savannah. She could even hear his growling voice when his wife objected to the obnoxious contraband in the parlor. "Damned if any government is going to regulate my smoking habits, so you might as well stop your blasted nagging, Lucy. The day I'm expected to take orders from any woman is the last day she'll see my face."

Mary Scarlett shuddered involuntarily at the memory. Bolt slipped his arm around her. "You're sure you want to go inside, honey?"

She nodded. "Just a passing anxiety attack. That's all it was, Bolt. I'll be fine in a minute."

In order to detach herself from all unpleasant memories, she concentrated on the familiar aromas. She could smell the fine old woods, the warmth of lemon wax old black Delsey had always applied lavishly to the furniture. The odors of dust and mildew wafted from the lace curtains and velvet drapes that hung longer than the windows, bunching on the floor to show that this was a household of wealth, a household that did not have to limit window treatment or anything else to prescribed parameters. Overlaying the musky lace odor was the good smell of their washwoman's homemade starch, carefully prepared in the old manner with flour, water, and scented soap to make the curtains not only board-stiff, but as fresh as a meadow after a spring rain.

The odor of stale grease from generations of Southern fried dinners tricked Mary Scarlett's memory into smelling thickly battered chicken and shrimp sizzling in great iron skillets. Turnip and collard greens swimming in pools of bubbling pork fat. Green tomatoes, okra, squash all dancing and popping in bacon drippings.

"The place needs airing out bad," Bolt said as Mary Scarlett's mouth watered with remembered childhood feasts.

"I'm going to learn to cook," she announced, seemingly out of nowhere.

Bolt laughed. "Well, good for you! You ought to check and see if the gourmet class is still in session at the college."

"No, no! I mean cook the *real* way, the old Southern way. Fried chicken every Sunday, pork chops, big juicy hams, and greens and fresh vegetables and butter-smothered grits and coconut cakes a mile high and pecan pies to go with them."

"Mary Scarlett, you're making me fat just listening to you."

"But you love Southern cooking, Bolt. I remember when you used to wolf down a whole plate of Delsey's biscuits with butter and gallberry honey."

He laughed. "I also love my present cholesterol level and my nice, unclogged arteries."

She turned, her hands on her slender hips, and stared him right in the eye. "If I have to go, Bolton Conrad, and I assume I'm no different from anyone else, I'm going to go well-fed and well-greased!"

Bolt was glad to see that her grim mood had lightened. They laughed together, then turned to enter the dim, musty foyer.

The moment she stepped over the threshold, Mary Scarlett gasped, then cried out. "It's gone! Oh, no!"

"What, Mary Scarlett? What are you talking about?"

Silently, she pointed at a dark oval on the wall over the petticoat table to the left of the door. The huge mauve and purple cabbage roses of the wallpaper retained their original brilliance in that one spot. Something had hung there for many years. Bolt suddenly remembered what it was.

"The mirror," he said, frowning.

"Granny Boo's mirror," she amplified. "Who could have taken it, Bolt?"

"Calm down, honey. It's probably somewhere else in the

house. Didn't you tell me that Miss Beulah used to take it up to the attic sometimes? Maybe that's where it is."

She shook her head. "No! I brought it down from the attic after she died. I remember! I had it in my room."

"Then it must still be there. We'll find it. Don't you worry, honey."

Bolt had called the day before and had the power turned on. In the foyer, the English chandelier of small, delicately-shaped crystals glowed with weak, yellowish light, but only for a few seconds. With another lightning strike, the electricity flickered and failed. The house shook, then they were standing in deep shadows.

"Damn!" Bolt said. "We can't do anything without power. Maybe we'd better come back on a better day."

"I'm not budging until I locate that mirror. Mama used to keep hurricane lanterns in the pantry. Come on. Let's find them."

Holding Bolt's hand and moving determinedly ahead of him through the deep shadows, Mary Scarlett headed down the hallway that bisected the house, passing the parlors, the dining room, and the library until she came to the huge kitchen that had been added to the back of the main building after the detached cook house burned back around 1900. The butler's pantry was between the kitchen and the dining room. Sure enough, in the glass-doored cabinets they found several kerosene lanterns and a number of candleholders with hurricane shades.

"The lanterns are empty," Bolt said. "We'll have to use candles."

Mary Scarlett flicked her cigarette lighter to torch the wicks. "There! That's much better," she said.

"Too bad there aren't any flashlights around."

"Mama wouldn't allow one in the house. She was afraid of battery acid. Never mind that she could have burned the place down with all these candles and kerosene lanterns. You know how she was."

"That was Miss Lucy," Bolt said with a nod. "Eccentric to the nth degree."

"I won't argue that point. Lord, she was something! I guess she had to be a bit balmy, though, to stay married to Big Dick all those years."

It was on the tip of Bolt's tongue to ask at that moment what it was that had turned Mary Scarlett against her father. He knew when it had happened, but she had never told him exactly what caused the rift between father and daughter. From that day in Mary Scarlett's thirteenth year she had never again called him "Daddy." Always "Big Dick" to others, nothing to his face.

"Bolt?" Mary Scarlett said. "Did you take Granny Boo's pearl-handled dessert forks and put them in the safety deposit box?"

"No, honey. I haven't been in the house since your mother's wake. As far as I know, the place was locked up tight the very next day. No one's been in here since."

Mary Scarlett had pulled out a slender, green felt-lined drawer. It was empty. "Maybe Mama put them somewhere for safekeeping. They were always right here."

"Miss Lucy wasn't too stable after the accident. She did a lot of peculiar things. We'll probably find the dessert set hidden in her mattress upstairs or in a shoebox in one of the closets."

Mary Scarlett noted that Bolt still called Big Dick's disappearance "the accident." He probably knew as well as everyone else in Savannah that her mother's husband, as she always thought of him, had run off with another woman. It was kind of Bolt not to mention that fact.

"Let's go up to my room and see if the mirror's there," Mary Scarlett insisted. "I won't feel easy until I have it in my hands again." She had to find out whose face she would see in it now, after all these years. What if she didn't see Bolt's face? She knew it sounded foolish and superstitious, but Granny Boo had believed. And so did she.

As they climbed the stairs, Mary Scarlett stepped higher out of lifelong habit to avoid the single trick stair, a sort of nineteenth century burglar alarm. Bolt, right behind her, tripped on it.

Mary Scarlett laughed. "You'd make a terrible thief," she chided. "You know all these old places have that one higher step to trip up anyone who breaks in and alert the family."

"I've never been up these stairs before. Remember? Miss Lucy would have had apoplexy if I'd ever dared come up to your bedroom. Any other tricky spots?"

"No. You managed to find the only one."

They came to the landing where the stairs turned to go up the rest of the way. A mummified potted palm in an old Majolica jardiniere had long ago moldered onto the frayed carpeting. The dead plant reminded Mary Scarlett suddenly that her mother had fallen to her death from the railing above. She glanced down to the first floor hall, half expecting to see a chalk drawing where Lucy Lamar's body had landed. Still hesitating she looked up into the darkness above, to the spot where her mother had stood before she fell. She shivered.

"Don't think about that," Bolt whispered, tuned in to her every change of mood.

"Hard not to," she said. She continued upward, her eyes fixed on the dull brass carpet rods across each stair. "I should have come back for her funeral."

"Don't punish yourself. There was no one left here to console."

"I wanted to come. Raul refused to allow it."

Bolt could hear tears in her voice. Pained tears, angry tears. What had this Raul done to her? What kind of monster must he have been?

"The mirror, Mary Scarlett. Just focus on finding the mirror. Don't think about all the rest."

She nodded, not trusting her voice to answer. Bolt was

right, of course. There was no need to torture herself over things long past.

In the wide hallway of the second floor, she paused and glanced about. The door of the master bedroom, which her mother had occupied alone for as long as she could remember, stood open. Down on the far left, the guest room that had been Big Dick's lair was closed. Her own room, too, was shut up tight. She wondered if her mother had closed the doors as each of them left her life for good, signaling an end to those relationships. And maybe she'd been glad. Neither relationship had been ideal. In fact, both had been stormy for many years before Lucy Lamar's death.

Mary Scarlett took some comfort in knowing that she and her mother had made peace with each other through letters while she was in Europe. Writing home was the one concession Raul had allowed, her only link with her past.

"Which room first?" Bolt asked.

She nodded toward the one across from the master bedroom. "That's mine," she answered. "The mirror should be there."

When she made no move toward the door, Bolt walked over and turned the knob. The hinges creaked from years of disuse in Savannah's high humidity.

"Mary Scarlett?" Bolt prompted. She seemed to be a million miles away.

She gripped his hand. "Come with me," she begged. "I'm scared, Bolt."

"No need to be," he assured her. "The two of us are the only ones here."

She gave him a twisted smile. "You're *sure* of that?"

Mary Scarlett could hardly believe her eyes when she walked into the room and raised her candle. She might have stepped back to the night of Granny Boo's funeral, the night of her parents' terrible fight, the night she had fled Savannah. The bed was unmade and rumpled, just as she'd left it. Clothes were strewn about from her hasty packing. She had spilled a bottle of perfume on the vanity while she was gathering up her cosmetics that night. A pale oval of wood surrounded the tipped over bottle where its contents had eaten away the finish. Dust lay thick and powdery over everything in the room. Her brass bed gleamed dully from lack of polishing.

"I think I shoved the mirror under the edge of the bed. I was going to take it with me, but I was afraid it would get broken. Also, it was pretty heavy to be carrying in a backpack."

Mary Scarlett scrambled to her knees and searched the darkness under the bed. She stretched her arm as far as it would go. Nothing. Just more dustballs and an old pair of bedroom slippers.

"Oh, Bolt, it's not here!" she cried. "What am I going to do?"

"Come on, honey." He raised her gently from the floor. "I'll buy you a new mirror. Any kind you want. It's not the end of the world, you know."

"You don't understand."

"I might if you gave me a chance. Why won't you tell me about the mirror?"

"You'll think it's silly."

"Maybe so. But we won't know that until you tell me, will we?"

He sat down on the edge of the bed and drew Mary Scarlett down beside him. She sat in silence for several moments, eyes downcast, hands folded in her lap.

Without preamble, she said, "Mama always said it was nonsense. She fussed at Granny Boo for filling my head with 'old wives' tales,' as she called them." She turned and stared into Bolt's eyes, her own wide and shining in the candlelight. "But there's something to it, Bolt, I know there is. I once saw a face. It scared me." She paused as if she had said all there was to say.

"Please, Mary Scarlett," he urged gently. "Tell me about the mirror."

Heaving a great, shuddering sigh, she went on. "Granny Boo first told me the story when I was just a little girl. It was one of her bedtime tales, so I never believed it back then. Not until . . . but I'm getting ahead of myself. The mirror has been in our family forever, since way back in the seventeen hundreds when a young craftsman from London came to Savannah with General Oglethorpe and the first settlers. He was a poor man, but very skilled. Granny Boo said he could take the sorriest stick of wood and turn it into something beautiful. His name was Will Johnston. He fell in love with a serving girl, Annie, who'd come over with one of the wealthy families—one of the men who planted mulberry trees to raise silkworms. Often, Will would visit the people Annie worked for."

Again, Mary Scarlett looked down, her voice quivering when she continued. "Will should never have visited her there. You see, there was a spoiled daughter in the family. The story goes that she wasn't nearly as sweet or as beautiful as Annie and she was jealous of the serving girl. She told her father that she wanted Will for her husband. Things were different back then, far different from the way they'd been in England. Savannah was raw and new, and none of the old rules applied.

"The girl's father went to Will's shop to look him over and found Will working on a lovely frame for a mirror. His carving was excellent—all flowers and scrolls and angels and hearts. The man tried to buy the mirror, but Will told him it was not for sale. You see, he was making it as a gift for his Annie. He couldn't afford a ring, but he would give her the mirror as a token of his undying affection.

Matters progressed quickly. Before Will knew it, he was being wined and dined by the gentleman and his family. Annie served the table with tears in her eyes, knowing what her young mistress was up to. But poor, unsuspecting Will hadn't a clue. He believed, as he was told, that the gentleman wanted him to carve the mantelpieces for the fine new home he was planning to build."

Mary Scarlett paused, thinking about the sad conclusion.

"Well?" Bolt said. "Tell me what happened."

"The spoiled rich girl realized that Will loved Annie and she didn't have a chance. Used to having her way, she set a trap to snare the man she wanted. She managed to lure Will away from the family one evening, telling him she had a broken writing desk that needed fixing. She took him to her bedroom. When her mother came in, she found her daughter in Will's arms, the bed rumpled, and the young woman's bodice torn. There was no way out for him, of course. Even though he was totally innocent, the young woman's father insisted that they marry. In fact, he sent for the minister that very night."

"Poor Annie," Bolt said, shaking his head, knowing in his own heart how the deserted girl must have felt. "And the mirror?"

"Will gave it to Annie after his marriage. He promised her that he would always love her, even though they could never be together. He told her that whenever she looked into it, she would see his face and know that she was his one true love. Ever since then, each woman in Annie's direct line has only to gaze into the mirror to see the face of her true love."

Bolt could certainly understand why Lucy Lamar had claimed this was nonsense. "Have *you* looked in the mirror, Mary Scarlett?"

"Not for a long time," she whispered.

"Have you ever seen a face?"

She nodded.

"Whose was it?" He held his breath, waiting for her answer.

"A man I've never met."

A flash hit Bolt out of the blue. "Don't tell me that's why you ran away eight years ago."

"I thought that was at least part of the reason." She turned and looked at him solemnly. "But I know better now. Back then, I was so torn, Bolt. I didn't know what love was. I knew about parties and flirting and petting and trousseaus. Love and marriage were just this kind of smoky, indistinct dream. I was scared, too," she admitted. "The only marriage I knew anything about was my parents'. That wasn't what I wanted. Not with you, not with Allen, not with any man. I couldn't stand the thought of spending the rest of my life with someone like Big Dick." She uttered a laugh completely devoid of humor. "Ironic, isn't it? I ran away and wound up with . . . *Raul!*"

"The man you saw in the mirror—you don't know who he was?"

"Now you *will* think I'm crazy. I told you I had a visit from Granny Boo's ghost that night and she took me to a party at Bonaventure. Remember?"

Bolt nodded, not wanting her to hear the total disbelief in his voice.

"Well, I met the man there. His name was Jacques St. Julian. He died in New Orleans back around 1800, but I saw his face in the mirror that night in 1988."

Bolt took Mary Scarlett's arm. "I think it's time we got out of here. This place is giving me the creeps."

"No, wait!" she said. "Let me tell you the rest. Jacques was in love with another ancestor, Miss Louise Manigault Robillard, Granny Boo's great-grandmother. He died before they could marry. According to Granny Boo, his spirit lives on in some other man, and I won't be happy until I find Jacques St. Julian, whoever he is in *this* life."

"God, Mary Scarlett! You actually believe that?"

She shrugged. "I don't know what I believe any longer."

"Well, I tend to side with Miss Lucy on this one. Let's go. I've had enough."

"You go on down. I'll be there in a minute. I want to get some of my things."

"I'll wait and help you carry them down."

"No. Go on. I want a few minutes alone here."

Bolt hesitated, uncertain about leaving her alone for a minute in this place. Finally, when she insisted, he went downstairs to wait.

He waited impatiently in the hallway, hearing shutters rap and boards creak in the storm until he almost convinced himself that the old house *was* haunted. When he heard a sound above, he went to the foot of the stairs. He opened his mouth to speak, but found the words frozen in his throat. Perspiration beaded his brow. His hands went clammy.

"Mary Scarlett?" he whispered at last, gazing up at her. *"What the hell?"*

"Aren't you pleased? I thought you'd like this." Mary Scarlett's voice was that of a stranger. Her face was totally colorless, her eyes glazed as she came slowly down the stairs. "I wanted to make you happy. I wanted you to love me the way you used to."

Before Bolt could move or speak again, Mary Scarlett's scream split the silence. In her trancelike state, she forgot the trick step and lost her footing. In a tumble of white lace and satin, she crashed down the stairs, landing in a limp pile at Bolt's feet.

"Mary Scarlett!" he yelled.

Then he was kneeling over her, gathering her into his arms, and seeing her for the first time in the gown she would have worn at their wedding.

Mary Scarlett swam back to consciousness through a gray haze of swirling, disorienting images from her past. When she opened her eyes, Bolt's troubled face staring into hers chased away all else.

"Darlin', can you hear me?" His voice sounded loud in the silent old house.

"I fell," she whispered. "Just like Mama. I fell!"

"Don't think about that. Are you all right, Mary Scarlett? I'm taking you to the hospital."

She pushed out of his arms and sat up. "You're doing no such thing! I'm fine. I've had worse falls off horses. Just give me a minute. I feel a little dizzy."

"It's a concussion. Who am I? What day is this? Where are we?"

"Of course I know you, Jacques. What day is this? Why, the day of the party!"

Bolt winced when she called him Jacques, but released an anxious, pent-up breath when she mentioned Overman's party. Her next words threw him into another panic.

"The party at Bonaventure. That's where we are. That's why I'm all dressed up."

He gripped her shoulders, staring into her eyes to see if her pupils were dilated. "Mary Scarlett, listen to me. My name is Bolton, not Jacques. Good God, we should never have come here!"

She hugged him with anxious desperation. "Bolt, I know who you are. I don't know what came over me, but it's gone now. I'm back in the present. I only wish I knew what I'm supposed to do next."

"Go to the hospital, that's what."

"No, Bolt," she said firmly. "I'm fine. Really!"

He drew back and stared at her, frowning. "If you're fine, whatever possessed you to put on that damn dress?"

She was taken aback by his gruff tone. Only then did she look down and realize how the sight of her in the wedding gown must have shocked and wounded him. Did he think she was playing a cruel practical joke—parading around in the gown she had bought for their wedding? That hadn't been her intent. Actually, she didn't quite know what had come over her once he left her alone in her old bedroom. She had gone to the closet to see what clothes she might still wear since most of her things were somewhere between Spain and Savannah. The long, plastic garment bag had caught her eye immediately. At first, she hadn't remembered what it contained. She had eased the zipper down, thinking it might be something appropriate for Allen's party. But when she spied the white lace shimmering in the glow from her candle, she was overwhelmed by a great urge to try it on.

"Why did you do it, Mary Scarlett?" Bolt asked in quiet agony.

Tears filled her eyes. "Oh, Bolt," she whispered. "The last thing I *ever* want to do is hurt you. You're the only person in the world I've always been able to count on."

"Then *why*, Mary Scarlett?"

She shook her head and stared down at his hand on her wrist. "You know how I said earlier that I wish everything could be the way it was?"

He nodded even though she didn't look up to see.

"Well, when I saw the wedding gown in my closet, I got this wild notion that if I put it on all the terrible years would fade away. It seemed like a kind of magic would flow into me if I was wearing this dress. I'd be back in my room eight years ago, back when you were still in love with me and I was still a sweet, innocent girl who thought she was about to have the marriage, the husband, and the life she'd always dreamed of. Granny Boo and Mama and even Big Dick would still be here, but there would be no Raul, no terrible memories of my years away from Savannah, away from you, Bolt."

She looked up at him, her eyes pleading, tears making silver streams down her pale cheeks.

"I wish it worked that way, Mary Scarlett."

"But it doesn't," she whispered. "There's no magic. It's just a dress. An old, faded, never-worn wedding gown that smells of mothballs, decay, and sadness. I'm sorry, Bolt."

Silently, he took her into his arms and held her close. For a long time, they sat on the floor of the empty house, holding each other and listening to the beat of their hearts and the raging storm.

After a time, Bolt helped Mary Scarlett to her feet. He brushed the damp hair back from her face, then caressed her cheeks with his palms. Looking frightened, hopeless, lost, she stared into his eyes—questioning, begging.

"Would you believe me if I said I've never stopped loving you, Mary Scarlett?"

Again her tears flowed and she closed her eyes against the torrent. Through trembling lips, she whispered, "No, Bolt. We mustn't lie to each other any longer. I know I was never good enough to deserve your love. That's part of the reason I had to leave."

Bolt uttered a groan of sheer pain, then crushed her in his arms. "Don't say that, darlin'. Don't ever even think such a thing!"

Bolt and Mary Scarlett clung to each other for support, both feeling wounded by life, by love, and by the past.

Seven

After a silent ride back to Bolt's apartment, Mary Scarlett thanked him almost formally for going with her to the house on Bull Street. He accepted her thanks in like manner. Neither of them mentioned the wedding gown incident or the things Mary Scarlett had said after her fall down the stairs.

She went straight to her room and closed the door. She didn't come out for the rest of the day. After her sleepless night and the fall she had taken, Bolt assumed she was resting.

He could use a nap, too, before the party, but he was too keyed up. Hurt and bewildered by Mary Scarlett's words and actions at the old house, Bolt buried himself in paperwork for most of the dull, rainy day. It was far easier not to think about her, not to try figuring out what was going on between them. Nothing much seemed to have changed since she ran away from Savannah. He still didn't know where he stood with her or what to expect next.

If Bolt was confused, Mary Scarlett was distraught. She hid out in her room because she simply couldn't face Bolt. She knew she had hurt him deeply.

Stripped of her soaking clothes, wrapped only in her robe, she stood at the window and gazed out over the river. The water was a flat, dull gray, pounded down by the wind and rain. Clouds scudded low on the horizon, looking dirty and angry. The weather mirrored her state of mind. Could she do nothing right? Was it her fate always to hurt and disappoint those she loved?

Somehow she had to pull herself together and get ready for the evening at Allen's house. God, how she dreaded it! All those people that she hadn't seen in years. All those gossips who had whispered about her and were still whispering. At least she could count on Allen to be the cheerful and accommodating host. None of his guests would dare make any remarks about her under his roof. He simply wouldn't tolerate it.

If Bolt had always been her rock, Allen had been her protector and defender, her perennial escort since Miss Felicia's Cotillion classes back in sixth grade. Maybe if she had narrowed her sights to Allen a long time ago, things might have turned out differently. She would be standing by his side tonight—married, smiling, confident—welcoming their guests to their home. There would have been no lingering feelings for Bolton Conrad, no hasty flight to Europe, no past with Raul.

"Mary Scarlett Overman." She tested the sound of the name aloud. It had a good, solid ring that smacked of old Savannah, blue blood, and Southern aristocracy. Maybe she should go after Allen, put Bolt out of his misery once and for all. With her out of the picture, Bolt would marry Kathleen and live happily ever after.

She stretched out on the bed with a sigh, staring up at the ceiling, focusing on nothing at all, trying to make her mind a blank.

"If only I'd found the mirror."

Somehow, if she had it, she could find her way again. She might even be able to sort out her life and her feelings.

"Where could it be?" she said in a drowsy whisper.

A moment later, her eyes closed and she slept.

Or was she sleeping?

Her dream journey began immediately. She found herself running down Bull Street. It was unpaved, muddy, strewn with filth and the carcasses of dead animals. With all the able-bodied men gone to war, Savannah had a serious sanitation problem.

She pulled her black cloak closer against the chill breath of December. She knew instinctively *which* December this was—that fateful month in 1864, the year Sherman came and a whole way of life changed in the South.

She passed two ragged boys playing soldier in the street. One of them sang out, "Jeff Davis rides a very fine horse and Lincoln rides a mule. Jeff Davis is a gentleman and Lincoln is a fool!"

She smiled in spite of Savannah's dire situation. *Little Rebels to the last,* she mused, hurrying on. Before she was out of earshot, she heard the other boy sing a snatch of another popular song. "All de Rebels gone to hell, now Par Sherman come!"

Her smile faded. This youngster had hit the nail on the head. Sherman's troops were poised outside Savannah, ready to attack and torch the city at a moment's notice from their general. The secret meeting called by Mayor Richard Arnold concerning the defense of the city was the reason for her haste. She would be the only woman there. But then she was the only female in Savannah who had spent much of the war traveling through enemy lines, carrying messages back and forth for the Confederacy. Not one to sit at home and roll bandages while her lover was off fighting with General Lee, Lilah had volunteered for her dangerous missions. Now that she was back in Savannah, she had one last mission to accomplish, her most important of the entire war.

As she neared the cotton warehouse on the river, she sent up a silent prayer that Mayor Arnold might have received some news of Captain Brandon Patrick's whereabouts. It had been months since one of his letters had reached her. For weeks, praying that she would not find his name, she had scanned black-bordered casualty lists as they were posted.

Her prayers had been answered, but that left her knowing nothing at all. The uncertainty nagged at her day and night.

She mustn't think about Brandon now. She must put Savannah first.

Thanks to her whining Cousin Amalee, she was late for the meeting. Mayor Arnold was already speaking by the time she slipped into the dank, gloomy warehouse. "I don't see that we have any other choice, gentlemen. General Hardee's plan seems to make good, solid sense to me. He'll build pontoon bridges across the river to Hutchinson Island and then across Back River to South Carolina. All troops will be evacuated from the city under cover of darkness."

"The hell you say!" a man shouted. "You mean to leave us here undefended against Sherman's cutthroat hordes?"

"If you'll kindly allow me to finish," Arnold said in a strained voice. "Once our troops are out of harm's way, I'll personally lead a delegation to Sherman's camp. Welcome him to Savannah. Present the city to him as a Christmas gift."

"Shit!" cursed another man. "We'll be the laughingstock of the whole damn Confederacy. I say we fight!"

"With what, sir?" Lilah spoke up boldly. All eyes turned to her. Few of the men had even noticed the lone female in their midst. She lifted her chin to a defiant angle and continued. "Would you rather preserve our city or your own pride?"

"What does a woman know about war?" the first man grumbled. Others joined in the fray, arguing against a female even attending such a crucial meeting, much less being allowed to speak her mind.

Mayor Arnold raised his hands for silence. "Gentlemen, please! Miss Lilah has been riding secret missions for the Cause. She holds an honorary major's commission signed by Jeb Stuart himself, received for her valuable services to the Confederacy. If we are able to carry off this deception, we will need the help of our ladies once the Yankees arrive in Savannah. Miss Lilah has agreed to coordinate their efforts."

Angry voices interrupted the mayor once again, but they were little more than mutterings now.

"As for our pride," he continued, "I believe the rest of the South will understand and appreciate our plan. We'll be freeing up troops needed elsewhere—troops that will most certainly be captured or killed should they stay to defend Savannah. A needless loss against Sherman's superior forces. And even Sherman, monster that he is, could hardly burn his own Christmas gift. If there's no more discussion to be heard, shall we vote now?"

Vote after vote was taken, but no decision was reached. Heartsick and disgusted with the stubborn leaders of the city, Lilah waited until they all filed out so that she could have a private word with Mayor Arnold.

"Is all lost, sir?" she asked him.

"They'll come around. They must! They simply need more time to think about it."

"There's not much time," Lilah reminded him.

"Less than anyone can calculate," he admitted. "Sherman is even now surrounding the city. My scouts have reported that guns are in place, their trajectory aimed at the very heart of Savannah. Everything is quiet now, but they could begin firing at any time. But that first shot will be to our advantage, Lilah. I think the men will see the hopelessness of trying to defend our homes once the barrage begins."

"Let's hope it doesn't take them too long to see our peril." Lilah stared up at the tall man, her indigo eyes misted with a trace of hopeful tears. "Have you any news for me, Mayor Arnold?"

He pressed her hand gently. "I'm sorry." His deep voice cracked as he uttered those two words.

"Still no news," she whispered, turning away.

"Wait, Miss Lilah. That's not what I meant. I'm afraid I do have news for you—not the best, but neither is it the worst. Captain Patrick has been taken prisoner. My sources tell me he is even now at Point Lookout Prison in Maryland. The fight is over for him, dear lady."

Lilah pressed Mayor Arnold's hand in thanks. Tears filled her eyes as her emotions battled within her. "Is he wounded?"

The mayor shook his head. "I don't know. But if so, he'll be given care. Have no fear of that."

"Thank you," she whispered. She turned and fled the dark warehouse before a sob could escape her. Mayor Arnold considered her a brave woman. She didn't want to damage that opinion by showing him a woman's weakness.

The very next day, the citizens of Savannah heard the first guns. Heavy artillery shells pelted Fort McAllister for hours. Terror reigned in the city. At any moment, Sherman could turn his guns on the civilians in their homes. But still the town fathers haggled, holding pride more precious than life. On December 19, General Beauregard settled the matter. His order read: *Evacuate all troops from the city to assemble at Fort Jackson to be transported to Screven's Ferry.*

That bitter cold night, Lilah watched from her window as the silent troops passed through the dark streets. Muttered curses filled the air. After four years of duty, the soldiers wanted to stand and fight. They hated retreat. A few of them sang "Dixie" as they trudged toward the river and their flight into South Carolina. It was a final defiance before they had to give up the beautiful old city to the hated Yankees. Many of the men left behind sweethearts, wives, and children, not knowing if they would ever see them again. But Lilah felt only triumph. If Mayor Arnold's offer was accepted, they would have outsmarted Sherman and thereby extinguished his dreaded torches.

"You would be proud tonight, Brandon," she whispered into her antique mirror, hoping to catch a glimpse of her lover, hoping the magic mirror might send her words clear to Maryland. "Proud of our men, proud of Savannah, and proud of our Cause."

On December 21, Mayor Richard Arnold formally surrendered his beloved city to General William Tecumseh Sherman. The mayor asked "the protection of our lives and property of the citizens and of our women and children."

Sherman accepted the city, granted the request, and sent a telegram to President Lincoln. "I beg to present you as a Christmas gift the city of Savannah, with 150 heavy guns and plenty of ammunition, also about 25,000 bales of cotton."

On Christmas Eve, Lincoln wired back, "Many, many thanks . . . and my grateful acknowledgments to your whole army, officers and men."

For a time, after reading President Lincoln's telegram in her dream, Mary Scarlett drifted in nothingness, half herself, half Lilah. When her vision cleared again, Lilah was arguing with another woman, her married cousin, Amalee Dupree.

"Heaven only knows what will happen next!" Amalee sobbed. "Just look out the front window. The darkies and the Yankees have taken over our city—stealing, insulting decent folks, why, they're even pitching their tents right in our square. I may lose my mind!"

"Would you prefer that they burned down your house?" Lilah answered with deadly calm. When Amalee made no reply, Lilah said firmly, "You *will* attend General Sherman's party at the Pulaski House tomorrow night."

"Why, I'd rather die!" Amalee cried. "Let me see that invitation."

Lilah handed her the white card, addressed to them personally, which amounted to a command performance to celebrate Sherman's good relations with the citizenry of Savannah. A messenger had delivered it only moments before.

A hint of a smile flitted over Amalee's thin lips. She hadn't been to a party in over three years, not since her husband rode off to war. "Mercy, I don't have a decent thing to wear. What *will* General Sherman think of us in our old rags from before the war?"

Repulsed by her cousin's obvious delight at the thought of the Yankee soiree, Lilah replied, "I'm wearing black—for Brandon, for Savannah, for the Confederacy. We will *all* wear black from now on."

"I'm wearing black." Mary Scarlett came awake with a jolt as she spoke the words aloud.

She glanced toward the mirror. She was herself again. Every trace of Lilah's long, silver-blond hair had vanished. And the eyes that stared back at her were a brilliant, true blue, unlike the violet-shaded indigo of Lilah's.

Mary Scarlett sat thinking through her dream for several moments. She knew Lilah's story; she had heard it from Granny Boo all her life. "Major Lilah" had been a heroine of the War Between the States, a brave spy for the Confederacy. And she had, indeed, kept the women of Savannah in line while the occupation forces were in the city. Lilah herself had decreed that no woman would wear anything but black until the Yankees left. That was their one small defiance. Otherwise, they treated their unhonored guests with only mild contempt rather than the all-out hatred they felt in their hearts. It was all meant to keep Savannah safe. Lilah and her ladies did a wonderful job. Sherman never suspected the depth of their loathing.

Mary Scarlett remembered how Granny Boo used to chuckle when she told that part. Yet there were things about the dream that Mary Scarlett had never heard before. She knew nothing of this cousin, Amalee Dupree. Nor had she ever heard the songs that the little boys sang as Lilah was rushing to that first meeting.

One thing she did know. Lilah's lover, Brandon Patrick, had come home from the war, but he had died of his wounds and harsh life in a Yankee prison only days after his return. It was almost as if he willed himself to live long enough to see her one last time.

Tears sprang to her eyes. "Another tragic love affair in my family. Poor Lilah!"

A soft knock at the door drew Mary Scarlett's attention. "It's almost seven," Bolt said from the hallway. "Do you still want to go to Allen's party?"

"That *damn* party!" she muttered. To Bolt she called, "Yes, I'm getting ready now." Then she added, softly to herself, "I'm wearing black!"

Bolt had had a rotten day. He figured Mary Scarlett was punishing him by staying in her room, not talking to him, not even wanting to set eyes on him for hours. He felt as little like going to a party as he ever had in his life. He didn't think he could smile and be cordial, make small talk or shower the ladies with the expected compliments.

All that changed the minute Mary Scarlett walked out of her room. She had a glow about her that he hadn't seen in years. It took him a moment to realize that the light shining around her like a magnificent, golden aura was the sun coming out at last. A brilliant rose and vermillion sunset lit the heavens and backlit Mary Scarlett. Her gown was clinging black silk—long, cool, and slender like Mary Scarlett herself. The jewel neckline gave way to an open back that draped to an astonishing depth. Her bare shoulders and arms made him want to caress the pale silk of her flesh. When she moved toward him, his gaze shifted to the thigh-high slit up the right side of her skirt. He could feel his temperature rising as she moved closer.

"Shalimar," he whispered, closing his eyes and taking a deep breath.

Mary Scarlett uttered a little purring laugh when Bolt took her hand and kissed it. She let her gaze roam his trim figure, clothed in a tailor-made tuxedo, his pleated shirt front gleaming with gold and onyx studs. "As Mama used to say, 'You clean up real nice, honey!' "

They both laughed, sounding almost relaxed with each other. Mary Scarlett thought about apologizing for the wedding gown incident earlier, but decided she'd rather not bring it up again. Not when Bolt seemed to be in a party mood. Instead, she had a totally different topic on her mind.

"Bolt, do you remember the story about how Mayor Arnold handed Savannah over to Sherman?"

He looked perplexed at this change of subject, seemingly out of nowhere. "Sure. Every schoolkid in Savannah knows about that. Arnold held his meetings right here in this building, right below my apartment."

"So that's it!" Mary Scarlett said.

"That's what?"

"Oh, it's nothing really. While I was napping I took another one of my dreamtrips. I went back to 1864. I was here in Savannah when the plans were made to give the city to Sherman. I guess being here must have triggered the memories, even though I didn't know this was where they met."

Bolt looked anxious. "Who were you this time?"

"A young woman named Lilah. She was in love with a Confederate captain named Brandon Patrick."

Bolt went to a bookcase next to his desk and pulled out a leather bound volume that looked old and worn. "Let's see what this says about Captain Brandon Patrick, CSA. This old registry lists the names of all the Georgia men who fought in the war. Here he is. He wasn't from Savannah, though. He owned one of the island plantations, Fortune's Fancy on Rainbow Hammock."

"I've never heard of it," Mary Scarlett said.

"I think the name was changed sometime after the war. Seems to me it's one of the smaller islands down near St. Simons and Jekyll. Some millionaire probably bought it and built condos and golf courses all over it."

"You're probably right. I was just curious. I don't think he and Lilah ever married. You see, they were in love, and in my family that's the kiss of death."

"Interesting tidbit of history," Bolt said, trying to lighten her mood. "It will make good cocktail conversation at the party."

"Yes, we'd better go," Mary Scarlett agreed, but the last thing she wanted to chitchat about at Allen's party was poor Lilah's loss.

As Bolt held the door for her, Mary Scarlett felt his warm hand brush her bare back. She shivered with pleasure.

She turned in the doorway. "Bolt? Do you forgive me?"

He stared down at her, puzzled. "For what, honey?"

"Don't you mean, for what *this time?* Seems I'm always hurting you without meaning to. The wedding gown . . . the way I acted . . . the things I said."

He leaned down and brushed his lips softly against her high cheekbone. "Nothing to forgive," he whispered. He placed his hands on her bare shoulders and let his palms slide down over her cool arms, then up again.

"I've wanted to do that for years," he whispered. "The night Allen escorted you to your debutante ball, you were wearing a white dress with bare shoulders. All I could think about all that night, while I was parking cars, was how it would feel to run my hands over all that gorgeous bare flesh."

"And how does it feel?" She was trembling, burning from his touch.

Mary Scarlett went up on tiptoe and pressed her mouth hard against his. He stepped away after only an instant, as if her lips had scorched his.

"We'll be late."

"We don't *have* to go to the party," she purred.

With a low chuckle, Bolt propelled her through the door. "Oh, yes, darlin'. I think we do. Can't keep your adoring public waiting."

* * *

"It's almost time!" Allen Overman checked his watch as he paced the front parlor, peering out the windows every few seconds. "Where is everybody?"

"Take it easy, Allen," Kathleen told him. "You know no one in Savannah wants to be the first to arrive. They'll be here. Stand still and take a few deep breaths, won't you?"

He did as his hostess ordered, then grinned at her. "Love your gown, Katie."

She nodded her thanks. It was Bolton Conrad's favorite, the rose chiffon with a plunging neckline and full, swirling skirt. It had an Old South look about it, even without hoop-skirts.

While she was still smiling, pleased with the way she looked and with Allen's compliment, he said, "Could I make a suggestion, though?"

"Yes. Of course." The frost in her reply did not invite suggestions, but Allen rushed on anyway.

He hurried over to an antique secretary beside the parlor door and opened the front. When he turned, he held a pair of white, opera-length gloves and a flat, gray velvet box. "Put these on." He handed her the gloves. "And this."

Kathleen grimaced at the gloves, then gasped when he opened the box. "Tell me that's not real."

"As real as they come," he answered. "I have it on consignment from a rich-bitch over on Isle of Hope who's selling everything she owns and plans to take off across country in a RV. She's one of those back-to-nature freaks. If I owned jewels like these, I'd be happy to stay right at home and just fondle them."

"It's a fabulous necklace, Allen. I've never seen anything like it."

"And you've got a fabulous chest, Katie. These diamonds would draw all eyes."

Kathleen turned and lifted her hair so Allen could fasten

the cascade of diamonds around her neck. She would gladly give in and wear the gloves for Allen in order to have the jewels for the evening.

"I feel like a queen," she said, touching the sparkling stones reverently as she gazed into the mirror over the mantel.

"As you should. Those diamonds once belonged to Napoleon's Josephine."

"My God!" she gasped.

The doorbell chimed just then. 'Gator White, pressed into service by Allen's threats and turned out to look the perfect butler, glided through the hallway to answer the call.

First to arrive was Aurelia LaMotte. Allen's fourth ex-wife had dropped the "Overman" after her divorce in order to avoid confusion. Savannah was becoming overrun with "Overman women." The petite, honey-haired woman with a face many times tucked, entered on the arm of a tall, distinguished looking antiques dealer whose dark good looks reminded Kathleen of Gregory Peck.

"Miz Aurelia LaMotte and Mr. Talliaferro Fitzhugh," 'Gator intoned grandly, bowing the couple into the parlor to be greeted by their host.

Allen threw his arms wide, preparing to hug his ex. "Aurelia, you look ravishing. Give us a kiss, love."

The small woman giggled as Allen embraced her and showered her heavily remade and madeup face with butterfly kisses.

"Oh, Allen, you sweet boy!" Aurelia gushed. "You're still the light of my life."

Kathleen stood by, observing. She guessed that Allen was still making it with Aurelia. There was something in the woman's eyes that hinted at secret rendezvous. And, too, Miss LaMotte had recently returned from a clinic in the Southwest. Rumor had it that Aurelia, fast approaching sixty, had had a boob job to please her young lover. Kathleen nodded approvingly. Aurelia certainly did fill out her low-cut champagne satin to full advantage.

"Talli, old fellow!" Allen exclaimed, glad-handing his ex's date while he slapped him on the back. "Haven't seen you in ages. Where've you been?"

"In France on a buying trip."

Kathleen noted that Mr. Fitzhugh's dark gaze hadn't left her throat since he entered.

"That's the Josephine, isn't it?" He moved closer to Kathleen and leaned down to peer at the diamonds.

"Right you are, my man!" Allen beamed with pleasure. "The very necklace. I have it on consignment. Bids will soon be coming in from all over the world."

Still peering, making Kathleen quite uncomfortable, Talli said, "It's not been on the market in over fifty years."

Allen nodded. "And once I sell it, it probably won't be again in our lifetime."

Kathleen suddenly realized what was going on. Allen hoped to sell the necklace to Talliaferro Fitzhugh. She was not only his hostess, but his model for the evening.

More and more couples began arriving. Soon all of Allen's ex-wives were there with their current lovers. A number of the guests were from the crowd Allen, Kathleen, and Mary Scarlett had gone to school with. Bolt hadn't really been a member of that group; he had lived in the wrong part of town. But through his prowess as an athlete and Mary Scarlett's patronage, he had been grudgingly accepted by the others.

There were Missy and "Roach" Carlisle, Annabelle and Lawton Winthrop, Cecelia and Pryce Jasper. All Old Savannah, Oglethorpe Club, and, of course, the ladies had been debutantes with Mary Scarlett.

They oohed and aahed over Allen's new digs. He played the role of the suave country planter showing off his ancestral home in town. A fair-haired Rhett Butler, charming the ladies and joshing with the men.

'Tator White, every bit as formal and polished as his twin, moved silently among the guests passing flutes of champagne and silver trays covered with crab balls, shrimp paté, petite tomato sandwiches, Russian caviar, and an array of other colorful and mouth-watering offerings.

When the doorbell rang again, all heads turned. This could be it—the moment everyone had been waiting for.

"I heard she's a blonde now," Cecelia whispered to Missy.

"And probably put on twenty pounds," Missy said. "All that rich food in Spain."

Big, red-headed Roach Carlisle leaned close to the two women and said, "You girls will know any minute. As for me, my guess is Mary Scarlett's probably more gorgeous than ever. Her mama was a knockout to the day she died."

It was hard for the anxious guests not to let out a collective groan of disappointment when 'Gator announced Frankie and Donny. With their cummerbunds and ties of matching lime-and-lavender print, the two hairstylists added the only touch of color among the midnight-blue gentlemen at the party. More than one adoring and regret-filled female eye turned on gorgeous, tanned, blond-maned Donny.

"God, Allen, you really let Katie wear it!" Frankie cried before even accepting a greeting from his host. "The Josephine," he said in a hushed tone that sounded almost like a prayer.

"Hey, you're not going to fall down on your knees, are you, Frankie?" Allen laughed while Talli Fitzhugh moved closer to Kathleen as if to protect the necklace from the lusting hairdresser.

"It's just the most beautiful thing I've ever seen, man," Frankie moaned. "Put that against stark black and it would knock your eyes out." He turned pleadingly to Allen. "Can I touch it?"

Grinning from ear to ear, Allen granted his consent. But when Frankie reached toward Kathleen's chest, she slapped his hand away.

"No way, Frankie!" She whirled out of his reach. "This is me inside this necklace and I won't be pawed."

Everyone laughed but Frankie. He whimpered softly and went to Donny.

Meanwhile, "the girls," Missy, Cecelia, and Annabelle had huddled a short distance away from the others.

"Did you see the notice in the paper?" Annabelle whispered.

"What notice?" Cecelia asked.

"The obituary. She's a *widow!*"

Annabelle shrugged elegantly in her off-the-shoulder designer gown. "No details. Maybe she screwed him to death."

"Well, she's not adding my Pryce to her list of conquests," Cecelia announced. "I've a good mind to take him right home before she gets here."

"Too late!" Missy said, peering out through the front window. "They're coming up the walk right now."

"Oh, God! And we all have to be *nice* to her," Annabelle replied.

"It won't be easy," Missy said.

"Not after what she did," Cecelia finished.

Just then, Mary Scarlett came through the door on Bolton Conrad's arm. All the girls—Annabelle, Missy, and Cecelia—rushed to Mary Scarlett, each pushing and shoving to be the first to throw herself on their long-lost friend's neck for "a big ole bear-hug," as Missy squealed.

Frankie and Donny were next, both exclaiming over how good Mary Scarlett's new hair color looked and swearing that they knew who she was all along when she came to them as "Mrs. Miguel."

Only Kathleen stood back, gazing at her competition, sizing her up from all angles. With an inner cringe, she realized that even decked out in the fabulous Josephine, she couldn't hold a candle to the glitter and shimmer of Mary Scarlett Lamar.

Kathleen transferred her gaze to Bolt. He hovered close to Mary Scarlett, one arm protectively clutched about her ever-so-slender waist. Kathleen would kill to have Bolt look at her with that passionate light in his eyes. She was about to flee the room and the party when Allen slipped his arm around her and urged her forward.

"They're here at last, Katie. Come say hello to our honored guest. Mary Scarlett is really, truly back!"

The two women faced each other. After a moment's hesitation, Mary Scarlett offered her hand. Another uncomfortable moment passed before Kathleen took it.

"Good to see you again," Kathleen managed.

"What a gorgeous necklace!" Mary Scarlett answered. "Maybe Allen will let you wear it sometime."

Kathleen turned away then on the pretense of getting champagne for the late arrivals.

Only Mary Scarlett noticed the brief, intimate glance that passed between Kathleen and Bolt. It cut her to the quick.

Eight

Allen had taken great care in arranging the seating for dinner. Kathleen would be on his right and Mary Scarlett on his left. He placed Bolt on the other side of Kathleen, and put dull, harmless, and balding Pryce Jasper at Mary Scarlett's left. Cecelia Jasper was fuming when she read the placecards until she realized she would be sitting between Lawton Winthrop, who had wooed her all through high school, and the glorious Donny. With a sweet smile, she let Donny hold her chair, the thought crossing her mind that, if she played her cards right, she might lure him away from his present lover.

The table was set to perfection. Intricately carved English sterling flatware gleamed against the white-on-white damask. The cloth was worn but elegant, freshly starched to give it stiffness and sheen. Twelve perfect white tapers glowed, crowning the graceful twin candelabra on either side of a fragrant, sprawling centerpiece of rubrum lilies, white gladioli, and waxy green magnolia leaves. The Waterford crystal sparkled as brightly as Empress Josephine's diamonds while the antique china—rimmed in blood-red and edged in eighteen karat gold—shimmered with the reflected aura of candlelight.

The ladies' gowns rustled as they seated themselves. Once at the table, that soft sound gave way to murmurs of awe and delight. Allen Overman sat at their head, beaming like an Eastern potentate presiding over a feast for his subjects.

"You've done well for yourself, Allen," Mary Scarlett said, bestowing a smile of genuine delight on her host. "All this . . ." She gestured toward the table, the room, the whole mansion. "You must be very happy here."

"You know it's what I've always dreamed of. But, ah, Mary Scarlett, no man can be happy with mere possessions, not alone, with no one to share the pleasure."

Overhearing his remark, Aurelia said, "It's too bad you didn't have all this before our amicable parting, dear boy. I'd never have left you."

His other ex-wives nodded their agreement. It was obvious to everyone in the party that they, too, would have ignored Allen's flings and his black moods in order to enjoy such grandeur and wealth. At the moment, all these ladies could have kicked themselves for suing for divorce. But how could they have known that someday Allen would actually amount to something?

'Gator and 'Tator moved silently and efficiently around the table, serving the first course, she-crab bisque, a delicate concoction of cream, sherry, and pure white crabmeat, shredded as fine as angel's hair.

"Tell us about your travels, Mary Scarlett," Annabelle insisted. "You're a brave one to take off to Europe all alone. I shudder at the thought of leaving Savannah. If it weren't for the Georgia-Florida game, I doubt Lawton and I would ever set foot out of Chatham County."

The other women at the table agreed. The outside world held no wonders for the true Savannahian. Many had never traveled even as far as Charleston, although they would on occasion force themselves to take the short run down the coast to Sea Island for a weekend of being pampered at The Cloister.

"I think of Spain as always being hot and dusty," Cecelia commented. "Is it, Mary Scarlett?"

"Not always," she answered, nervous at being the focal point of this interrogation, afraid where it might lead. "Not nearly as hot as Turkey. But then all the countries I visited had their seasons. I found that especially true in Italy."

"Really?" Missy said, her silver soup spoon poised, pinky arched elegantly. "How is Italy different?"

Gaining confidence from this mundane topic, Mary Scarlett answered, "It never rains all summer. Can you imagine? Not a cloud in the sky. Just vast stretches of brilliant, sunny blue. And the dust! You have to wipe the fine powder from your plates before you eat. Then in September, the bottom drops out. Once I was flooded out of my hotel room. Then all winter, you hardly see the sun. Rain, mist, and a cold wind that howls down from the Apennines." She held her arms and shivered to reinforce her point.

"I can see why you left Italy for Spain, then," Annabelle said.

No, Mary Scarlett thought, still smiling, you can't see at all. Annabelle and the others had no idea what her "romantic adventures" in Europe had been like. Nor did she plan to tell them. They needn't know that when she was flooded out in Naples, she lost everything she owned or that her parents flatly refused to send her any assistance, even money for a ticket home. She had her passport and the clothes she was wearing, nothing else. She had to bum her way to Spain with an expatriate from Queens who was ten years her junior but light years her senior in experience. They had met shortly after the flood while standing in a soup kitchen line at a church in downtown Naples, the only two Americans among the hungry. That in itself had made them seem like distant relatives.

"Stud" he had called himself, and she should have taken that as advance warning. But she was too desperate and alone to be wary. He had told her he had enough money to get them both to Sardinia by tramp steamer. Once there, he said they could work in the artichoke fields until they had enough to buy passage to the Spanish island of Ibiza. He told her fabulously colorful tales of the Gypsies who lived in the caves along the shore and the Americans who flocked there for the history, the beauty, and the ambiance of this one special place on earth.

She closed the door on thoughts of Stud and Ibiza. Once more she turned to her dinner partners. While she had been lost in reverie, the conversation had moved on to other topics. A vast relief. But she realized she must have missed a comment from Bolt.

"Is what Bolt says true? You're *really* going to move back into that old place on Bull Street?" Again, Annabelle was her inquisitor. "You said when we were in high school that if you ever got away from there you'd never go back."

Mary Scarlett forced a small laugh. "We said a lot of things back in high school, didn't we, Annabelle? But times change and we change with them. If I don't move back in, I'll lose the place."

"Oh, that's right. Miss Lucy's will," Cecelia chimed in.

Did *everyone* know her private business? Mary Scarlett wondered.

"Actually, I think I'll enjoy it. Bolt's going to help me move in and get settled. It will be different now that it's *my* house."

Allen reached over and squeezed her hand. "I'll help, too, darlin'."

She smiled and nodded. "Of course, Allen. We'll have the old place in shape in no time. Then *I'll* throw the party and you're all invited."

Missy giggled and immediately covered her mouth with her snowy napkin, a slave to her debutante training. "Do you all remember when Miss Lucy used to let the tour groups in?"

Mary Scarlett remembered, all right. Big Dick kept his wife on a strict household budget. When Lucy blew her weekly allowance on clothes—her passion—instead of food, she would open up the Bull Street house and charge admission so she could buy groceries to feed her family until her next payday.

Annabelle rolled her eyes. "God, how could we forget? Especially that one time when we were still in junior high. We'd all spent the night with you when she decided on the spur of the moment to give a tour. Remember, Mary Scarlett?"

Mary Scarlett felt a flush creeping into her cheeks. She had always known Annabelle for the viper she was, but how *could* she bring this up? Mary Scarlett had been so embarrassed that she had refused to go to school for days. She might never have returned if the truant officer hadn't come to the house to find out what was going on. Then she'd been marched back to school, practically under armed guard, adding insult to injury.

"I can see your mama now in that hoopskirt and old ruffled gown, with that sausage-curl wig on," Missy said with another giggle. "Of course, not a word of that scandalous stuff she told the tourists about your ancestors was true."

If you only knew, thought Mary Scarlett.

"Then right in the middle of the tour, Granny Boo came flying down out of the attic, pistol in one hand and battle flag in the other, dressed in that old moth-eaten Confederate uniform, threatening to shoot any damnyankee that didn't clear out of her house."

Now all three women—Cecelia, Annabelle, and Missy—were giggling fit to kill and not even bothering to cover their mouths with their napkins. Mary Scarlett tried to keep smiling, but it wasn't easy.

Between gales of laughter, Annabelle managed to say, "But Granny Boo didn't clear the Yankees out soon enough. Your daddy got home about then. Remember? We were all hiding upstairs on the landing, watching everything that happened."

"I think he'd been at the Club with our daddies," Missy whispered. "He had that likkered-up gleam in his eyes and he smelled a good bit of gin. And when he came in and saw Delsey passing the hat, collecting money from those tourists, and your mama in her Southern belle getup and Granny Boo waving her Confederate flag and her pistol, he blew sky-high."

"It was a very embarrassing scene," Mary Scarlett said loudly, in order to be heard. "But I thought you wanted to hear about Spain."

Ignoring her, Missy hurried on. "When Granny Boo yelled, 'The biggest damnyankee of 'em all is about to meet his Maker' and leveled that gun at your daddy, I figured it was all over for Big Dick."

Mary Scarlett bristled. It was fine for her to call her daddy that, but it rankled deeply to hear it from the lips of one of these prissy, stuck-up socialites.

Missy was leaning over her empty soup plate, her eyes gleaming in the candlelight. "Well, sir! When I heard that gun fire off, I just knew he was a goner. But she missed."

"It wasn't her aim," Mary Scarlett said grimly. "It was that old pistol. It hadn't been fired since the war."

"But it sure cleared the Yankees out of the house," Annabelle said with a very unladylike horselaugh.

"Then the police came," Cecelia said, "then my daddy. Then half the town. What a sight that was to see. The battle of Bull Street!"

Mary Scarlett added nothing to Cecelia's windup of the story. Their daddies had come all right, to get their precious, innocent daughters out of "that lunatic asylum on Bull Street," as she had heard Missy's father describe her child-hood home. He might have called it a lot worse if he'd stuck around for the real finish.

Missy was right. Big Dick had come home likkered up. And there was nothing worse—until Raul—than the combi-nation of Richard Habersham Lamar, gin, and vermouth, with an olive for good measure. Once the smoke from Granny Boo's pistol cleared, and the tourists, gawkers, and policemen as well, Big Dick was in one of his most towering rages. His foul curses, shouted down on the heads of the womenfolk under his roof, had sent Granny Boo racing back to her attic to bolt her door and read her Bible to calm herself. Then Mary Scarlett's mother had ordered her to her room, sure that a scene was imminent and not wanting her daughter to witness it. Mary Scarlett had only partially obeyed Miss Lucy. She had gone as far as the landing, where only a short time before she and her friends had hidden themselves to watch the Yankee tourists.

To this day, Mary Scarlett wished with all her heart that she had gone to her room when she was told to.

"Mary Scarlett?" Allen's voice interrupted the beginnings of her most terrible childhood memory. "Won't you join us? You're a million miles away."

"Forgive me." She forced a bright smile, which Allen happily returned.

"You were going to tell us about Spain."

"Do tell us about your bullfighter!" Frankie begged. "I've never even met one. He must have been brave, and passionate beyond words."

"Frankie, behave yourself," Allen warned.

"Do you have any children?" Annabelle cut in. The rumor that Mary Scarlett had gone to Europe to give birth to a bastard baby had run rampant in Savannah after her sudden disappearance.

"Alas, no," Mary Scarlett said, her face that of a martyred madonna.

The salad was served almost unnoticed, even though it shone like a rainbow with its fresh greens, tiny slices of purple-brown figs, wedges of mandarin orange, and slivers of iridescent Vidalia onion.

"Children tend to bore me," Allen said. "Tell us more about your life and your marriage."

Mary Scarlett steeled herself to lie—fabulously. "What can I say? Bullfighters lead the most romantic lives imaginable. They make our movie stars pale by comparison. And Raul Miguel was indeed a star in his country and all over the Continent. Women threw themselves at his feet and showered him with expensive gifts while the men raised flags and statues to his bravery." She turned to Frankie and smiled sweetly, shyly. "Was he passionate? Oh, yes, my friend."

The other women at the table went dreamy-eyed. Mary Scarlett saw Missy Carlisle cast a look of distaste toward her overweight husband Roach, who unfortunately deserved his nickname.

"Where did you live?" Donny asked. He had been quiet all evening, except when Cecelia tried to draw him out.

"Raul had a house in the country outside Barcelona. He had a villa on the *Costa Brava* and another on a small Spanish island that he owned off the *Costa del Sol.*"

"Which island?" Annabelle demanded to know. "I have some cousins who vacation in that area."

Mary Scarlett fluttered her eyelashes demurely. *"Isla Maria Scarletta,* of course. Before we were married, it had been called *Isla Raul,* but my husband changed the name. We spent a good deal of time on the yacht, too."

"God, what a life!" Frankie moaned. "And I think I have it good when me and Donny can close the shop for a weekend and sneak off to Myrtle Beach."

The smile remained frozen on Mary Scarlett's face. If only they knew that Raul had kept his Spanish mistress at the Barcelona house, his French mistress at the *Costa Brava* villa, an ever-changing selection of women on *Isla Raul*—she'd lied about the *Isla Maria Scarletta* part—and kept Mary Scarlett herself a virtual prisoner on that damned yacht.

Kathleen had remained apart from all this. She much preferred her quiet conversation with Bolt to the adventures of Mary Scarlett, past or present. Ignoring the conversation that so entranced her tablemates, Kathleen said to Bolt, "I'll gladly help Mary Scarlett get settled in. Just let me know if there's anything I can do, Bolt."

"That's sweet of you, Katie. I know she'll appreciate it. It will be nice for her to have another woman's opinion. You were certainly a great help when I was redecorating. I don't know what I'd have done without you."

Kathleen beamed into Bolt's dark eyes and touched his hand. "You know I loved doing it."

Bolt coughed, an excuse to draw his hand away from hers. Kathleen's touch was a bit too warm, a bit too intimate with Mary Scarlett sitting so near, yet out of reach. Allen was up to his old tricks. Divide and conquer seemed the strategy for the evening. There was no doubting that Allen had set himself and Mary Scarlett up as the royal couple tonight. All she lacked was the Empress Josephine diamonds around her neck.

Talli Fitzhugh had entered the general conversation in order to change the subject back to his main point of interest. "I would really like to know how you beat me to that necklace, Overman. I've been on its scent for years. I knew its owner would eventually sell. I thought I had her in the palm of my hand."

Allen chuckled and reached over to fondle the sparkling gems at Kathleen's throat. "You were off, God knows where, haggling over trinkets when she made up her mind. I happened to be in the right place at the right time." He turned and winked at Mary Scarlett. "Then, of course, there's the matter of my unequaled charm and charisma, Talli old chap. That goes a long way in convincing ladies that I'm the right man . . . for almost anything."

"But you don't have the connections to dispose of a piece like that, Overman. It should sell in New York at auction. Sotheby's or Christie's."

"Exactly my plan, Fitzhugh. The Josephine will be the centerpiece of Sotheby's next sale." He leaned toward Kathleen and reached for the clasp. "Do you mind, Katie dear?"

He gave her no time to answer before he removed the necklace, then turned to Mary Scarlett. "May I?" he asked, holding up the waterfall of diamonds. "I'd like to see how it looks against black."

Murmurs of admiration were heard around the table when the others saw the dramatic effect. Mary Scarlett fingered the cold stones nervously.

"There!" Allen breathed. "Have you ever seen anything more magnificent?"

All eyes turned to Mary Scarlett. Their stares set her nerves on edge. She reached back to undo the clasp. "I've always thought it indecent for a woman under forty to wear diamonds," she said with a forced laugh.

"No, please!" Fitzhugh objected from across the table. "Don't take it off. Allow me the pleasure of gazing at it a bit longer. What a fantastic sight! The beauty of the necklace is outshone only by your own, my dear."

"Watch it there, buddy!" Allen said with a leer. "That's my girl you're flirting with."

No one but Kathleen noticed when Bolt stiffened at Allen's words.

The main course arrived—a fragrant, spicy lava flow of shrimp creole atop a mountain of fluffy white rice. Silence reigned as 'Gator and 'Tator served the *pièce de résistance.*

"I want you all to know that these shrimp slept in the Atlantic last night. Old Sam brought his boat in early this morning and I met him at the dock at dawn," Allen said. "And the peppers and tomatoes slept—if veggies can be said to sleep—in my garden until only hours ago."

Mary Scarlett looked at him askance. She couldn't imagine Allen up at dawn to buy shrimp or up at any time to work in a vegetable garden. The others laughed and exchanged knowing glances. They didn't believe a word of it either.

Not until demitasse and dessert—a magnificent trifle, oozing rich cream, nutmeats, raisins, and blackberry brandy—did the conversation return to Mary Scarlett and her secret life of the past eight years.

"Well, I just think Spain must have been glorious," Missy remarked. "I don't understand how you could bear to come back to little ole Savannah, honey."

"How *did* your husband die?" Annabelle asked bluntly. "The item in the paper wasn't real clear on that point."

Bolt shot the woman a quick, angry look.

Mary Scarlett set down her spoon and stared at it. "In the bull ring," she whispered.

"Oh, God!" Annabelle and several others gasped. "How terrible!"

"An honorable death for a brave *torero*," Mary Scarlett said softly. "He will remain forever a hero in the eyes of his countrymen."

"Why don't we have our brandy in the front parlor?" Allen suggested, attuned to Mary Scarlett's need for a change of venue, even if she wouldn't get a new jury.

He stood and eased her chair back. "Need some air?" he whispered.

She pled her case with her eyes, unable to trust her voice.

"Come on. I'll get the others settled with their after-dinner drinks, then I'll show you my vegetable garden."

That brought a smile from her as he knew it would. She had always known when he was lying—"yanking her chain," as she used to say. Still, she looked like she could use a breath of air and he desperately wanted to get her alone.

"The powder room?" she asked.

He motioned down the hallway. "Third door on the left."

Allen had the very ticket to keep the others occupied while he slipped outside with Mary Scarlett. He saw that everyone had a drink, then pulled out his collection of high school and college yearbooks and old photograph albums.

"Oh, my word!" Missy shrieked. "Here's a picture of Roach in the third grade! And our kids wonder how their daddy got his nickname." She turned and called, "Roach honey, come look at this."

But Roach Carlisle had found a comfortable chair and was enjoying his brandy and cigar.

"Here we are, the belles of the prom," Annabelle cried excitedly. "Look! Mary Scarlett's the only one not wearing falsies with her strapless gown. I was *so* jealous! I craved boobs in the worst way."

"And now we both do, darling," Lawton Winthrop said, smiling coolly at his wife.

"I wasn't wearing falsies," Cecelia sniffed, then glanced nervously over at Lawton Winthrop, remembering suddenly that he had been her date that night.

He only chuckled and raised his snifter to her in salute. Her secret was safe with him. He had found out that there was nothing false about plump Cecelia when they had parked by the river after the dance. As his wife had just put it so aptly, he, too, had craved boobs ever since.

Even Kathleen got in on the action. "Bolt, come look at this. It's you on your bike, delivering papers. That goes *way* back."

He sauntered over and draped his arm casually across her shoulders. "Damn, I was an ugly kid! Let's see what you looked like, princess."

Flipping through one of the yearbooks, he found Kathleen's freshman picture and stabbed at it with one finger. "There! Take that, my pretty!"

"Oh, no," Kathleen moaned, covering her eyes. "How could you, Bolt? Look at that hair! Those braces!"

"Those falsies!" Cecelia said with a broad grin.

Seeing that his guests were up to their eyeballs in nostalgia, Allen slipped out of the room and down the long hallway. He met Mary Scarlett as she came out of the downstairs powder room.

"How 'bout that stroll in the moonlight, darlin'?"

"You're on, Mr. Overman."

The night air in the parterre garden between the mansion and the carriage house was cool, scented with green perfumes and exotic Confederate jasmine. After the day's storm, the sky was perfectly clear, the stars a mirror of Josephine's diamonds against Mary Scarlett's black silk. The quarter moon cast just enough silver to enchant the garden and bring memories flooding back of other soft Savannah nights.

Mary Scarlett took a deep breath. "Ah, it smells like home."

Allen slipped his arm around her waist. "It is home, honey. It's where you belong. You should never have gone away."

"I had to," she answered absently.

"Why? I still don't know."

"I'm not sure I do either. I was confused, unhappy."

"But you were fixing to get married. I thought you and Bolt were all set. I was jealous as hell, of course."

"I don't know why everyone assumed that. There'd been no engagement notice in the paper, no invitations mailed out. I wasn't wearing a ring."

"But you would have been if you'd stayed. My God, Mary Scarlett, he was building a house for the two of you!"

"Bolt's idea," she said, and the picket fence flashed through her mind.

"Come on now. This is ole Allen you're talking to. And I know Bolt. He'd never have started such a project if you hadn't said you'd marry him. We were both in love with you. But of course you know that."

She reached up and touched his face, a mask of light and shadow in the pale moonlight. "You're sweet, Allen. You always have been."

"Shoot, there's nothing sweet about the way I felt when I found out you meant to marry Bolt. I wanted to kill the bastard with my bare hands."

"But Bolt was your best friend."

"And a lot bigger than I was. That's why I didn't kill

him. A second-best friend with a little less muscle would have been in his grave long since."

"You're joking." She chuckled.

He sighed. "Yeah, that's me—ole Allen-the-joker. Good for a few laughs, a few steamy dates, but not good enough to marry Mary Scarlett Lamar."

"Allen, you know better than that. All through school I thought we'd be married someday. Why, we'd be man and wife now if I'd listened to my mama."

"Ah, Miss Lucy! How I adored that woman! I think I wanted to be her son-in-law almost as much as I wanted to be your husband."

"I know that," she said quietly. "Maybe that was part of the problem. I was a little bit jealous of the relationship you two had. I wanted a man all my own. I didn't want to share my husband with my mother. And when I imagined us married, I also imagined Wednesday night suppers and Sunday dinners, command performances at Mama's house, with her making over you and Big Dick drunk out of his skull and picking fights with all of us. It just made me sick, Allen. I didn't want to live like that or raise kids like that."

"That's a weird reason to turn a guy down. A guy who was—is—crazy in love with you."

That stopped Mary Scarlett short for a minute. She stared at him. "You don't really mean that. Maybe one time, long ago. But not still."

"Oh, no?"

Before Mary Scarlett knew what was happening, Allen drew her into his arms and kissed her deeply. This wasn't one of his frantic, hot-to-trot high school kisses, but a sweet caressing of flesh, a pleading for love and trust. She came away as shocked as she was breathless.

"Give me another chance, Mary Scarlett," he said earnestly. "That's all I ask. I know I botched things last time. But we're older now, more settled. We've both been married and we know the pitfalls. We could make it work."

"Allen, please . . ."

Before she had a chance to turn him down, he kissed her again. This time he moved his hand from her waist to her hip, then lower until he found the slit at the side of her skirt. He shoved the slithery fabric aside to caress her bare thigh. His other hand worked its way up to the diamonds, stroking them with his fingertips while his palm rubbed her breast.

When she was breathing hard and returning tongue thrust for tongue thrust, Allen released her so suddenly that her weak knees nearly caved in under her.

"If you're finished with my date, I think it's time I took her home." Bolt's gruff voice cut through the silence in the garden like a knife blade, startling them both.

"Bolt!" Mary Scarlett said. "We just came out for a breath of air."

"So I saw," he answered sarcastically.

Allen shrugged. "You can't begrudge a guy a kiss for old time's sake."

"If you wanted something for old time's sake, you could have stayed inside and looked at the pictures of you groping Mary Scarlett at the prom. You didn't have to come out here and recreate the scene."

"Bolt, that's unkind," Mary Scarlett snapped.

"It's been a long day, Mary Scarlett. I'm ready to go home. Do you want to go with me or stay here? I'm sure Allen wouldn't mind bringing you home later."

"Hey, she's welcome to stay all night."

Mary Scarlett was just about to say that she was tired and ready to go, too, but Bolt never gave her a chance.

He turned to go back to the house. "Fine! Stay, then. I'll see Kathleen home."

When Mary Scarlett made a motion that told Allen she was about to call out to Bolt, he quickly took her into his arms again and silenced her with another kiss. Furious with Bolt and unable to escape Allen's embrace, Mary Scarlett let herself relax in his arms.

But the spell was broken. This was like her school days all over again. Allen and Bolt. Bolt and Allen. Each of them tugging her this way and that. Never letting her make up her own mind about either of them.

She pushed out of Allen's arms and headed back to the house. But by the time she reached the parlor, Bolt was gone. So was Kathleen.

Nine

Bolt peeled rubber, anxious to be away from the party. Away from Allen Overman and Mary Scarlett.

"Do you mind explaining to me what's going on?" Kathleen asked, staring at Bolt's grim profile lit by the greenish dashboard lights. "What is this? Musical dates?"

"You didn't have to come," he snapped.

For a time they were silent, Bolt intent on breaking the speed limit and Kathleen nursing the hurt from his angry reply.

"Hey, I'm sorry, Katie. I'm not mad at you."

"I know that," she answered, tears threatening. She wished he cared enough to get this mad at her. "What happened, Bolt? Can't you tell me?"

Instead of answering her question, he said, "Feel like a nightcap?"

"Sure." She smiled in the darkness. This would be her first visit to Bolt's place since Mary Scarlett's return. A week ago, she'd thought of his apartment as her second home.

But instead of parking on Bay Street, Bolt drove down the steep incline to River Street. The CRX bounced and bumped over the rough cobbles—ballast from century-old ships—as it inched its way toward the waterfront with its strip of shops, restaurants, and bars. The smells of fried shrimp, pralines, beer, and river mud permeated the damp night air.

The popular tourist area was packed, the cars jammed

tight. Bolt parked at a precarious angle, then came around to open the passenger door and help Kathleen out.

"Watch your step now," he warned. "It's rough out here."

Kathleen thought to herself that he didn't know how rough.

He took her arm to help her negotiate the cobbles in her high heels, not an easy task, especially in the dim light from the street lamps. At this hour most of the restaurants and bars on River Street were ablaze with hot music and awrithe with sweaty bodies. Bolt guided her down the street toward a small, rustic lounge called Harbor Lights. With no live band to draw a crowd, the place was practically deserted, except for one quietly romantic couple and a few solitary drinkers at the bar.

"Let's take that table by the window, in the corner," Bolt suggested.

As they crossed the threshold into the murky den of candlelight and cigarette smoke, a tired-looking blond waitress came from the shadows to show them to their seats.

"What'll you have?" she asked in a bored tone.

"A draft for me," Bolt ordered, then nodded toward Kathleen.

"Vodka tonic," she said.

They waited in silence until their drinks were set before them. Then Bolt got right to the point. "So tell me, Kathleen, did you and Overman cook this up together?"

She blushed. It was on the tip of her tongue to deny any knowledge of what he was talking about. But she knew. And he knew she knew. She nodded.

"Allen called me at the last minute and asked if I'd be his hostess this evening. I agreed."

"That was it? No motive behind his madness?"

"Oh, he had motive all right. Mary Scarlett. He wanted to make her jealous. He thought having me there would do the trick."

"What does he think this is, high school?" Bolt puffed out his cheeks, then blew a long blast of breath.

Unable to look Bolt in the eye, Kathleen stared out the window at the reflected lights on the river. "It's my fault as much as Allen's. I went along with his scheme." Then she shrugged. "I guess I should be happy. I got what I wanted. I'm with you."

"But you aren't happy." It wasn't a question.

"No, because you aren't. When I'm out with a man, I like to think that I'm the only woman he has on his mind. What happened, Bolt? Did you go out and catch them in the garden star-gazing?"

"Yep!"

"And?"

"They looked like they were trying to eat each other alive." He shredded his cocktail napkin. "I shouldn't have gone out there."

"No, you shouldn't have. You need to give her some space. Mary Scarlett's not herself, Bolt. She needs time to fit back into the picture. Here in Savannah, she's lost her place in the scheme of things. With you and Allen both giving her the big rush, she doesn't know which way to turn."

When Bolt made no reply, Kathleen shook her head and said, "God! Will you listen to me, of all people, making excuses for her. What am I doing? Forget what I just said, Bolt. You should be mad as hell at her."

He threw back his head and laughed.

"Hey, I don't see anything funny."

Bolt stopped laughing and rubbed his hand over his eyes. "I don't either, Katie. I just can't believe any of this is happening. Life was so calm and pleasant a week ago. It seemed like I was on the verge of forgetting that Mary Scarlett Lamar ever existed." He reached over and touched Kathleen's hand. "I really thought we had something good going, you and I."

"Isn't it still good?" she asked, holding her breath.

He waited a long time to answer. "I have to explain something, Kathleen. Then you tell me if it's still good. Something's happened to Mary Scarlett. Or, I should say, something's happening to her. I still haven't gotten her to tell me why she ran away from Savannah. I think I'm at least partly responsible and that makes me feel guilty as hell. From what she has told me, her time in Europe wasn't the lark she described tonight at dinner. Her bullfighter husband was a sadistic bastard. He refused even to allow her to come home for her own mother's funeral."

"But that's all behind her. He's dead now."

"He's dead. Yes. And Mary Scarlett was there to see it all when the bull tore into him, then trampled his body into the dust."

Kathleen covered her face with her hands. Even imagining such a thing was more than she could bear.

"It had to be awful for her," Bolt continued. "I can't think of anything worse. Unless she'd been wishing he were dead, which is very possible, and believes now that she brought about his death."

"She couldn't believe that."

"I think she does. A couple of nights this week, she scared me out of my wits, woke up screaming from a nightmare. The thing is, the bad dreams don't go away after she wakes up. She's carrying a lot of baggage at the moment and Raul's ghost is only a part of that."

"You mean she actually believes that his spirit's come back to haunt her?"

Bolt chewed at his bottom lip before answering. "That's hard to say. The first time it happened, she told me he wasn't really dead, that he'd faked his death and followed her back to the States. When she calmed down a little, she admitted that he had to be dead. But she seems totally convinced that his ghost is stalking her." Bolt stopped there, not wanting to admit to Kathleen that he and Mary Scarlett would have made love that first night had it not been for the menacing presence of Raul Miguel.

"Shouldn't she see a good psychiatrist, Bolt?"

"There's no way she'll do that. You know how Miss Lucy was—scared senseless of battery acid and shrinks to name only two of her phobias. Mary Scarlett's had it drummed into her all her life that anyone who needs a psychiatrist is crazy. And that's another thing that has her worried. Everyone always thought Granny Boo was insane because she wanted them to think that. Mary Scarlett's afraid madness is in the blood, that she'll go right off the deep end one of these days and there's not a thing she can do about it."

"Good grief! She sounds like a mental case already."

"She very nearly is, thanks to Raul, Big Dick, and Miss Lucy. It's got nothing to do with Granny Boo, though. She was the one strong influence in Mary Scarlett's life." He raised an eyebrow. "And by the way, she's also been conversing with her granny's ghost."

"Bolt, she needs help."

"Right now, more than anything, she needs someone she can depend on. I don't think Allen Overman quite fits the bill. Do you?"

"But you do?" There was hopelessness in her voice; she knew the answer.

"I think I'm the only one who can help her right now. And I feel like it's my duty to do what I can."

Kathleen sat up straighter and brushed her hair back off her face with both hands. "Come off it, Bolton Conrad! Who do you think you're talking to? I wasn't born yesterday. Don't talk to me about *duty*. You *want* to be back in her life." She paused and swallowed the rest of her drink, then raised her empty glass to him in mock salute. "This wasn't just a nightcap. It was a farewell toast. Admit it."

He stared down in his beer. "Not farewell. I just thought you deserved an explanation. I'm sorry, Katie."

"Save your apologies." She picked up her evening bag

and stood. "I'd like to go home now and it's too far to walk in heels."

"Sure, Katie," he said miserably. "Whatever you want."

She didn't reply to that. She *wanted* Bolt Conrad. But it was clear she wouldn't get what she wanted. At least not right now.

The party got wild after Bolt and Kathleen left. Allen brought out tapes of their high school and college "oldies but goodies" and turned the volume of the tape deck up full blast. The liquor flowed like the eternal tides at Tybee Beach. Before long his fashionable guests got down, kicking off their shoes and doing the dirty bop, a dance that brought back memories of youth, hope, and eagerness for all the golden years yet to be lived. More memories than any year-book could supply.

Mary Scarlett felt the years rolling back as she was passed from one guy to the next, each wanting his turn with the best dancer of them all. Bolt's hasty departure with Kathleen had left her crushed and depressed, but no one would have guessed. More champagne and all that old music had her flying high.

"Just like old times, eh?" Allen shouted above the music as he gyrated rhythmically, sending pelvic thrusts toward Mary Scarlett's thighs.

"Right on, man!" she answered in that deep smoky voice—low, sexy, and inviting.

She reached the very peak of her euphoric intoxication around one in the morning. From there the drop was straight down, with the dark jaws of hell waiting at the bottom. She looked up suddenly and saw him leering at her from the stairs.

Raul!" she gasped.

"Say what?" Lawton Winthrop shouted over the music and laugher. "Couldn't hear you, honey."

But Mary Scarlett didn't stay to repeat anything. She broke away from her gyrating partner and ran for the front door. Allen was in the kitchen at the time, but even if he had been in the room, she wouldn't have bothered with the formalities of saying good night or thanks for a great party. She shed his diamonds and tossed them on a table by the door. Then she vanished into the night before anyone could stop her.

The others shrugged and bopped on. Mary Scarlett had long been known for her abrupt departures.

Without even knowing where she was going, Mary Scarlett turned toward Bull Street. Shoes in hand, she hurried barefoot, leaving Lafayette Square and heading west along Charlton Street. She was conscious of the cool, misty air of night on her face and the day's trapped warmth in the pavement beneath her feet. She quickened her pace until she was almost running, glancing over her shoulders now and again, checking to see if Raul was following.

By the time she reached the wrought-iron fence around her childhood home, she was out of breath, exhausted, and shaking with fear. With a final burst of energy, she flung the gate open and ran up the weed-choked brick path to the veranda. She had taken the key back to Bolt's apartment earlier in the day, but she knew where an emergency key lay hidden. Surely, it would still be there. Only her family had known of its existence.

It took all her strength to raise the molded concrete planter by the stairs. Her effort was rewarded when her hand closed around the heavy key to the front door. Fumbling at the lock, she seethed, "Ollie, ollie, oxen free. You can't touch me once I'm home, Raul."

She burst inside, slamming the door behind her and leaned against it, breathing heavily. After a moment, she felt for the switch beside her on the wall. With a click, the foyer was bathed in soft yellow light.

"I'm home!" she called out to the empty house, the same

words she had always used when she entered, unless she was sneaking in after curfew from a date.

There was one difference. No one answered her call this time. With a jolt she remembered that they were all gone . . . all dead.

She stayed where she was for several minutes, listening to the silence, trying to figure out what disturbed her about it. What sound did she expect that was missing?

"The clocks," she said. "They aren't ticking."

She tiptoed slowly down the hallway to the spot where the grandfather clock had stood for well over a century. The pendulum hung motionless, the hands positioned at five minutes after twelve. For some reason that hour seemed significant. She knew that it was five minutes after midnight, not noon. But how did she know? What did it mean?

She reached inside the back parlor door and switched on the lights to check the delicate French clock on the mantel. Again, five past midnight. But now she remembered the significance of that time. Her clue came from the long mirror above the fireplace. It was draped in black bunting.

Suddenly, she heard a voice, her mother's voice, ringing soulfully through the house. "Stop the clocks, Delsey. Cover the mirrors. She's breathed her last."

"Granny Boo," Mary Scarlett whispered, chill bumps covering her arms. "She died at five minutes after midnight."

She remembered something else, too. She turned and ran her hand over the satiny wood of the wide parlor door—the cooling board door. Unlike the others in the house, this one was smooth on one side, with two boards nailed across the other side so that it could be placed on sawhorses without danger of slipping. Its other oddity was the ease with which it could be slipped off its hinges whenever it was needed.

Mary Scarlett heard her mother's voice again. "Take down the door, Delsey. We'll be laying her out as soon as she's bathed and dressed."

Another voice from the past boomed through the silent

house, making Mary Scarlett cringe. "What the pluperfect hell do you think you're doing, Lucy?"

"You know she wanted it this way. Besides, it's time Mary Scarlett learned about preparing the dead for burial. Now you just go back to bed and leave us be, Richard. Your bellowing will wake up the dead."

"Damned if I will! I'm going to call the funeral home," he yelled. "I won't have this voodoo going on under my own roof."

"It's not voodoo, Richard, and you know it. It's tradition. She wanted to be laid out the same way as all her ancestors. That door's coming down!"

"The hell you say!"

"Calm yourself, Richard. You'll wake Mary Scarlett. Here, have a drink."

Mary Scarlett smiled, remembering. She had been awake already, listening and watching all the while. She knew that the drink her mother had made for Big Dick was liberally laced with Lucy's own sleeping powders. Give it ten minutes and the cooling board door would be in the front parlor while Big Dick slept like a drunken baby. Richard Lamar might be more than a match for his tiny wife when it came to a physical struggle, but she could outmaneuver him mentally without breaking a sweat.

A short time later, Mary Scarlett heard his telltale snoring from the library.

"Mary Scarlett? Is that you up there on the stairs?"

"Yes, Mama."

"She's gone to her reward."

"I know, Mama." The child was suddenly sobbing.

"It's all right to cry for her," Lucy Lamar said, climbing up to the landing. "But you're really crying for yourself, you know. She lived a good, long life. Granny Boo's happy now, released from this earthly plane to fly with the angels. Why, she's probably already up there, planting her Confederate flag at the gates of heaven."

That image brought a smile to Mary Scarlett's lips. She could just see her great-grandmother, storming the Pearly Gates, dressed in her father's old Confederate uniform and flying his tattered flag of battle.

"I know what she told you, Mary Scarlett, but I won't have it. It wouldn't be proper to put her in her grave wearing that moth-eaten uniform. We'll pick out one of her nice Sunday dresses. Come along now. We have a lot to do before dawn."

Reliving the past, Mary Scarlett climbed the stairs all the way to the attic, to the room Granny Boo had claimed as her own. The door squealed from lack of use when she opened it, but inside everything looked the same. Dominating the room was the bed where Mary Beulah Robillard had been born and where she had died over a century later. The bedstead was intricately fashioned of wrought iron, painted white. Since the piece predated the use of electricity, each bedpost formed a candleholder to light the chamber at bedtime.

Mary Scarlett smiled, remembering the stormy nights when she would sneak up the stairs to climb into bed with Granny Boo. When lightning flashed all around the house, the old woman turned off her electric lights and lit her candles. The two of them would huddle close on the soft feather mattress and whisper tall tales by the flicker of bayberry candles. It was here on such nights that Granny Boo had begun telling Mary Scarlett about the family, about the good times and the bad.

She lit the candles and the room filled with the familiar scent of waxy bay. She touched the iron rosettes and curlicues of the headboard, remembering that she used to imagine fairies and elves perched there, eavesdropping on their conversations. Now only dust lay thick and dormant in the metal curls.

"Are you here, Granny Boo?" she called softly, almost afraid she might hear an answer. She listened closely, but the only sound was the whisper of the rising wind outside the house.

She moved to the cottage-style vanity. Here, too, the mirror was covered with black cloth as it had been since the night of Granny Boo's death. Her great-grandmother's most personal belongings remained in place on the dresser top. A box of Pond's face powder. A small blue vial of Evening In Paris *eau de toilette.* Long silver-gray hairpins in a Nippon china dish. A comb and brush, their sterling silver backs gone black from time and want of polish. Then Mary Scarlett spied something she had neither seen nor thought about in years. In fact, she herself had brought it up here the night her great-grandmother passed away. Granny Boo had always thought the silver dollar-sized piece of polished mahogany was a lucky token.

Holding the relic in her palm, Mary Scarlett climbed onto the bed. She stretched out and closed her eyes, smoothing her fingers over the circle of wood that felt as smooth as satin to the touch.

"A mere bit of trash from the steamship *Pulaski,* but the plank it was cut from saved a life, you know." In her drowsy state, Mary Scarlett could hear the faint echo of the old woman's chuckle as she began her tale. "Yes, it served Captain C.A.L. Lamar well, that broken beam. He held on to this shred of flotsam after the boiler blew until he was dashed through the breakers and onto the white sands of a North Carolina beach. Nearly drowned like so many others, he was. Makes a body wonder—why was he saved to do such deeds? He was a roundabout, all right. A thinker, a dreamer, a *scoundrel,* truth be told. 'Twas the War that took him finally. He's always been known by folks as 'the last man to fall.' "

"Oh, tell me about him, Granny Boo!" Mary Scarlett heard a child's excited voice—her own from years gone by. She looked down, not at all surprised to find herself dressed in a soft white flannel nightie instead of her black silk gown.

The old woman began in a faraway voice that called back

the years. "Charles Augustus Lafayette Lamar, his name was, born on the pretty first day of April back in 1824 to Jane Meek Cresswell and Gazaway Bugg Lamar. His mama was a sweet, pretty thing, so I've heard tell, and his daddy was rich as a lord, a banker by profession, well respected. So much so, in fact, that the Marquis de Lafayette, that hero of our Revolution, came to little Charley's baptism at Christ Episcopal Church and even stood as his godfather. You can't get much more distinguished than that, honey."

Mary Scarlett had heard the tale a dozen times, but she remained silent, eager as always to hear it again.

"When Charley was in his early teens, his whole family took a pleasure trip on the steamship *Pulaski*, under Captain Dubois, bound from Savannah to Baltimore, with a stop in Charleston to take on more passengers that first afternoon. They sailed at six the next morning, with one hundred and eighty-two souls aboard, passengers and crew. They never made Baltimore, though. And that's when Charley's whole life changed. You know the story, I vow."

"It sank, Granny Boo."

"That's God's own truth, honey. It sank out deep in the ocean on the fourteenth of June in 1838, only a day out from Savannah and Charleston. There were forty five women on that ship and many children much younger than Charley. Some babes in arms. A great tragedy! Jane Lamar and all five of her other children died. Only Charley, his daddy, and his Aunt Rebecca McLeod survived in their party."

Granny Boo paused to utter a deep, mournful sigh. Then she looked down at the little dark-haired girl sitting beside her and shook her head sadly. They shared a silent moment to honor the dead.

"Having no mama and losing all his brothers and sisters probably accounted for some of Charley's wildness in his later years," the old woman continued. "But who's to say?"

"How would a child get by without a mama, Granny Boo?" The idea struck terror in Mary Scarlett's young heart.

"Well, back then, just as now, it was real hard. So his daddy married again only eleven months later. Harriet Cazenove, Charley's new mama's name was. She wasn't a Savannahian, but from a fine old Virginia family. I reckon she looked down her nose at Savannah because a few years after their marriage, they moved off to New York City."

Granny Boo was usually good at recalling dates, but she squinted a minute thinking about it before she went on. "Let's see, that would have been back in 1846 that they moved up North, the same year Charley married Caroline Agnes Nicoll of this city. They stayed here and set up house-keeping. It looked like Charley was finally going to settle down and make something of himself as a cotton and rice factor. Especially once Caroline started having children. People were big on having younguns back then, Mary Scarlett. Not like today when one or two will do. Charley and his wife had five daughters. Caroline tried her best, but I reckon that was a disappointment to Charley, too. No son to carry on the family name."

"The same as our family," Mary Scarlett said with a sigh of remorse at her own girlhood.

Granny Boo patted her hand. "Don't you fret, honey. Girls are better, smarter, and a whole lot prettier than old hairy-legged, foul-mouthed boys."

Mary Scarlett was frowning. Granny Boo had taught her a lot about genealogy. "If all Charley Lamar's brothers drowned and if Charley himself had no sons, then what line did I spring from?"

Granny Boo winked at her. "You're a smart one, missy. Ask your daddy, and he'll tell you he came down from one of Charley's cousins. But I've always figured that our Charley had a roving eye. It's my belief he had a son right here in Savannah that his wife never knew of."

Mary Scarlett giggled. "What happened next?"

"From the day Charley's daddy and stepmother moved back to Savannah, Charley and old Gazaway never saw eye-to-eye on another thing. 'Cal,' as some of his friends called Charley on account of he always signed his name 'C.A.L. Lamar,' was a real firebrand. He fought to bring duelling back. Why, he shot and nearly killed his best friend, Henry du Bignon, of Jekyll Island, after they got into an argument at Ten Broeck racecourse. He was all for Georgia's secession from the Union, and he had a scheme about setting up a fleet of blockade runners with the state footing the bill. But the biggest thorn under his saddle was slavery. He was all for it, of course, being a cotton factor as he was. No slaves, no cotton, no money to line Charley's pockets. He wanted the law against importing more slaves repealed. Since that wasn't going to happen, Charley decided to take matters into his own hands and that's when he hit on his wildest scheme ever. He went up to New York City with some of his buddies and they joined the New York Yacht Club and partied with their new Yankee friends for a time. Then they bought the *Wanderer* from one of the other members. She was a beauty—the sleekest, fastest yacht you ever laid eyes on."

"But they didn't plan to sail her for sport, did they, Granny Boo?"

"For nary a minute, honey. No, those fellows had their sights set on illegal slaving. In the spring of 1859, they sailed the *Wanderer* to Charleston and outfitted her for what they told everyone was a pleasure cruise to China. Instead, they headed for Africa and Brazzaville on the Congo River. There Charley made a deal with the Portuguese slave traders to buy seven hundred and fifty souls between the ages of thirteen and eighteen, eighty of whom died during the long voyage back to Jekyll Island. They were only children really, kidnapped from their homes."

"That's sad," Mary Scarlett whispered.

"Not for Charley. He had the whole scheme planned out. When he landed on the Jekyll beach that dark night, small boats were waiting to deliver the cargo to plantations in Georgia, South Carolina, Florida, and as far away as Mississippi. Nearly a hundred went to the Carolina plantation of one of his Lamar cousins. Charley came out of it a rich man, indeed."

"But he got caught!" Mary Scarlett cried with a pleased grin.

Granny Boo nodded. "That he did. But he never spent a day in jail. Instead, he was put under house arrest in his own offices on Bay Street. He lived like a king while the trial was going on. It was like a big party here in Savannah. The ladies came every day and brought him fancy baked goods and lavish meals, which they served him on their best china plates. He drank the finest wines, even magnums of French champagne. Seemed like Charley was a hero instead of a criminal, at least to the citizens of Savannah. Of course, he was acquitted. The worst that happened to him was that he was thrown out of the New York Yacht Club. They didn't figure slaving was a proper vocation for one of their members."

"But he did himself proud in the War, Granny Boo. Tell that part," Mary Scarlett begged.

The old woman nodded solemnly. "Yes'um, Charley gave his all to the Cause. He organized and was Captain of the Savannah Mounted Rifles. Later, down the coast at Brunswick, he was elected colonel of Twenty-fifth Regiment Georgia Cavalry. But then after getting through the whole war, he was shot and killed near Columbus *after* General Lee's surrender. *The last man!*"

"Does he come to your parties at Bonaventure?"

Granny Boo shook her head wearily. "Haven't seen him. I think they have their own doings over at Laurel Grove where he's buried. Caroline's over there with him. She probably keeps a right tight leash on him." She chuckled, then sighed. "All this talking's got me wore out, honey."

"Granny Boo?" Mary Scarlett opened her eyes. She was once more alone in the bedroom. All signs of the little girl in the long nightgown had vanished. She was dressed in the black silk she had worn to Allen's party.

She lay back against the musty pillows thinking about Charley Lamar. What part did she have in his story? Had she been his wife? His lover? Or simply one of the ladies who visited him while he was under house arrest?

"Maybe none of those," she whispered, rubbing her fingers over the smooth token in her hand. "Maybe his lucky piece is our only connection other than blood."

She was nearly asleep when she heard a crash. The noise, close at hand, made her shoot up in bed. The rusted hinges of an old cupboard door had given way, falling to the floor. She cried out as she stared through the dim candlelight reflected in a mirror.

"There it is! Granny Boo's mirror!"

She hurried across the room to retrieve her treasure, but closed her eyes as she picked it up. Silently, she begged to see the love of her life when she opened her eyes again.

"Let him be here with me. *Please!* Let me see his face."

She opened her eyes and gasped. Allen Overman's gray eyes stared back at her from over her shoulder. In her shock, she almost lost her grip on the mirror's gilt frame, but he reached out to steady it.

"So, here you are," he said. "I've been searching the whole house. I was about to give up and leave when I heard that crash. What are you doing up here in the attic, Mary Scarlett? Why'd you leave the party?"

"God, you scared me out of ten years' growth, Allen. What are *you* doing here? How did you get in?"

"I was worried about you, honey. You just dashed off into the night. It's storming out there. The wind blew the door wide open. I figured you must be in here somewhere. Come over here and sit down. You look as pale as a ghost."

Mary Scarlett let him lead her to the bed. She smiled weakly, wondering what Allen would say if she told him she had indeed been in the company of a ghost after leaving his party.

"Are you okay?" he asked, genuinely concerned.

"I'm just *so* tired, Allen."

"Lie down and rest for a while. I'll stay here with you. When the storm lets up, I'll take you back to the house."

"I can sleep here," she argued. *"This* is my home."

"I'm not leaving you here all alone. The place gives me the creeps."

"Suit yourself."

She was already drifting off to sleep. He leaned down and kissed her softly. That and the fact that he asked where she had found the mirror were her last memories of that night.

The bright sun in her face woke her the next morning. She was still clutching Charley Lamar's lucky piece, but both the mirror and Allen were gone. She glanced toward the cupboard. The door was on its hinges and closed, just as it had been when she entered Granny Boo's attic room. A quick inspection of the interior showed that it was used only for storing bedding. No mirror!

Mary Scarlett sank down on the bed, bewildered and depressed. Had she only dreamed everything that had happened last night? She knew she had imagined the part about Granny Boo. She certainly had not been here in a long, long time. But Allen had been here. Hadn't he?

She rubbed a hand over her dry lips. She remembered his kiss, even if she had been half asleep at the time.

Someone banging at the front door jolted her from her troubled thoughts. She hurried down to see who was there. She was surprised to find the door locked. When she opened it, she had to squint against the bright sunlight outside.

"Thank God you're here, Mary Scarlett! I've been searching all over for you. I figured you'd gone to Bolt's place. When I called and he hadn't seen you, I panicked."

"Allen?" The sight of him left her totally baffled. "But you knew I was here."

"And just how would I know that? You left the party without even saying goodbye."

She glanced back up toward the attic. "But weren't you . . . ?" Her words trailed off. Allen would think she was crazy if she mentioned anything about seeing him in the mirror—which wasn't there—that had come from a broken cupboard door—which wasn't broken—to kiss her in the attic—where he had never been in his entire life.

She offered him a weak smile. "I'm sorry, Allen. I wasn't feeling myself last night. I shouldn't have run out the way I did."

He grinned back. "Hey, don't mention it. I was just worried about you, that's all. Come on now. I'll take you home."

"Home?"

He shrugged and laughed. "Well, how about my house? We'll have some breakfast."

She shivered, thinking of Raul's ghost on Allen's stairs. "Thanks, but I'd rather go to Bolt's place."

When Allen's smile changed to a frown, she quickly added, "I need to change clothes and all my things are there."

"Well, okay, honey. Whatever you say."

He took her arm and led her down the stairs toward his car. As they walked away from the house, Mary Scarlett turned and glanced up at the attic window. She was sure she saw a face peering down at her through the bubbled-glass panes.

On the drive to Bay Street, she tried not to think, not to feel, not to remember that finding Granny Boo's mirror had been only a figment of her dreams.

Allen glanced over at her. "Why the frown, darlin'?"

Shielding her eyes from the sun and from Allen, she said, "Too much champagne, I guess."

Ten

As Allen turned into Bay Street, Mary Scarlett—silent during the whole ride—let out a burst of high-pitched laughter. Allen glanced at her, puzzled.

"What's so funny?"

"I was just thinking about a story Mama used to tell me before I was old enough to start dating. She said once one of her girlfriends spent the night with her after a prom and forgot to bring any clothes to change into to go home the next day. When the neighbors saw her sneaking into her house early in the morning, still dressed in her prom gown, they all assumed she'd out all night with her date. And, of course, as Mama used to say, 'That could mean *only one thing!*' She would always end the tale by saying, 'Mary Scarlett, that poor girl's reputation was *ruined!* Not just in Savannah, but throughout the South. Don't you ever, ever forget about appearances. They count for *everything!*' "

She turned to Allen and feigned an expression of total mortification. "Just look at me! Do you think it's going to ruin my pristine reputation when all the neighbors see me coming in at this hour in my evening gown?"

They both laughed, then Allen reached over and patted her hand. "I don't think you need to worry, honey. That story is one of Savannah's sacred myths, handed down for generations. Every girl I knew in high school had been told that same story by her own dear mama."

"It's not as if I had any reputation left to ruin," she said with a sigh.

Allen pulled up to the curb. "Want me to come in with you?"

She shook her head. "You'd better not, Allen, but thanks. I have some explaining to do and I think I'd better do it alone."

"You're sure, honey?"

She nodded, then climbed out of the car. "Great party, Allen. See you around."

"You'd better believe it, darlin'!"

He pulled away as Mary Scarlett headed the short distance across the small park to Factor's Walk. She was almost hoping she would catch Kathleen still in Bolt's apartment. Then she could take the stance of the injured party. That was a much easier role to play than repentant date and house guest.

She noticed with a mixture of relief and annoyance that not one person gave her a second glance as she crossed the park. Savannah had changed; her mama could sleep easy in her grave. Her little girl's reputation was safe in this city that had once been called a "garden of good and evil."

Bolt must have been watching from the window. Before she could touch the bell, the door swung open. He stood there, dressed only in paint-smeared jeans, scowling at her.

"Well? Aren't you going to invite me in, Bolt?"

"I'm deciding," he answered, his voice chilly. "And, believe me, it isn't an easy decision, Mary Scarlett."

"Please, Bolt," she said softly. "Let's not stand here in the doorway and argue. We'll have all of Savannah discussing our dirty laundry."

"I don't have any," he snapped. "I washed everything in sight last night when I couldn't sleep for worrying about you."

He held the door wide and motioned for her to come in. She glanced about, expecting to see Kathleen lounging on the sofa or in the kitchen fixing breakfast. But there wasn't a sign of her. Maybe she hadn't spent the night with Bolt after all. That would account for his dark mood. He had taken Kathleen home, but he thought Mary Scarlett had spent the night with Allen.

She decided to meet the problem head-on. "I know you expect me to apologize, Bolt, but I'm not sure for what. You're the one who left me stranded at Allen's last night."

He had gone to the balcony door where his easel stood, supporting a large canvas with the first palette knife strokes of a fiery sunrise taking shape. Turning away from her and back to his work, he added great blobs of alizarin crimson with quick flicks and angry slashes of his narrow blade.

"I didn't hear anyone begging me to stay." His words were directed not to Mary Scarlett, but to his canvas.

"Is that what you want?" she asked in a cold voice that matched his. "You want me to *beg?*"

From where she stood, a few feet behind him, she saw his broad shoulders slump. His head drooped forward. He set aside his paints and knife.

"Why are we doing this to each other?" he said in a defeated tone, without turning to look at her.

"I wish I knew, Bolt," she whispered. After several moments' hesitation she added, "I *am* sorry about last night. But not for the reasons you may think."

He turned around slowly. He wasn't smiling, but there was a certain, unmistakable glint in his dark eyes. Reaching out, he wiped a smear of mascara from Mary Scarlett's cheek.

"You've been crying. Tell me what Allen did to make you cry."

"Nothing, Bolt, I swear it. I wasn't even with Allen last night."

He arched an eyebrow in surprise. Or was it disbelief? "Where were you, then?"

"At the house on Bull Street. I had to go. It was the only

place that was safe. After you left, I saw Raul." Her voice was quivering, breaking with every word. Tears came again.

"Mary Scarlett." Bolt drew her into his arms, against his warm, bare chest. "Honey, we've been all through this."

"I know! I know!" she sobbed. "He's dead. So why do I keep seeing him? What am I going to do, Bolt? I'll never be able to get my life back together if I'm always looking over my shoulder, expecting to find him staring at me with those cold black eyes."

"I wish there was something I could do to help, honey." He kissed her temple; that helped a little.

She drew back and looked up at him. "There's something else, too, Bolt. Granny Boo was there last night. I went up to her room, looking for the mirror. I was sure it had to be there."

"Was it?"

She had to fight for control to get the words out. "Yes. But then it was gone. I guess I only dreamed I found it. Everything about last night is fuzzy in my mind. I don't know what was real and what wasn't. I'm so confused, Bolt. And I'm scared. *Really scared!*"

"Come on into the den and sit down before you fall down. You look like you've been through hell. I'll get you some coffee. We'll talk."

Bolt took Mary Scarlett's hand and led her to the soft couch in the den. The morning sun washed the pale walls in yellow, making the whole room look cheery with springtime light. The minute she sank into the deep cushions, Mary Scarlett found herself fighting sleep.

"If you want to talk, you'd better get me some coffee. Fast! And make it strong or you'll lose me to the sandman."

He reached down and stroked her cheek. "I don't want to lose you to anyone, Mary Scarlett. That's why we have to talk."

He left, but returned seconds later with a tray of coffee

and a plate of cheese danish. Before he even sat down, he said what he knew he had to say.

"Mary Scarlett, you need to get some professional help."

"No!" she cried. "I will *not* go to a shrink and have him poking around inside my head and dissecting my dreams. I refuse!"

He handed her one of the mugs. "Drink your coffee and hear me out. Please, Mary Scarlett!"

She sipped the hot coffee and gave him her attention, but her eyes beamed defiantly.

He sat down beside her and took her hand. "I know how you feel about psychiatrists, honey. I don't think you're right, but I do understand. I had something else in mind. What are your feelings about hypnosis?"

"I don't have any," she said, frowning. "What are you getting at, Bolt?"

"There's this man I know in town, Dr. Schlager. I've done some legal work for him. Mary Scarlett, he's a licensed hypnotherapist. I think he might be able to help you."

She said nothing, just kept drinking her coffee and staring at Bolt.

"They've learned that through hypnosis all kinds of ills— physical and psychological—can be helped and sometimes cured. Would you be willing to see him, at least talk to him? You don't have to commit if it doesn't feel right. But I really think it's worth a try."

She took so long to answer that Bolt thought she had fallen asleep with her eyes wide open. Either that or she was so furious at the idea that she couldn't think of anything to say. Finally, she set her cup down and turned to him.

"Will you go with me?"

Bolt broke into a relieved grin and hugged her. "Of course, honey, I'll go with you. I'll be there the whole time."

She stared up at him, her eyes still wide with fright, but with a glimmer of hope as well. "We'll just talk to him. Right? He won't force me into anything?"

"Not with me there to look out for you. No one's going to force you to do anything, not ever again. Trust me, Mary Scarlett."

She closed her eyes, snuggled close, and kissed his naked shoulder. She realized in that moment that Bolton Conrad might be the only person in her life she could trust, totally and without reservation.

A short time later, Mary Scarlett was in bed, fast asleep. Bolt was on the phone, dialing Dr. Manfred Schlager's number.

"His office is in his home," Bolt explained as they drove past the graceful Victorian houses along East Hall Street.

Mary Scarlett had slept from noon Sunday right through the night. She had spent this whole day at Bolt's apartment, alone while he was at work. With no one to talk to, she had managed to work herself into quite a state, worrying about this evening and her first meeting with Dr. Schlager. Now she felt ready to jump out of her skin. Bolt's proposed solution seemed almost as distressing as her problems.

"I've never heard of any doctor seeing patients at night. Are you sure he's on the up and up, Bolt?"

"He often arranges appointments at night for working people. I told him I had to be in court all this week, so we both thought tonight would be best when I explained how anxious you are to meet with him."

She grimaced. The word "anxious" certainly described her feelings—eager, but with pronounced fear. Why had she let Bolt talk her into this?

"Here's his place," he announced, turning into a wide driveway that terminated under a carriage drive at the side of the massive stone mansion.

Mary Scarlett stared up at the turrets, gargoyles, and the many-hued gleam of light shining through stained glass windows.

"Isn't this *some* place?" Bolt asked. "It was about to be demolished when Dr. Schlager moved to Savannah a few years ago. He came to me for help to stop the wrecker's ball. We saved it with a last-minute stay of execution. Schlager says it reminds him of the castles along the Rhine that he remembers from his childhood."

"He grew up in a castle?"

"No, no! Peasant stock all the way, he insists."

"For a peasant, he's done well for himself," she mused, staring up at his imposing home with its fancy stone, brick, and terra-cotta ornamentation. "Who in the world would build a house like this? It must have cost millions!"

"It's one of the masterpieces of the post-Reconstruction era, built around 1887, I believe. The Victorian Age. There was lots of money here then, huge fortunes based on cotton, lumber, naval stores, and phosphates. That's when your family recovered its fortune, isn't it?"

She nodded. "I guess you could say we were lucky. At least my family still had a home at the end of the war, even if all the money was gone. Granny Boo's husband, my Great-grandaddy Horace, was the business-wizard on Mama's side of the family. He was in lumber. He owned thousands of acres of 'worthless' timberland west of Savannah. When he went into the lumber business, he made a fortune practically overnight."

"Hey, I'll bet Granny Boo and old Horace used to come to parties here. According to Dr. Schlager, this house was the center of social and cultural activity back in the 1890s."

At Bolt's words, the scene shifted for a moment as if a haze had drifted over the great house. Mary Scarlett heard music and the laughter of guests at a party. She thought she saw a beautiful young woman peering out of the front parlor window. *Granny Boo!* she thought.

The magical mist faded when Bolt squeezed Mary Scarlett's arm. He had led her around to the front of the Gothic mansion.

"You aren't shivering, are you? There's nothing to be nervous about, honey. You'll like Dr. Schlager. He's been everywhere, done everything. He's quite the Renaissance man. You'll probably fall madly in love with him."

"Yeah, right," she muttered grimly.

"Come on, Mary Scarlett. You've always been thirsty for new experiences. Think about this as another of life's exciting adventures."

She had no time to respond—they were at the huge, iron-banded front door. Bolt gripped the ring that hung from the mouth of a hideous brass gargoyle and rapped sharply. Immediately, an attractive woman who appeared to be in her mid-forties answered.

"Good evening, Mr. Conrad," she said warmly. "You are right on time. And this must be Miss Lamar."

She extended her hand to Mary Scarlett, who hesitated only briefly before she accepted the tall, blond woman's firm handshake.

"I am Helga," she said. "Please, won't you come in."

Mary Scarlett shot a questioning glance at Bolt. He hadn't mentioned Helga. Who was she? Dr. Schlager's wife, daughter, assistant, mistress?

Before she could ask, the doctor himself appeared in the hallway. "Ah, good. You have arrived. Come! Come! Everything is ready in my library."

When the short man with salt-and-pepper hair and beard turned toward Helga and asked her to bring tea and join them, the gleam in his charcoal eyes ruled out her possible roles as daughter or mere assistant. There was obvious passion between the two.

Manfred Schlager, Mary Scarlett noted, was not a handsome man, but he had a warm, paternal charm. That thought amused her. How could she tag him that way when the only measuring stick she had was Big Dick, who had been anything but paternal? She concluded that the doctor was the kind of man she had always *wished* she had for a father.

She began to relax, but not completely. Her fear of the unknown refused to be banished.

Noting Mary Scarlett's obvious nervousness, the doctor turned his attention to Bolt. "So, how goes the lawyering trade, my friend?"

"Busy as ever," Bolt answered with a laugh. "Too many divorces, too many petty quarrels, and far too many murder cases, to my way of thinking."

Dr. Schlager shook his head and clucked his tongue as he stood back and raised his arm in invitation at the door of his den. "The drugs," he sighed, "always the drugs and the shootings and the knifings. It is most distressing. The plague of our times."

"With no cure in sight," Bolt agreed.

Mary Scarlett felt surprisingly calm and comfortable, listening to the two men. She realized what the doctor was doing—pointing out to her, without saying it in so many words, that her problems were dwarfed by those of the city and the world. Even though she understood the tack, it worked. Suddenly, the plagues in her life seemed small by comparison.

They entered the doctor's office-den, a large room, lined with books, hung with expensive paintings and tapestries. It could have been a castle on the Rhine.

"How have things been going for you, Dr. Schlager? Is Savannah still to your liking?" Bolt asked.

"Oh, good, good!" Schlager nodded. "I have had some luck tracing my former self recently."

That caught Mary Scarlett's attention. His *former self?*

"I told Mary Scarlett you had come here by an unusual route. Is there time to explain to her briefly?"

The doctor smiled broadly. "There is always time to speak of Prophet Jones. I have followed him this far—from the darkest part of Africa, to where the Portuguese slave traders captured him at Brazzaville, to take him on board the vessel *Wanderer,* and on to Jekyll Island. Now it looks as if I might soon locate his grave right here in Savannah."

"The *Wanderer?*" Now Dr. Schlager had Mary Scarlett's *full* attention.

"Yes. It was a slave ship, owned by—"

"Charles Augustus Lafayette Lamar," she cut in. "He was one of my own ancestors." Her excitement faded when she realized that Charley Lamar had sold Prophet Jones—Dr. Schlager's former self—into slavery.

"Ah, you know your history well." Schlager beamed at her. "It seems that in my most recent past life, I was a prince among my own people, but a slave once Lamar transported me to America. Many died on that voyage, my own sisters among them. It was a sad time, but not such a sad life for Jones. You see, Prophet, as he was named by his owners, brought great knowledge with him from his land. Some called it magic. Some called it voodoo. But no one denied that he had a special sight, a gift for healing. Even now, I am studying the old ways to try to learn all that I knew in that past life. He fathered many children, too. I am in search of some of his descendants who might still live in the Savannah area." He leaned back, his face aglow. "Imagine meeting my own grandson from a previous life. What a marvel that would be! He might even have known old Prophet and heard tales from his own lips of those old days back in Africa." He paused and closed his eyes as if he had drifted off. Then he jerked back, all business again. "How I ramble! You have not come to hear about my lives. You are here to find out more about *your* lives."

Bolt tried to hide a smile as he shook his head. Schlager saw his reaction.

"Always the skeptic, eh, Conrad?"

"I just find it hard to believe that I've lived more than once. Maybe this is my first time around. Did you ever think of that?"

"Not a likely theory. From my dealings with you, I believe you to be an old soul. Old and very wise."

Bolt laughed aloud at this. "How I wish!"

While the two men talked, Mary Scarlett had been giving the room a closer examination. She noticed one of Bolt's seascapes among the old European masterpieces on the walls. Bolt's painting held her attention. It disturbed her. The style was unmistakably his, but the hues contrasted starkly with the usual rich colors he favored. The fierce, angry sea was done in grays, black, and somber shades of purple and ultramarine. She wondered when Bolt could have painted this tortured scene and what had so troubled him at the time.

"Ah, Helga is here with our tea." Dr. Schlager rose from his desk chair to take the heavy tray from her. "You will join us, of course, my dear."

Helga smiled and passed the cups of fragrant Darjeeling, then took a seat on the sofa beside Mary Scarlett.

"I see you recognize Bolton's work," Schlager said to Mary Scarlett.

"It's hard to mistake his unique style," she said. "But this one is different from any of his others. More violent, jarring to the senses."

The doctor gave a quick nod. "It is!" he said emphatically. "Tell me more about this difference you observe. How does the painting make you feel, Miss Lamar?"

She thought through her words carefully before she answered. She didn't want Bolt to think she hated his painting. "I believe he was angry or depressed when he did this one. His fury flowed into his strokes." She stood and walked over to the painting, completely caught up in her explanation and in Bolt's stormy sea. "Look here." She touched the canvas gently. "His strokes are always bold, but these go beyond that. Slashes, jabs, strikes. It makes me think that if he had held a real knife in his hand instead of a palette knife, he might have committed murder instead of creating art." Embarrassed by her own dramatic words, Mary Scarlett uttered a nervous laugh. "I'd say he was mad as hell at somebody when he painted this."

An uncomfortable silence followed. She resumed her seat and sipped her tea, trying not to meet Bolt's stare.

"You hit the nail on the head, honey," he muttered under his breath.

"Explain to her, Bolton," the doctor urged. "This could be a good starting point for our first session."

Mary Scarlett saw Bolt flash Schlager a dark look. "We're not here to discuss *my* problems. Mary Scarlett is the one who needs your help."

"It has been my experience," the doctor said, "that one's problems are most often intertwined with the problems of those closest. Miss Lamar might take hope from learning that others have suffered because of her own suffering. No one is alone in life, isolated from those around them."

Hanging on the doctor's every word, Mary Scarlett stared right at Bolt's profile. What *did* this painting of pain and fury have to do with her?

"Won't you at least tell us the title of this work?" Dr. Schlager prodded gently.

Bolt shrugged. "I called it 'Gone To Hell.' Bad title," he added. "Means nothing."

"And when did you execute this unusual work?" Schlager pressed.

Bolt was losing patience, something rare for him. "Listen, we didn't come here to discuss art, especially bad art."

"When did you paint it?" Mary Scarlett begged softly. "Tell me, Bolt. I really want to know."

He turned slowly, until he was facing her. When she saw the pain in his eyes, she had to look away. It was too much to bear. The suffering on the canvas mirrored some dark, hidden place within him, some scar on his soul.

"I painted that the day after you left Savannah," he said bluntly, tonelessly.

Mary Scarlett gasped. Never, until this minute, had she realized the depth of Bolt's angry hurt. And she had caused it by leaving without a word of explanation.

"It's my worst nightmare," he said. "You have Raul; I have this hell of sea and sky. I've painted it over and over—endlessly in my dreams—for the past eight years. I gave it to you, Dr. Schlager, because I thought getting it out of my sight might end the nightmares. And you were the only one who ever liked it. I hate the thing!"

Again, silence descended over the four people in the room. Mary Scarlett felt tears near the surface. She had been relieved when Dr. Schlager began this seemingly innocuous discussion of Bolt's artwork, thinking this would shield her from becoming the main topic for a time. Now she wanted to blurt out all her own problems. She would tell the doctor anything he wanted to know. *Anything!* But she could not bear to see Bolt's pain—pain *she* had caused.

Helga finally broke the brittle tension in the room. "We are all linked to one special other in each life," she said quietly. "We share that partner's pain as well as his joy. Neither man nor woman was created to exist alone. Manfred and I were lucky enough to discover the link between us. We have shared many lives and many relationships through all eternity."

The doctor nodded gravely and stroked his beard. "Helga speaks the universal truth," he answered solemnly. "She and I once fought side by side in Hannibal's elephant corps. We existed as brother and sister in the ancient Mayan civilization. In China long ago, when Helga was a poor peasant woman, I was her eldest son."

"And the dearest of my children," she answered meekly, eyes cast down as if she was remembering.

"Lovers we have been in many lives. Most recently, when I was Prophet Jones and she was the Princess Zoldza. We came from the same village and were betrothed from birth.

We shared passage on the *Wanderer*. We shared shame and pain, but always love."

It was on the tip of Mary Scarlett's tongue to ask if the same was true in this life, but she kept the question to herself. The answer seemed obvious.

"As for you and Bolton Conrad, Miss Lamar, I believe it is the same with you. I sense a closeness between you, a sharing, and deep affection. But I see a wide gulf that could swallow you both. There is danger between you—and misunderstanding."

The doctor's words sent a shiver through Mary Scarlett. How could he tell all this from simply looking at them? And, if he was right, what could they do about it?

As if sensing her unspoken question, Schlager said, "Through dual hypnosis and regression to past lives, we can discover the truth and so patch the wounds from previous existences."

Bolt's head shot up. His eyes narrowed. *"Dual?* I didn't know I was going to be a part of this. You never mentioned that, Schlager." His voice rose as he spoke.

Mary Scarlett put her hand on his arm. "Hear him out, Bolt. What can it hurt?"

"Yes, do hear me out, Bolton," the doctor said, still calm and quiet. "You asked me to see your friend, to help her. You must be willing to submit to this if you truly wish Miss Lamar to be able to work through her problems—problems that have come with both of you as excess baggage through time." He smiled warmly. "It will be most enlightening. And painless. I promise."

Mary Scarlett squeezed Bolt's hand in a silent plea. Suddenly, she was no longer nervous, but eager to begin.

"Well, Conrad?" he asked.

All eyes turned to Bolt. He looked uncomfortable under the fierce scrutiny. Finally, he heaved a great sigh. "Okay. You win, Doc. I'll do it. But only for Mary Scarlett's sake.

To tell you the truth, I don't believe all this reincarnation bunk."

Schlager smiled benignly and tented his fingers in front of his beard. "I, too, was a skeptic long ago. Understanding and knowledge will come through experience. A whole new world is about to open up for both of you. A world that has been with you all your lives without your realizing it. I envy you that joy of first knowledge. It will be a journey of beauty and light."

Mary Scarlett glanced toward Helga. Her face glowed with intense joy. Her eyes never left those of Dr. Schlager. In that moment, Mary Scarlett wanted desperately to feel what Helga was feeling. She wanted to know that each time she looked at Bolt he was seeing her with that overwhelming light of love shining through her whole being.

"What do we have to do, Dr. Schlager?" she asked, leaning toward him, more than eager now.

"Bolton?" It was the doctor's final plea for permission. "You must be as willing as Miss Lamar for this to work."

Bolt only nodded in reply.

Dr. Schlager smiled at them. "Then let us waste no more time. Shall we begin?" He motioned to his assistant. "Helga, if you please."

She rose and walked quickly to open a door at the back of the room. She looked at Mary Scarlett, then at Bolt. "Come with me, please."

They rose, still holding hands, and followed Helga into the unknown.

Eleven

Bolt hadn't bargained for this. Schlager had set him up, but good! Helga was definitely in on it, and maybe Mary Scarlett was, too. She had had plenty of time and opportunity while he was at work today to call the doctor and have a cozy chat.

As they followed Helga into the adjoining room, he gave Mary Scarlett a quick glance. No, he decided, she hadn't been in on the scheme. She was too caught up in her own problems to do any behind-the-scenes plotting.

It's Schlager, he thought, *and that damn painting!*

Bolt knew he never should have shown that horror to the good doctor. He certainly shouldn't have given it to the man, even though he had admired it. And as much as Schlager had wanted it, Bolt had wanted it out of his sight even more. He dreamed about it often enough—he didn't need the original hanging around to haunt him. He should have burned the damn thing right after he poured his guts out onto that canvas. Now he was caught . . . in a trap of his own creation.

For more reasons than one, he didn't want to submit to hypnosis, either alone or with Mary Scarlett. This wasn't one of those deals where he feared the doctor's control over him once he was in a hypnotic state. No, his was a fear that ran deeper than that. There were things about his early life that he never wanted to relive. He certainly didn't want anyone to know about his "good ole days," especially not

Mary Scarlett. She had enough skeletons in her own closet; she didn't need his rattling around. Besides, he loved Mary Scarlett—always had, always would. In spite of everything, he still wanted to marry her.

As for *past lives* they might have shared, who the hell cared? He couldn't be held responsible for what some dude back in the tenth or the nineteenth century had done. Even if Schlager conjured up some former lives, who was to say that the doc wasn't just putting on a magic mirror show for their benefit? *Reincarnation? Bullshit!*

"If you will each take your place on one of the couches, please."

Mary Scarlett tugged his sleeve. "Bolt? Are you with us? Helga wants us to lie down. Which couch do you want?"

"Makes no difference," he muttered.

For the first time, he became aware of the room. He wasn't sure what he had expected—a crowded, airless cubicle like his childhood bedroom or maybe a dark closet like the one where he had been locked away as punishment when he was a kid. This was far different from either. The walls were done in deep, restful green with matching drapes patterned in swirls of crimson and gold. The furniture was simple, but comfortable looking—twin leather couches, each with a pillow at one end and a light blanket folded neatly at the other, a desk, two chairs. The place looked harmless enough. No electronic torture machines or a video camera with its probing, all-seeing eye.

Bolt flopped down on the couch nearer the windows. "Not bad!" He looked over at Mary Scarlett and forced a broad grin. "Don't worry, honey. Everything's going to be fine." He hoped she couldn't tell that he was lying through his teeth. None of this was fine with him.

Mary Scarlett picked up on Bolt's nervousness. She knew he wasn't happy about this proposed dual hypnotic journey. He obviously hadn't planned to come along with her into the past. He had said he would be with her all the way, but he hadn't meant the statement quite so literally.

She reached across the small space separating the couches and took his hand. Her smile matched his—bright, but shaky. "It'll be okay, Bolt. Really."

"Indeed it will," Dr. Schlager echoed as he entered the room and took his place behind the desk.

"Yeah, right!" Bolt mumbled. "You aren't going to force us to tell all our deepest, darkest secrets, are you, Doc?"

Schlager chuckled, then turned serious. "You have nothing to fear, Conrad. Or you either, Miss Lamar. There will be no force of any sort involved. You will retain your free will at all times. You will say only that which you choose to divulge."

"Once I'm under, you won't make me bark like a dog or anything?"

"Bolton! I am shocked you would ask such a question. I am no stage show mesmerist. I am a scientist, an historian, a seeker of truth and knowledge. Calm yourselves now. Close your eyes and try to clear your minds. Only listen to the sound of my voice."

As they closed their eyes, Helga silently covered each of them with the blankets on their couches. "You will lose body heat under hypnosis," she explained in a whisper.

Then all sounds faded except for the velvet-smooth voice of Dr. Manfred Schlager. "We are going on a voyage. As with any extended trip by sea there will be smooth sailing at times, but some rough water. Do you wish to be aware of all that happens or would you prefer a state of forgetfulness? I will, of course, tape record each session for future reference."

"I want to know *everything*," Bolt answered. "The smallest details."

"Yes," Mary Scarlett agreed in a drowsy voice.

"Very well, then. We shall begin. Relax for a moment. Keep your eyes closed. Feel your bodies losing weight and substance. You are like smoke blowing in the wind. Your minds are quiet, resting. You hear only my voice and it soothes you, comforts you."

For what seemed like a long time to his two patients, the doctor did not speak. Bolt grew fidgety during the extended silence. Mary Scarlett, however, slipped into a deep state of relaxation. She became aware of the rhythms of her body, the flow of her blood, the quiet beating of her heart. She became the smoke in the wind.

Once Bolt and Mary Scarlett both went perfectly still, Helga tiptoed to the doctor's chair. She leaned down to whisper into his ear, trying not to break the hypnotic spell. "I think you must know this, Manfred, before you go any further. I have been studying them closely all the while. Now that they are still, I can read their auras clearly. His seems normal enough, but hers is most unusual. There is a dark-shrouded figure hovering over her, some soul who has gone on to the other side."

"Man or woman?" he asked.

"I cannot tell."

"Good or evil?"

She shook her head. "Again, I do not know. But I feel that this entity is always with her, an integral part of her aura and her life."

With a worried frown, Schlager said, "You are right, Helga. This demands exploration before they go back. This spirit could prove a danger to both of them."

Turning his attention back to Mary Scarlett and Bolt, he instructed, "On the count of three, you will open your eyes. Slowly. You will feel refreshed and happy. Your troubles have blown away with the smoke. You will awake, but remain lying still."

Both Mary Scarlett and Bolt snapped back to wakefulness the moment they heard Dr. Schlager say, "Three."

"That wasn't much of a trip," Bolt said, starting to rise to a sitting position.

Helga placed her hand on his shoulder, gently pressing him back down.

"Do not rise yet," the doctor repeated. "Give your body a few moments to regain its equilibrium. As for your journey, this was what we might call a dry run. I needed to know that each of you *could* be hypnotized before we begin our regression."

"Well, it didn't work on me. Sorry, Doc!"

Helga and Dr. Schlager exchanged knowing smiles.

"Perhaps if I hypnotize Helga for you to see, Bolton, then you will understand the technique better. Shall we try it?"

Helga sat down in a large reclining chair, tipped it back, then pulled a thin blanket over her body. "I am ready, Manfred."

"Are you going to take her back to when you were both on the *Wanderer?*" Mary Scarlett asked, hoping for a negative answer.

"No, my dear. Don't worry about that. Actually, this experiment is more for your benefit than for Bolton's."

"But I *was* hypnotized—*I think.*"

"Indeed you were. You are a most willing and able subject. However, Helga brought something important to my attention while you were under. Are you familiar with the existence of auras, Miss Lamar?"

"I've heard of them. I don't think I've ever seen one, though."

"Not everyone has the power," he explained. "Helga is gifted in this area. She has just told me that there is something rather curious about yours."

"Oh, no!" Mary Scarlett cried, truly distressed. "It's deformed, isn't it? That's why my life is such a mess."

"Not at all," Schlager soothed. "Most auras are like rainbows. They are simply formations of light, which signify by their color the sort of energy being released from the body and the soul. However, in your aura Helga sees a shape, a cloaked figure of someone connected to you who has passed over."

"A man?" Mary Scarlett demanded, thinking instantly of Raul.

"It is difficult to distinguish the sex of a spirit. Is there someone you think it might be?"

Mary Scarlett was trembling. She clutched her arms. Bolt moved quickly to her side and held her. "It's okay, honey. Take it easy."

"Bolt, what if it's Raul? I know it's him. I told you I've been seeing him. No wonder, if he's in my aura."

"You also told me you've talked to Granny Boo. She watched over you all your life and I'll bet she's still at her post."

"Have no fear," the doctor said. "Helga will find out for us. Now you must be silent so I can put her under. Once she is hypnotized, she will contact the other side for us and let the spirits speak through her."

"How does that work?" Bolt wanted to know.

Dr. Schlager scowled at this interruption, but Helga smiled and explained. "It's like a very long distance phone call. I am the receiver. Manfred will place the call by putting me under hypnosis. Those on the other side will answer."

"You mean you'll be able to tune in to this spirit in Mary Scarlett's aura?"

"Perhaps. Perhaps not," Helga replied. "We have no way of knowing which spirits are present when the channel opens. But whoever responds will be able to give us answers."

"May we begin now?" Schlager said. "Or is this needless discussion going to go on all night?"

Bolt resisted the urge to ask Helga more questions. She leaned back in her chair and closed her eyes.

"You will go deep and deeper, Helga," the doctor said in an even tone. "Beyond the here and now, on to the other side. You will bring the messages of the spirit world back to us."

All eyes in the room focused on Helga's face. Almost instantly, she seemed to fall into a deep sleep. Not the slightest twitch of an eyelid betrayed the fact that she was even alive. Then, slowly, the corners of her mouth curved into a grin.

"Is someone there?" Schlager asked.

"We are four in number." Helga's voice when she answered was her own, but slightly deeper—huskier.

"May we know who you are?" the doctor asked.

"I am Teaujac the baker. I was among those who stormed the Bastille," Helga answered with gruff pride.

Next came a voice as distinctly feminine as Helga's own, but with an Italian accent. "Signora Sophia Costaño, a poor woman of Napoli. I lived with my ten children in a cave near the foot of Vesuvio. We had little except a lovely view of the bay and our love for one another."

Helga lapsed into silence after the first two spirits spoke.

"The others?" Schlager prompted. "Are they still there?"

The baker's voice once more issued from Helga's lips. "One is an infant. He passed over in the great flood, before he learned words to speak. The other is a holy monk from Tibet, Chin Su Singh. He still honors his vows of silence, even here. But he will sign his answers to your questions and I shall pass them along. Advise us with whom we are speaking."

Schlager quickly complied with Teaujac's wishes, identifying the four of them and their place and time. Then he added, "You are speaking through my dear friend Helga."

"And you wish answers to what questions?" the spokesman from the other side asked.

"The entity Mary Scarlett wishes to know in which direction her life should flow."

"Ask him about her aura," Bolt hissed in a loud whisper.

"Sh-h!" the doctor cautioned. "We must work up to that. First, we will get some general information."

Sophia from Napoli answered. "That truth she will find in the mirror. Only there."

Dr. Schlager turned to Mary Scarlett. "Does that make any sense to you?"

She nodded. "I'm afraid so. The only problem is, I don't know where to find the mirror. It's missing."

Bolt shot a glance at the ceiling and called out, "Where is the mirror?"

"They can't hear *you*," Schlager said, annoyed. "They will only respond to questions I put to Helga."

"Then *you* ask them where it is," Bolt demanded.

"Do you know where the entity Mary Scarlett can find this mirror?"

A long silence followed. In her own voice, Helga explained, "They are discussing the matter. It seems they all know exactly which mirror you mean, and they knew its location until very recently."

"The cupboard is bare," Helga said in Sophia's voice after a time.

"The cupboard," Mary Scarlett whispered excitedly. "This is real! They know what they're talking about."

"I'm afraid I'm rather in the dark," the doctor admitted. "What should I ask them next?"

Mary Scarlett whispered her query into Schlager's ear. He nodded. "The entity Mary Scarlett wishes to know if it is true that she will see the love of her life in the mirror."

"The mirror shows only what is true," answered another female voice—neither Helga's nor Sophia's.

"Might I ask your name?" said the doctor.

"I was christened Annie in my most recent existence." This spirit had a pronounced English accent. "My own love, Will, fashioned that mirror for me. But, alas, I lost both Will and the lovely mirror to another."

Mary Scarlett gasped. Bolt and Dr. Schlager stared at her.

"You know this woman?" Schlager asked.

"I do."

"I can back her up on that," Bolt said. "She told me the story of Annie and Will. They were early settlers right here in Savannah."

"Don't tell me you've not seen a face in my mirror, Mary Scarlett Lamar. I know better!"

"How could Annie know?" Mary Scarlett whispered to the doctor.

"There is not much they don't know, my dear."

"Admit it, Mary Scarlett," Annie's spirit persisted. "Tell us the name of the man you saw."

After a moment, Mary Scarlett whispered, "Jacques St. Julian."

"We others do not know of him." Teaujac had returned. "He must be on your side now, on the earthly plane."

"What is his name now?" Mary Scarlett held her breath as she asked.

Dr. Schlager repeated her question to Helga. Another long silence followed.

"Without the mirror, we cannot say," Annie answered.

The doctor then posed the question Bolt had been so impatient to ask. "Where can the entity Mary Scarlett find this mirror of truth?"

After a few more moments, Helga said in Teaujac's voice, "We are confused. We see the mirror, but we cannot tell you where it is at the present time. It seems to be moving with great speed from one place to another."

"Who has it?" Schlager persisted.

"No one. Many!" Sophia answered, obviously bewildered by her own reply.

In an aside to Mary Scarlett and Bolt, Schlager whispered, "This is highly unusual."

"Ask them if they can tell us *anything* about the mirror's whereabouts," Bolt insisted.

In answer, Annie said, "It is over the great sea I crossed to come to America."

"No, over the land," Teaujac corrected. A babble of different answers ensued, keeping Helga busy.

Finally, Annie came through loud and clear. "A huge bird has it."

With a sigh and a shrug, the doctor said, "This is getting us nowhere. Obviously, they can't tell us where it is."

Bolt had an idea. "That bird Annie mentioned. Could she mean an airplane? That would explain what she said about it being out over the Atlantic. It's flying, en route to another place."

The doctor's eyes lit up. "I think you've got it, Conrad!"

"Never mind the mirror for now. Ask them about the person in my aura," Mary Scarlett begged. "I have to know."

"May we move on?" Schlager asked through Helga.

All those on the other side agreed that might be a good idea.

"But if you happen to locate the mirror, do let us know," the doctor said.

"You wish to know about the spirit in the entity Mary Scarlett's aura, do you not?" Sophia said before the doctor even posed the question.

"Indeed we do!"

"There is no evil in this guardian from the other side," Sophia explained. "The woman wishes only good for the entity Mary Scarlett."

"It's Granny Boo! It has to be!"

"We can't be sure," the doctor said. "Let me ask a few more questions."

"All right, but I know it's Granny Boo."

"Has this spirit of the aura been at her post for a long time?"

"She took her place in the aura while the entity Mary Scarlett was still in the womb. She has never deserted her post."

"Then she passed over long ago?"

"In your year, 1828."

Shock registered on Mary Scarlett's face.

The doctor looked at her quizzically. "Does that date mean anything to you, Mary Scarlett?"

"Nothing," she answered. "Not a thing."

Schlager nodded sagely. "This will bear some exploring once you go back in time. We shall learn the identity of your guardian."

"Why don't you just ask them?" Bolt suggested.

When the doctor did just that, the spirit of Annie answered, "You know in your heart, Mary Scarlett. She wishes you to remember without our telling you. The truth will come, and so will the mirror."

"That damn mirror again!" Bolt muttered under his breath. "Why don't we get some information from them. Something we can use. Like what next week's winning lottery numbers will be? We could all get rich."

"Tell the entity Bolton Conrad that we heard that," Teaujac said in an angry voice. "We are not amused!"

"I do apologize for Conrad," the doctor said, casting a scathing look at Bolt.

"What must I do to learn the identity of the woman in my aura?" Mary Scarlett asked.

One after another, the spirits called through Helga, "Go back! Go back! Go back!"

"It seems they are ending our conversation," Dr. Schlager said. "Helga has gone still and silent once more."

"But they didn't tell us anything." Mary Scarlett sounded disappointed almost to the point of tears.

"I think they told us a great deal, my dear. You know the spirit Helga saw in your aura is a woman who means you no ill."

She nodded. "That's true. I was so afraid the figure was my former husband, Raul Miguel."

Dr. Schlager gave her a fatherly smile and patted her

hand. "How sad to be widowed so young. If you like, Mary Scarlett, we can try to contact him."

"No!" she cried, frantic at the thought. Then she smiled back at the doctor. "I'm not sure where Teaujac and Annie and the others are, but if that was Heaven we were talking to, I don't think we'll find Raul there."

The doctor raised a bushy eyebrow. "Oh, I see."

"One thing I do know—I *must* find that mirror!"

"If we're right about the plane, and if you're right about seeing it in the cupboard, then someone must have stolen it," Bolt said. "And whoever took it has sent it away from Savannah. No doubt to sell it."

"Oh, no!" Mary Scarlett cried. "Bolt, we have to do something. It could be lost forever."

Dr. Schlager chuckled. "I think not! You see, my dear, once it arrives at its destination, those on the other side will know where it is. Think about it—have you ever mailed a letter to some distant city and tried to guess as it was en route where it might be at any given moment? Such is their dilemma. We will contact the spirits in a few days and they will give us the answer you seek. Until then, I think we must concentrate on discovering the identity of this mystery woman who crossed over in 1828."

"But where do we start?" Mary Scarlett asked.

"At the cemetery?" Bolt suggested ironically.

"Sometimes you surprise me, Conrad. That's exactly what I was about to say."

"But there are several here in Savannah. And what if she's not buried here, but somewhere else?" Mary Scarlett looked defeated already.

"Bonaventure." It was the last word Helga spoke before she woke from her trance.

The session at Dr. Schlager's ended shortly after that. Midnight was fast approaching and they were all exhausted from the evening's work. They agreed to meet again on Friday evening.

The drive home was fast and silent.

"I wish I'd thought to ask the spirits what I can do to get rid of Raul," Mary Scarlett said as they entered Bolt's apartment.

"Hey, you know what they would have said—their answer to everything. *'You must find the mirror!'* " he intoned in a deep, ghostly voice. "They're really hung up on that thing."

"Don't make jokes, Bolt. This is serious. To me, at least."

He draped an arm around her shoulders and drew her close. "I know that, honey. I guess my problem is that I don't really believe in any of this stuff. Reincarnation, spirits, voices from the other side."

She turned and stared at him. "Bolt? If you don't believe, why on earth did you insist that I see Dr. Schlager in the first place?"

"He's a nice fellow. I knew you needed to talk to somebody and I also knew you'd never open up to a psychiatrist."

"Just coddling me, huh?"

He pulled her gently into his arms. "No. But coddling sounds like fun."

When he kissed her, Mary Scarlett was sure for the first time that he was no longer mad about finding her in the garden with Allen. As the kiss progressed, all thoughts of Allen, or any other man, fled from her mind. Bolt was here, right now, holding her, making her feel loved and needed and wanted. She wanted him, too, she realized. But could she . . . ?

"Are you too tired or would you like a nightcap, honey?"

She smiled into his eyes and nuzzled his chin. "A glass of wine would be nice. I'm too keyed up to sleep. I want to talk about what we experienced tonight."

"You're on!"

He went to the kitchen and uncorked a bottle of Madeira.

By the time he came back, Mary Scarlett had taken off her blazer and her shoes. She was stretched out on the sofa, looking absolutely her most desirable in her tight white slacks and black silk blouse, opened far enough to show a tantalizing hint of cleavage.

Bolt handed her her wine, then sat down and lifted her bare feet to his lap. She sighed deeply as he began massaging her toes.

"Ah, that's wonderful!"

"The wine?"

She smiled at him—a lazy, sleepy, sexy smile. "The wine, too."

Bolt slid the leg of her slacks up and kneaded the muscles of her calf. Mary Scarlett felt every touch of his strong fingers send warm jolts through her blood. Parts of her body that had lain dormant for months began to throb with sweet urgency.

Little by little, he slid toward her on the couch until she was practically in his lap. He moved his magic hands up her thighs, on to her hips.

"You should give up the law and go into another business, Bolt. You're good. *Real good!*"

He laughed. "I'd never make a living at this."

"I don't see why not."

Leaning closer, he brushed her lips. "Because you're the only customer I'd ever want to work on."

She tingled all over when his hand went to the top button of her shirt. A moment later, he was stroking her breasts above the tight restriction of her black lace bra.

"What was it you wanted to talk about, honey?"

Head thrown back, eyes closed, Mary Scarlett whispered, "I forget."

Another button. Another tingle.

"You should have married me," he whispered, tracing the edge of the black lace and smiling when he saw her tremble at his touch.

"I know. But if we were old married folks, we'd probably be sleeping in twin beds by now and you'd be fast asleep, snoring, and keeping me awake."

"I don't snore!"

"Maybe not. But if we weren't in bed already—separate beds—you'd be watching a Braves game while I knitted."

"I didn't know you could knit."

"I can't. But I'd have to take it up so I'd have something to do every night while you watched the games and ignored me."

He certainly wasn't ignoring her at the moment. Now all the buttons were undone and Bolt was drawing a design on her flat midriff with one teasing finger. Finishing that tantalizing game, he moved his hand back to stroke the black lace.

He leaned down and kissed the soft, deep valley between her breasts. Mary Scarlett caught her breath.

"Do you know what you're doing to me?" she murmured.

"Good things, I hope."

"*Too* good!"

He stared into her eyes, unsmiling. "Nothing's too good for you, Mary Scarlett."

"You are," she murmured.

She couldn't imagine what she'd said that struck a nerve, but Bolt pulled back. He sat on the sofa, head drooping, staring down at his hands, now at rest.

"Mary Scarlett, there's a lot you don't know about me."

"Nothing that really matters, Bolt. Why, I've known you forever."

"No, you haven't. And that's what scares me. You're going to find out things about me if we go through this dual hypnosis. Things that I'm afraid you won't like. This could be the end of us—*period!*"

She leaned forward and stroked his cheek. "Bolt, you know that's not so. Besides, remember what Helga and Dr. Schlager said? They think we belong together and have shared many lives in the past. So you just stop that talk. Come back here!"

She shrugged out of her silk shirt and pulled him toward her until his cheek rested against her breasts. His warm breath felt wonderful through the thin lace.

A moment later, the lace vanished. In one deft motion, Bolt unsnapped the center clasp and the little bra fell away. Now he was kissing hot bare flesh, cooling it with his tongue, squeezing it in his hands. Mary Scarlett felt as if she were floating somewhere above the couch.

Raul appeared momentarily to stand over them, scowling. Bolt's loving attention banished him as quickly as he had appeared. Mary Scarlett forgot all about her brutal Spaniard. All she could think about was how wonderful Bolt's body felt next to hers.

Before she realized what was happening, they were naked, in each other's arms, their bodies kissing from lips to toes. Sometime during that long, lazy kiss, he entered her, filling her with a heat and a power like none she had ever known. Slowly, gently, he urged her to join his rhythm. Soon they were moving together, taking off for a heavenly flight.

All the while, they kept their eyes open, staring in wonder at what was happening between them. Mary Scarlett watched Bolt's eyes grow darker as the pleasure grew. She could see the reflection of her own face there—lips smiling, nostrils flared. It was like looking into a mirror that softened and complemented her image.

Bolt leaned down, blocking the sight as he covered her lips with his. His kiss was hard and deep and hot—the final thrust to send her spiraling off into space. She clung tightly to him, trying to make the feeling last forever. He arched hard against her and cried out her name.

Then no one moved. They lay together, wondering if this had finally happened, after so many years of longing for it, dreaming of it.

After a long time, Bolt kissed her softly, then whispered, "No Raul?"

Mary Scarlett smiled up at him and brushed the damp hair off his forehead. "He wouldn't dare intrude on such a moment. You scared him away, Bolt. I think you may have chased him off forever."

"Good riddance," he answered.

Neither of them spoke again for a long time. They were content to lie together, kissing softly, touching, caressing.

"Mary Scarlett?" Bolt said at length. "Do I need to say I love you?"

"Always," she whispered dreamily.

She touched his lips with her fingertips. After what had happened between them tonight, the words seemed superfluous, but she still loved hearing them. She closed her eyes, still smiling, and drifted off to sleep.

It was much later when she woke. Bolt had covered her with a patchwork throw and gone to his bed. She dragged herself up, feeling her muscles ache wonderfully, and went to her own bed. For a time, she lay there in the darkness, wondering what would happen now. There were so many decisions still to be made, so many problems to be worked out. But Bolt had solved some of them tonight. He had banished the ghost of Raul. Maybe Dr. Schlager could put the rest of her house in order.

Finally, when she couldn't keep her eyes open any longer, she drifted off. She slept deeply the rest of the night, without her usual nightmares.

Twelve

To Mary Scarlett, Bonaventure seemed exactly the same as it had been that long-ago afternoon when her family had gathered under the moss-weeping oaks to say goodbye to Granny Boo. But in reality everything was changed. For the first time, she would be visiting her mother's grave, and returning to visit Granny Boo. This was now her family's real home. Mary Scarlett had changed, too. No longer an innocent young woman, she was a life-scarred widow, searching the past for a clue to her future.

Just outside the cemetery gate they had come upon an enterprising vendor selling bouquets and wreaths. Bolt had stopped the car, sensing Mary Scarlett's need to bring flowers to decorate the graves of her relatives. As they drove through the gate, she clutched two newspaper-wrapped sprays of carnations—white for her mother, red for Granny Boo.

Neither of them had spoken of the night before. It seemed almost like a dream by the light of day, far removed from this visit with the dead.

"Park here by the gate, Bolt. I'd like to walk to the plot."

"Are you sure? It's mighty hot this morning."

"Please," she said softly.

He pulled in and cut off the engine. They both sat in silence for a moment, staring out toward the river through the oaks and azaleas, dotted with monuments that created the illusion of an ancient city in all its springtime glory.

"It's so peaceful here," Mary Scarlett whispered. "This place must surely be a comfort after all the chaos of life."

Bolt made no comment, even though her remark troubled him deeply. He didn't like to hear Mary Scarlett voicing such morbid thoughts.

"Ready?" he asked.

She nodded. A minute later they were walking along the road that had once led to the magnificent Tattnall mansion. Mary Scarlett's thoughts wandered back to the party the night the house burned. Had Granny Boo actually brought her here or had she only dreamed it?

"I wish you could have seen the old plantation, Bolt. It was quite a showplace, palatial and elegant, constructed of the finest English brick. Every room was like a museum of European treasures. Now it's gone, all gone."

She seemed to be off in a world of her own. Bolt felt left out. He needed her back here with him, in the present.

"There's an old piece of the foundation," he said, hoping to snap her out of it.

Mary Scarlett leaned down to place her hand on the crumbling block of tabby, all covered with vines that were eroding it even more. She looked up at Bolt, a melancholy smile on her face. "Yes. This was definitely part of the house. I can still feel the vibrations of the past when I touch it."

Bolt placed his palm next to hers. He felt nothing except the sharp edges of broken oyster shells and the subtle heat from Mary Scarlett's flesh. He inched his fingers closer until his hand covered hers. For a moment, their eyes met and visions of the previous night flashed through their minds. Then she stood straight and looked away.

"Well?" He glanced around, trying to orient himself in the confusing maze of footpaths and roads. "Which way first?"

Mary Scarlett's answer shocked him. "I'd really like to see the Conrad plot, Bolt. You know my whole family's darkest secrets, but you've never told me anything about your ancestors."

His collar felt too tight suddenly. There was a good reason he'd never discussed his ancestors with Mary Scarlett or any of their friends. He wasn't sure who they all were. He did know that if they had ever visited any of Mary Scarlett's forebears, his people had gone to the back door, not the front. It was a sign of prestige to be buried at Bonaventure. Not one of his relatives had enough status to be laid to rest in this lush garden of the dead. Then he remembered something and grinned at her.

"I had a great-uncle who was put in the Stranger's Tomb for nearly a year."

Mary Scarlett's eyes lit with interest. She turned to look back at the large marble mausoleum near the gate. William Gaston died on a trip north and had to be buried far away from his beloved Savannah. To honor his memory, his family built the vault back in the 1800s, providing a tomb where visitors to Savannah who came to death unexpectedly might have a place to rest until their remains could be returned to their homes. So William Gaston, famous for his hospitality in life, continued to entertain guests after his death.

"I've never known anyone who was entombed there. Tell me about this great uncle of yours, Bolt."

"There's not a lot to tell. My grandfather's brother was a sailor on a whaling ship out of Nantucket. After an especially long and profitable voyage, he came home to Savannah for a visit with his kin and died unexpectedly, so the story goes, from drinking rot-gut whiskey. A rather ignoble end, but some of the Gastons saw him as a romantic figure since he had sailed all over the world in pursuit of whales. I guess it was something of a philanthropic gesture to put the old boy up. You know, give the poor bloke a place to rest his bones for a time. There was another story passed down in the family, but I've never believed it."

"Tell me!" Mary Scarlett begged.

He shook his head and laughed nervously. "It's just bunk. You know how people here in Savannah talk."

"Please, Bolt!"

"Well, my daddy used to say that one of the Gaston ladies took a shine to Uncle Delbert. I find that hard to swallow, considering the fact that while the Gastons were socially prominent, my great-uncle's favorite hangouts were dockside bars and his favorite ladies strolled River Street after dark. The tale was always a big hit in the family, though."

"I think it's a wonderful story."

They walked on, Mary Scarlett's desire to see the nonexistent Conrad family plot diverted for the time being, to Bolt's vast relief.

"Granny Boo is just over there," she said, pointing to a vast enclosure that held the remains of a variety of her far-reaching family ties.

"Look at this," Bolt said. "What a pretty child!"

He was standing at an enclosure dominated by the pure white marble likeness of a girl of six or seven. Staring straight ahead, the child had bangs and soft curls draped over her shoulders and was dressed in Victorian style—all smocked and tucked and ruffled. She sat with her neatly buttoned hightop boots crossed at the ankles, her right hand curled in her lap while her left rested on a broken column, the symbol of a life cut off in its prime. At the base of the monument, a dime-store-variety papier-maché bunny peeked out of the pot of ivy, its leathery green leaves dotted with bright plastic flowers left by visitors who had never met the long-dead child. Most unusual of all, the little girl wore strings of colored beads about her neck and a blue satin ribbon tied round her stone hair. A rag doll lay in her lap along with smaller toys and a whole piggy bank's worth of coins.

"Why, it's little Gracie!" Mary Scarlett cried with delight. "I'd forgotten she was here. Mama always used to bring me to visit her grave when we came to tend the family plot."

"Was Gracie one of your relatives?"

Mary Scarlett walked to the stone image and stroked her hair as she might greet a real child. "Gracie's sort of a part of everybody's family. Everyone in Savannah loved her during her short life. And everyone has loved her since as well. I wish I'd remembered to bring her a gift."

"I don't think she'll miss it from the looks of all her pretties." Bolt fingered the long strand of pink beads around the statue's neck.

"When I was little," Mary Scarlett said, "I used to spend hours searching through my favorite possessions before coming out to Bonaventure, trying to decide what I'd give Gracie. Every Easter I'd bring her a colored egg from my basket. At Halloween she'd get candy corn. And Christmas was the best time of all, so I'd choose something special from my stocking."

"What happened to her?" Bolt asked.

"She died suddenly—one of those childhood things like whooping cough or measles. Her father was the manager of the old Pulaski Hotel. Gracie used to meet all the guests and welcome them. Then one morning the hotel guests came down to breakfast to learn that she had died during the night. It must have been a terrible blow to everyone who knew her."

Bolt spun the tiny wheels on a shiny new Matchbox car, one of Gracie's many treasures. "What happens to all this stuff? It must pile up here after a while."

"I believe the toys are collected periodically and distributed to needy children." She dug into her purse and fished out two quarters and a bright copper penny. She placed the coins in Gracie's lap in the curve of her fingers. Two carnations—one red, one white—went into the pot of ivy. "I'm sorry, little friend," she whispered. "This is all I have for you today."

Bolt noted that the pile of coins in the statue's lap probably added up to three or four dollars. "What about the money? Anybody could just steal it."

Mary Scarlett flashed him an arch look. "Could *you* steal Gracie's money?"

"No, but somebody might."

"Anyone who needs it is welcome to it. That's part of the mystique surrounding Gracie. She gave of herself when she was alive. She's still giving. The poor of Savannah all know her, and know that if they're hungry, they can count on Gracie for enough change for a sandwich and a cup of coffee."

Bolt was smiling now. He caressed the child's shoulder. "Savannah has some nice traditions."

"And some nice people," Mary Scarlett added, slipping her arm through his.

They said goodbye to Gracie and wandered down the aisles of pink and white azaleas. Some of the ancient bushes grew as high as Bolt's head, while Spanish moss drifted down from low-hanging oak limbs to brush against his face. They approached a wrought-iron spear fence, identical to the one that surrounded the house on Bull Street. An arch at the entrance proclaimed the name "LAMAR" in fancifully scrolled letters entwined with metal leaves and lilies. Beyond the fence and gate stretched an eclectic collection of stone angels, table tombs, obelisks, crosses, lambs, and one Gothic mausoleum stained dark with age.

Bolt glanced at the dates on the earliest graves. A number of them predated 1869, the year Bonaventure Plantation became Bonaventure Cemetery. Before that date, Mary Scarlett's people had been buried at the Colonial Cemetery in Savannah proper. Many of the graves had been removed to this quieter and more idyllic setting.

Mary Scarlett seemed oblivious to the graves of her ancestors as she hurried to a newer section of more modern and more subtle markers. There, off to the right, facing the river, stood the stones of her mother and great-grandmother, side by side. Bolt noted that Lucy Lamar's stone was twice the width of Granny Boo's. On the left half of Miss Lucy's stone, he read the inscription: "RICHARD HABERSHAM LAMAR, Born December 20, 1938." A blank space next to his birthdate awaited the unknown date of his death, just as the empty earth beside his wife awaited the discovery and burial of his remains. Not a likely possibility since he had been missing these past six years.

Mary Scarlett knelt before the two graves, said a silent prayer, then placed the flowers in the two brass vases. She knew they had remained empty until now unless some kind stranger had passed this way and, noticing the sad and lonely tombs, had offered gifts even as strangers bestowed presents on little Gracie.

She remained where she was for some time, pulling dandelions and patches of chickweed from the graves.

"Do you want me to scout around and see if I see any tombstones with 1828 on them?" Bolt's question was a gentle reminder that they were really here on other business.

Mary Scarlett kept at her work. "I know where to find her grave."

"You do? How?"

"It stands to reason that she's buried with or near the Tattnalls. They're all together over there." She motioned with the dandelion she had just pulled and its ballerina-like seeds drifted on the breeze toward the original Tattnall burying ground, the very place where Jacques St. Julian had kissed a pretty maiden long ago.

"What if there's more than one grave with that date?"

Mary Scarlett rose and dusted off her slacks. "I think I'll know when I find her."

"How?"

She smiled and shook her head. "That I can't tell you. I just feel like I'll know."

Bolt offered his hand. They strolled at a leisurely pace, following the flight of the dandelion seeds.

Inside a stone coping, surrounded by towering Indian azaleas that burned like fuschia flame in the sun, they found the Tattnall plot. Mary Scarlett and Bolt moved cautiously among the gracefully weathered monuments, searching for the right date. All the clan were gathered there. *For one final party,* Mary Scarlett mused. *An eternal family reunion. Sleeping silently, side by side.*

"Harriette Fenwick, wife of Commodore Josiah Tattnall, Jr.," Mary Scarlett read aloud. The Commodore himself lay next to his wife. His stone was engraved "US & CSN," a man who had served on both sides.

"Look here," Bolt said. "The Commodore died in 1871. His wife remarried—a fellow named Edward Fenwick Neufville. I'll bet they were cousins. She outlived the Commodore by thirty-three years. Wonder why they called him 'Commodore'?"

"Probably because he served in the Confederate Navy. Bolt, you're not sticking to business. It's a woman's grave we're searching for."

"Well, that woman could be Harriette, couldn't she?"

"No. Look at the dates. You said yourself that she outlived her husband. See, she died in 1904. Wrong century." Mary Scarlett paused with her fingers still touching the cool stone. "You know what? We may be getting close. I believe the Commodore must have been the son of the master of Bonaventure Plantation."

"He'd be Josiah Tattnall, Sr."

"Yes! And here he is." She read from the stone excitedly, " 'Josiah Tattnall, Esq., who after having enjoyed the highest honours of the state, died at the age of 38, in 1803, an honest man, rich in the estimation of all who knew him.' "

"His wife's right here. She died December 3, 1802, at the age of thirty-three. Folks sure didn't have much time to live their lives back then."

"They didn't have modern medicine," Mary Scarlett replied. "It can cure almost anything except old age."

"Here's another Josiah," Bolt said, still grave-browsing. "He was born in 1794, the year before the Commodore. Poor little fellow. He only lived a few months."

"They lost more than one child," Mary Scarlett said softly. "Mary Mullryne Tattnall died at age eight that same year. They lost Sally at six months and Charlotte at a year. It seems only Josiah survived to adulthood."

"What about this one—Claudia Tattnall? She lived to be seventeen."

"I don't think she's one of the children, Bolt. Look at the dates. Claudia was born when Josiah Sr. was only fourteen himself. I'll bet she was his younger sister."

"Could she be the woman in your aura?"

"No. She died too early, 1806."

Then Mary Scarlett spied it—an urn finial mounted on a dark pyramid atop a columned base. Without a word, she moved swiftly toward the striking monument, which was set a short distance away from the others in the plot. She stroked the age-pocked pyramid with trembling fingertips. When she read the inscription, she knew for sure that this was the figure in her aura, the woman who had fallen instantly and forever in love with Jacques St. Julian. Her name was Louise Manigault Robillard Fenwick.

Her epitaph—in beautifully engraved script—brought tears to Mary Scarlett's eyes.

Fair Stranger
whose feet have wandered
to this land of silence
Contemplate this Stone.
Near it is interred Dust
which once a lovely Form
inhabited by a Mind,
Superior in Intelligence,
worth and Amiableness,
to most of her sex,
as a Daughter, Sister & Friend,
as a Wife and Mother,
few whom she left behind
can boast
so bright an example.

"Bolt," she whispered. "I've found her."

He moved to Mary Scarlett's side, took her hand, and quickly scanned the words on the tablet. "Beautiful words, but who was she?"

"Granny Boo was her great-granddaughter. Remember the party here at Bonaventure, the night the mansion burned?"

"I remember what you told me about your dream."

Fully aware of his skepticism, she said, *"When I was here,* she and I were one. I know how much she loved Jacques St. Julian because I fell in love with him that night, too. Granny Boo told me she married someone else, but I assumed it must have been an empty, unhappy marriage. I figured she must have just made the best of the rest of her life. She wasn't like that, though. She was much stronger than I am. From the epitaph, I'd say she went on to marry, raise a family, and live an exemplary life."

Bolt said something then, but Mary Scarlett's thoughts were elsewhere. The two women had lived over a century apart and their losses had come in different ways. Mary Scarlett wondered how this young woman had reacted to Jacques St. Julian's death. Surely she had been heartbroken, but she had picked up the pieces and gone on with her life. Mary Scarlett, on the other hand, had allowed herself to stagnate. It was time she made some decisions, found some direction in her life.

She looked up at Bolt through a mist of tears, but they were happy tears, determined tears. "I'm ready to go now," she said. "I want to see Dr. Schlager. Right away! I think I understand everything now."

"You do? Well, I wish you'd explain it all to me."

"There's no time for that, Bolt. You'll know everything before long. Let's get going."

* * *

Mary Scarlett called Dr. Schlager from Bolt's car phone. The hypnotherapist didn't seem surprised in the least to hear from her.

"I have been expecting your call. Helga sensed earlier that something was happening in your life and that a great transition was in the offing."

"Can you see us right now?"

"Certainly. Come immediately."

Bolt reached over and touched Mary Scarlett's arm to get her attention. He frowned and shook his head. "Not *us*," he said. "I have an appointment with a new client—R.A. Tollison from Sea Island."

Mary Scarlett gave him a disappointed, pleading look.

"I'm sorry," he said, "but I can't cancel it. He's an important man and his message sounded urgent. Won't this evening do just as well?"

"No," she said. "This can't wait."

On the other end of the line, the doctor had overheard their discussion. "Mary Scarlett, come without Bolton. I have a feeling his presence will not be needed for this session."

She hesitated, nervous about going alone, but her need was too strong to wait. "Fine," she answered.

Bolt leaned over and said into the phone, "I'll have her on your doorstep in half an hour. You treat her nice, now. I'm going to get a full report later this afternoon."

They both heard Schlager's deep chuckle through the phone. "I will be waiting, Mary Scarlett."

"What's going on, honey?" Bolt asked when she replaced the phone. "Why all the rush?"

"I'm not sure, Bolt. I do know, though, that I've been spinning my wheels for far too long. I've accomplished nothing, wasted a good bit of my life. I got such a powerful feeling when I touched that stone. It was almost as if she was trying to speak to me. If I'm ever going to make contact, now is the time. There are so many questions I need to ask her, so many things to understand about our relationship. And most important of all, I need to know more about Jacques St. Julian. If he's here, alive right now on this planet, then I mean to find him."

The car phone rang as they cruised back into heavy traffic along Victory Drive. Bolt picked it up, still concentrating on his driving. Mary Scarlett noted both the frown on his face and the slight tone of displeasure in his voice.

"She's right here, Allen. No, we haven't been hiding out from you."

Mary Scarlett rolled her eyes as she took the phone. She didn't want to talk to anyone right now, least of all Allen Overman.

After preliminary greetings, Allen expressed his concern for her and said he had hated leaving her to face Bolton's wrath alone.

"There was no problem, Allen. We've just been real busy the past couple of days, that's all. I know I should have called and thanked you again for the party. No, please don't plan another one for this coming weekend. I'm going to be moving."

Bolt grinned when Mary Scarlett preempted Allen's plans for more trysts in his garden, but frowned when she mentioned moving.

She assured Allen one last time that all was well, promised that they'd have lunch sometime soon, then clicked off.

"Moving?" Bolt demanded without preamble.

"Yes. I was going to tell you."

"But instead you told Allen. I thought after last night things had changed."

Mary Scarlett felt her face flush with pleasure and a bit of embarrassment. Last night was not a topic easily discussed in broad daylight while cruising beneath the tall palms of Victory Drive.

"It's time, Bolt. You need your space and I need mine.

You were a true friend to take me in and put up with me this long."

"True friend?" he muttered. "I figured our friendship was a given. I thought last night had brought at least a subtle change in our relationship."

Mary Scarlett slipped her arm through his and leaned her head on his shoulder. "Bolt, you're a dear, and, yes, last night changed everything. What happened between us was precious, too special to be discussed just yet. Give me some time, won't you? Let me sort out my feelings before I have to talk about them openly. I think my visit with Dr. Schlager today will make it easier to . . ."

When her words trailed off, Bolt glanced down at her, his dark eyes smoldering. "To *what?* To decide whether last night meant anything or if it was just a one-night stand?"

"Hey, I don't think you want to go there, Bolt," she warned. "Just let it lie for now. We'll talk this evening."

His expression softened. "Promise?"

She nodded. How could she tell him she hoped to discover the identity of her own true love before this evening? Bolt simply wouldn't understand, especially after last night. How could she have let her emotions and desires run away with her? And how could she have stopped what happened?

Glancing over at his strong, handsome profile, she smiled. Silly question! Who wouldn't have gotten carried away under the circumstances, with this man who knew all the right things to say, all the tenderest spots to touch . . . to kiss? By the time they pulled up in front of Dr. Schlager's, she was squirming in her seat from reliving her memories of the night before. It was a good thing Bolt had an appointment that he couldn't break. Otherwise, she might have canceled her session with Schlager and suggested they go to Bolt's apartment.

She leaned over and kissed him solidly before she got out of the car. Her actions clearly surprised him, but he joined in with enthusiasm.

"Will it keep till tonight, Bolt?"

"After *that?* I don't know."

Before he could say any more, Mary Scarlett was out of the car and on her way to the front door. She turned and waved as Bolt drove off.

She followed the fiery blaze of the CRX as it melted away down the street into the vibrant spring green of the landscape. Some of her confidence vanished with him. She stood at the door for several minutes before she could gather the courage to knock. The moment she did, Helga's calm, smiling face chased all doubts from her mind.

"Good afternoon, Mary Scarlett. Do come in."

"I hope I'm not inconveniencing Dr. Schlager."

"Not at all. I had told him to expect your call." She focused her gaze above Mary Scarlett's forehead. "Your aura is absolutely brilliant. One needs sunglasses to look at you."

"Is *she* still there?"

Helga nodded.

Mary Scarlett could hardly wait to share her discovery with Dr. Schlager. Sensing her eagerness, Helga ushered her to his library immediately.

When they entered the room, the doctor was leaning over his desk, a magnifying glass in his hand as he studied what looked to be a large map. He glanced up and smiled when he heard them come in.

"Ah, good! You have come, Mary Scarlet. And what news do you bring?"

She gave him a quizzical look. "How did you know I'd have news?"

He and Helga exchanged knowing glances. "Simply a speculation, my dear. But, tell me, did you go to Bonaventure?"

"Yes, we did." She eased into a chair near the desk and leaned toward the doctor. "We had just left there when I called you. I knew I had to see you right away."

"I am glad you called."

Once more Helga brought tea before she joined them. "Her aura is perfectly glorious this afternoon, Manfred. I believe she learned something vital."

"Yes!" Mary Scarlett exclaimed. "Maybe the most important thing I've ever learned in all my life."

Dr. Schlager arched an eyebrow. "Indeed!"

She was about to rush ahead, telling him all about the Tattnalls and the party and Louise Manigault Robillard Fenwick, but he held up his hands to silence her.

"Let us search out all the details of your experience," he suggested. "If you are ready to submit to hypnosis, we can learn much more than what you remember. The subconscious retains infinite details that the senses pass over or forget."

Mary Scarlett glanced toward the door to the other room. "You mean *now?* Without Bolt?"

The doctor nodded. "I told you he would not be needed today. Well, Mary Scarlett? Are you willing? I truly believe this to be the perfect time."

"With your aura so bright, there could be no better time," Helga urged.

"All right," Mary Scarlett agreed, feeling her palms grow sweaty even as she said the words.

"Good!" said the doctor, rising from his desk. "If you will help to ready her, Helga?"

"Of course, Manfred. Give us only a moment, please."

Mary Scarlett's heart was thundering. Her legs felt shaky as she followed Helga through the door. Lying down on the couch came as a blessed relief.

"Make yourself comfortable," Helga said in a soothing voice. "I will cover you with the blanket. Close your eyes for a few seconds and take a deep breath. Then focus your gaze on the prisms of the chandelier. When the doctor arrives you will feel calm and prepared."

Mary Scarlett did as Helga instructed. Her suggestions helped. She felt herself relax. Her heartbeat slowed to its normal rate.

"Thank you, Helga," Schlager whispered when he entered the room. "I see that she is ready." Then he turned his full attention to Mary Scarlett. "You are feeling well, my dear?"

"Yes," she answered, drowsy already.

"You are studying my lovely chandelier, I see. A precious antique which I brought from my homeland. Notice how each crystal is perfectly formed to catch the light. See the colors, like a rainbow dancing before your eyes. Let your spirit soak up the colors. Let them flow through you. You are growing sleepy. Soon, it will be impossible to keep your eyes open. When they close, you will continue to see the beautiful colors. You will drift with them, dance with them, float in time like a leaf upon a river."

Mary Scarlett felt as if she were weightless, drifting up and up until she became a part of the colors and the light. All anxiety, all tenseness fell away. She felt free to roam as her spirit moved her.

"Can you hear me, Mary Scarlett?" Dr. Schlager's voice came to her from far away.

"Yes."

"Do you know who I am?"

"Dr. Manfred Schlager."

"Do you trust me?"

"Yes."

"Do you wish to tell me about Bonaventure Cemetery?"

"Yes. I was there. Before today. Before eight years ago when we went to bury Granny Boo. I went there long ago." The voice was Mary Scarlett's, yet she had an unusual accent. European, decidedly, but with hints of both French and English.

"And when was that? Can you give me a date?"

"The month 'twas November," she said dreamily. "In the first year of the glorious new century."

"Which century? Tell me the year, please."

She laughed giddily, flirting like a young girl. "Guess, if you can. John Adams is our new president since our dear and illustrious George Washington passed on last December. Did you know he visited Savannah once?"

"I'm afraid I am poor at guessing games, my dear. The date, please."

"Why, 1800, of course."

"Who was there with you at the party?"

She laughed again as if remembering that night brought her great pleasure. *"Everyone!* See how the boat torches light up the river like a ribbon of fire? They are coming to Bonaventure from Savannah and from all the great plantations up and down the coast. Hear the voices of the slave boatmen? They ring through the soft night air. Oh, it is going to be a grand evening! I might even fall in love."

Dr. Schlager and Helga glanced at each other. She made a brief note on her pad. "She is no longer remembering," he whispered to his assistant. "She is *there."*

"Your name, dear lady?" he asked Mary Scarlett.

"I am Mademoiselle Louise Manigault Robillard, a distant cousin of Josiah Tattnall, the master of Bonaventure."

"Where is your home?"

"Savannah now, but I was born in Paris, my father's home, while my parents were on holiday."

"And your connection to the Tattnalls?"

She pondered a moment before she answered. "Vague, yet valid. Third cousins twice removed or such."

"Tell me more about the party, please."

"There is a handsome young man here," she whispered. "He has danced with none other all evening. When the house caught fire, I thought to myself that it must be his passionate nature which struck the fatal spark. He is from New Orleans—as beautiful as a prince, tall, devilishly dark of hair and eye, but soft of voice and nature. His name is Jacques St. Julian and I believe I will marry him."

"Has he asked you?"

"The evening is still young."

"Will you accept if he asks?"

"Most certainly! Even now he owns my heart."

"Where exactly are you at this moment, Mademoiselle Robillard?"

"We have left the others," she whispered, as if not wishing Jacques to hear her private conversation with the doctor. "He is leading me toward the old burying ground. It is dark and silent here, although we can hear the shatter of crystal as the other guests drink toasts to the ruined house, then dash their goblets against the oaks."

Suddenly, Mary Scarlett seemed to drift deeper still under Dr. Schlager's spell. Or was it the spell of Jacques St. Julian?

"I should not allow you to be so bold," she purred. "No man has ever held me in his arms this way."

She paused, breathing heavily, making soft sounds that hinted at intimacy and desire.

"Mademoiselle? What is happening?" the doctor asked.

"Jacques," she answered breathlessly. "His arms are around me. He is embracing me most tenderly. I both fear and hope that he might kiss me."

"Why should you fear his kiss?" Schlager asked.

"I have never been kissed by a man. Perhaps I will swoon."

"Oh! Oh!" The two sharp little cries were followed by an extended silence. Mary Scarlett writhed on the couch, but she was smiling.

"Please tell me what is happening?" Schlager demanded.

"He did it!" She touched her smiling lips with her fingertips. "I have *truly* been kissed. But how can I explain the feeling to you? It was as if fire raced through my blood. My head felt light. My heart pounded. My slippers no longer touched the ground. I will never be the same. *Never!* Jacques is my soul, my life!"

"What now?" Schlager asked excitedly.

"He has asked my forgiveness for his boldness." She gasped. *"He loves me.* He told me so. He wishes my hand in marriage. Oh, I may die of happiness! 'Yes, my darling

Jacques, yes! We will be married as soon as you return to Savannah.' "

Suddenly, the smile faded from Mary Scarlett's lips. She twisted on the couch, seemingly in pain. When she opened her mouth, a keening sound—awful in its anguish—filled the room. She began tearing at her hair and her clothes, beating her breasts, screaming.

Helga was out of her chair, trying to restrain her. "Quickly, Manfred, do something!"

He leaned close, trying to make himself heard through her screams. "Mary Scarlett, listen to me. I will count now. When I reach *three,* you will awake refreshed and happy, removed from what you have just experienced. But you will remember it all."

"No!" she screamed. "No, I can't live! Not without him. Jacques . . ."

"Manfred!" Helga was holding Mary Scarlett down, but it took all her strength. "Bring her out of it!"

"I am trying. *Mary Scarlett Lamar. Mademoiselle Robillard is gone! Do you understand? Gone! You must return now.*"

Still, she seemed not to hear as he counted quickly, "One! Two! Three!"

Thirteen

"No, no, no!"

Mary Scarlett couldn't hear Dr. Schlager's counting or Helga's frantic pleas. Gray mists wrapped her and cruel lightning flashed about her. Under hypnosis, Mary Scarlett had slipped away to some dark, unknown region—a place she had never visited even in her blackest nightmares.

The howling wind died. The clouds parted. She stopped thrashing on the couch. Still she refused to respond to the doctor's voice. She remained hypnotized, wandering in a world where she had existed long ago.

Before anything came clear to her, she sensed the ooze of primordial soup inhabited only by lurking carnivores. She heard the groan of great, black trees as a storm wind whipped their heavy limbs. She felt the moist air of a wide river that seemed to stretch on forever, bringing scents from all over the world.

Suddenly, light suffused her mind, turning the evil swamp bright with green velvet duckweed and swooping white birds. The great oaks and cypresses looked like ancient wise men, all bearded with moss. And the river—what a marvelous river! The Mississippi, flowing in all its glory, bringing ships down from Vicksburg, St. Louis, and Memphis. A never-ending circus parade of colorful sails.

And then she was part of the scene, strolling along Charters Street on the arm of a handsome gentleman. She wore a lovely blue satin gown with a matching velvet coat and plumed bonnet. Nothing seemed the least bit odd or out of place about her world. Not her old-fashioned costume or the horse-drawn carriages in the street or the sight of the city as it had appeared over a century before Mary Scarlett's time.

"Is it not fortunate that I have cousins in New Orleans, Jacques, and that they invited me to come for the holidays?" she asked.

As they promenaded down the street, the old city bustled around them, a magical carnival of color and a babble of languages, from French to Spanish to Creole *patois.*

He smiled down into her glowing face. "More than fortunate, I'd say. I think Fate brought you here. What surprises me most is that your Maman and Papa allowed you to travel so far with only one servant and your old auntie as chaperone."

She squeezed his arm gently. "They trust me."

His dark eyes smoldered when he looked down into hers. "Ah, but can *you* trust *me?*"

She trilled a gay laugh, trying to cover the wild fluttering of her heart brought on by his teasing words.

They soon arrived at their destination, a new town house owned by two of Jacques' married friends, Adelaide and Demonde Beauchamps.

Louise felt a twinge when the beautiful and uninhibited Adelaide threw her arms around Jacques and kissed him soundly before he even had an opportunity to introduce Lou to their hostess.

"Watch her, Jacques," Demonde said with a twinkle in his dark Creole eyes, "or she'll do something truly outrageous and I'll be forced to invite you to the duelling oaks."

Jacques laughed heartily and clapped his host on the back. "You know I'm too much of a scoundrel and far too poor a shot to accept any such invitation. How are you, you old barnacle?"

"Home from the sea for good, thanks to Adelaide's gentle persuasion."

"Ha!" she laughed in most unladylike fashion. "There was nothing gentle about it. I told him simply, 'Marry me and stay on dry land or forget it. I'll marry Jacques!' "

"Ah, my loss, dear lady." He bowed over her hand and kissed it. "However, I'm afraid your threat to Demonde was a ruse. You see, my heart is spoken for. Allow me to present my fiancee, Mademoiselle Louise Manigault Robillard of Savannah."

"Enchanté, mademoiselle," said Demonde. He kissed her hand and, looking up, gave her a sly wink. "Are you sure this *gentleman* has told you *everything* about himself, my dear? I have known him for years and can tell you in all truth that he is no better than a snake oil salesman."

"Do not listen to him, Louise," said Adelaide. "He is only jealous that Jacques has won you when he himself never had the chance. Now that Demonde has finally given up his freedom for marriage, it pains my darling husband that he must confine himself to only one woman. Were the choice his, he would keep a harem."

Shocked by this bold talk, Lou forced a smile, then allowed herself a small titter behind her fan while the other three laughed uproariously.

"You must forgive my wife," Demonde apologized. "You see, she and Jacques were children together—undoubtedly, very naughty children. They revert to their former mischievous selves whenever they see each other. Now do come to the parlor and let's all sit and catch up. How ever did you convince Jacques to settle down? I was the last, save he, among our crowd to give in to marriage."

"And not without a fight," Adelaide said loudly and laughed again.

Demonde, taller than Jacques, and slender as a reed, leaned down to whisper to Lou, "She chased me until I caught her. I only pretended to love the sea. While on board, *mal de mer* was my constant companion. I considered marriage to Adelaide the lesser of the two evils."

"I heard that!" his wife called again. "You *must* stop your lies, Demonde. What will Jacques' young lady think of us?"

Jacques answered for his friend. "She will think exactly what I think—that you are the two most amusing people in all New Orleans, perhaps in all the world. You know how to enjoy yourselves." Casting a mournful gaze toward Demonde, he added, "Even if you *are* married."

Once they were seated and Demonde was passing around thimble-sized goblets of sherry, Adelaide said in a whisper, "Marriage, my dears, is only the start of all the fun. The life of an innocent virgin is, alas, so *boring!*"

Lou felt her face go scarlet. She dared not look at Jacques. Instead, she sipped her sherry and kept her eyes downcast.

"Adelaide, really!" Demonde said in a sharp whisper.

"Well, you are hardly a child, are you, Lou?" She was on the very verge of saying, "Or a virgin either, I'll wager, if you've known Jacques for long." But Demonde cut her off in the nick of time.

"The others will be arriving soon. Is everything ready, Adelaide?"

She nodded, obviously miffed at being interrupted. "Of course! That's what we have servants for, dear."

They were saved from further exposure to Adelaide's outrageous opinions by the arrival of the other guests. Lou had never seen such a gathering of handsome young people—all with dark hair, flashing eyes, and possessed of cutting wit to match that of their hostess. Most were the newly married sons and daughters of planters—wealthy and exuberant. A few in the group were still single, brothers and sisters who had accompanied their married siblings.

During the afternoon call, every gay blade in the group cast his gaze longingly in Lou's direction, but she had eyes only for Jacques. Over *petit fours* and *café brûlot* the young people exchanged gossip, talked about the latest fashions, and discussed the merits of the new soprano at the Opera. Lou smiled and made small talk, as she had learned to do so well in Savannah, but again and again her gaze drifted longingly to Jacques. It seemed every eligible female in the city had her cap set for him, and Adelaide's words about boring virgins continued to haunt her. Lou could hardly wait to get him all to herself again, away from these sighing Creole beauties. She had been with her cousins nearly a week now, and all she and Jacques had managed were two brief kisses on the very first evening of her visit.

As she sat watching a dark-eyed siren openly flirting with Jacques, Lou burned with desire and jealousy. She wondered how many of the young women present were still innocent . . . if any were. She began to feel like an oddity.

Finally, it was time to say their *adieus.* Louise took Jacques' arm possessively as they descended stairs to the street.

Both Adelaide and Demonde called out to them repeatedly from the doorway. They turned and waved back to their hosts several times.

"They liked you," Jacques said admiringly.

"Well, I can't speak for the men, but all the women *adored you!*"

"Ah, *ma petite*, is that jealousy I hear in your sweet voice?"

"I cannot stand seeing other women look at you that way! Even Adelaide, the way she kissed you." Her admission came in a sudden, violent outburst. "It makes me want to tear their hair and scratch out their eyes."

Jacques stared at her, shocked. Then he threw back his head and laughed.

"I do not jest! If we are truly to be married, Jacques, we owe each other certain privileges. And I for one would like an opportunity to enjoy some of those. Why, if I could get you alone this minute, I would—"

"Yes?" he said. "You would *what*, my darling?"

Blushing furiously, she stammered, "I would . . . I would *kiss you!* That's what!"

"Do you really mean that?" he asked seriously. "If I could arrange for us to be alone for a while, would you give me a kiss?"

"Oh, yes, Jacques. I would kiss you over and over and over again!"

He pulled her closer to him and whispered, "Then shall we see what I can do?"

Leading her to a closed carriage on the square, he helped her in, then went to speak with the driver. A moment later, he was beside her, alone in the cab, with darkness coming on.

"See how simple that was, my darling?"

"But, Jacques, we mustn't! I was to stay overnight at Madame Eugenie's guest house until tomorrow when my cousins come for me."

He slipped his arm around her and drew her close. "I have your cousins' permission to see you home this evening. All the way back to the plantation. They were worried about your staying alone in town, but they trust me to see you safely home."

"And should they?"

In answer, he drew her close and lavished a kiss on her lips. All the pent-up desire she had felt simmering for hours and days came bubbling to the surface. She tried to hold back; they both did. Their love, however, would not be denied. Lou parted her lips and he kissed her deeply, making her body ache to know more of his.

Fate again stepped in. No other explanation serves. No one could have predicted that a wheel would come loose on their carriage along a deserted stretch of the dark road. Had it been a bitter cold December night, they might have huddled together close to the cab while the driver fixed their conveyance. Had there been a bright moon, they might have been less tempted than they were by the cover of darkness. But the wheel *did* break and it *was* a balmy night for December and the sky *was* like inky velvet. Conveniently, the woods bordered the road. So, leaving the driver at his work, they strolled off into the shadows, following a red fox that dashed into a thicket at the edge of the forest.

Jacques spread his cloak. "Shall we rest while we wait?"

They exchanged looks through the darkness, both knowing that rest was the last thing on either of their minds.

After only a moment's hesitation, she sank to the black velvet that held the warmth and the scent of her lover's own body. When they kissed this time, he was lying next to her. She trembled slightly, Adelaide's words still echoing in her mind and heart.

Jacques moved closer, pressing until she felt the heat and strength of his loins. His arms slid around her, pulling her ever nearer, until her aching breasts were tight against his chest. Before she knew what was happening, he was making her mindless—kissing her eyelids, stroking her neck, fondling her breasts. It took a bit of maneuvering and fumbling at clothing for them to get to each other, but moments later she felt the cool night air on her bare thighs, followed by Jacques' gentle touch.

Soon, Lou understood fully what Adelaide's words had meant. Before the driver called out to them, Louise Manigault Robillard had become Jacques St. Julian's wife—by deed if not by word. She felt marvelous! She could hardly wait to become Madame St. Julian, to lie with Jacques each night for the rest of their lives and do the heart-bursting, soul-blazing things they had done in the woods.

As they rode on toward the plantation, Jacques held her gently and whispered words of love and assurance. It was meant to be. They had nothing to be ashamed of. They would be married in the spring, as soon as he returned to Savannah. They would have a glorious life together. He would build her a fine mansion on one of the squares. They would fill it with children and happiness and love.

Louise could only smile at his words. She needed no mansions to be happy with Jacques. She would love him in a cottage or a hut on a desert island. All she needed for happiness was the man himself holding her close, kissing her senseless, making her his own.

She knew she should be totally happy at this moment, but it seemed that despite all Jacques' promises and pledges of love, a dark shadow had passed over her heart.

"You do love me, don't you?" he begged when she remained silent.

"Oh, yes, Jacques! More than a woman has a right to love any man. I fear I may make God Himself angry, I worship you so."

They held each other tightly then, knowing that only a few more minutes remained to them before they would turn off the levee road and into the long *allée* of oaks that led to her cousins' plantation house.

Suddenly, they heard a sound thundering in the distance, growing louder every moment. Jacques raised the window curtain and peered out. Just then their horse reared and screamed, almost upsetting the carriage. They could hear the driver yelling, trying to gain control of his frightened beast.

" 'Tis a runaway, sir. Coming right for us," their driver yelled down.

Jacques leaned out the window and looked ahead. "Good God, he's right!"

Lou watched in horror as Jacques opened the door and leaped out. His timing was flawless. He managed to grip the side of the driverless carriage as it hurtled past. She screamed his name, but too late.

When their own driver finally stopped the horse, she jumped down onto the road atop the levee. In the distance, she saw Jacques clinging to the side of the careening carriage. He wrenched the door open just as horse and vehicle plunged off the levee into the angry water swirling below. Lou ran toward the scene of the accident, screaming Jacques' name with every breath she took.

Almost at once, she saw a woman's head bob to the surface. The driver jumped from the levee into the water to lend aid.

"Take my child!" the frantic mother cried.

The driver plucked the baby from her arms and all but tossed the infant to Lou. She caught it and held it—wet, squalling, and wriggling—in her arms. Next the hysterical young mother was hoisted to the bank. Her heart pounding until it ached, Lou waited for Jacques to swim to the surface. Again and again their driver plunged beneath the murky water, searching.

The sobbing woman, clinging to Lou and her baby, cried over and over, "He saved us. Your husband saved us. God bless him, he saved my baby!"

But God had no earthly blessing for Jacques St. Julian that night. He never resurfaced. His body was found, days later, downriver. He was still tangled in the carriage lines along with the dead horse.

As the realization came to Louise, there on the levee, that the man who had made love to her such a short time ago would never take her into his arms again, she grew still and cold.

Mary Scarlett, too, stopped her thrashing and wailing and settled into grim silence on Dr. Schlager's couch. She was shivering so that Helga covered her with a second blanket.

"On the count of *three,* Miss Lamar ! One, two, *three!*" Dr. Schlager repeated for the tenth time. "You *will* awaken!"

Her tear-swollen eyes blinked open. She stared at Helga and the doctor blankly. "Where am I?"

"Thank God," the doctor said.

Helga sat down beside Mary Scarlett and took her cold hands. "How do you feel?"

"Strange."

"Do you remember what happened?" Helga sounded perfectly calm, but Schlager, who never drank in the daytime, poured himself a stiff shot of brandy to settle his nerves.

"Jacques," Mary Scarlett whispered. "Jacques is dead."

"He died long ago," Helga said. "Long before you were born."

Mary Scarlett shook her head slowly. "No. He made love to me. I remember."

"In another lifetime."

She frowned and blinked several times, trying to clear her senses. "Yes," she said at last. "But I remember."

"He loved you deeply."

"As I loved him. I must find him." Mary Scarlett sat up suddenly and the room spun around her.

Helga pressed her back down. "Slowly. Gently, Mary Scarlett. Your first experience at regression was not an easy one. Give yourself time to recover. Doctor?" Helga looked toward Schlager. "I think a drop of that brandy might be in order."

Both women watched the doctor's shaking hands as he filled a small snifter. Mary Scarlett took it from him and sipped it slowly.

"I want to go back," she said, handing him the empty glass. "I want to know the rest. What happened to Louise? How could she live after Jacques drowned? I have to know."

Dr. Schlager removed his glasses and cleaned them with his handkerchief, stalling for time. "I am not sure that would be a good idea. Not this afternoon. You have been through a tragic episode. It could do you great harm to rush—"

"It could do me greater harm *not* to know. I insist, Dr. Schlager."

Mary Scarlett flattened herself on the couch again and stared up at the chandelier. She replayed in her mind the very words Dr. Schlager had spoken to hypnotize her before. He was still talking to her, pleading with her to wait, when he realized that she was already beginning her journey back.

"Good God, she has left us again!" Schlager cried. "She's performed self-hypnosis."

"Guide her, Manfred," Helga urged. "She mustn't do this alone. We must help."

"Mary Scarlett? Can you hear me?" he asked.

Eyes closed, she nodded slightly.

"Very well. You are back in Savannah. What happened in New Orleans is still a painful memory, but life goes on. Tell us what is happening, please."

A smile lit her face. "I am happy. There is a new man in my life."

"Ah, you are in love again?"

"No. Jacques was the one and only love of my life and I have faith that we will meet again sometime in the distant future. But he has left me a gift. Even now, his son's heart beats beneath my own. I do believe that Jacques' spirit will live on with me through this child of our love."

"And will you raise this love-child alone?"

"No. I am married now. My cousins arranged it. When I returned to Savannah, I was accompanied by my betrothed, a gentle man twice my age. Auguste LeFont Fenwick. He lost his wife two years ago in childbirth. He has a son older than I and three younger children as well, two girls and a boy. Jacques' son will be but one more in my ready-made brood. It is for the best that this child of our passion will have a father to guide him and brothers and sisters to love and protect him. Jacques would approve."

"And what does your husband think of this child that you carry?"

"He believes it to be his own. A small deception on my part for the sake of his happiness."

"Will you ever tell him the truth?"

"Never. What good could such a confession bring? Auguste will be my son's father in every way save one."

"Move ahead through the years," Dr. Schlager instructed. "Beyond the birth of your child. A son?"

"Of course," she answered. "As I knew he would be. A brighter boy you never saw—glossy dark curls, eyes wide with wonder at all the world, and a temperament as sunny as the skies in June. I see Jacques in little Julian—his mannerisms, his laugh, the way he smiles at the slightest provocation. He is a strong, handsome lad of six now." Mary Scarlett paused. Her expression changed to one of sadness.

"What is troubling you, my dear?" Schlager asked.

"*Seven years* have passed since that dreadful night. Why can I never put it out of my mind? Auguste is so good to me. I love all his children almost as much as I love my own son. We have a wonderful life—a lovely house in the city, a summer haven on the Salts at the Isle of Hope. We have friends galore and young people in and out of our house every day. I am never idle, with my family, my church, my charity work. So why must my heart remain forever a prisoner in the dust of the past?"

"What year is this?"

"Eighteen hundred and twenty-seven. The country is at peace again after the terrible second revolution. Would that I could know such peace. I hear Jacques calling to me, urging me to join him. How can I, though? I must stay with little Julian."

Helga whispered, "Her death will come soon, Manfred. Perhaps that is why she hears Jacques calling to her."

He nodded. "Tell us how you left this world, but without actually reliving it or experiencing the pain."

"There was no pain," she answered in a calm, quiet voice. "It was in the summer of the following year at our cottage by the sea. The night before had been too hot to sleep. I had tossed and turned in a fever for two days and nights, unable to eat the smallest morsel. I could only sip water a few drops at a time. I became delirious, my mind wandering old familiar paths. Long after midnight, his voice began calling me. Softly at first, then louder, with more urgency. He offered relief from my misery and my pain. I rose an hour before dawn, following the sweet echo, trying to find my love. I crawled from my bed, stumbled out of the house and down the stairs. I fell and had to lie in the sand for a long time to regain strength enough to go on. Had it not been for the sound of his voice, urging me on, I might have stayed where I fell. Slowly, I dragged myself to my feet. Clinging to bushes along the path, I made my way unsteadily to the beach. There a cool, clean breeze eased my burning flesh. I sank to the damp sand, grateful for the relief. The first light of dawn was just breaking when I saw a figure coming toward me."

"Who was this person?"

"At first, I didn't know. I could not see his face. As he drew closer, I recognized him, and, oh, the joy! It was Jacques come to take me with him. He leaned down and kissed my forehead with cool lips. Then he slipped his arm around my waist and raised me from the water's edge. He took my hands in his and smiled down at me. His wonderful kiss seemed to chase away the last of my fever. He nodded toward the water, where the sun was rising like a great fiery ball out of the sea. We walked into the waves. I could feel his love, as alive as it had ever been. I knew he meant to have me with him at last. Deeper and deeper we went until finally the gently lapping water closed over us both. As the sun rose in all its glory, I passed into an even brighter light—the sweet light of eternity."

Helga looked at Schlager, her eyes sad and troubled. *Suicide,* she mouthed silently.

The doctor frowned at Helga and shook his head. "She was ill, out of her mind with fever." To Mary Scarlett he said, "You left your son. How sad that he had to grow up without his mother."

"I did not leave him. I was there with Julian always. His father and I both were. You must understand that love as great as Jacques and I shared simply could not be denied. Without him I was a mere shade moving through life."

"Where are you now?"

"Right here, with the entity Mary Scarlett. She now wears my soul. Since I did not finish my full span of years of the earthly plane, it has been my task to watch over those who have been unfortunate in life. I have been a part of her since the terrible night she was conceived, since her father in a drunken rage forced her mother to submit to his angry lust. No fruit of such a coupling can enter into life with an easy road ahead. Life is difficult at best—our period of trial and pain. A wise man has said, 'We are not human beings having a spiritual experience. We are spiritual beings having a human experience.' "

Schlager nodded. He knew the quote from Pierre Teilhard de Chardin.

"What do you see ahead for the entity Mary Scarlett?"

"Happiness . . . or sadness. It all depends. She is living a delusion."

"Explain please."

"She has found our Jacques. But she will not admit this to herself until she finds this mirror she believes in. She must see his face there in order to know the truth."

"You are saying the mirror has no real power?"

"The power is in the belief. Mary Scarlett believes. Therefore, the power is real, at least to her."

"Like voodoo," Schlager said in an aside to Helga. "The true believer can actually be killed by a conjure."

"Exactly," Helga answered.

"So, she must find this mirror?"

"She must."

"Do you know where it is?"

A long silence followed. Mary Scarlett went very still.

Only the slightest rise and fall of her chest revealed that she was still breathing.

Finally, in her protector's voice, she said, "I knew for many years. It was there where it had always been. But now? I am not certain. Someone sent it away. No one here on this side seems to know its whereabouts. We have all been searching, but a mist of clouds seems to cloak its hiding place."

"Will you keep searching?"

"We will."

"We shall remain in touch to hear your progress on this matter. Have you any words of wisdom for the entity Mary Scarlett?"

"*Beware!*" The word echoed in the silent room.

Mary Scarlett stirred on the couch. She was coming out of her hypnotic state.

"Gently, Mary Scarlett," the doctor soothed. "I will count. You will awake refreshed and feeling well and happy."

Mary Scarlett's eyes shot open. "I knew I was right about the identity of the woman in my aura."

"And a very delightful spirit she is," Helga said with a smile.

Mary Scarlett nodded her agreement. "But she's wrong about Jacques. I *don't* know who he is in this life. I won't know until I find the mirror."

"She explained that," Dr. Schlager reminded her. "But the knowledge is yours, Mary Scarlett, even without seeing his face in the mirror."

Helga frowned at him and shook her head gently. He could no more reverse Mary Scarlett's beliefs than he could undo a voodoo curse. It would be folly to try.

"Lou will find it for me," Mary Scarlett said confidently, "and then I will know for sure."

It was already dark outside. The session had been long and exhausting. Dr. Schlager and Helga both looked frazzled and weary. Only Mary Scarlett looked fresh, wide awake, and alert.

"Shall I call you a taxi, my dear?" Schlager wanted nothing so much as a drink, a light supper, and bed.

Mary Scarlett was considering his offer when the telephone rang. Helga went into the next room to answer it, then called to Mary Scarlett.

She looked to Dr. Schlager. "Is it all right for me to get up now?"

"But of course, my dear. You are fine."

When she took the receiver from Helga, the sound of Bolt's voice brought a smile to her lips.

"You're finished?"

"Yes."

"How did the session go?"

Mary Scarlett could hardly hear him for the loud, brassy music in the background. Where could he be? "It went marvelously! I spoke with Louise, the woman in my aura. Actually, I guess she spoke through me. Anyway, I know who she is and she's a friendly spirit. She's with me for my own protection."

"Well, that's a relief," Bolt said. "Are you ready—?" His final words were drowned out by a loud burst of music and raucous cheers.

"Bolt, I can't hear you. Where are you?"

"Still working," he answered.

"Not at your office, that's for sure."

"No. I'm with a client, but we've finished our business. I'll be leaving here soon. Want me to pick you up? We could grab a quick bite somewhere, then I have to get home and pack."

"Pack? Where are you going?"

"To Atlanta on business."

"You didn't mention taking a trip."

"Didn't know until I met with this client. It's urgent, Mary Scarlett. I don't have any choice in the matter." Again the music and the cheers swelled to a deafening roar. "Look, I'll explain when I see you. I can be there in about twenty minutes."

"Never mind, Bolt. I'll call a cab back to your place. See you in a while."

"Shortly," Bolt answered, then hung up.

Seeing the troubled look on Mary Scarlett's face, Schlager asked, "Is something wrong?"

"I don't know. Bolt said earlier that he had to meet a new client, a Mr. Tollison from Sea Island. But it certainly sounded like he was calling from a nightclub."

"Tollison! Well, I am impressed. R. A. Tollison is a man of great wealth and distinction, a rising star in state politics. Perhaps destined to be a presidential hopeful at some time in the future. Conrad has done well to secure him as a client."

On the taxi ride home, Mary Scarlett kept thinking about what Dr. Schlager had said about Bolt's high-powered new client. A man of stature he might be, but unless her senses had failed her, she was almost sure that thumping, grinding beat in the background could only be the musical accompaniment to a strip show. She would reserve judgment on Mr. R. A. Tollison until she met him for herself.

Fourteen

While Mary Scarlett slipped under Dr. Schlager's hypnotic spell, Bolt paced his office. Tollison was late for his appointment. That should have been Bolt's first tipoff.

When Mr. Radley Axel Tollison III finally did show up, Bolt damned himself for not canceling or postponing in order to go with Mary Scarlett to Schlager's. Either his secretary had failed to emphasize "the Third" on the end of his name, or Bolt, preoccupied, had simply missed it.

Conrad had expected to meet with the father, R. A. Tollison, Jr., a high-powered Georgia businessman and politician from Sea Island. Instead, he got the son, obviously a SCAD student by his purple-spiked hair and the plethora of studs, hoops, and satanic symbols poking through his ears and nose. Not until the pale, bone-thin student sauntered into the office twenty-eight minutes late and said, "The name's 'Rat,'" did Bolt note that his tongue, too, was pierced to accommodate a small gold ring.

"Have a seat, Mr. Tollison." Bolt swallowed his revulsion and tried to sound business-like.

The kid flopped in the chair opposite Bolt's desk and slouched down on his backbone. Bolt wondered what Rat's rich, powerful father thought of his son's ragbag wardrobe—torn jeans, ripped tank top, runover high-tops, all black and smeared with paint. Bolt tried to conjure up a picture of this alien-looking young man entering the Spanish Lounge at The Cloister with his prominent parents for an afternoon tea dance. No way!

"How can I help you, Mr. Tollison?"

Rat wriggled around in his chair, as uncomfortable as if he were on the witness stand in court, but trying to appear nonchalant. He draped one leg—knee protruding from a foot-long tear in his jeans—over the arm of the chair before he said, "Hey, I gotta problem, man."

You've got that right kid! Bolt thought. Aloud he said, "Why don't you tell me about it?"

"Yeah, I guess. That's why I'm here. I gotta tell somebody. It's buggin' the hell outta me, man. I've never been in a mess like this."

Bolt figured it must be something serious—probably trouble at school. The Savannah College of Art and Design had had problems with some of its students over the past years, most notably the pair who had decided to experiment with bomb-building in their spare time.

"You go to SCAD, right?" Bolt prompted.

The kid brushed a hand through his purple hair and gave a quick, humorless laugh. "How'd you guess? But that's got nothing to do with my problems. Well, almost nothing. I met her at SCAD."

Bolt nodded. A girl, then. Pregnant? Wanting to get married, but not up to Dad's standards? Needing funds for an abortion?

"I came to you 'cause I know you're not on my old man's payroll. I don't want this getting back to him." The kid leaned close and glared at Bolt. "You got that, Conrad?"

Bolt hadn't liked this kid on sight. And he was liking him less and less as the minutes ticked by.

"You don't have to worry about client confidentiality, Mr. Tollison. That goes without saying."

"Okay! Just so we got that straight."

Bolt's thoughts wandered to Mary Scarlett. If Rat didn't get to the point soon, he was going to toss him out on his pierced ear and rush over to Dr. Schlager's. Right now the kid was rambling on about his girlfriend and how good she was in bed and how much she'd taught him about love and life and blah, blah, blah.

The word that drew Bolt's thoughts back to his client was *murder.* He sat up straighter and gave young Mr. Tollison his full attention.

"Let me see if I have this straight," Bolt said, snatching up his pen to make notes. "You met this woman, Magnolia, when she was posing for a life class at SCAD? You moved in with her when you got kicked out of your apartment for not paying your rent?" He looked skeptically at Tollison, imagining the palatial "cottage" on Sea Island where his parents lived and where he must have been raised, despite all the evidence to the contrary.

"You're figuring my old man has enough money so I don't have to worry about funds—right?"

Bolt nodded.

"Well, the bastard keeps me on such a tight allowance that I don't have money to buy toilet paper to wipe my ass. If I called and told him I'd run out of funds, I'd get the usual lecture and he'd figure I'd blown all my cash on drugs."

Bolt didn't ask, but the quizzical look on his face must have told the kid he wanted to know if that was the case.

"It's none of your damn business what I do with my money, man. But just so's you know, I been holding back rent so I could pay a lawyer. Is it gonna be you?"

Bolt only stared at Rat, not yet ready to commit.

"See, the problem is, I've got to find out something. Can I get in trouble for just *knowing* about a murder even if I had nothing to do with it?"

"This woman—Magnolia—was she involved?"

"Naw. 'Nolia's a nice lady. She's just got lousy taste in men."

Bolt had to agree. She'd allowed this young punk to move in with her and taken him as her lover, hadn't she?

"If she wasn't directly involved, how does she know about this murder? Why did she tell you about it?"

Rat uttered a frustrated sigh, as if to indicate that Bolt was a total bonehead. "I told you, man, my lady's a big time boozer. She gets in these moods when she's on the sauce. She'll laugh till you think she's going to have a stroke or something, then she'll start in on a crying jag. Once she gets all weepy, that's when she talks. For hours she'll go on and on about this rich dude she used to hang with and how he was crazy about her and how they ran off from Savannah together and how he left his old lady and his kid." Rat paused and chuckled. " 'Nolia, she's always saying, 'Rat honey, I was hot stuff back then. You shoulda seen me.' " He leaned forward and gave Bolt a wink and a crooked grin. "I'm here to tell you, boss, she's *still* hot stuff!"

"How old is this woman?" Bolt asked, trying to fit dates to Tollison's weird tale.

The kid shrugged. "Hell, I don't know. She's old—maybe thirty-five, forty. She's been around the block a time or two. That's for damn sure!"

"And exactly when did this murder take place? Where? Who was the victim?"

"Man, don't bug me," Rat whined. "You want the details, go talk to 'Nolia. All I wanna know is can I get in deep shit for knowing what I know?"

"You could," Bolt answered evenly. "It all depends."

"Oh, ma-a-an!" he groaned. "Depends on what?"

"I can't say until I know more about the case. Maybe this woman is just jerking you around. Maybe she made the whole thing up. Or maybe she just saw something and imagined she had witnessed a murder."

Rat leaned forward, propping one elbow on Bolt's desk. He narrowed his eyes and pursed his lips. "Listen, Conrad, she ain't making *nothing* up."

"How can you be so sure?"

" 'Cause I checked her facts, that's how. I figured, just

like you, that it was the booze talking. So I went to the library and did me some research. I looked back through old newspapers until I found it. There ain't no doubt. Everything 'Nolia told me was right on target. Only difference was that nobody called it murder. Papers said the old broad got likkered-up and fell over the banister of her stairs. Broke her neck when she hit the deck."

Bolt shot to his feet, then turned to gaze out the window, trying to cover his reaction to Tollison's words. "Do you know the victim's name?" he asked, trying to sound casual.

"Yeah, I know it. What's it to you?"

Bolt ground his teeth at the teenager's insolent tone. He turned slowly, his face set in a threatening scowl. "The question is, Mr. Tollison: *What's it to* you*?"*

"I don't getcha. Can't you just answer a simple question? I thought that's what lawyers do."

"What I do is protect my clients. If you wish to be my client, you'll have to tell me *everything,* Mr. Tollison."

"Awright! Awright! Her name was Mrs. Richard Habersham Lamar."

"Miss Lucy?"

"Yeah, that's what 'Nolia said folks called her. You know who I mean?"

Bolt nodded. "Go on."

"Well, like I said, her husband ran off with Magnolia, only back then she wasn't using that stage name. She was just plain Jenny Flower, a cocktail waitress at the Moon River Pub. They took off one night after Lamar spread the word that he was going on a fishing trip. He hoped people would figure when he didn't come home that his boat sank and he was fish food. I guess everybody pretty much went along with that 'cause nobody came looking for him. He and 'Nolia were real careful just in case. They took off in her old car until they could get far enough away from Savannah to sell it and buy a new one. Big Dick had plenty of money, she said. They went all over—New York, Las

Vegas, San Francisco. They lived the high life till his cash started running out. Then he got this idea. He said he could get money in Savannah, if they were careful not to let anybody see them while they were in town. So they sneaked back one night and went to his house."

"Why on earth would they do that?" Bolt asked.

" 'Nolia said Big Dick told her he had cash hidden somewhere at his house. He figured he could slip in on the maid's day off and get the money while his wife was sleeping and she'd never know he was there. They ran into a couple of problems, though. The money was gone and his wife was awake. She heard him out in the upstairs hall and came charging out of her room, swinging a bottle of brandy like a club. 'Nolia said—she was watching downstairs at the front door—that Big Dick picked up his wife and just tossed her over the railing like a sack of potatoes."

"Good God," Bolt muttered, visualizing the scene.

" 'Nolia got hysterical—started screaming her head off. That's when Big Dick ran downstairs and slugged her to shut her up. The next she knew, they were back in the car, heading out of Savannah. And she said he'd piled all this junk from the house in the backseat."

"What kind of junk?" Bolt asked.

"Aw, I don't know. Stuff he could pawn. Silver, jewelry, some paintings, she said."

"Did Magnolia mention an antique mirror?"

Rat squenched his eyes up, thinking. "Not that I recall, but you'd have to ask her."

"Yes. That's what I should do. Where can I find Magnolia?"

The kid grinned. "That's easy, man. Where've you been? She's the star at the Blue Note, that nightclub out near Pooler. She's an exotic dancer and she's *good,* I'm telling you."

Pooler was a small community on the outskirts of the city. The Blue Note was a new one on Bolt. As for Magnolia the stripper, the star's fame had not reached beyond her rural milieu.

Bolt's thoughts turned back to Miss Lucy's murderer. "What happened to Dick Lamar?"

Tollison shook his head. " 'Nolia ditched him the first chance she got. She said she wasn't sticking with any guy who knocked her around, no matter how much money he had. She was scared, too, that the cops would come after him once they found his dead wife. 'Nolia figured they might arrest her as his accomplice. She figured Big Dick wouldn't dare show his face again around Savannah, so she hightailed it back here. She's been here ever since."

"I have to talk to her. As soon as possible."

"Right now's as good a time as any, but I better go with you," Rat suggested. "If a strange guy comes sniffing around, she's sure to think you're the law or somebody Big Dick sent looking for her. She's real squirrelly about that. Keeps a little pistol on her all the time, just in case."

"Then, by all means, come along, Mr. Tollison."

The Blue Note was a grungy little dive out near the airport, far off the city's well-worn tourist route. Nor was it one of the "in" places with the upper crust of Savannah society. One side of the cinder block duplex featured a smiling winged pig-angel "BAR-B-Q Made In Heaven," while the other half of the building had dirty windows outlined in blue neon and its name glowing over the bright blue door. It was early yet, but the happy hour crowd had already gathered. The unpaved, pot-holed parking lot was lined with muddy pickup trucks, one eighteen-wheeler, and a couple of mean-looking Harleys.

"Man, I'd like me one of them hogs!" Rat said, drooling over the shiny bikes.

"Where do we find Magnolia?" Bolt asked, sliding out

of the CRX into a twilight filled with the aromas of hickory smoke, basted pork, mud, gasoline, and beer.

"There's a door to her dressing room around back. But she ought to be doing her first show by now. Let's just go in the front way and catch the rest of it."

Bolt gave his client a quick glance. "Are you old enough to get in there?"

"Ma-a-an!" Rat groaned. "They don't even card me. These fellows know I'm 'Nolia's guy."

Tollison was wrong—not about getting carded, but about 'Nolia's show. She hadn't come on stage yet. The gloomy club—its smoky, cobwebby walls decorated with beer signs and girlie posters—was populated by blue-collar types in plaid shirts, jeans, and boots, along with the two bikers, who stood out in the crowd in their black leather, chains, and studs. Not if he had tried could Bolt have looked more out of place in his three-piece suit and conservative tie.

The owner-bartender, Pinky, a barrel of a man with a tangle of black beard, gave Rat a high-five and yelled over the blaring country music, "She's in back. Go talk to her, kid. This ain't one of her better nights."

Bolt nodded self-consciously to the men they passed, most of whom simply offered him surly stares, then went back to their beers. Ahead of him, Rat slipped through a black curtain that led to the back of the club. Bolt followed.

The restrooms on the right were marked "Dudes" and "Babes." To the left was a storage room and then Magnolia's "dressing room," not much larger than a broom closet.

When Bolt reached the open door, Rat was leaning over his lady love, whispering something. She sat slumped forward in a bent folding chair, her elbow on a packing crate that doubled as a table and her forehead resting against the palm of her left hand. Bolt couldn't see her face for the riot of electric-blue curls that tumbled to her shoulders. A cigarette burned in an overflowing ashtray on the table beside a lipstick-smeared glass and a half-empty fifth of Jack Daniels.

"I don't wanna see nobody, Rat," she moaned as Bolt came within earshot. "It ain't been a good day. That guy called again."

"That's why you've got to talk to Mr. Conrad here, honey." Rat motioned toward Bolt. "He's gonna help you. He'll make sure the bum leaves you alone."

Still sniffling and whimpering, 'Nolia dragged the damp blue curls out of her eyes and looked up at Bolt. He was surprised to see that she was truly a beauty. What age had robbed from her looks, artfully applied makeup had restored. She looked Italian—almond-shaped eyes as blue as her wig, black batwing eyebrows, and full pouting lips tinted blood-red. When she turned toward him, he glimpsed the deep cleavage between her breasts above the open V of her flowered kimono.

"Is that true?" She drilled Bolt with her ice-blue eyes. "You can really keep this creep from bugging me?"

"I'll do my best, ma'am, but you'll have to tell me everything about the problems you're having with him."

She shot a glance at Rat. "You little pissant! You told, didn't you?"

" 'Nolia honey, I had to. You can't go on looking over your shoulder the rest of your life. It's driving you crazy."

She snorted a laugh and took a slug of bourbon. "I must have been crazy to spill my guts to you, kid. It's a wonder you didn't run right home and tell *Daddy*."

"You know I'd never do that, sweetie." Rat reached out to stroke her shoulder, but she shrugged away from his touch. "Come on, baby, tell Mr. Conrad so he can help. He's my lawyer, so he's honor-bound not to go to the cops or anything."

She looked Bolt up and down, then threw back her head and laughed. *"A lawyer?* God, Rat, what'd you have to do to hire a guy like this—pawn the family jewels?"

When she reached for the bottle again, Bolt decided he had better step in before she got too drunk to talk. "Miss Magnolia, hear me out. Please."

His ploy worked. Her hand stopped just short of gripping the bottle. He had her attention.

"Mr. Tollison came to me because he is deeply concerned for your safety and for his own. *If* Richard Lamar truly murdered his wife—"

"Ain't no *if* about it, mister! I was there. I seen the whole damn thing, start to finish. He said if I ever blabbed, he'd do the same to me. Rat—running around, shooting off his mouth—is going to get me killed."

"How do you know Lamar is still alive?" Bolt asked.

" 'Cause he's got this guy who calls me now and again, just to remind me that I should keep my trap shut."

"This is the man who called you today?"

She nodded. "That's him! Only today he upped the ante. He claimed Big Dick needs money. He gave me a post office box in Marietta where I'm supposed to send the cash. Like I had five hundred dollars! Ha!" She slumped down and hid her face in her crossed arms. "So I guess he'll kill me and that'll be an end to it."

Rat patted her shoulder clumsily. "No, honey. Don't say such a thing."

"Do you know this man's name?" Bolt asked.

She sat up, turned toward Bolt, and let her robe fall open to show a blue sequined G-string. "Yeah, I know his name. I even know what he looks like. He came right to the club in Savannah where I was performing one time last year. That's why I'm out here now in Pooler at the Blue Note. I figured I'd be harder to find. But he's tracked me down again. His name's Lumpkin Quincey and he looks like a 'possum—shaggy gray hair, big pointy nose, and little beady eyes."

"What's his connection with Richard Lamar?" Bolt asked.

'Nolia shook her head. "I'm not sure. Once he mentioned something about their college days together. Quincey don't look like no university man to me, though."

"Looks can be deceiving," Bolt commented, casting a glance at Rat.

"Yeah! You got that right. Looking at me, you'd never guess I was an honor graduate of Jones Business College down in Jacksonville, would you?"

"You're a businesswoman," Rat insisted.

She chucked him under the chin. "Right you are, honey boy!"

"When was the last time you saw Lamar?" Bolt persisted, determined to get the facts.

"The night I was holding a gun on him, threatening to blow his balls off if he made a move to stop me from leaving." She smiled sweetly and twirled a gentian-colored curl around her finger.

"When and where was that?"

"About a week after he killed his wife. We were in a motel in Arab, Alabama. We'd been running for days, sort of zigzagging back and forth through Georgia, Florida, and Alabama since that night in Savannah. He wasn't stopping for anything but gas. I'd run to the john, then grab a Dr. Pepper and a sandwich while he gassed up. He didn't talk to me. Wouldn't answer when I asked him where we were headed. He just kept muttering to himself, mostly things that didn't make any sense, but every now and then I'd hear him say, 'She's not dead, just knocked out. Takes more than that to kill Lucy. Tough little bitch!' Stuff like that. Then he'd look at me like he didn't even see me, like I wasn't right there with him in the car. My jaw was aching where he'd hit me. I was afraid it was broken, but I knew if I said anything he'd probably slug me again. I was half out of my mind, I was so scared." She broke down and had to pause to regain control.

"Just take it easy, Magnolia. Take your time, but you have to tell me what happened," Bolt prodded gently.

"All of it?"

He nodded. "Everything."

She swiped at her eyes and blew her nose. "Oh, God," she sighed. "Where to begin?"

"How did you meet Big Dick?"

Magnolia stared in her mirror, a distant look in her eyes. Carefully, methodically, she began repairing her ruined makeup as she talked. The familiar ritual seemed to calm her.

"I wasn't no kid," she began. "I shoulda known better, but I'd just been dumped by a guy I was nuts about. It seemed like my whole world had come to an end. I guess you could say I was vulnerable when Big Dick walked into my life. I was working at a cheesy little joint down on River Street—singing some, but waiting tables mostly. My thirtieth birthday was coming up and with no guy and a lousy job I was feeling like I was over the hill. Then *he* came in one slow night. It was raining like all hell. My last table had just paid and left. The boss was talking about closing early. I was more than ready. The whole street was dead. I hadn't even made cab fare that night, so I was going to have to walk home in the rain. I was feeling lower than a snake's belly.

"When Big Dick walked in, he looked worse than I felt. He's a big, good-looking man, but that night he looked like somebody who'd tried to drown himself, and couldn't even do that right. He took a seat at the bar and ordered a double martini. I fixed it for him and kind of hung around. The boss was in the back, so it was just the two of us. I'll never forget how he started the conversation. He threw down that first drink, then looked up at me and smiled. He lifted his empty glass to let me know to hit him again.

"While I was fixing him another one, he said, 'You ever feel like the whole world's a toilet and you've just been flushed?' Well, that really tickled me. He'd hit the nail on the head.

"I stopped what I was doing and stared at him. I'd been trying to think all night how it was I was feeling. Then he walks in and puts my whole life into those few words. I felt a little better. I realized all of a sudden that my face wasn't frozen in a scowl. I grinned back at him and said, 'Mister, I know *exactly* what you mean. And you know that commercial on TV—the little guy in his boat in the toilet bowl?' He nodded that he knew the one I meant. Then I says, 'Well, it's *a damn lie!* There *ain't* no boat!'

"He threw back his head and just filled up that gloomy place with his big old laugh. That sound made me feel good all over. I guess it'll come as no surprise to you that he drove me home after closing and stayed most of that long, rainy night."

'Nolia paused again to outline her full lips with quick, precise strokes. Her hands seemed steady enough, but Bolt noticed a twitch at the corner of her mouth. She was fighting for control again.

She spotted Bolt staring at her reflection in the mirror. "Don't worry. I'm holding it together. I'll tell you the whole story. But I got a show to do and those boys out there aren't gonna wait all night."

"Want me to go tell Pinky you'll be ready in a few minutes?"

She turned a brilliant smile on her eager young lover. "You do that, Rat honey. And tell the guys I'll give 'em a special show since I've kept them waiting so long."

Magnolia waited until Tollison left the room before she continued. "Dick Lamar and me, we hit it off right from the start. We crawled in the sack together that night, I'm not denying it. But there was a lot more to our relationship. He'd spend hours telling me about his stuck-up, ditzy wife and his kid who hated his guts. I'd be real nice to him, trying to let him know that not everybody was as bad as them. And in trying to help his feelings, I helped my own. It felt real good to be needed for a change. Before then, I'd always been the taker instead of the giver. I used to think it would be the most wonderful thing in the world if him and me could just chuck it all and run off together. So when he suggested that very thing, I had my bags packed in an hour.

"We hit the road with no looking back. Had a ball, too! New York, Vegas, San Francisco, and all points in between. He showed me places I'd never hoped to see. But then the money ran out. He'd started out with a bundle and a wallet full of credit cards. He hadn't thought about the fact that dead men can't use plastic. See, he'd told everybody that he was going on a fishing trip. The only other person who knew he wasn't fishing was his buddy Quincey. He took out the boat Dick had rented, sank it, then came back in a small boat he'd towed out. A bad nor'easter blew in the next day so that helped the story along. The whole town figured him for dead—lost in the storm."

Bolt nodded. He remembered that time well—the search and recovery boats, the divers, and Miss Lucy, popping tranquilizers and washing them down with brandy—half out of her mind with Mary Scarlett gone and Big Dick "missing at sea."

"Tell me about the night the two of you came back to Savannah."

Magnolia sort of moaned before the sound became words. "I've tried so hard to forget that night. There's no way. Dick told me the maid was always gone on Sundays and we could sneak in the house and get a wad of cash he had hidden in a wall safe in his bedroom. So we drove into Savannah a little before midnight and he parked the car around back, off the street. Somewhere along the way, he'd lost his house key, but they kept one hidden on the front porch, under a heavy planter."

Bolt nodded. He knew the place, had used that very key.

"I wanted to stay in the car. He said no, that he needed me to watch the front door just in case somebody showed up. I went inside with him and stayed downstairs in the foyer. Things went just like clockwork at first. His wife was in her room—sleeping, we figured—and there wasn't a soul in the rest of the house. It seemed like everything would be all right. He tiptoed up the stairs and into his room. I was nervous as a cat, especially after he disappeared upstairs. Finally, I heard a sound—maybe a board creaking, I don't know—but when I looked up he was at the head of the stairs, starting down. I knew, though, that something was wrong. His face was fishbelly-white. Then—*God A'mighty!*—you never heard such a sound. It was like some demon from hell got loose. I saw the blur of white coming at Dick—she was all over him. He grabbed her arms and just picked her up like she didn't weigh nothing. I started screaming when he dumped her over the railing. I couldn't stop. It was like I was watching her fall and fall and fall in slow motion. I even remember her looking right at me with that startled expression on her face as she fell. It was almost like she was saying, 'Well, who are you and what are you doing in my house and why don't you catch me before I hit the floor and break my neck?' "

Magnolia paused to take a deep, gasping breath.

"And then?" Bolt said, almost whispering.

"I was still screaming when she hit the floor right in front of me. I was just frozen where I stood, yelling my fool head off. I never saw Big Dick coming at me, not till I saw his fist in my face. He hit me a good solid shot to the chin. If that wasn't enough to put my lights out, I must have hit my head on the door frame from the force of his punch. The next thing I knew, I woke up groaning. I felt like I was the one he'd tossed over the banister. My whole body hurt, but my jaw and my head mostly. It was still dark. I couldn't tell where we were, but I knew we were miles from Savannah. I tried talking to him. He wouldn't say a word, just hunched over the wheel with his face angry and all green from the dashboard lights, looking like something out of a horror movie. The next couple of days were just a blur. I was hurting real bad, and it was raining—hour after hour, all gray with fog and rain. Oh, another thing— he'd hauled off a bunch of stuff from the house on Bull Street."

"What kind of stuff?" Bolt asked.

"Anything he could grab fast and pawn faster. Silver, some small paintings, jewelry, even a set of golf clubs. Whenever we passed through some little town that had a pawn shop, he'd stop and take something in, then come back a few minutes later with some cash."

"Do you remember an antique mirror?"

Magnolia thought for a minute, then shook her head. "I don't think so. I can't recall anything like that. Seems like he grabbed mostly small stuff that wouldn't break."

"Go on," Bolt instructed. "Tell me how you got away from him."

"Well, finally, when he'd pawned everything, he pulled into a cheap motel in Arab, Alabama. I wasn't sure how far we were from Savannah, but I could tell he was heading north. He'd driven by a fried chicken place and bought us a family-sized bucket. Man, that was the best food! I hadn't had a square meal in a couple of days. Anyway, while we were scarfing down drumsticks, he finally seemed to realize again that I was with him. He looked at me real mean-like and said, 'You don't remember what happened in Savannah, *do you?*' It wasn't a question. It was an order. And he sort of hinted that my remembering could be hazardous to my health. I tried to act real casual. I asked him what he was talking about, told him I didn't even remember being in Savannah for a long, long time. He kind of smiled. I think he thought he'd knocked the memory of that night right out of my head—like I had amnesia or something. That suited him fine, I could tell. Then he starts in telling me we're heading for Canada first thing in the morning. He was talking real crazy and looking wild-eyed. I knew then what I had to do. I wasn't about to go off to no Canada with a murderer!"

"How did you get away?"

"I waited till he was sleeping. He'd been drinking a good bit so he was snoring away. I had this little pistol I always carried for protection from back in the days when I used to have to walk home alone after work. Lucky for me, I brought it along, 'cause while I was going through his pants, looking for his money, he woke up.

" 'What the hell you doing?' he wanted to know.

" 'Just getting me some traveling money,' I told him, real sweet-like.

"Well, he came roaring up out of that bed like a bull that just saw red. He'd have killed me right then and there if it hadn't been for that gun. I never shot anybody in my life and I was shaking all over. I couldn't bring myself to shoot to kill, so I aimed it right for his ding-dong and told him he better back off or else. When he saw I really meant it, he turned into the old Dick—talking nice, smiling, telling me all the great things we were going to do once we got out of the country. I wasn't buying any of it. I kept that pistol steady while I got the car keys and the money, several hundred dollars. I left him enough for food for a couple of days and bus fare back to Savannah or wherever. He kept on threatening—said if I took the car he'd call the cops. I didn't figure that was too likely, considering what he'd done in Savannah and me being an eyewitness. Just before I backed out of the room, he looked at me with murder in his eyes and said, 'You ever tell *anyone* what you saw and, I swear to God, I'll kill you, too.' "

"You got away?"

"I'm here talking, ain't I? If he'd caught me, I sure wouldn't be. He may get me yet. That's why I'm staying in

Savannah, dancing at the Blue Note, and hanging with a kid almost young enough to be my son. So far, so good."

"Have you heard anything from Lamar since you left him in Arab?"

"Not directly. Only through his buddy Quincey."

"When did he first contact you?"

"Not long after I'd got shed of Big Dick. I figured he was just a crank caller at first. Then he said some things to me that he could only have heard from Lamar. Things *about* me." She looked away, almost shyly. *"Real personal things.* He knew details about the killing, too, that no one who wasn't there could have known unless Big Dick had filled him in. He said Big Dick just wanted to stay in touch and that he wanted to make sure I knew he was still around. Scared me shitless, I can tell you. The calls have come every few months since that first one. This Quincey character is really beginning to get on my nerves."

"Hey, 'Nolia honey," Rat called and leaned in at the door. "Pinky says he can't stall those guys much longer. You better hustle it up."

"Coming right now, darling. Tell Pinky to put on my music."

Magnolia rose grandly from her beat-up chair. She shrugged out of her flowered kimono, displaying an ample figure clothed only in G-string, mesh stockings, and blue sequin pasties.

"If you'll excuse me now," she said, "I got to finish dressing. And, Mr. Conrad, I'll be most obliged if you can get this Quincey guy off my case. I'd really like to see Big Dick behind bars, too. I won't breathe easy until I know he's been put away—one way or another."

"One last thing," Bolt said. "I'll need that post office box number Quincey gave you."

"Sure thing!" She grabbed her eyebrow pencil and wrote down the number on a paper towel. "I wish you luck."

Bolt slipped out and went to find a telephone. It was late,

past nine. He had told Mary Scarlett he would call as soon as he wound up his meeting. She was still at Dr. Schlager's. He tried to make himself heard over the blaring bump-and-grind music and the whoops of Magnolia's enthusiastic admirers. Glancing over his shoulder, he watched her shimmy across the tiny stage, shedding gloves, earrings, scarf, and finally the slinky see-through gown she had donned after he left her dressing room. By the time he hung up, Magnolia was once more down to the bare, blue sequin essentials.

She was quite a woman, he mused, watching her stalk the stage like a lioness with a blue mane.

"Quite a woman, with quite a story."

He turned and walked toward the door, wondering how in the world he was going to break the news to Mary Scarlett that her father had murdered her mother.

Fifteen

When Bolt arrived home thirty minutes later, he found Mary Scarlett packing her bags. Naturally, he jumped to the conclusion that she planned to go to Atlanta with him. That wouldn't do at all. He had decided, at least for the time being, to keep everything he knew about Big Dick and Miss Lucy's death to himself. If Mary Scarlett went with him—as much as he would enjoy her company—there would be no way to keep his mission a secret. Besides, he had more than one purpose in mind on this trip. Once he located this Quincey character, he meant to find Richard Lamar and bring him back to Savannah to stand trial for his crime. The man only *thought* he had gotten away with murder.

"What are you doing?" Bolt asked as he met Mary Scarlett bringing one of her bags into the foyer. "Packing for me?"

She laughed. "You'd look real cute carrying my flowered tapestry suitcases through the Atlanta airport. No, Bolt. I've decided this is my cue to clear out. I don't want to stay here alone, and the obvious place for me to go is to my own house. It's high time I got busy putting that in order. The rest of my stuff should arrive from Spain any day now. Believe me, you don't want to have to fit all of it in here." Changing the subject abruptly, she asked, "How long will you be gone?"

"I'm not sure," he said honestly. "Not too long. I have

to be in court with another case next week. I'll be back by then, regardless."

She looked at him oddly. "Regardless of what? What kind of business do you have to take care of."

"I really can't talk about it, Mary Scarlett. All I can tell you is that I'm looking for someone."

"A missing person?"

He answered evasively, "You could say that."

She laughed softly. "That makes two of us. I'm searching for a missing person, too. Jacques St. Julian. But I'm afraid I'm a lot less likely to succeed than you are since my guy's been dead for over a century."

Bolt made a move toward the kitchen. "How about we have a drink and rustle up some grub? Or would you rather go out?"

"No. I'm bushed. A martini would be wonderful, then maybe those cold stone crab claws left from yesterday. I'll fix a salad and you can nuke the sourdough bread."

Bolt busied himself at the bar while Mary Scarlett tore cold, crisp lettuce for their salad. When he handed her her glass, he slipped his arm around her waist and kissed her cheek.

She turned slightly and smiled at him, feeling last night's tingle of intimacy rekindle. "What's that for?"

"Just decided I'd like an appetizer."

"Me, too," she whispered, turning into his arms.

This time they shared a *real* kiss—slow and deep and wonderfully arousing. Mary Scarlett clung to him after it was over.

"I hate your having to leave," she whispered. "I'll miss you, Bolt."

"I'll miss you, too, but it can't be helped. Business is business, as the saying goes. Really, though, you'll be so busy at the house on Bull Street that you won't know I'm gone."

"Is Mr. Tollison going with you? Dr. Schlager says he's a real important guy."

Bolt threw back his head and laughed. "The joke's on me! My client isn't Tollison of Sea Island, but his purple-haired, tongue-ringed son from SCAD."

"Oow!" Mary Scarlett shivered at the very thought of having anything stuck through her tongue.

"Yeah," Bolt agreed. *"My* Mr. Tollison goes by the name of 'Rat' as in R. A. Tollison III. I doubt he's even welcome at the old homeplace on Sea Island."

"Poor kid!" Mary Scarlett went serious suddenly. "I know how he must feel."

Bolt stared at her, his brow creased in a frown. "Mary Scarlett, you were never unwelcome in your home."

"Oh, no? Why do you think I took off for Europe?"

"Good question."

Turning away from Bolt, back to the salad, she said, "I wasn't ready to get married. I've always let myself believe that I really talked to Granny Boo that night and she's the one who told me to go." She chuckled. "I guess I needed someone to blame for all my mistakes. I think I'm beginning to face the truth now at long last. Mama wanted me out of the house. That's why she was pushing me to get married. Big Dick wanted me gone, too. I don't know what all went on while I was away at college, but once I returned, I stood up for Mama against him. He despised me for that. He was always lord of his castle. He wouldn't take any backtalk or interference from anybody. One night shortly after my graduation, I truly believed he was going to kill Mama. He was drunk and she made some comment about his drinking and staying out all hours. The look in his eyes when he came at her was murder, pure and simple. I jumped between them and stood my ground."

"You never told me about that." Bolt caressed her shoulder soothingly. "It's a wonder he didn't go after you."

Mary Scarlett laughed humorlessly. "He did. But I pulled

Granny Boo's gun on him and he backed off and stormed out of the house. He didn't come home for three days and nights. He claimed he was staying at his club, but I heard rumors he had a woman on the side. Probably the same one he took off with when he supposedly went on that fishing trip."

Bolt didn't comment. Mary Scarlett obviously knew a lot more about her father's affairs than she had let on. She might not know Magnolia's name, but she was certainly aware of her existence.

"How's that salad coming?" he asked. "Should I put the bread in the microwave?"

"Any time. I'm all ready with my part of the feast."

Bolt was glad to hear a different tone in her voice. She had pushed Big Dick out of her mind to concentrate on the pleasures of a quiet supper, just the two of them.

A few minutes later, they were settled comfortably on the little balcony that hung out over River Street. The breeze was fresh and the music drifting up from one of the bars below was soft, cool jazz.

"Ah, this feels good," Mary Scarlett said, drawing in a deep breath.

"Have you noticed that *everything* feels good when we're together?" Bolt had cracked a stone crab claw for her. He held it out and she sucked the rich white meat from the shell.

She nodded her agreement. "When are you going to come back to Dr. Schlager's with me, Bolt? I really need you to participate in one of the sessions with me. I've reached a point where I know my way around that other world, back in time. But there's something—someone— missing. I need you with me . . . *soon.*"

"Especially after last night, you mean?" He was staring at her, giving her a drowsy, sexy look.

"Yes," she answered quietly. "Last night made all the

difference. I think you may be the one, Bolt. The Jacques St. Julian I've been searching for all my life."

She felt a change in his emotions. He looked away from her and stared out over the water. His shoulders seemed tense. His hands tightened on the arms of his chair.

Without looking at her, he asked, "Mary Scarlett, isn't it enough for me to just be myself—Bolton Conrad, the guy who's been in love with you for most of his life? Why do we have to connect everything? Why must we only think of the past, the distant past, at that? I want to look to the future, the living. I want to think about *us*."

She reached out and touched his hand. "Give me some time, Bolt. I'm carrying around a lot of baggage from my past lives. I need to sort through the junk before I know what's of value and what needs to be trashed. I have to figure out what's real."

He reached for her suddenly and kissed her hard, then released her just as quickly. Still staring right into her eyes, he demanded, "Tell me that's not real! Right now, it's almost too real. I want you so bad that I'd like to jerk you up from that chair this minute, carry you to my bed, and make love to you till you beg for mercy. After last night, the thought of leaving you to go to Atlanta, even for a few days, tears me up inside. I don't know how I'll last till I can get back here to you. *I want you*, Mary Scarlett! Not just last night or tonight or next week. I want you right here with me for the rest of my life."

He paused for a moment and looked out over the river. "You said we needed to talk about what happened between us last night. Well, that's what I have to say on the subject. How about you?"

Mary Scarlett felt breathless by the time he finished. She couldn't find words for a reply. Last night had been wonderful, but was it real? Was it love? Or had she been without a man for so long that any red-blooded male who showed her that tender side of passion would have sent her into orbit? There was only one way to find out and no time like the present.

Without a word, she rose from her chair. Bolt looked at her quizzically. "Where are you going? You haven't finished your supper."

"I'm not hungry . . . for crab." Her voice was a breathy whisper.

She stood there, unbuttoning her blouse while Bolt watched. Still on the balcony, standing beside him, she let the garment slither down her arms. She was now wearing only her slacks and a blue lace bra. Bolt's gaze never wavered as she reached her hands up behind her back.

"Damn," she cursed softly. "My hair's caught in the hook."

She sat down on Bolt's knee with her back to him. "Undo me, please."

"I don't know what's gotten into you, Mary Scarlett, but I think I like it."

He stroked his cool hands over her back, then slid them around to cup her lace-covered breasts. She trembled when he squeezed.

"Good thing there are no lights on up here," she said with a laugh. "We'd be giving the tourists quite a show."

"Damn the tourists," Bolt said, brushing his lips against her shoulder.

While she sat astride his leg, Bolt continued gently stroking her breasts and bare midriff. He kissed her back and shoulders, giving her delicate little flicks with his tongue. Before long, Mary Scarlett was moving sensually as her desire rose with his every touch.

Finally, she felt his fingers at the back hook of her bra. He played with the thin strip of elasticized lace, pulling it tight, sliding the straps slowly down from her shoulders, doing everything *but* unfastening it.

Mary Scarlett reached behind her and braced her hands

on his thighs. She leaned her head back so that her cheek pressed his. "Are you going to play with me all night?"

He kissed her cheek, then uttered a low, growling laugh. "Could be. I think I'd like that."

She chuckled back. "I think I would, too, but I don't know if I can take much more."

He chose that moment to unhook her bra. The froth of lace fell into her lap. She gasped softly and, remembering all the tourists strolling directly below them on the street, tried to bring her arms forward to cover her nakedness. Bolt caught her wrists and held her hands in place on his thighs.

"Don't!" he said. "I like your hands right where they are."

"Bolt," she pleaded, "people will see me."

"And think you're gorgeous. Don't worry, honey, this is Savannah. Remember? Relax! Enjoy!"

He was right. What did it matter? The playful breeze on her bare breasts felt wonderful. She leaned back farther, tilting her face to the night sky. Bolt reached around and grasped her midsection just beneath her breasts, lifting them higher, massaging the undersides gently.

Mary Scarlett moaned and tilted her head for another kiss. "You're driving me wild."

"Good," he whispered. "I do enjoy a wild woman after dry martinis and cold crab." He nipped at her earlobe and let out a long sigh.

She held very still, wondering what he would do to her next, almost afraid to move she felt so aroused. As she suspected, Bolt had other surprises in store. He slipped his fingertips slowly up her breasts until he was touching her nipples, erect now with her need. Caressing, pinching, probing, he brought another moan from her. Then, coming as a total shock, he removed his hands from her breasts. Once more, she felt only the humid breeze fondling her. With her back still to him and her face to the river, she could feel him moving, but had no idea what he was doing.

"Turn around," he said in a husky voice.

She stood, turned, and straddled his lap. They were now face-to-face. Bolt had removed his shirt and tie. He, too, was bare to the waist.

"What now?" she asked breathlessly.

"Just sit there. I want to look at you."

There was no light on the balcony, but a lamp in the room behind Bolt functioned as a spotlight to bathe Mary Scarlett in a soft, golden glow. For a long time, he only sat with his hands on her hips, gazing at her breasts. She became very conscious of their rise and fall with each breath she took. Bolt was smiling, nodding slightly as if to let her know he approved of what he saw.

When he raised his hands toward her, she held her breath for a moment, waiting to feel his touch. But he held his palms away, only a half-inch. His flesh was close enough so' that she could feel his warmth before he actually made contact. Neither of them moved for long moments.

The suspense grew. *When would he move? When would she feel his touch?*

She started to lean forward, to rush the moment of contact.

"No!" Bolt ordered. "Wait!"

She stared down at her bare breasts, the nipples straining to feel his palms against them. She took deeper breaths, expanding her chest, yearning for flesh to meet flesh. Unable in her need to stay silent, she began to moan softly. The sound was animal-like, low and throaty, filled with desire.

"Now you know," Bolt whispered.

She was beyond speech. She simply stared, wondering what he meant.

"You know what it feels like to want something the way I've wanted you since the first day we met. You want me to touch you, don't you? Nothing else in the world matters right now, does it? At this moment, you'd do anything for that sensation—that intimacy, that togetherness, wouldn't you?"

"Please, Bolt!" she cried out.

He chuckled. "Now you've aroused the curiosity of a couple of tourists down below. They're watching, Mary Scarlett. They know what we're doing."

That snapped her out of it for a moment. Her thoughts turned back to her prim and proper upbringing. *What would Mama think if she knew I was up here half-naked with a man while strangers watched?*

She was about to reach for her blouse, when Bolt made contact—fierce, hot, passionate contact. He closed one hand over her right breast while he sucked her left nipple into his mouth. A smattering of applause reached them from below. Mary Scarlett ignored the sound. She ignored the whole world. Bolton Conrad was her only reality at this moment in time.

"Take me to your bed," she begged in a ragged whisper.

His free hand went to the waistband of her slacks. She felt the button snap off, heard the zipper glide down.

Did he mean to make love to her right here on the balcony?

Her body refused to acknowledge her thoughts. She didn't care where they made love as long as they did. As Bolt had said earlier, *Damn the tourists!*

He released her long enough to whisper, "Take 'em off, darlin'."

Mary Scarlett rose from his lap quickly and stepped out of her slacks. Now she wore only blue lace panties, French cut. She looked at Bolt for further instructions. He nodded, smiled, and patted his lap.

With more of her flesh at his tender mercy, he drew invisible pictures on her bare hips and belly until she quivered all over. He pulled the elastic tight, then let it snap loose. He slipped one hand down over the thin lace until he was cupping the narrow crotch. Mary Scarlett squirmed against his hand, trembling from the sensations he aroused with such intimate fondling.

"You'd better take me to bed," she begged in soft, panting gasps. "Time's running out. That feels *too* good, Bolt."

"Really?" he said with a chuckle. "Then how about *this?"*

Taking her by complete surprise, Bolt lifted her and maneuvered her body until she was sitting side-saddle on his lap. He held her with one arm, leaning down to kiss her breasts again. Once he had her totally distracted, he used his other hand to ease her panties down, lower and lower. By the time he lifted his head, she was wearing only blue lace anklets and the breeze was teasing her whole body.

"How's that?" he called down to the street below. But the crowd had moved on and no one was aware of the passionate scene taking place just over their heads.

"You're *so bad*," she whispered in a quivery voice.

He chuckled. "Would you have me any other way?"

"Right now, Bolton Conrad, I'd have you any way I could get you."

She found the rise in his trousers and gave it a good squeeze.

Moments later they were in his big bed together, their naked bodies pale against his forest-green sheets. The very smell of the room aroused Mary Scarlett even more. The piney, smoky, musky-male scent that was different from any other part of the house.

They didn't make love immediately, however. Instead, Bolt stretched out beside her and propped up on one elbow, gazing down at her, toying with her breasts.

"What's all this about?" he asked.

"I don't know what you mean." She was touching him, stroking him, trying to make him take her.

"Yes, you do. One minute we're eating crab and the next minute, without even a change of conversation, you're doing a striptease for me. Wouldn't you say that's just a bit unusual?"

"You didn't like it?" She drew a line down the center of his chest and belly with one finger.

He shuddered with a low groan. "Don't try to distract me. I want to know. What are you up to, Mary Scarlett?"

"Don't you want me?"

"What do you think?"

She smiled. "I'd say all appearances seem to point in that direction. So, what's your problem?"

"You are, dammit! I never met a woman like you in my life. You twist me and turn me and keep me off balance till I don't know if I'm coming or going. What's the game tonight, Mary Scarlett?"

She leaned forward and kissed his chest, teasing his nipple with her tongue. "No game, darling. I just want to make sure last night wasn't a fluke. It had been a long time since any man touched me. And, Bolt, no one ever touched me the way you do. So maybe last night was only so good because I was purely starved for love. Or maybe because it was our first time. I've thought about you all day and the more I thought, the more I wanted you again. I have to make sure, Bolt. I have to know that the second time will be as good as the first."

"Ah, so this is a test."

"Don't make it sound that way. You know what I mean. And I know very well that you want me, too."

He leaned down and whispered in her ear, "I thought I'd already admitted that, darlin'. You want more proof? Fine with me. Hey, I'll give you proof three times a day for the rest of your life if you'll let me."

His hands played over her while he talked. Soon she was writhing on the deep-green sheets. When he came into her, she was more than ready. They moved perfectly together this time. No missed cues, no loss of rhythm. They were together all the way.

The night before had been wonderful because it was Mary Scarlett's first time with a man who truly cared for her. Tonight was even better because she knew no fear. Raul was dead—dead and gone forever. Only Bolt was here, loving her with a tender fierceness that took her straight to the promised land.

When the stars had burst overhead and the heavens had clashed with sweet music, they lay still in each other's arms, their bodies fused with the sweat of passion.

"Well?" Bolt whispered after a time. "What's the verdict on last night? A fluke?"

"No fluke!" she purred. "Three times a day, you say? How about four?"

Bolt pressed his mouth over her ear and whispered, "Will one more for the road do for now?"

Remembering suddenly that he would be leaving in the morning and this would be their last chance for at least a week, Mary Scarlett gave that one more for the road her all. Afterward, they slept in each other's arms until the alarm clock roused them with its demanding buzz.

Later, Mary Scarlett would remember that Bolt kissed her goodbye and promised to be back as soon as possible. Exhausted and drugged with satisfaction from the night before, she never came fully awake before he left.

When she finally woke up, it was past ten. By now, Bolt was somewhere over middle Georgia, winging his way to Atlanta. She missed him already. Grabbing his pillow from the other side of the bed, she buried her face in it and breathed in Bolt's scent.

Sighing softly, she cuddled the pillow close to her body, closed her eyes, and let her thoughts drift back.

"So good," she murmured. "So right."

She had never felt this way before. It almost seemed as if she had just shed her Mary Scarlett-skin and stepped into someone else's. If Granny Boo was right about all the women of the family for generations losing the men they loved—a pattern, a tradition—then Mary Scarlett figured she must have been left in a basket on the doorstep of the old house on Bull Street. Surely she couldn't be related to a line of broken-hearted females that stretched back clear to the founding of Savannah. *Or,* she thought, frowning, *Have I finally found Bolt only to lose him again? Is this just the beginning of the end?*

She tossed her head, refusing to allow any senseless gloom to linger. "Anybody who tries to come between me and my man will have to deal with me and Granny Boo's gun!"

Something was nagging at her, though—one of those "no-seeums,"—gnats so invisible you don't know they're there until they draw your blood.

"What's your problem?" she demanded. It came to her immediately. *"Kathleen!"*

Yes, that was it! She still couldn't be sure how far things had gone between Bolt and Kathleen. She didn't think they had seen each other since the night of Allen's party, but she really had no way of knowing.

On sudden impulse, Mary Scarlett reached for the phone. The best way to find out what a woman had on her mind was to invite her to lunch. A couple of martinis, some cozy girl-talk, and secrets often slipped out. Now, while Bolt was gone, was the perfect time. She opened the phone book to look up Kathleen's office number. To Mary Scarlett's chagrin, she found it circled in the Yellow Pages with her home number written beside it in Bolt's squared-off handwriting.

Mary Scarlett jabbed angrily at the numbers on the phone. After the very first ring, a man with a mellow Southern drawl answered.

"I'd like to speak to Kathleen O'Shea, please."

"I'm sorry, ma'am," he answered. "Kathleen's not in today. She had to take an early flight this morning. She'll be out of town for the rest of the week on business. Would you like to speak to one of our other agents?"

"No. Thank you."

Mary Scarlett felt the no-see-'em drawing still more blood. Forcibly, she shook off her suspicions. It was simply a coincidence that Bolt and Kathleen had both left town this morning and would be gone for the rest of the week. Still, there was only one airport in Savannah and that's where the two of them had headed. Maybe they even ran into each other and had breakfast together. Or maybe, just *maybe* the two of them shared a common destination and common plans for the week.

Determined not to let such a silly notion spoil her day, Mary Scarlett got out of bed, showered, dressed, and packed the rest of her things. Within the hour, she was in a cab on her way home to the Bull Street house. Now more than ever, she missed Bolt. It would be difficult to go back alone. She felt nervous, almost scared. Once again, she forced down her feelings. She was being foolish. Why, hadn't she gone there alone in the middle of the night not so long ago? And, besides, this time she knew she had the lady in her aura watching over her. She smiled and brushed her hand over the top of her head as if she were smoothing her hair.

"We here, ma'am," the driver said. "I'll he'p you with them heavy bags."

"Thank you," she answered offhandedly, staring up at the house as if she were seeing it for the first time in years.

"This place been empty a *long* time, ma'am. Shore needs a good yard man. And I reckon the inside gone need some tidyin' up, too. You could use yo'self one of them *do*mestic engineers. You got anybody to help you, ma'am?"

"What?" Mary Scarlett's thoughts had been elsewhere. She had heard the cabbie's voice behind her, but she hadn't really been concentrating on his words.

"A maid, ma'am, and a yard man. Look like you gone need both and then some."

She nodded. "Yes, I suppose I'll have to call an agency."

The driver set down her bags and whipped two business cards out of his shirt pocket. He grinned as he handed them to Mary Scarlett. "Best workers in town, my sister-in-law and her boy."

She looked at the smudged cards, nodded, and thanked him. "I'll call them right now."

Heading for the flowerpot, she changed her mind abruptly. It wouldn't be wise to let a stranger see her take the spare key from its hiding place. Instead she dug in her purse for the other one. She opened the unlocked door and he hauled her bags into the foyer.

"Want I should take these upstairs for you, ma'am?"

"No, thank you." She handed him the fare and a generous tip. "I can manage from here."

He doffed his cap and gave her a wide grin. "You have a nice day now, ma'am."

The door closed. Suddenly, she was all alone with the house and her memories. The place looked different this morning. She had been here only twice before since her return to Savannah—the first time on a dark, stormy day and the second time at night. In the bright, unforgiving sunshine of late morning, the house looked shabbier than it had seemed before. She walked from room to room downstairs, taking a quick inventory.

"A lot of work," she murmured. "This is really going to take some time and effort."

She glanced down at the cards in her hand. Checking the wall phone in the kitchen, she was delighted to hear a dial tone. Bolt had told her he would have the phones reconnected. Quickly, she punched in the number on the card of "Domestic Engineer" Pearlene Jaudon. Minutes later, Mary Scarlett had the woman's assurance that she and her son Egmont would be "up to Bull Street in no time a-tall."

Mary Scarlett hung up the phone feeling like a beleaguered Confederate general who had just been told that reinforcements were on their way. When she looked at the dusty, moth-eaten drapes, the grimy windows, and the tapestry of cobwebs in every room, the task seemed slightly less than humanly impossible.

She had come dressed for battle in jeans and a tee-shirt. Leaving her bags in the hallway for the time being, she pitched right in with the clutter in the kitchen. Since the Lamar household had always had a maid, there was no dishwasher. A good starting point, she decided, was emptying all the cupboards, scrubbing them out, and washing every glass, dish, and piece of cutlery on the place. That would give her a chance to sort through things, too. She wanted to see if anything besides Granny Boo's dessert silver was missing.

Her search didn't take long. When she went to the dining room to bring her mother's best blue-and-gold-trimmed Limoges china into the kitchen for washing, she found only empty shelves inside the carved oak breakfront doors. She stood staring at the circles in dust where the dishes had sat until quite recently, by the looks of things. If Lucy Lamar had moved the china herself, dust would have gathered over the years, leaving no imprint. In addition to this piece of evidence, Mary Scarlett knew that her mother would never have parted with that china. It had belonged to some distant ancestor who brought it from France by way of Nova Scotia.

Suddenly, Mary Scarlett remembered her vision of Marie, the young woman Jean Lafitte had loved. She had said her mother came to Savannah from Nova Scotia. Had Marie herself eaten from those delicate china plates?

Next she checked the silver drawer and the heavy old English sterling that had graced Lamar dining tables for generations. Worth a king's ransom at the price of sterling these days, she mused.

The thief had realized that. The silver was gone, too. Only a few pieces of late Victorian silverplate remained in the felt-lined, camphor-scented drawers that had once dazzled the eyes with the rich gleam of sterling.

Mary Scarlett was still pondering the thefts when the back doorbell rang. She hurried to the kitchen to see who it might be. She found an enormous black woman in a crisp blue uniform accompanied by a tall teenager wearing overalls and no shirt. Although the young man had not inherited his mother's mountainous shape, the facial resemblance left no doubt that he was her son.

"Well, if this ain't a treat!" Pearlene's chocolate-colored face split in a grin. "I don't reckon I've been in this house since I was knee-high to a grasshopper." Seeing the confusion on Mary Scarlett's face, she said, "Why, you don't remember me, do you, ma'am?"

"No. I'm afraid not," Mary Scarlett admitted.

"I come from Delsey's brood. I was the second youngest. And this here's my baby boy, Egmont." She leaned closer and whispered, "His pa and me always call him 'Eggie,' but now he's got a eye for the girls, he don't like that no more. He want to be 'Monty' now. Don't that beat all?" She laughed and slapped one ample hip.

Mary Scarlett stared at the woman. "You're Delsey's daughter?"

"Shore am! She used to bring me to work with her sometimes. I played many a hour on this here kitchen floor. Lord! Lord! Just look at it now! When Ma was in charge here, she kept it so clean you could eat offen it."

"I've been away," Mary Scarlett explained, Pearlene's words making her feel personally responsible for the decay and disarray all about them. "The house has been closed up since my mother's death."

Pearlene pulled a solemn face. "I was sorry to hear about that. Such a sweet lady, Miss Lucy. She was mighty good to us all her life. Many's the time she sent a box of your own lovely clothes home to us girls. Why, we was the best dressed at our school, thanks to you and your dear mama."

Egmont hung back, shifting from one foot to the other,

awaiting his instructions on the yard, eager as any teenager to get started, get finished, get paid, and go spend it.

"Eggie, meet Miss Mary Scarlett," Pearlene said. "Why, she's 'most like family. You best do a good job for her, now. You hear me?"

"Yeah, Ma," he answered in a bored tone. Then he nodded, unsmiling at Mary Scarlett. "Ma'am," was all he said.

"Well, I reckon it's time we all rolled up our sleeves. We got a heap of work to do. Eggie, you get that lawnmower outten the truck and get at it. I brought everything I'll need in here, Miss Mary Scarlett, including elbow grease. I see you done started emptying shelves in the kitchen. Good! I'll get right to that. Lordy, my ma would die all over again if she saw her kitchen in this mess!"

Mary Scarlett had wondered what ever happened to Delsey. It saddened her to learn that the old woman had died. "Your mama's passed on, too? I'm sorry, Pearlene. She and Granny Boo practically raised me."

Pearlene smiled her gratitude for the kind words as tears gathered in her eyes. "She always said you was a joy to have around, Miss Mary Scarlett. Loved you like one of her own, she did, to her dying day." She cast her gaze down, shaking her head sadly. "What they did to her was a crying shame. I won't *never* get over it. Not never!"

"Are you talking about Delsey?"

Pearlene nodded and dabbed at her eyes with the corner of her apron. "Yes'um."

"What happened to her, Pearlene?"

She glanced over her shoulder to make sure Egmont was out of earshot. Stepping into the kitchen, she closed the door firmly. "They done her in with the mojo," she whispered. "Killed her dead."

"Mojo?" Mary Scarlett repeated. It was a word she hadn't heard in years, not since her childhood at old Delsey's knee. "Pearlene, are you talking about voodoo? Do you mean to tell me someone put a conjure on your mama?"

Her round face strained with remembered grief, Pearlene nodded until her double chin jiggled. "You right about that, Miss Mary Scarlett! Buried a conjure bag somewhere on the place, they did. And, worse than that—you remember them frizzle chickens Ma used to keep for protection?"

Mary Scarlett almost smiled, remembering the funny looking chickens Delsey raised. All their feathers grew in backward, making them look like one of God's mistakes or at the very least proving that He had a bizarre sense of humor. Supposedly, these frizzle chickens were the only sure safeguard against conjures. They could seek out and destroy any bag of grave dirt and bones, no matter how powerful its spell.

"Yes, I remember Delsey's chickens."

"Well, ma'am, before they put the mojo on my ma, they sneaked up and kilt every one of them frizzles. Wrung their poor, scrawny necks. They wasn't taking no chances. Without the chickens for protection, Ma was as good as dead by morning, even though she lingered on, suffering the agonies of the conjure for weeks."

Mary Scarlett felt goosebumps crawl up her arm. "Who did this to her, Pearlene? When did it happen?"

"They put the spell on her right after your own mama died. See, Ma was still working here then. In fact, she's the one found poor Miss Lucy. Ma reckoned it was the man and woman that came to the house that night what put the conjure on her."

"Someone came here to visit the night of her fall?"

"Yes'um, least that's what my ma told me. That was her day off, but she come by the house that night late on her way home from church just to check was Miss Lucy doing all right. She'd been a mite poorly, you see. Ma told me that when she was coming in the back way, she heard a woman scream and then a man yell at her."

"Probably Mama and Big Dick having a fight," Mary

Scarlett said, remembering the terrible row the night she had left home.

"No'm, it couldn't have been. Your daddy had been gone a good while by then. And Ma said it wasn't Miss Lucy she heard screaming. Anyway, she hid out by the carriage house till she saw a man carry a woman out to a car in the alley. Then he went back inside and brought out a bunch of stuff from the house, put it in the car, and drove off with no headlights on. Ma rushed on in the house then. That's when she found poor Miss Lucy, lying there in the foyer, all busted up from her fall."

"Did Delsey tell this to the police, Pearlene?"

She looked mortified. "Oh, no, ma'am. Ma knew how touchy Miss Lucy was about gossip concerning the family. She'd have never let on that there was a man in the house, and Big Dick gone and all. Besides, the *po*lice wouldn't have believed a crazy old black woman."

"Pearlene! I'm surprised at you. Delsey wasn't crazy."

"Neither was Miss Boo, but everybody figured those two women had spent so many years together that they both had a few bats in the belfry."

"Who else knows about this?" Mary Scarlett demanded.

"Not another soul but me and my man. See, me and my family was living with Ma then. All my brothers and sisters had moved off the place and Pa'd been gone since right after my baby sister was born. Ma told me about it when we found the yard full of dead chickens a couple of days later. She knew she'd be next after them frizzles. She had me go to every mojo doctor in the county. They all said the same thing—without her knowing who done it, they couldn't fix it. So she just commenced withering away."

"That's terrible!" Mary Scarlett exclaimed. "Poor old Delsey!" There wasn't much else she could say. It would be a waste of breath to try to convince Pearlene that her mama had succumbed to anything other than a voodoo spell. Besides, from what Dr. Schlager had explained to her about his studies, mojo was very real, a case of mind over matter. If a person thought she was going to die from a spell, she died. Simple as that. *Scared to death.*

"Don't fret yourself, Miss Mary Scarlett. Ma went real peaceful at the end. That day she'd dragged herself up from her deathbed to bake a dozen lemon and pecan pies for the church homecoming." Pearlene shook her head sadly. "But she didn't never get to taste a one of them pies. Died that night in her sleep, real peaceful after all her suffering. I reckon the angels took pity on her at the last and just floated down from Heaven and carried her sweet soul home. It's the way she woulda wanted it. But I know she woulda liked to stay long enough to have a piece of one of them pecan pies. At her burying service, the preacher made a point of saying how like Ma it was to bake pies for her own funeral dinner. We had the burying during the church homecoming and everybody who came said it was the best one ever."

Mary Scarlett didn't ask "the best what?" Homecoming or funeral? Instead, her thoughts remained on the man and woman Delsey had seen the night of her mother's death. Maybe it hadn't been accidental after all.

To keep her mind off so many nagging questions, Mary Scarlett ushered Pearlene over to Delsey's deep sink and they both got busy, Mary Scarlett emptying cabinets and Pearlene washing dishes.

When the phone rang, Mary Scarlett jumped so she almost fell off her step ladder. She was emptying the highest shelves, pulling out old crockery and copper pans that had not been used in her lifetime. Pearlene was up to her elbows in soapsuds, singing hymns as she washed.

"I'll get it, Miss Mary Scarlett."

"No, let me," she answered. "I'm almost finished up here. I wonder who in the world it could be? Nobody knows I'm here and the phone was just reconnected."

Allen Overman knew. His grapevine never failed him. Pearlene's brother-in-law, who had driven Mary Scarlett from Bolt's place to Bull Street, had run into 'Gator White down on River Street performing for the tourists. 'Gator had wanted to know what was new, so the cabbie, for lack of any better gossip, had told him about his fare to the old Lamar house on Bull Street and that a right nice lady was moving in today. 'Gator had taken an emergency break from his banjo-picking to call Allen.

And, as Mary Scarlett soon found out, that wasn't all Allen Overman knew.

Sixteen

Earlier that morning, while Bolt had been tiptoeing around his apartment trying not to wake Mary Scarlett, Allen Overman was lying naked in Mrs. Hampstead's huge antique bed and staring up at the lovely old canopy.

Every day the elderly widow was gone from Savannah, Allen congratulated himself on his good luck. The only thing more fortunate for him would be the dear old lady's demise before she could return to her home. She had no close relatives as far as he knew—no one to lay claim to her valuables. And wasn't possession nine-tenths of the law? Before her estate was settled, he could enjoy a good, long stay in this wonderful mansion.

"Maybe it's time to start planning another party?" he mused aloud. "Bigger than last time. I'll have it right after my trip to New York—then I'll be able to announce the sale of the Josephine necklace. Yes. I like the drama of it."

His mind moved on quickly from one thought to the next like a train making whistle-stops. Soon, he would have to enlist 'Gator and 'Tator's assistance again, and there was a pending deal with his man in North Georgia, a new tux to be fitted, and a big poker game next week that he really shouldn't miss. Then there was Mary Scarlett.

"What to do about Mary Scarlett?" he muttered aloud.

She would certainly move back to Bull Street soon. Before she did, he had other problems to face. All his worries

would be over, however, if he could just get her to himself
for a while, with Bolt completely out of the picture.

"Doesn't he ever leave town?"

He had his big seduction scene all planned. He would
invite Mary Scarlett to an intimate dinner at the mansion,
just the two of them. He'd tell her the dress was casual.
When she arrived, they'd have a few drinks; then he would
spring his surprise on her—an elegant picnic on the beach
at Tybee. He would pack silver candelabra, chilled champagne, oysters on cracked ice, feta cheese, and plump, ripe
peaches.

Once they were well along with their gourmet picnic, he
would say, "Hey, remember all those wild, crazy things we
said and did when we were kids?" She was sure to give
him a sexy laugh—a little high on champagne and moonlight, and feeling kittenish from the oyster. Then she would
say that of course she remembered. That's when he would
move in for the kill. By this time he'd have their blanket
cleared of all food and dishes, ready to serve another purpose. He would move over close to Mary Scarlett, drape
his arm over her shoulders, and play with her hair while he
whispered, "Remember what I told all the guys the night
of your debutante ball?"

He pounded his heels and elbows on the mattress and
yelled, *"Yes! Perfect! Go, Overman!"*

Then letting his daydream drift on, he imagined Mary
Scarlett saying something like, "You were *bad,* Allen!" That
would give him the opportunity to whisper close to her ear,
"I still am, darlin'. Just can't help myself when I'm around
you. I've never given up my dream of making love to you
on the beach in the moonlight."

This would be the perfect time to kiss her and feel her
breasts. By the time he finished with her, she'd be all turned
on and ready for their big love scene.

"Oh, yes," he breathed, eyes closed, smile a mile wide.

He lay there for a while, creating the whole scene in his

mind—pale thighs parted and quivering against the dark blanket, heaving breasts, parted lips. All for him. Her slender body gleaming like old English silver in the light of the moon. He would tease her for a long time, make her beg to have him, then ease into her.

"Yes, Mama! Come to your papa," he moaned in an ecstasy of anticipation.

The fantasy he created was perfect. That, however, created a problem. He got an arousal that wouldn't be refused.

"Dammit," he muttered. "The maid's not even here yet."

He reached for the phone, trying to think who he could get to come over at seven-thirty in the morning. Somebody who might be as needy as he was. With a slow smile, he dialed Kathleen O'Shea.

When she answered, he said, "Katie, I apologize for calling you this early in the morning, but it's sort of urgent."

"No problem, Allen. I've been up since six. How can I help you?"

He grinned. "Are you heading for the office soon?"

"As a matter of fact, I was just walking out the door. What's up?"

He chuckled. "A lot! I want to talk to you about the possible sale of this property," he improvised quickly.

"You mean Mrs. Hampstead has finally decided to put it on the market?"

"I believe so. She adores Europe, may stay forever. If so, she'll sell this place. I thought you'd like first crack at the listing. If you could just stop by—I'm right on your way—I can tell you all about it." Allen's mind rushed ahead. He would lure Kathleen up to the bedroom when she arrived, then offer her the best of him.

"Gee, Allen, any other time. But I have to catch a plane to Atlanta at nine-thirty and run by the office to pick up some papers first. You won't let anyone else have it before I get back, will you?"

Sorely disappointed, he muttered, "I can't make any promises."

"I'll only be gone a few days. I'll call you the minute I get home. I promise. I'd better run now. Take care of yourself."

It looked like that's what Allen would be forced to do. He slammed the phone down in frustration, half-tempted to call Bolt's and try to lure Mary Scarlett over with some fantastic lie. Maybe he could tell her he knew something about her mirror. After some thought, he decided against that. Too risky.

He closed his eyes and went on with his beach fantasy. Before long, both Mary Scarlett and Kathleen were with him on the blanket in the moonlight, each begging for her turn. The clock ticked away as his imagination ran rampant—champagne poured over bodies slick with love-sweat, the three of them in the ocean with both women clinging to him for protection in the rough surf, husky lifeguards jogging down the beach to gather around the blanket and watch, with envious eyes, Allen in all his erotic glory. He drifted off to sleep letting dreams pick up where fantasies left off.

A couple of hours later, the jangling phone jerked him rudely awake.

"What?" he answered angrily.

"Hey, boss, it's me, 'Gator. I got some news might interest you."

"Well?"

"That lady you throwed the party for? She done moved in at Bull Street this morning."

Allen stared at the receiver in stunned silence. After a few seconds, he demanded, "How do you know?"

"Bubba done tol' me. He drove her there. She tol' him as how she be moving in for good—gonna call Pearlene and her boy Egmont to get the place in shape."

"Damn!" Allen cursed. "Hey, 'Gator?"

"Yeah, boss?"

"You stay in touch, you hear? You and 'Tator both. I'm gonna be needing you real soon."

"We ain't going nowhere, boss. Be right here shuckin' and jivin' the River Street crowd."

"Good! You'll hear from me. *Soon!*"

Allen sat on the side of the bed, staring down at himself. He no longer needed a woman. 'Gator's news had scared him limp and useless.

"Damn!" he repeated.

He dragged off to the bathroom, showered, and dressed before he called Mary Scarlett. By the time he dialed, he was already sipping his second vodka and orange juice—his breakfast.

"Allen, how on earth did you know I was here?" Mary Scarlett asked.

He chuckled, a sexy sound. "Oh, darlin', I have my ways. You don't think I'd let my favorite girl move in alone, do you? I'll be over in ten minutes to help you."

"Well, I won't deny that I need all the help I can get. There's more work than Pearlene and I can do. We'll be watching for you. And, Allen?"

"Yes, hon?"

"Thanks. Bolt's gone to Atlanta for the week and I can sure use a man around here."

"Really?" he said, his mind working furiously. "Well, I'm just the man for you. See you shortly."

After she hung up, Mary Scarlett went back to her task on the step ladder. She finished hauling the last of the dishes from the high shelves. "There! I think that should keep you busy for a while," she said to Pearlene. "I'm going upstairs and see what's to be done in the bedrooms. If you hear a knock at the front door, let Mr. Overman in, won't you? I don't like leaving it unlocked."

"You a smart lady, Miss Mary Scarlett," Pearlene assured her. "The things that go on in this town. Mercy! Makes a person scairt of her own shadow. Why, just last week my Cousin Luther got hisself shot in the leg in a car-jacking, and the old heap he was driving wasn't nothing but a junker. Them guys that shot him was on drugs, no doubt in my mind about it. Wouldn't nobody in his right mind want Luther's car. Even Luther don't want it! You just go on about your business now. I'll listen out for Mr. Allen."

Mary Scarlett gave her a quizzical look. "You know Allen Overman?"

Pearlene laughed. "Ain't nobody in Savannah who don't know Mr. Allen. He a good man, but tricky sometime."

"Tricky?" Mary Scarlett repeated.

Pearlene ducked her head in shame. "I shouldn't ought to have said that. If I was white, you'd see me just a-blushin', I'm so embarrassed this very minute."

"What do you mean by tricky, Pearlene?"

"Aw, nothing, ma'am. It's just, well, Mr. Allen, he don't do things like normal everyday folks. Always figuring out ways to twist everything his own way. Ain't nothing exactly bad about it, just different. Seem like he must have been birthed by a root doctor or something, the way things always go his way."

Mary Scarlett smiled. "Maybe it's just the luck of the Irish, Pearlene. I'll be upstairs if you need me for anything."

Crossing the foyer, Mary Scarlett couldn't keep her gaze from the spot where she knew her mother had died. Pearlene's tale of Delsey's death was still bothering her, too. She knew that voodoo had always been a powerful force among the lowcountry Gullah blacks, but she had never actually known anyone who was killed by a conjure. It seemed to her that Delsey had been too strong a woman to believe in the powers of mojo. Still, she was dead for a fact.

The wide hallway upstairs was dim and shadowy. Mary

Scarlett reached for a light switch. The twin pair of electrified sconces at each end of the hall offered little relief from the darkness. Three of the bulbs were burned out and all of the etched glass shades needed washing. She and Pearlene would have to tend to the lighting problem sometime today.

Big Dick's was the one bedroom Mary Scarlett had yet to enter. She decided to check it out first. When she opened the door, the sight that greeted her made her breath catch in her throat. Things were strewn about as if a tornado had passed through. The antique painting that had always hung over the chest of drawers hiding the wall safe was gone. The door of the empty safe stood wide open. Drawers were pulled out, clothes scattered, and the mattress was half off the bed.

"Mama must have been really mad the last time she was in here." She turned on a lamp to inspect the damage more closely. Also missing were a pair of antique duelling pistols that had hung in a shadowbox over the bed. She went to the armoire and searched inside for the secret panel that slid open to reveal a hidy-hole where her father had always kept a pouch of antique gold coins. That, too, was empty.

"Somebody really cleaned the place out," she murmured aloud to herself. "But who?"

"Shoot! I meant to surprise you."

Mary Scarlett jumped when Allen spoke from the doorway. She turned quickly, her hand over her heart. "Allen Overman, you scared me out of ten years' growth! I didn't hear you come in."

"Sorry, hon." He walked over and gave her a peck on the cheek. "I figured you'd heard me coming up the stairs and were talking to me when I walked in." He glanced around. "God, what a mess! Who did this?"

"That's exactly what I was wondering when you sneaked in."

"I didn't sneak!" he protested.

"Whatever. At any rate, this room has been ransacked and everything of value was stolen. Paintings, antiques, gold coins, even the contents of the safe."

"Maybe your daddy did it before he left. You know how wild he got at times. Or maybe Miss Lucy trashed the place after he went away."

Mary Scarlett nodded, but she was thinking that more likely the couple who had been in the house the night of her mother's death had done it. Who were they? How could she find out?

She turned to him, frowning. "Allen, were you here for Mama's wake? Bolt told me a lot of her friends came and sat with her body the night before the funeral. He said that the house was locked up when the casket was taken to the church and not opened again until I came home."

He nodded, his face solemn. "I came to pay my respects, but I didn't stay long. Why?"

"I was wondering if there was anyone here that night who might have done this."

"Oh, Mary Scarlett, of course not! You don't come into someone's home to pay your respects to a corpse, then slip upstairs to rob them blind."

"I guess you're right."

"Besides, most of the people here that night were members of the UDC. Can you see the illustrious Daughters of the Confederacy doing this? I think not."

Mary Scarlett couldn't stifle a giggle, picturing those elderly matrons in their hats and white gloves, still worshipping their great-grandfathers' unsuccessful efforts fighting for the Cause, coming up here to Big Dick's bedroom to wreak havoc. Come to think of it, she had trouble picturing any of them in any man's bedroom for any purpose.

"You're right, Allen," she repeated. "I'm just having a hard time putting all this together in my mind. If Big Dick had been gone so long, why wasn't his room cleaned in case he returned or for guests if he didn't? Mama might have gone off the deep end when he disappeared, but Delsey was still here. The woman waged a lifelong battle against dirt and disorder."

Allen shrugged. "Who knows? Maybe Miss Lucy had too much peach brandy one night and tore the place up. Does it matter after all these years?"

"It matters that so many valuables are missing. Somebody's helped themselves to a fortune that belonged to me. I mean to find out who."

Mary Scarlett motioned Allen toward the hallway, then followed him out and slammed the door on the mess. She would worry about it later. Right now her own room was her main objective since she planned to sleep in it.

Allen helped her strip the musty sheets from the bed, take down her curtains, and make a pile of the hooked rugs. By the time they finished, the air was thick with dust.

Mary Scarlett began to cough and opened the windows. "Let's get out of here till the dust settles. Help me carry these down to Pearlene. I sure hope the washer and dryer still work."

Allen hauled the heavy rugs out into the hallway. Mary Scarlett winced when he dumped them over the railing at exactly the spot where she imagined her mother had fallen—*or been thrown*—to her death.

He reached for the linens in Mary Scarlett's arms. "That's all right," she said. "I'll carry these down."

Back in the kitchen, piling the bedding by the laundry room alcove, they found Pearlene just finishing up at the sink. Allen gave her an affectionate smack on her broad backside. "Hey, gal! Where you been keeping yourself? You're still as pretty as a swamp flower."

Pearlene giggled and said, "Go on with you, Mr. Allen. I ain't pretty as *no* flower. How you been?"

As the two bantered back and forth, it didn't dawn on Mary Scarlett that this was obviously the first time Allen and Pearlene had laid eyes on each other for a while. Her

302   Becky Lee Weyrich

mind was too filled with other things to wonder how Allen had gotten in if Pearlene hadn't unlocked the door for him.

Mary Scarlett stepped out the back door to see how Egmont was coming with the yard. She was pleased to see that a lawn was emerging from the jungle. Allen followed her out.

"It's going to be a hot one, honey. Want to take a break and go somewhere for a tall cool drink and some lunch? You name it—Pirate's House, Pink House, Mrs. Wilkes's Kitchen."

His last suggestion made Mary Scarlett's stomach growl with desire. Mrs. Wilkes's fried chicken, cornbread, rice and gravy, candied yams, and turnip greens would taste wonderful about now. But half the tourists in town would be lined up, waiting to get into the popular restaurant by this time of day. That crunchy chicken would have to wait for another, more leisurely time.

She turned to smile at him. "Sounds great, but no, Allen. We'll have to settle for a pizza by phone today. Too much work to do."

He leaned close and touched her temple with his. "Ah, I finally get you alone and all I get is dust and pizza. What a waste, darlin'!"

She laughed. "The sooner I finish, the sooner I'll be ready to start leading a normal life. *Then* you can take me to lunch anytime you please, Allen."

"Promise?"

"Promise!"

Out of the blue, he asked, "What kind of business do Bolt and Kathleen have in Atlanta together this week?"

The shock factor he had hoped for registered on Mary Scarlett's face. Her eyes narrowed, her nostrils flared, and her lips parted as if she couldn't quite get her breath.

"What are you talking about, Allen? They aren't together."

"Oh, my mistake." He sounded as innocent as a babe.

"When you said Bolt had gone to Atlanta this morning, then I talked to Kathleen and she was leaving at the same time for the same destination, I just assumed . . ."

"Well, you assumed wrong," Mary Scarlett snapped. "What business could they possibly have together?"

Allen smiled and brushed a wisp of hair back from Mary Scarlett's damp forehead. "Forget it, darlin'. Atlanta's a big town. You're probably right. I'll bet they were surprised to find themselves on the same flight this morning. I doubt they'll even have time to see each other all week."

He had chosen the perfect words to ignite Mary Scarlett's jealousy. She could deny it all she liked, but he could tell from the look in her eyes that he had planted more than a bit of doubt in her mind—a doubt that would plague her every minute until Bolt returned. Before then, Allen had other plans for Mary Scarlett.

While they were working side by side in the attic the next day, Allen said, "Want to go to New York with me Friday?"

She only stared at him over a stack of papers she was sorting.

"I'm serious. The Josephine necklace is going to be auctioned at Sotheby's. I've already reserved a suite at the Plaza. You could come along, do some shopping, see a few shows. You deserve a break after all this."

"Thanks, Allen, but you know I can't."

"The offer's open if you change your mind. I'll be leaving Friday and I sure would love to have your company. Shoot, honey, if Bolt can drop everything to take a little vacation, you can, too."

Allen didn't mention Kathleen; he didn't have to. No more was said about it, but that didn't put a stop to Mary Scarlett's nagging suspicions.

* * *

Mary Scarlett and Allen spent the next few days working at the house. Things were coming along nicely as far as the housecleaning and repairs were concerned. But every day that passed gave Allen more opportunity to needle Mary Scarlett—gently, of course—about Bolt and Kathleen. Bolt didn't help matters by not phoning Mary Scarlett for several days.

When he finally called on Thursday, she was in no mood to be cordial. It was around eleven o'clock one night after a long, hot day of cleaning and sorting in the carriage house. She was already asleep when the phone rang.

"Honey, did I wake you?"

"Bolt?" She listened closely. Again, she heard bar-sounds in the background—music, laughter, and glasses tinkling. Her suspicions deepened. Her jealousy flared. "Where are you?"

"In Atlanta," he said. "Still working. But I have some leads on the guy I'm looking for."

"Oh, good," she said sarcastically. *Like I care!* she added silently.

"What's wrong, Mary Scarlett? Everything all right at the house?"

"Just dandy! If you don't count the fact that someone came in here while I was away and robbed me blind."

"Are you serious? My God! Have you called the police?"

"Yes, but they claim the theft took place so long ago that there's no hope of finding any leads."

"Well, we'll just see about that. I'll talk to them when I get back."

All of a sudden, Mary Scarlett desperately wanted to see Bolt, to have him hold her and make love to her again. "Bolt, when are you coming home?"

There was a brief hesitation at the other end, then she heard him sigh. "I'd hoped to be back tomorrow or Saturday, but this may take longer than I planned. I just can't tell you right now, honey. There are some details I still have to wind up."

"How's Kathleen?"

"What? How did you know she was here?"

Mary Scarlett felt real pain shoot through her heart. "I have my sources."

Hearing that tone in her voice, he said, "It's nothing, Mary Scarlett. We just happened to be on the same flight. We both had a free evening tonight so we decided to have dinner together."

Stony silence on Mary Scarlett's end.

"Believe me, darlin', I'm ready to finish things up and get home as soon as possible. I miss you!"

"Don't hurry things on my account," she answered archly. "I'm leaving anyway."

"Leaving?"

Mary Scarlett smiled at the panic she heard in his voice. *Tit for tat, my love,* she mused.

"Honey, what are you talking about? You can't leave. Not now! Not when everything's just starting to make sense between us. Come on, Mary Scarlett, give it a chance."

A chance like you're giving it with Kathleen? she thought.

"I'm going to New York for a few days, Bolt. Allen's invited me to go with him to the auction, to see that diamond necklace sold."

"Mary Scarlett, don't do this."

"Give my best to Kathleen." Then she hung up. Then she cried.

What on earth had possessed her? She hadn't the least desire to go to New York with Allen. She didn't give a damn about that necklace. If she had only thought to ask Bolt where he was staying. If only she'd gotten his number. She could call him back this minute and tell him she wasn't going to New York with Allen, that she had never had any intention of going. That she only wanted to be with him.

If, if, if!

But she didn't have his number. So, still visualizing Bolt and Kathleen at their cozy dinner, she dialed Allen's instead. "Count me in on the New York trip," she said, then hung up.

When Bolt returned to the table from making his phone call, he looked as upset as he felt.

"Trouble?" Kathleen asked.

"How'd you guess?"

"Well, the fact that you look like somebody just shot your favorite bird dog gave me a clue. Want to talk about it?"

He sat down and struck the table with his clenched fist. "Damn! I knew I shouldn't have left her alone so soon."

Kathleen tried to hide her hurt. She had had high hopes for this dinner date. Neither she nor Bolt had known about the other's planned trip to Atlanta until they boarded the plane in Savannah. They had sat together and talked on the flight, the talk consisting mostly of Bolt telling Kathleen how well things were going between him and Mary Scarlett, and Kathleen grinning and bearing it. At the Atlanta airport, they had gone their separate ways, but not before Kathleen had given Bolt the name of her hotel and he had promised to call sometime during the week.

The week had been half over when he finally phoned. She had gone all out, even had her hair and nails done and bought a new dress for the occasion. What a waste of red silk! All Bolt had talked about all evening was Mary Scarlett. Still, Kathleen had hopes for after dinner, when she planned to get herself invited back to his hotel room, but the last glimmer had faded when he excused himself to call home.

"Calm down, Bolt." Kathleen glanced around the quiet dining room, sure everyone was staring at them after his outburst. She covered his fist with her hand to keep him from permanently scarring the antique table. "Tell me what's happened."

His eyes flashed dark fire. "Allen Overman! That's what's happened. He must have moved in on her before the plane even took off. Now he's taking her to New York. Can you believe this?"

"And?"

He flashed an angry look at Kathleen. "*And* they'll probably get real cozy while they're there."

"Like we have while we've been up here in Atlanta together, you mean?"

"Dammit, it's not the same and you know it, Kathleen. We're both here on business and we didn't know we would be here at the same time. Why, we've hardly laid eyes on each other all week."

She nodded, afraid a reply might betray her disappointment.

"Allen *invited* Mary Scarlett to go with him. But, by damn, she didn't have to accept. I've a good mind to drop everything and fly home tonight."

Kathleen couldn't stifle a laugh. "*You men!*"

"What do you mean by that?"

"Well, it's just that you're all so gullible. I suspect that's exactly what Mary Scarlett's hoping you'll do. She probably has no intention of going to New York with Allen. Or, if she does decide to go— just to make you jealous— she'll insist on separate rooms and keep her door locked. She's figuring, though, that you'll come running home to her. A little white lie never hurt. I'd probably do the same thing in her shoes."

"I don't understand. She knows I'm here on business. And actually, it's business that has to do with her. I'm hot on Big Dick's trail."

"You're kidding, Bolt! You mean he's still alive?"

"I'm not certain yet. But I know for a fact that he didn't die in any boating accident."

"Mary Scarlett doesn't know anything about this?"

"No. The way she felt about her father, I thought it was better to keep it to myself."

"Does she have any idea why you're up here?"

"Not really."

Kathleen shook her head. *"Men!"* she said again. She stared Bolt square in the eye. "Look, I'm going to level with you, ole buddy. I haven't given another man a second glance since Jimbo died. But finally I decided it was time. I haven't been just dating you, I've been laying the groundwork for a marriage. Well, all those plans caved in on me the morning I read in the paper that Mary Scarlett was back. I knew before I ever saw her again that my chances were all washed up."

Bolt looked at her with sympathy in his eyes. "I'm sorry, Kathleen. I never meant to lead you on. And I certainly didn't mean to hurt you. I guess I was just so damn lonely."

She laughed. "Weren't we both! Don't apologize, Bolt. We never really fell in love. We fell in *like*. Our relationship was so comfortable that we let it continue. Both of us were just going to settle because we hadn't found anyone else to light our fires. At least I hadn't. As for you, you've never gotten over Mary Scarlett, probably never will. If you don't marry her, you're a prize idiot."

He chuckled. "You've got me pegged, all right. So what do I do next?"

"First of all, you turn me down flat when I try to worm my way into your hotel room later tonight. I'll probably still try, even though I know it's hopeless."

He grinned at her. "You were really going to do that?"

"I most certainly was and I'll probably still try, as I said. But it wouldn't be a good idea, no matter how horny we are."

"You *are?*" He gave her a crooked, sexy grin.

"Don't you dare flirt with me, Bolton Conrad! If you're

going to marry Mary Scarlett, the fun's over between us. And it has been fun."

"Who says I'm going to marry Mary Scarlett? I want to—sure—but she's got this idea about that damn mirror and some guy who's been dead for years. Unless I can prove I'm him, there's no way she'll marry me."

"What a crock! And you know it, Bolt. All Mary Scarlett or most any other woman wants is a man to sweep her off her feet. You keep giving her room, allowing her space to get away from you."

"I crowded her before and I lost her. I've learned from that."

"Pardon my French, darling, but you didn't learn shit! Mary Scarlett's not the same person she was back then. She's changed; we all have. And we're not getting any younger. If you want her, go get her."

Bolt motioned to their waiter for the check, in a hurry all of a sudden. "Thanks, Kathleen. I know what I have to do now. I'll drop everything and fly back tonight."

"No, you won't!" She gripped his hand as if to stop him physically. "Have you listened to *anything* I've said, Bolt? If you rush back to Savannah, it will be like waving a white flag. No woman wants a man who's been humbled. We like winners, white knights who come to our rescue. That's what takes the breath away."

Bolt remained silent for several moments, a plan forming in his mind. The waiter came and took his credit card. A few minutes later, they were out in the parking lot, each waiting for the other to speak.

"I guess this is goodbye," Kathleen said at last.

"Sure I can't lure you back to my room?"

"In a heartbeat, but please don't try, Bolt. I'm not a strong woman."

He chuckled and kissed her cheek. "I guess I'll see you back in Savannah next week then."

She shook her head. "I doubt it. I've been offered a job

with our Atlanta branch. I think the change will do me good. I'll be back, but only long enough to pack up and head to the big city. You look surprised, Bolt."

"Not really." He hugged her, a definite farewell embrace. "You know I wish you luck, Katie. And thanks—for everything."

Bolt stood in the parking lot until he saw Kathleen's rental car vanish into the night, thinking of all that might have been and all that was still possible for the future.

He glanced at his watch. Twelve-twenty. "The perfect time to pay a call on Mr. Quincey," he said.

Returning briefly to the restaurant, Bolt placed a local call. Minutes later, he was speeding toward an apartment complex on the outskirts of Marietta. The manager had told him earlier that Lumpkin Quincey had moved in last week and that he usually came in from work around midnight. With any luck, Bolt would find the subject of his search snoozing away, unsuspecting and unarmed.

He wasn't disappointed. His heavy knock at the door was answered by a short, rumpled, bleary-eyed man. Magnolia was right—he did look like a 'possum.

"Lumpkin Quincey?" Bolt demanded.

"Who wants to know?"

"Bolton Conrad," he answered. "I'm Magnolia's lawyer."

"I don't know no Magnolia," the 'possum whined. "Get the hell outta here!"

"Sorry, but I'll have to stick around for just a bit. You see, you're expecting more company, whether you know it or not."

"I ain't expecting *nobody* this time of night."

"It's a surprise party," Bolt said with a friendly chuckle. "And here they are now."

The flashing blue lights of the two police cars, responding to Bolt's call, brought a low curse from Quincey. Once the uniforms reached the door, it was all over in minutes.

Search warrant in hand, one of them handcuffed their prisoner and put him in the back of a squad car.

Among the cardboard boxes, still packed from his recent move, the investigators found letters from Richard Lamar, an address book with Magnolia's name and various numbers in it, some of the jewelry Big Dick had stolen from the Bull Street house. They also found a cancelled check written to the boathouse where Lamar had rented his ill-fated fishing boat, credit cards belonging to Richard H. Lamar, and keys to Mary Scarlett's house. There was one more thing, too, that especially interested Bolt. A letter written to Lumpkin Quincey by Allen Overman. Bolt frowned as he read the brief note. There was really nothing incriminating in its content, but still, the connection between the two men was there. What was Overman doing with a friend like Quincey?

Around three in the morning, Bolt followed the police cars to the station. With Quincey in custody, he would soon know the whereabouts of Big Dick. Then he could concentrate on more pleasant business, like the woman with hair as black as midnight at Bonaventure.

"Mary Scarlett," he whispered. "You don't know it yet, darlin', but you've got a wedding to plan."

Seventeen

Mary Scarlett woke up the next morning with a pounding headache. As wonderful as it had been to hear Bolt's voice on the phone the night before, their conversation had left her anxious and upset. She shouldn't have lied to him about going to New York with Allen. It was a cheap schoolgirl trick to make her lover jealous. He had damn well deserved it, but she felt bad just the same.

She had barely finished dressing when Allen arrived on her doorstep, beaming excitedly. "Mary Scarlett, darlin', do I have a surprise for you!"

"Do you mind if I get a cup of coffee first?"

"I'll allow that. Then you'd better get your bags packed for New York."

His mention of the trip stabbed at her again. "Allen, I've changed my mind. I'm sorry, but I really can't go. There's just too much to do here."

"No argument, honey! Not yet." He took her arm and led her to the kitchen, heated a cup of last night's coffee in the microwave, then set it before her. "Drink up. Then look at this."

He flashed a colorful magazine before her eyes. "What is it?"

"Sotheby's catalogue. And you'll never guess what's in it."

"The Josephine," she said dully.

"Yeah, but that's not all."

Quickly, he flipped through the pages of beautiful colored pictures until he found the one he was searching for. He held it out for her to see.

"Take a gander at *this!*"

Mary Scarlett set her mug down so suddenly that it spilled, pouring coffee all over the table and her lap before it pooled on the floor. "Allen!" she gasped. "It can't be!"

"But it is, isn't it?"

"Granny Boo's mirror! How did it get to New York? What's it doing for sale? It belongs to me."

"Search me, honey. Maybe whoever stole all the other stuff took the mirror, too. But that doesn't matter. We'll go to New York and buy it back. I have to warn you, though, it's likely to carry a pretty fancy price tag."

She glanced up at him, frantic. "Allen, I don't have a lot of cash right now. Everything's still tied up until Raul's estate is settled. He has some relatives back in Spain, and the Spanish courts are so slow. What if I don't have enough?"

He leaned down and kissed her, then smiled into her eyes. "Don't you fret, sweetheart. I'll buy it for you. Even if I have to sell my house, I'll get that mirror back for you."

"Oh, Allen, I don't want you to do that. Maybe I can get a loan or something." Her face turned stormy. "Why should I have to buy it back anyway? It *belongs* to me. It's stolen property."

"That's going to be hard to prove, since it's for sale at Sotheby's. They check out their items thoroughly. Somebody—whoever's selling it—must have firm proof of ownership. But don't you worry, Mary Scarlett. It will be a pleasure for me to buy that mirror back for you. Everything I have is yours, if you'll accept it."

Before Mary Scarlett realized what he was up to, Allen was down on one knee, holding her hands in his. While he was proposing marriage, all she could think about was that he was messing up his crisply laundered chinos in the pool of coffee she had spilled.

When he finished his long, rambling proposal, which included some wild fantasies about taking her to Tybee to eat oysters and make love in front of lifeguards on the beach under the moon, Mary Scarlett felt totally confused.

"Well, Mary Scarlett?" he finished hopefully.

"Get up, Allen. You're ruining your pants."

He rose slowly, grinning down at her, still holding her hands. "You weren't listening to a word I said, were you? Why, you were a million miles away. Mary Scarlett, I just asked you to marry me!"

"I know, I know," she said impatiently. "But right now I have to call the airlines and see if I can still get a flight to New York."

"Then you agree?" he whooped.

"To New York. Not to marriage." She tossed her words over her shoulder as she dialed the phone.

"Hey, I'll take what I can get for now," he answered with a lusty chuckle. "But once I get that mirror for you, I'll expect more than a simple thank you."

Mary Scarlett missed this last bit from Allen. She had someone on the phone and was making arrangements to go to New York. When she was put on hold for a moment, she suddenly recalled what the spirits on the other side had told her through Helga at Dr. Schlager's—that the mirror was with a great "bird." As Bolt had suspected, it had been on a plane at the time, winging its way from Savannah to New York.

To Bolt's vast relief, Lumpkin Quincey was not a tough nut to crack. Once he was in custody, he spilled his guts about everything. Bolt stood outside the mirror-window of the interrogation cell, drinking bad coffee from a styrofoam cup while he watched the thin, mean-tempered thief and extortionist squirm under two detectives' unrelenting questioning.

"I never heard of Richard Lamar or any woman named Magnolia," the pointy-faced punk said, shying away from the direct gaze of the "bad cop" officer firing questions in an angry snarl. "You got the wrong guy. I'm just an honest, hardworking security guard, trying to get along. You gonna mess things up so I lose my job. I don't know nothing."

"If you're the wrong guy," the second detective said almost pleasantly, playing the "good cop" role to the hilt, "perhaps you'd care to explain to us how all that stuff in those boxes got into your room, Mr. Quincey."

His narrow head twitched to one side with a nervous tic. "Don't know," he mumbled. "I guess somebody broke in and left all that junk at my place. He's the guy you ought to be looking for. Why don't you arrest him for breaking and entering?"

Bolt noted that Quincey glanced up quickly to see if the officers were buying his story.

"Well now, Mr. Quincey, I guess it could have happened that way, but, you see, the manager of your apartment told us he saw you hauling all those boxes from your van the day you moved in."

"He's lying!" Quincey snapped.

The big, farmboyish officer nodded slowly, as if considering that possibility. "That brings up a problem, doesn't it? Your word against his. I guess we've got no choice but to call in our polygraph expert and let him run tests on you and the apartment manager." Detective Edgerton sounded bored, world-weary, but still amiable. "Then we'll have to run fingerprint comparisons, phone all those numbers in that book we found and check them out, find this Lamar fellow and his lady friend Magnolia. It'll be a whole lot of work, but if you won't cooperate, we can do it. And we will. And we'll get to the bottom of all this. And you'll likely have time to get a library card all your own down at Reidsville, where guys who don't cooperate tend to wind up for a *long* stay."

Bolt watched Quincey squirm under Edgerton's calm gaze.

No one said anything for several minutes. The only

sounds coming from the room were Quincey's jeans rubbing the wooden seat of the chair and the nervous cracking of his knuckles.

"Well, Haggard, what do you think?" the nice cop said to his surly, short-tempered companion.

"What do *I* think, Edgerton?" Haggard's deep voice boomed inside the small cell. He sounded angry enough to rip Quincey's 'possum-head from his scrawny body. "I think he's a goddamn liar. I think we oughta lock him up down at Reidsville and throw away the fucking key! He's too dumb to help himself, so why should we try to make it easy for him? The bastard ought to see by now that he's peanuts . . . that it's Lamar we want, the brains of the operation. But if he says he don't know no Lamar, then I guess Mr. Q here will have to serve time. If he had the brains God give a billygoat, he'd tell us where to find Lamar and we'd cut him a deal."

Quincey looked up quickly to see if Haggard was serious.

"He's right, you know," Edgerton said in that velvet voice. "If you helped us find Lamar and explained to us what all this is about, we'd go easy on you."

"How easy?" Quincey wanted to know.

Edgerton smiled sweetly. "That depends on you, on what you can tell us and how much it helps."

Once Lumpkin Quincey started running off at the mouth, it seemed to Bolt that he just couldn't stop. He had known Big Dick Lamar since college. They had been fraternity pledges together, but Quincey hadn't lasted into a second quarter. Over the years, he'd always been at Lamar's beck and call, for the right price. He was the one who had arranged to smuggle Big Dick's Cuban cigars into the country. He was the one who found women for Lamar when he couldn't find his own. He had talked to the right people to fix DUI charges against Lamar, to hush things up when Big Dick got caught with a teenage girl whose mother threatened to blow the whistle on him. And when Miss Lucy had had all she could take and had threatened to divorce her husband, Quincey had come up with the idea of Lamar's ill-fated fishing trip.

Bolt set aside his coffee cup and leaned closer to the window when Quincey got to that part of his story.

"You're telling us that Lamar would have been *embarrassed* if his wife had divorced him and on account of that he faked his own death?" Edgerton exchanged an exaggerated look of disbelief with Haggard.

"Naw, that's not what I'm saying," Quincey added quickly when he saw the anger in Haggard's ugly face. "Big Dick had this gal. He wanted to run off with her. It just so happened that was at the same time that Miss Lucy started threatening divorce."

"And this *gal* . . ." Haggard paused and smiled—a frightening sight to see. "Her name wouldn't happen to be Magnolia, would it?"

Hypnotized by the evil gleam in Haggard's eyes, Quincey first shook his head, then nodded. "Uh, well, I guess that's what she calls herself now. Back then she was just plain Jenny Flower. A waitress down on River Street. But she was a looker."

"Let me get this straight," Edgerton interrupted. "You are telling us that you set up everything so the two of them could take off on a joy ride all over the country. That kind of cut you from the pattern, didn't it? I mean, without Big Dick around, what did you do as a means of support?"

The 'possum grinned. "I ain't so dumb as you think. I let Lamar know before he left that I'd be needing some funds from time to time to keep my mouth shut."

"And?" Haggard demanded.

"And he give me a bag of gold coins to tide me over till he got back."

"Got back?" Edgerton asked. "You mean Lamar returned to Savannah?"

"Just once. Long enough to visit his wife one last time and get some of his stuff from the house." Quincey's nervous, lopsided grin betrayed him. He obviously wasn't telling everything he knew.

Haggard quickly wiped the smirk off his suspect's face. "That's it, Edgerton! I ain't giving this louse no more time. He's playing with us, kidding around, thinks he's so god-damn smart. Well, he *ain't!* And I say we throw the book at him for wasting our time."

Bolt watched Edgerton reach out and grab Haggard's arm to keep him from throwing a punch at their prisoner, who was now cowering instead of grinning. "Hold on now, Haggard. He was just fixing to tell us the rest. Weren't you, Mr. Quincey? I can tell from that look on your face that you're just dying to tell us everything. Right, ole buddy?"

He nodded vigorously, leaning as far away from Haggard as possible. "Yessir! But, you see, the part you want most to hear, I wasn't there to see. That's why I didn't tell it. I wasn't holding out on you guys. Honest!"

"We know you weren't, Mr. Quincey. Now, just take your time and tell us the rest," Edgerton prompted calmly.

"Yeah!" Haggard growled, then slammed his fist down on the table. "And you better be quick about it, butt-head!"

"He killed her!" Quincey yelled. "He killed Miss Lucy!"

Bolt stood riveted to the spot, listening to Quincey's second-hand account of Lucy Lamar's death, almost the same in every detail as Magnolia had told it to Bolt. He also told how Big Dick had torn up his room in a rage when he found most of his valuables missing. He had then carried off anything pawnable—silver, paintings, jewelry. After that, Quincey had been hanging around Savannah, keeping an eye on Magnolia for Lamar and extorting money from her for himself, a scheme that had been financially satisfying for years. It kept Big Dick happy and kept Magnolia paying for her blackmailer's silence.

In his talks with the police during the week, Bolt had told them, too, about old Delsey's death by conjure. So it was no surprise to him when Haggard demanded to know "What about the Lamars' maid? What happened to her?"

"The mojo got her," Quincey muttered.

"And who arranged that?"

"I didn't do it!" he snapped in a scared tone. "Big Dick gave me a number to call in Savannah. I delivered the message—don't even know the guy's name."

"What did you tell this man?" Edgerton asked.

"To get them chickens, then throw a little grave dirt old Delsey's way. That's all! I swear it! I don't mess in no voodoo. That's mean stuff!"

Finally, Haggard asked the question that Bolt had been waiting to hear. "Where is Richard Lamar now?"

A deep silence fell over the scene. Then Quincey drew in a ragged sigh and let it out. "Dead!"

"Dead?" the two officers said at once.

"You kill him?" Haggard demanded.

For the first time, Quincey raised his voice to the tough detective. "Hell, no! What you think, I'm crazy? Shit, man, I had to go back to work once he was gone. Why you think I'm busting my ass as a security guard at that crumby mall? All I got left to show for all I done for Big Dick is that little bit of jewelry I was fixing to pawn. That's the last of it—the last there'll ever be. Man, I wouldn't kill my main meal ticket."

"Then what happened to him?" Haggard growled.

Quincey laughed. "He died in a fishing accident."

When Haggard let out a roar, Quincey covered his head with his arms. "Hey, I'm telling the truth! I almost went with him. Coulda been me out there feeding the alligators. He had this place down in the Okefenokee Swamp. Just a shack, but it was a good hideout. He even had a gal in there with him for a while, but she got bored 'cause there was no TV. About three months ago, I thought I'd go out to his place to spend a day or so, see if there was anything left I could get out of this relationship. If not, I figured I'd move on. He didn't have a thing left, not worth having anyway. He fried us some fish and rattlesnake over a fire. We ate, then he said he was going out in the boat with his pole for a while to catch breakfast. He asked me to come on along. Me, I ain't no fisherman. Can't even swim, so I stay clear of boats unless I'm getting paid to go. I would have left, but I couldn't do that either. It was dark by then, too dark to find my way back to civilization without his help. So I figured I'd get some shut-eye, have breakfast with him, then say so long for good. Find me some bigger fish to fry, so to speak. But I never saw him again. First light, I found his boat washed up a few yards from camp. It had a hunk chomped out of it by a 'gator. The teeth prints were right there to see. So, breakfast got caught that night, but not by Big Dick. He *was* breakfast!"

"You didn't report it?" Edgerton asked.

Quincey shrugged. "Who the hell would care? His kid was off in Spain or somewhere and they never got along anyway. Besides, I figured there wouldn't have been any remains to find once that 'gator finished with him. And I just plain didn't see no reason to get involved."

Bolt had heard enough. The sun was already up and he was dead on his feet. Haggard came out of the room for a minute.

"You still here?"

Bolt nodded and rubbed a hand over the stubble on his chin. "Had to hear it all," he said.

"So, what do you think?"

"I think he's a scrounge and a jerk and the scum of the earth, but it doesn't sound like he killed anybody. Sounds like that Okefenokee alligator took care of seeing that your killer was brought to justice."

"What about his daughter? Somebody has to notify her."

"I'll do it," Bolt said, feeling a pleasant rush when he thought of Mary Scarlett, even under such unpleasant circumstances. "I'm going to catch the first flight back to Savannah. I guess I've finished my business up here."

"Sounds like it, Mr. Conrad." Haggard extended his hand. "We really appreciate all your help. You have a good trip home now."

Bolt turned and left. He broke into a trot once he was outside the building. All of a sudden, he couldn't wait to get back to Mary Scarlett. He had to go to his hotel to pack and check out. He would call and tell her he was on his way.

But by the time Bolt got someone in Savannah, it was too late. Pearlene answered the phone at the Bull Street house.

"Naw, sir, Mr. Bolt. She done left to go up to New Yawk with Mr. Allen. They been gone 'bout a hour already."

Bolt sagged down on the bed and groaned.

"Allen, are you out of your mind?" Mary Scarlett whispered as they rode up on the roomy elevator at the Plaza. *"Fourteen hundred dollars?"*

She wasn't referring to the price of the mirror she had come to buy, but the cost per night of the suite Allen had reserved.

He chuckled and squeezed her hand. "It's only money," he said. "Besides, I want you to enjoy your stay in New York to its fullest. Nothing's too good for the woman I plan to marry." He failed to mention the fact that he was putting the bill on Mrs. Hampstead's account.

Champagne and a dozen red roses awaited them in their magnificent rooms—one of the corner turret suites that overlooked the busy traffic on Fifth Avenue, but was too high above it all for any city noise to intrude. Sipping champagne, Mary Scarlett strolled from room to room, admiring the ornate gilt decor, the fine velvets and tapestries of the furniture, the Roman bath, and the king-sized bed.

Allen came up behind her and kissed her neck as she stood staring at the bed.

"Great, isn't it?" he whispered.

"Lovely," she answered, "but where are *you* going to sleep?"

He chuckled, thinking she was making a joke. Not until after they had been to the Winter Garden to see "CATS," then shared a late dinner at the Russian Tea Room did Allen find out she was deadly serious. When they returned to their suite at the Plaza, Mary Scarlett went straight to the bedroom. Allen smiled, anticipating her return to the parlor after she had changed into something more comfortable. Instead, she returned—still dressed in the svelte black suit she had worn to the theater—carrying a pillow and a blanket, which she dropped on the burgundy velvet sofa.

"For you," she said sweetly.

Allen's blissful smile faded. "You can't be serious! Mary Scarlett, I've asked you to marry me. Don't tell me you plan to put me out in the cold."

Glancing around the lavishly decorated room, she answered, "I'd hardly describe it that way. I'm simply not going to share the bedroom with you. I'm sorry, Allen."

"Not even with us about to get married?"

She stared him straight in the eye. "I never said I would marry you or anyone else."

"Still can't decide between me and Bolt, eh?"

"This has nothing to do with deciding between you. Actually, I don't think I'm cut out for marriage. I came up here for one reason—to get my mirror back. The fancy frills are your idea, Allen. I'm sorry if I'm ruining your trip, but it can't be helped. I'll see you in the morning."

Allen flopped down on the sofa, all the wind out of his sails. It was a good thing he wasn't paying for any of this or he'd really be upset.

"I should have gone to see that voodoo woman in Thunderbolt before the trip," he muttered. "She deals in passion potions. Hell, it worked on old Delsey, so why wouldn't it work on Mary Scarlett?"

After a few minutes of stung contemplation, Allen rallied, left the suite, and headed downstairs to cruise the bar.

Mary Scarlett tried to feel bad about turning Allen down after he'd reserved this gorgeous suite and offered to buy back her mirror. But she couldn't. There was something about his attitude that irked her. It seemed almost as if Allen Overman thought he could buy her as easily as he bought anything else he wanted. It was an attitude that smacked of Raul and Big Dick. The comparison made her shudder.

Suddenly, she could hardly wait to be back to Savannah, back to Bolt. She was mad at him for seeing Kathleen in Atlanta, and he would undoubtedly be at least as angry with her for coming to New York with Allen.

She sighed and forced a mirthless laugh. "Maybe Bolt will figure we're even again now." A second chuckle died in her throat. "Or maybe this is the end for us. Maybe Bolt and I were just never meant to be."

She lay in bed staring up at the reflection of Fifth Avenue's lights on the ceiling, thinking about how good things had been between her and Bolt since her return to Savannah. What was she doing here? Why wasn't she home, waiting for Bolt?

The sound of the door to the suite opening and closing made her jump. She hadn't realized she was almost asleep. For a second she couldn't think where she was. Then she relaxed, realizing that Allen must have left to go in search of more compliant females. She wished him luck—tonight *and* tomorrow at the auction. Just before she dozed off, she told herself that the minute the auction was over and she had her mirror, she would be on the first plane back to Savannah . . . back to Bolt, if he'd have her.

THE mirror!

Thoughts of that one object consumed Mary Scarlett's mind as she swept into the second-floor sale room of Sotheby's that crystal-bright spring afternoon.

The mirror—listed in the catalogue as "American, Eighteenth Century, gilt frame handcrafted by Savannah master artisan Will Johnston"—might have been on the minds of many of the other buyers that afternoon. But it quickly lost its hold on their attention when the woman in the white Chanel suit entered the room on the arm of a man who was undeniably Hollywood-handsome. They made a striking couple, like a latter-day Scarlett and Ashley. The amazing thing—the detail that kept everyone staring—was that no one knew who they were.

Mary Scarlett felt their stares, but looked neither right nor left. Her gaze focused instead on the delicate angels, flowers, scrolls, and hearts that framed the silvery face of the mirror—her dream machine, her obsession since earliest childhood.

"How's this?" Allen asked, indicating two seats on the aisle only a few rows back from the massive hooded podium from which the auctioneer would conduct his business.

"Fine." Mary Scarlett took her seat, still staring at the mirror displayed on the stage. "How long before they begin?"

"The auction starts at five minutes past two. It's 1:40 now. I'll just have time to dash upstairs and see how things look for the Josephine. I won't be long, darlin'."

Allen left her then, stopping a moment to speak to a man wearing a blue Sotheby's blazer. They chatted for only a moment before Allen disappeared through a door.

All around her, the hundred-and-fifty-or-so buyers talked in subdued tones. A dapper, elderly gentleman seated next to her turned slightly and shielded his words with his bidding paddle. "Odds are your young man's set on buying the Josephine for you. Well, if it's not too forward of me, I'd like to say you'll look even more lovely with that fabulous bauble adorning your person."

Mary Scarlett smiled and nodded, not bothering to tell the man that Allen was selling, not buying, the necklace.

The silver-haired matron sitting to the man's right dug

bejeweled fingers into his arm. "Duffort," she said in a harsh whisper, "how many times must I tell you not to speak to strange women?"

Allen reappeared, drawing Mary Scarlett's attention away from the couple beside her. His deep frown sent a chill to her heart.

"What's wrong?" she asked.

He sat down and squeezed her hand. "Nothing to be alarmed about, honey. But it looks like we might have some stiff competition for the mirror. See the guy over there at the lectern talking on the white telephone?"

"Yes."

"Well, he takes phone bids. When I went up to the third floor, one of my buddies tipped me off that there's another party interested in the mirror. He'll be calling in bids against us."

"Who?" Mary Scarlett demanded a bit too loudly.

"I don't know. Some out-of-town collector. He's here in the building, just flew in and didn't have time to change or something. The whole thing sounds screwy. Anyway, he'll be watching and bidding from the board room up there." He pointed above to a row of windows that looked down on the sale room.

Mary Scarlett glanced up, almost afraid to see the face of their competition. But the windows looked blank, like wide, staring eyes.

"Then you don't think we'll get it?" Her voice trembled as she spoke.

"Yes, we will," Allen answered determinedly. "This just means we'll probably have to pay a lot more than I'd bargained for. But surely he won't force us over my limit."

Mary Scarlett's heart sank. Allen hadn't mentioned anything about a limit before. If only she had her own inheritance, she would pay *anything* to get the mirror back. She fully intended to repay Allen as soon as humanly possible.

Just then a hush fell over the audience. All heads turned

toward a tall man walking down the center aisle toward the stage.

"It's about to begin," Allen whispered. "That's the chairman and chief auctioneer."

"Lot Number twelve hundred," the auctioneer called in the voice of a game show host, and the sale began.

"Showing here," called the man in the blue blazer Allen had spoken to earlier.

"Showing on stage," the auctioneer said, indicating a Queen Anne sideboard.

The bidding began slowly, but even so Mary Scarlett had difficulty following what was going on. The price went up and up without her being conscious of any bidders. Finally, the man next to her raised his paddle slightly.

After a long pause, the auctioneer's gavel came down. *"Sold!* For twenty-seven thousand dollars."

The amount made Mary Scarlett shudder.

Meanwhile, the buyer upstairs was staring down at her, watching her reaction, his nerves as tightly strung as her own. He resumed pacing the green carpet, sipping a Scotch and water, waiting for the final item, Lot Number 1240, *the mirror.*

More and more items were sold. Time and again the auctioneer's gavel crashed down. Prices soared. A good day. The man on the podium was almost smiling.

Mary Scarlett felt Allen grow tense beside her as time neared for the Josephine to be shown. He muttered under his breath, praying one minute, cursing the next.

"Calm down, Allen," Mary Scarlett whispered at last. "You're going to have a stroke."

"A stroke's what I want—a stroke of good luck. This sale can make me if that necklace goes for top price like the rest has today."

Top price. The words chilled Mary Scarlett through as she glanced again from Granny Boo's mirror to the windows high above. What was the top price on this fragile antique that was part of her life, part of her heritage?

Bidding on the necklace went well, better than even Allen could have hoped for. When the gavel came down after a more than generous bid from Taiwan, Mary Scarlett could tell it took all Allen's control to keep from jumping up and giving the Rebel yell.

The gentleman sitting next to Mary Scarlett leaned over and whispered, "I'm so sorry. You were born to wear that necklace."

She smiled in response. Her smile faded a moment later.

"Lot Number 1240," the auctioneer announced.

"Showing here," said the man in the blazer.

"Showing on stage," called the auctioneer.

Allen started with a bid of five hundred, which only brought a scowl from the auctioneer. He set the floor at one thousand. That amount was quickly reached by a nod from the man on the white phone. The gentleman next to Mary Scarlett bid fifteen hundred, but dropped out when she gave him a pleading look.

"It belonged to my great-grandmother," she whispered.

Allen went to two thousand, cancelled out immediately by the anonymous bidder upstairs. Mary Scarlett turned a pleading gaze toward the windows.

At five thousand, Allen turned to Mary Scarlett and shook his head slightly.

"One more bid," she begged.

"You make it," he said.

With a shaking hand, Mary Scarlett raised her paddle. The auctioneer nodded. Silence fell over the room. It seemed that no one was breathing. The man on the phone remained motionless. Mary Scarlett, her heart pounding, stared up at the windows, then back to the auctioneer. His gavel was raised to strike.

Then came the quiet voice of the man on the white phone. "Ten thousand here."

"Sold!" To Mary Scarlett, the crash of the gavel sounded like a gunshot right through her heart.

Allen was saying something to her, but she couldn't concentrate on his words. She could only stare at the mirror with a sinking feeling. Slowly, she rose and walked toward the stage. She had to look into it one last time.

So, it was all over, she thought. Finished! Forever!

Mary Scarlett couldn't even cry. She felt numb and hopeless. Slowly, she made her way down the aisle to stand and gaze at her distorted image in the wavy looking glass. She thought about Annie and Elisabeth and Marie and Louise and all the other women who had looked into this same mirror just as she was doing now and had lost the men they loved. "A cycle of unhappiness," Granny Boo had called it. *A never-ending cycle,* she knew now.

Tears misted her eyes. Her own reflection blurred. She blinked rapidly, still staring at the mirror. She closed her eyes.

"So now it's over." She sighed, ready to turn away.

A hand touched her shoulder. Someone whispered her name. She opened her eyes and stared. There in the mirror, beside her own reflection was a man's face. Her lover's face. He looked so sad.

"I bought it for *you,* Mary Scarlett," he said. "I guess I knew all along that we never had a chance, but I wanted you to have something to remember me by. Will gave it to Annie out of love. Now I'm giving it to you for the same reasons."

Mary Scarlett wanted to turn and throw her arms around Bolt, but she couldn't move. She found herself mesmerized by his face and hers, together in the mirror. Chills and thrills ran through her. Tears brimmed in her eyes again. Tears of joy, not sadness this time.

When she couldn't find her voice, he turned as if he meant to leave. Mary Scarlett spun around and threw herself into his arms. "Oh, Bolt! Don't leave! Will you marry me? *Please!*"

After he grabbed her and hugged her, he threw back his head and laughed. "I thought you'd never ask, darlin'."

The staid crowd in the auction house applauded sedately as Bolt gave Mary Scarlett a million dollar kiss. She never noticed their admiring audience. She was too caught up in this new feeling, this sensation of belonging and cherishing and being loved.

"Bolt," she whispered between kisses, "thank you for the mirror. We'll take it back to Savannah and hang it on the foyer wall where it belongs. But I'll never, ever have to look into it again. You're the man I love. The man I've always loved."

"Do you mean that, Mary Scarlett?"

"I've never meant anything more sincerely in my whole life."

He drew her closer, kissing her again. But their embrace, reflected in the mirror, showed Will kissing Annie, Jean Lafitte caressing Marie, and, finally, Jacques embracing Louise.

By the time they looked again, Mary Scarlett and Bolt saw only two people in love, side by side, where they belonged and would remain for the rest of their long, happy lives.

Epilogue

During the month of June, Savannah is a city of weddings. Every weekend will find heavenly brides and handsome bridegrooms riding in limousines or horse-drawn carriages into brand-new lives, kissing for photographs in the city's green squares, speaking their sacred vows before robed clergy in any of a dozen ornate churches with stained-glass angels looking benignly on.

Bolton Conrad and Mary Scarlett Lamar joined these happy ranks on a softly sunny Saturday when all of Savannah was perfumed with roses, oleander, and bridal wreath, and a subtle, salt-tanged breeze blew the drifting beards of the ancient oaks. Dr. Schlager and Helga stood with them on that special day, making it a double wedding. The new Mrs. Schlager whispered to Mary Scarlett afterward that the woman in her aura no longer wore a dark shroud, but shimmered in bridal white.

In the previous weeks, much had happened. Detained by the New York Police Department on a warrant sworn out by Ida Hampstead, Allen Overman had not flown back to Savannah as soon as expected. His world-traveling benefactor had returned unannounced to her home in Savannah the very hour after Allen and Mary Scarlett left for New York. She found her bed unmade, her wine cellar depleted, and a number of her own valuables missing while someone else's English silver, jewelry, and Limoges china were now stockpiled in her cellar.

Mrs. Hampstead had also been surprised when she walked into her bedroom to find a robbery in progress. 'Gator or 'Tator White—she could never tell which was which—was busily removing the rest of her jewelry from a safe she kept in her closet. He didn't hear her come in or realize she was standing over him until an ugly ironstone pitcher that she had been meaning to dispose of for years crashed down on his skull.

Under interrogation later that day, 'Tator, as it turned out, confessed that he was not the brains of the operation—a fact that did not surprise Mrs. Hampstead in the least. What did surprise her was that he named as the mastermind behind this systematic looting of her property the very man she had trusted to guard it while she was away—Allen Overman. She found it difficult to believe that the "dear boy" could do such a dastardly thing, but not so difficult that it kept her from swearing out a warrant for his arrest.

Allen was picked up outside Sotheby's in New York immediately following the auction, returned under guard to Savannah, indicted on charges of grand theft, then released to the custody of one of his ex-wives until time for his trial. Aurelia LaMotte, more than happy to have her former husband and current lover under house-arrest, planned a series of parties to entertain her prisoner and show him off to her friends. Even Mrs. Hampstead, firmly ensconced once more in her mansion on Lafayette Square, attended one of the soirées. Of all the members of Savannah society who were invited, only Bolt and Mary Scarlett sent their regrets to Aurelia's lavish prison theme gala in Allen's honor on Memorial Day, where champagne was served in tin cups and the guests came dressed as gangsters, gun molls, guards, and inmates.

Lumpkin Quincey was having his own prison party that very night down at Reidsville. Detective Edgerton had been correct; the new inmate would have plenty of time for reading during his nine-month incarceration. He was soon to be joined by 'Gator and 'Tator White.

Kathleen O'Shea quickly made the Millionaire's Club at her new real estate position in Atlanta, selling one of the old Buckhead estates to an Arab sheik, who immediately had the fabulous landmark mansion painted hot pink and lined the long, curving drive with Cadillacs, Volvos, and BMWs in matching hues.

As for Richard Habersham Lamar, the alligator from those murky depths of the Okefenokee who had devoured him could have cared less that he was a member of the Oglethorpe Club or a wife-murderer. He had been simply breakfast, a fatty morsel, part of the food chain. Big Dick's remains—a few pale, cracked bones—were never recovered, but settled down and down into the primordial ooze to become oil to fuel the as yet uninvented machines of far off generations.

Magnolia, free a last of the men who had plagued her all her life, married young Radley Axel Tollison III in a brief ceremony at the Chatham County Courthouse on the very day he graduated from the Savannah College of Art and Design. After a few years of struggle, Rat placed his mark on the world of commercial art, lost the nose and tongue rings, and let his hair go back to its natural brown. The couple was finally accepted back into the fold when the elder Tollisons received word that their daughter-in-law was expecting. "Jennifer," as Magnolia began calling herself after her marriage, became the toast of Sea Island society, singing at charity functions and shepherding the Tollison triplets to ballet recitals, harp lessons, and to the elegant birthday soirees of the many future debutantes of island society.

Mr. and Mrs. Bolton Conrad settled into their glorious marriage with the ease of two people deeply in love who have known each other since the beginning of time. Together they finished the renovation of the old house on Bull Street, turning Mary Scarlett's childhood room into a nursery, since their first child was expected on St. Patrick's Day, barely a year from the moment Bolt had picked up the phone that bright March morning to hear a sultry-sweet, magnolia-flavored voice whisper, "It's Mary Scarlett, and *I'm back!"*

Well, she was back, all right! Back in his life, back in his arms, back where she belonged. Forever and ever. Back to raise the family he had always dreamed of. Back to accept the love he had always offered. Back to make dreams come true he had never thought possible.

As for the mirror, they hung it in the foyer where it had always been, and where it would remain for many generations yet to come. A symbol, a sign that love is never impossible when it comes straight from the heart.

Granny Boo and the ghosts of all the lovelorn ancestors smiled down on the Bull Street house and its new family. But the spirits never tarried long in Savannah because out at Bonaventure the party went on . . . and on . . . and on . . .

Here is an excerpt from
Becky Lee Weyrich's
next time-travel novel

SWAN'S WAY

Coming from Zebra Books in 1997

Prologue

"What a delight to have such a handsome couple before me, Miss Swan, Mr. McNeal. You must both hold perfectly still now and look directly into my lens."

Slender, dark-haired and -bearded Mathew Brady spoke to his subjects from behind the large, tripod-mounted box of his camera. He was a dapper gentleman in his black coat and doeskin trousers, topped off with a merino vest and silk scarf. Propped nearby was a handsome cane with a silver head fashioned like a tiny camera, a gift to the photographer from the Prince of Wales, who had had his own portrait done in this very room only five months ago, during his tour of America.

Of all Virginia Swan's extraordinary adventures on her first trip to New York City, this visit to Brady's uptown studio at 859 Broadway and Tenth streets to have her engagement portrait done ranked as the most unique. She didn't know what she had expected, perhaps a drab shop that recked of chemicals and cigar smoke. She had steeled herself for such a place —something between a sweatshop and a mortuary. Instead, she caught the faint aroma of expensive Atwood's cologne, the same scent her fiancé sometimes wore. And imagine her surprise when she had entered the reception room two floors below through doors of beautifully etched glass to find velvet tapestries, walls hung with silver and gold paper, banks of mirrors, crystal chandeliers that sparkled like stars in the mellow gaslight, and the most elegant rosewood furniture. The special "Ladies Parlor" was no less pleasing, with its green satin decor and fragile gilt-painted chairs. Examples of Mr. Brady's work hung everywhere—portraits of statesmen, European royalty, freaks from Mr. P. T. Barnum's museum, along with likenesses of everyday people like herself.

Now she stood one floor above "Brady's Famous National Portrait Gallery" in the studio, with her head firmly held in place by a metal support, waiting for the moment of truth when Mathew Brady would uncover his lens and magically imprint the image of herself and her fiance on his collodion-coated glass plate, stopping time for an instant and capturing forever the love that shone in her eyes for the man who would soon make her his wife.

Having her portrait done photographically was a new experience for Virginia. But then she was finding these days that life after betrothal was full of new experiences, each one more exciting than the last. She was engaged, but more than that—*in love*. And love, she found, made all the difference in the world.

She rested her hand lightly on Channing McNeal's shoulder and smiled down at him. He looked especially handsome this morning, dressed in his high-collared, brass-buttoned, gray cadet uniform from West Point Military Academy.

It swelled her heart with pride to think that in another four months he would graduate with the Class of 1861 and receive his commission in the United States Army, along with her eldest brother Rodney. The entire Swan family planned to travel with the McNeals from their plantations in Virginia to Upstate New York to attend the commencement ceremonies and the grand reception on the superintendent's lawn. There would be parties, too—teas, balls, and, of course, the traditional stroll along Flirtation Walk with her beau. Following that auspicious occasion, the two new second lieutenants would return to Virginia for a visit at home and for the wedding—a double ceremony to take place at Swan's Quarter at which Rodney Swan would wed his childhood sweetheart, Agnes Willingham, while Virginia exchanged vows with Channing McNeal. There would be no time for a honeymoon, but that didn't matter to Virginia. Becoming "Mrs. Lieutenant Channing Russell McNeal" would provide more than enough happiness for her. Wherever her husband's orders took him, his new bride would follow willingly. They would honeymoon as they traveled to his post, their first home together.

"Whither thou goest," she thought, smiling down at her darkly handsome fiance.

From behind the bulk of his camera, Mathew Brady peered out of his wire-rimmed, blue-tinted spectacles at the stiffly posed couple. "If you don't mind, Mr. McNeal, this is to be an engagement portrait, not a 'Wanted' poster. Do try to relax, won't you? You look as if you're staring into a hangman's noose."

Brady wasn't far off the mark, Channing thought. He felt as if he were staring into the barrel of a loaded cannon—as he might well be before long. The prospect of war did not frighten him. He was trained for battle. Something far more unsettling was on his mind this bright March morning.

He had wanted everything about Virginia's visit to West Point and his furlough to New York City to be perfect. Perhaps his fiancee had missed the tension at the academy but her father had noticed the dissension in the ranks immediately upon his arrival, and Jedadiah Swan had not been cheered by what he saw. Since South Carolina's secession from the Union back in December, the cadets had become polarized, North and South. The atmosphere at the Point these days was explosive. Many cadets had already resigned to go South. The first had been Channing's own roommate, Henry Farley from South Carolina, who left in November of 1860, even before his home state seceded. There had been many fights among the cadets, even one duel. On

Washington's Birthday, one of Channing's classmates, a flamboyant but unstudious fellow named George Armstrong Custer, had led the singing when the band in the quadrangle struck up the "Star Spangled Banner." Custer's roommate, Thomas Lafayette Rosser, had countered with a boisterous rendition of "Dixie." A near-riot had ensued. That was when Virginia's father had ceased keeping his silence to state his opinion clearly and succinctly to his future son-in-law. "I am raising a cavalry unit for the coming conflict, Channing. I expect *all* my sons will want to ride with me should the North be so foolhardy as to invade our homeland. We all know our duty and must answer the South's call."

A war was coming; there was little doubt of that. The only question in Cadet Channing McNeal's mind and heart was with which side—North or South—would he, a born and bred Virginian, cast his lot? He knew his own family's feelings on the matter. They were Virginians to the pits of their souls, the same as Jedadiah Swan. But Channing himself had other feelings, other loyalties. How could he fight against his own country? He had walked the hallowed halls of the Academy at West Point for the past four years in the very footsteps of Ulysses S. Grant, Class of 1843; William Tecumseh Sherman, Class of 1840; and Robert E. Lee, Class of 1829, a Virginian himself, yet rumored about the Academy to be the most likely candidate to lead the Federal forces in the "Southern rebellion," as his northern classmates termed it.

"Smile, dearest." His fiancee's soft voice interrupted his troubling thoughts. "If not for Mr. Brady, smile for our children and grandchildren. What will they think if they see you scowling so in our engagement portrait?"

Mathew Brady gave a short bark of a laugh. "Ah, Mr. McNeal, she has you there! Think of the wonder of it. A century from now, your children's children will gaze on my work and see you both just as you are today, flesh and blood, smile and scowl. Do you really want to be remembered this way? With such a lovely fiancee, it looks rather unseemly somehow."

Channing glanced up at Virginia. His heart never failed to thunder with joy at the sight of her. Dark gold curls draped her shoulders and framed a face as perfect as the finest French porcelain. Lips as delicate and soft as the petals of the first summer rose and a pert nose that tilted just enough to suit him. Her eyes, though, were her most bewitching feature. Dazzling now in the shower of sun from the windows with tints of blue, silver, and gold. Looking at her, he couldn't help smiling. She was his love, his soul, his whole world.

"Yes, that's better," Brady said. "Now, hold that pose. Don't move a muscle."

Virginia held her breath. She felt almost wicked, having this portrait made. Her grandmother had railed against such modern voodoo, claiming that to have one's image captured, other than in a painting, was the same as having one's very soul stolen by the charlatan behind the camera. But if there was any soul-stealing going on in Mr. Brady's Broadway studio, Channing McNeal was the thief. She had been in love with him since before she knew the meaning of the word. He had been born and raised on a neighboring plantation. Often it had seemed that he was the fifth son of the Swan clan or she the third McNeal daughter. Soon it would be so and the two families would be linked forevermore.

She had to force herself to keep from smiling wider when she thought ahead to the June day when she and Agnes would descend the elegant staircase to the main hall of Swan's Quarter to be married in the front parlor while their assembled families and friends looked on. Virginia planned to wear her mother's wedding gown, the same handstitched satin and lace that Melora Etheridge had worn twenty-eight years ago when she became Jedadiah Swan's wife. On that day, the happy couple had planted a tulip poplar sapling. Now a towering monument to their enduring love, it spread its branches to shade the swan pond on the plantation's front lawn.

Channing and I should plant a tree, Virginia thought. *A symbol of our love for each other and a vow never to be parted.*

"Done!" Mathew Brady announced. "You are now immortalized, my young friends. I hope you will invite me to your wedding. I'm opening a studio in Washington soon, and I would dearly love to create your wedding portrait."

"Oh, what a wonderful idea!" Virginia cried. "By all means, Mr. Brady. The date is set for the first of June. A new month for our new life together. Mama and Papa will approve of our inviting Mr. Brady, don't you think, Chan?"

Channing stood and took her hand. His dark eyes captured hers and the intensity of his gaze all but took her breath away.

"How could anyone not approve of whatever you want, Virginia?"

She fought for control before she could speak. When she did, her voice was a bare whisper. "Then it's all settled, dearest. We'll have another portrait on our wedding day."

A slow, lazy smile warmed Channing's dark features. "There can't be any wedding until I give you a token of my affection. Come along now, my love. We're going to buy you a ring."

Virginia knew it was rather unseemly, but she couldn't contain herself. Besides, no one but Mr. Brady was watching when she threw her arms around her fiance's neck and gave him a sound hug. He hugged her back, but even as he did, she felt him sigh deeply. It was a worried sigh, and she knew, even though she had tried to keep it from him, that the possibility of the coming war was uppermost in both their minds.

Why now? she wondered. *When our lives should be so perfect!*

One

The discreet wooden sign on the rolling lawn read in elegant gold script, "SWAN'S QUARTER." Smaller lettering below the name of the former plantation identified the current establishment as a "Rest Home and Sanatorium."

Beyond the sign stood the old mansion. On the veranda Pussy Pennycock, Elspeth McAllister, and Sister Randolph huddled together around the white wicker tea table, clutching their crocheted shawls close about their thin shoulders. They waited. They whispered among themselves. Nervous, excited, dry-throated bird twitters. All the while they talked, they watched the path that led out of the woods to the swan pond and up the hill, each hoping to be the first to catch a glimpse of Ginna.

Ginna always came on Mondays. *Always!* She came to laugh and chat and charm the inmates of the rest home. She came to hear how they had spent their weekend, to find out who might have had a surprise visitor, to inquire as to which of the three white-haired ladies had sung the loudest and most harmoniously at chapel on Sunday.

But this Monday was fading quickly, with yet no sign of Ginna. As the afternoon sun began its gentle descent, the three little ladies—two widows, one spinster, all mothers who had outlived their children—shifted uneasily in their cushioned wicker chairs, their hopes fading with the setting sun.

Why was Ginna late for tea? *Today of all days!* A day

when her three friends were absolutely bursting with anticipation at the special news they had to tell. News of a mysterious young man who had checked in since Ginna's last visit.

"She'll come," Elspeth stated adamantly, staring out toward the clearing west of the sun-spangled swan pond. She cradled an antique china doll in the crook of her mahogany-skinned arm and asked, "Did you ever know her to miss a Monday, Miss Precious?"

Sister, who didn't hold with talking to inanimate objects, snapped, "That old rag of a doll won't give you any answers. Don't act foolish, Elspeth. She'll either come or she won't and that's the long and the short of it."

"Oh, dear me!" Pussy's frail, blue-veined hands fluttered like moths before the flame of her cinnamon-brown eyes, focused on the line of woods. "There was that one Monday last January. We waited and waited and she never came until a whole week later. Remember, Sister?"

Sister had outlived all her six siblings, but still bore her nickname with pride and authority. She gave Pussy an arch look. "We had a blizzard, you ninny. The roads from Front Royal and Winchester were impassable that whole week long. Even the postman couldn't get through." She sighed. "Not that it mattered. No one ever writes to us nowadays."

"It's not their fault, dear." Pussy always felt it her duty to apologize for everyone, even the dearly departed, as she added, "They're all dead."

"And likely better off for it. You call *this* living?" Elspeth's scornful voice trailed off in a weary sigh.

"There, there now, Els." Pussy patted her hand. "We still have our moments. Mondays at least are special—when Ginna comes."

A tense, watchful silence fell over the threesome. Six rheumy eyes searched the clearing near the pond. But something was missing, something more than the first glimpse of Ginna. Elspeth would never have admitted it to Sister, nor Sister to Pussy, but a change in the atmosphere always preceded Ginna's arrival. It was a shifting of light, a modulation of shadow, accompanied by a delicate breeze, flower-scented even in the dead of winter. And most amazing of all, the old tulip poplar always materialized to spread its giant, ancient limbs over the pond, announcing Ginna's approach. They all knew, the tree had been wounded in the war, then blown down in a fierce storm back in 1924, over seventy years ago. Yet when Ginna came the tree materialized miraculously, rising tall and strong as if to banish the present and recall the past.

"Tea's getting tepid," Elspeth said through a scowl. "Miss Precious can't abide cold tea. Shall I pour out?"

"Please," said Sister.

Fluttering again, Pussy simpered, "Shouldn't we wait, dears?"

Ignoring her weak protest, Elspeth carefully tipped the heavy vessel toward Sister's blue-flowered china cup.

The late afternoon sun glinted off a disfiguring dimple a half-inch below the old English's engraved on the right side of the antique silver teapot. The dent was as much a battle wound as any suffered by the men of Swan's Quarter during the long ago War of Northern Aggression. The women of the Swan family had suffered their wounds as well, but they had worn them deep inside, unlike their men or their teapot.

The war might have been decided well over a century past, but all three ladies knew the conflict's history by rote. They knew the teapot's story as well, although each one told a different version of the bravely scarred vessel's history. For this reason, they seldom discussed the tale because of the disagreements the telling always precipitated. But today was different. Today Ginna had yet to come and there was little else to do besides retell old tales.

"Juniper really should have wrapped the teapot in a

croker sack or a quilt before he tossed it into the well to hide it from the Yankees," Pussy began.

Both Elspeth and Sister cut their eyes her way. Pussy met neither of their gazes, but kept her pointy chin tucked as she sipped her tea. They always scoffed at her story about the Swan family's butler dumping the silver service down the well. Still, it *could* have happened that way, she reasoned.

"Juniper would never have done such a thing and you know it. He was said to be a fine servant, a credit to his people. Besides, that's the first place anyone would have looked for valuables." Sister clucked her tongue and waggled a finger at Pussy, who pretended not to notice. "It was those crude Yankees who damaged the teapot. And after Miss Virginia offered it to them filled with a cool drink from the well. They imbibed of that sweet Southern water, then tossed Miz Melora Swan's prized teapot right here onto this very veranda and it bounced across the paving stones and got the dent in it. They rode off just a-laughin' afterward. And that's the truth of it!"

Replacing her fragile cup with such force that the saucer danced, Elspeth glared at her two companions. "Neither of you knows a blessed thing about it! You make up history as you go along to suit yourselves. If you're going to tell it, for pity's sake tell it right! My great-grandma was right here on the place when the Yankees came that day. I got the true story handed down to me though my own family. Great Gran told my granny and she told my mammy, who told it all to me, just the way it happened."

Sister and Pussy settled into a bored, but polite, silence. They had heard it all before, a hundred times, but they pretended to listen again as they kept their eyes keened on the verge of the woods, watching for Ginna.

"Now, as you all will likely recall," Elspeth began, "Colonel Jedadiah Swan rode off to war at the head of his own cavalry unit and all four of his sons went with him. They were a fine-looking passel of manhood—big, fair-haired, square-jawed, and strapping. The very steel and cream of the South. Back here at Swan's Quarter they left only Miz Melora and young Miss Virginia, the prettiest belle in the county, to look after the place and the hundred slaves."

"Last time you told it, they had *two* hundred slaves," Sister interrupted with a good deal of satisfaction at catching Elspeth in a mistake.

"Well, some of the sorry ones ran off with the Yankees. It was just my Great Gran and the other good ones that stood by the family. At any rate, Miz Melora Swan and her daughter Miss Virginia had their hands full taking care of all this land and this house and our people. It was early in the war, May and June of 1862, that the Yankees first showed up around here. Stonewall Jackson had been chasing them up and down the valley, trying to run the blue bellies far away from the Shenandoah. But he'd lick 'em one place and they'd pop up somewhere else. Well, with the Yankees tramping all over and burning whatever they didn't steal it was no easy task for Miz Melora and Miss Virginia, I can tell you. They had to be strong and stern to keep up their spirits and their faith. Those were no ordinary times."

Pussy loved this part of the story and couldn't help interjecting, "And Miz Melora Swan and her daughter Miss Virginia were no ordinary women."

Elspeth nodded her approval. She didn't mind interruptions when they added emphasis to her tale. "Right you are, Pussy. No ordinary women at all. They were the bravest of the brave. So when the Yankees came here on the twenty-fifth of May back in 1862 and burned their fields and threatened to set their torches to the house, the women of Swan's Quarter stood right up to them, as bold as brass. Miz Melora ordered them off her land. She had made pretty Miss Virginia dress up like a boy so the Yankees wouldn't be tempted by the sight of her. But one of them noticed a golden curl escaped from under her daddy's old cap and saw the tempting rise of her young bosom even though Miz Melora had ordered old Nanny Fan to bind her breasts tight. That lusting blue belly marched right up to Miss Virginia and snatched the hat off her head, freeing her long hair to tumble down like golden coins spilling from a money bag."

"And they all laughed and those that had turned to go turned back to see Miss Virginia," Pussy added, too eager to wait when Elspeth paused for a sip of tea.

"That they did!" Elspeth nodded solemnly. "But Miz Melora stood her ground. 'Y'all get on out of here now,' she warned them. 'My daughter is untouched and promised to another brave soldier.' "

"But they didn't listen, did they?" Sister asked, as she knew she was expected to at this point in the telling.

Elspeth shook her head sadly. "They were no gentlemen, those Yankees devils. They closed ranks around poor Miss Virginia and stroked her hair and *touched* her." Elspeth leaned close and whispered that one word.

"And one even tried to steal a kiss," Pussy added breathlessly, her pale cheeks flushed with dusty rose.

"They shamed the poor girl," Elspeth said with a sad nod. "And after she'd been so kind as to serve them cool water from this very teapot. Brutes they were, and some of them married men with children—*churchgoers,* mind you!"

"Tell what Miss Virginia did," Pussy begged. It was her very favorite part of the story, the part that purely made her swell up with Southern pride.

"Well," Elspeth drawled, lengthening the suspense. "You'll recall she'd just poured them water from this very teapot. She still had it in her hand. When the brute who'd snatched her hat off caught her about her slender waist and tried to press his rangy body to hers, she hauled back and cold-cocked him with this very pot. He gave a fearful yell, staggered backward, tumbled down the veranda stairs, and landed in a heap in the dirt of the carriage drive."

"Good for her!" Pussy crowed, clapping her arthritic hands.

"It's, a wonder those nasty Yankees didn't shoot Miss Virginia and Miz Melora Swan," Sister said with a shudder.

Elspeth's attention now seemed focused on something far away as her gaze searched the woods beyond the swan pond. "They might have," she said softly, "but for an accident of fate. The troop's captain, a member of General Nathaniel Banks's forces that had just been whupped by old Stonewall at Winchester, came riding up about the time that Yankee bastard landed at the foot of the stairs. All the others—a dozen or so—had drawn their pistols and had them aimed right at Miss Virginia's wildly beating heart. But the captain—a handsome fellow even if he was a Yankee—yelled, 'Halt! Put your guns away. Whoever harms a hair on the heads of these ladies will answer to me.'"

"And they backed right down, didn't they, Elspeth?"

"That they did, Pussy. They put away their guns and left the veranda The captain ordered them off the property, down beyond the entrance gate, out of sight of the house. They camped there for the night."

"But the captain didn't join his men in camp, did he, Elspeth?" Pussy said, a sly grin etching her thin lips.

"Sh-h-h!" said Sister. "That part of the story's a secret."

"Not to us!" Pussy insisted through a pout. She loved hearing the romantic ending of the tale. It reminded her of her own life and lost love. "Tell the rest, Elspeth. Tell it! Do!"

"Very well, but it's to remain among the three of us. Always. Swear?" She clutched her doll closer and looked hard at the other two.

"Always! I swear it!" Pussy crossed her heart, holding her breath after she spoke.

"Very well, then. You'll recall that Miz Melora had told the rude soldiers that Miss Virginia was promised and still a virgin."

The other two nodded, blushing at Elspeth's use of such a forthright word.

"Miss Virginia's mother spoke the truth. Her daughter had been betrothed not long before the war broke out to a fine young man who lived over at Belle Grove plantation. But she never married. The start of the war put an end to their plans and near broke Miss Virginia's poor heart. You see, the man she loved had graduated from West Point and felt obliged to join the Union forces."

"A turncoat in blue!" Sister said with disgust.

"A misguided young man," Elspeth explained. "But he did love Miss Virginia with all his heart and soul. They vowed to wed once the war was over. It was Colonel Jedadiah Swan who forbade the union, not wanting to divide the family and possibly meet his daughter's husband across the line of fire in the heat of battle."

"We know that," Sister broke in impatiently. "Get to the point, won't you?"

"The point is," Elspeth paused dramatically, "that Miz Melora held more with love than with war. She saw the look that passed between her daughter and the captain—the pain and sorrow and longing in their eyes. It proved more than a mother could bear. So she told my Great-Gran to prepare a feast of what little they had left to eat—one scrawny hen, a bit of bacon, a few dried beans, and some yams. Miz Melora invited the captain to dine with them. She even opened the last bottle of Colonel Swan's fine old French brandy, a surprise she'd been saving to celebrate the end of the war and her husband's safe return. She told Miss Virginia to put on the white satin wedding gown they had hidden in the attic beneath a loose board under the eaves. They had a jolly evening with the captain as their guest. After dinner Miz Melora told all the house servants to gather in the parlor. Then she instructed Brother Zebulon, a self-styled minister to the people, to perform a marriage ceremony. It was an odd affair, a combination of a Christian service and a broom-

stick jumping. Likely the Lord Himself had never seen anything to match it. However, what it lacked in orthodoxy, it
made up for in sincerity."

Pussy and Sister giggled, picturing the scene.

"Actually, it was a wartime wedding and not unlike many
another back in those times. It was certainly good enough
to satisfy all involved, especially the bride and the groom."

"And afterward?" Pussy said.

"Afterward, Miz Melora bade the happy couple a good
night. She sent the people back to their quarters, went to
her own room, and left the newlyweds to their one night
of bliss. Along about dawn, the captain kissed his bride and
told her goodbye before he rode away. His parting words
were a vow to return the minute the war was over and marry
her in proper fashion."

"But by then it was too late," Pussy said sadly, sniffing
back tears.

"You're wrong, Pussy. It's *never* too late for love," Elspeth added cryptically.

Just then, the breeze changed suddenly, bringing with it
the scent of spring flowers. Clouds shifted and the heavens
seemed to shine with more light. The three women sat up,
staring off toward the woods, their senses keen with anticipation.

ABOUT THE AUTHOR

SAVANNAH SCARLETT is Becky Lee Weyrich's twenty-first novel. She is also the author of four novellas. Since she began publishing fiction in 1978, she has written for various publishers in a variety of genres, including historical romance, fantasy, saga, Gothic, horror/mystery, contemporary, and time-travel. Her first novel, *Through Caverns Infinite,* is now a collectors' item among New Age aficionados.

In 1991, Weyrich won *Romantic Times* magazine's Lifetime Achievement Award for New Age Fiction. Several of her books have won Reviewers' Choice awards, including her 1993 time-travel, WHISPERS IN TIME, from Pinnacle. Her books have been translated into ten foreign languages and produced on tape.

Beginning as a non-fiction writer in 1960, Becky Lee Weyrich did freelance work for magazines while her byline was seen in newspapers in Maine, Maryland, and Georgia. She also wrote and illustrated two chapbooks of poetry before turning to a full time career in fiction.

A member of Romance Writers of America, Novelists Inc., and a board member of Southeastern Writer's Association, Weyrich is the originator of the Becky Lee Weyrich Fiction Award, presented annually at the Southeastern Writers' Workshop on St. Simons Island, Georgia. She established the cash award to aid and encourage new writers.

After roaming the world as a Navy wife, residing in such diverse locations as Maine, Florida, California, and Italy, the Georgia-born author now lives on St. Simons Island with her husband of thirty-seven years, several cats, and a Beagle named Barnacle.

If you would like to receive Becky Lee Weyrich's newsletter, please send a self-addressed stamped envelope to P.O. Box 24374, St. Simons Island, GA 31522.